The cries that had died briefly rose once more, growing louder and more frantic as the cause of their fear drew nearer. Jikun could see his soldiers running to the side, the clean marching line scattered like dust to the wind. A body sailed high into the air before it vanished into the mass of elves fleeing the carnage.

"*The Beast.*" Jikun's pale skin grew deathly white, his composure lost. He drew his sword swiftly from its sheath, aware of how naked the troops around him lay. "Captain, get the army north!"

There was no fighting this time.

Jikun turned away and hurried through the ranks of soldiers who were scrambling away in fear and disarray: he ran toward the beast. He could glimpse a shadow of the creature, even as the nearest males vainly attempted to block its path. The beast tore through them like a blade through water, dispersing their bodies to the side. Jikun was painfully aware that the chainmail on his body was more than all the armor his entire army had left.

STEPS OF POWER

THE KINGS

*Kings or Pawns*

-UPCOMING-

*Heroes or Thieves*
*Gods or Men*
*Princes or Paupers*

STEPS OF POWER

# KINGS OR PAWNS

THE KINGS: BOOK I

JJ SHERWOOD

EDITED BY ALEXANDRA BIRR

# Kings or Pawns



Cover art by Kirk Quilaquil
Cover design by J. Caleb Clark
Edited by Alexandra Birr
Map by J. J. Sherwood
First Printing October 2015
Library of Congress Catalog Card Number: 2015904200

Ebook ISBN: 978-0-9862877-1-8
Paperback ISBN: 978-0-9862877-0-1
Hardback ISBN: 978-0-9862877-2-5
Audio Book ISBN: 978-1-944006-00-6

Silver Helm
P.O. Box 54696
Cincinnati, OH 45245

(513) 400-4363 * SilverHelmPublishing@gmail.com

Visit the website at **www.StepsofPower.com**

Acknowledgements

For my dear grandmother, Carol Bundy. Without her influence, I would certainly not have finished this book when I did.

I would like to thank my friends and family who supported me, encouraged me, and offered insight and advice when I needed it the most. In particular, thank you, Alex Belshaw.

And above all, I want to thank my editor, Alexandra Birr. There have been many wonderfully helpful and insightful people in my life, but none have shown the devotion, love, and time that she has. Without her help, I could never have achieved the quality, consistency, or the depth you see before you.

And last but not least, my financial backer, my loving spouse, whom I could only repay with cuddles and smiles. (I *do* give great cuddles *and* smiles, though, and I'm fairly certain the conversion rate of cuddles-and-smiles to dollars makes us *nearly* even.)

# Glossary

| | | | | | |
|---|---|---|---|---|---|
| a – rack | e – wet | i – miss | o – lock | u – fur | ee – seen |
| ah – far | aw – call | ey – came | ahy – right | air – fare | uh – up |
| oo – soon | oh – rope | | | | |

Note: the "**h**" in all Sel'varian names is pronounced "breathlessly": ɦ
Note: the "**d**" in all Sel'varian is quick and almost "silent"
Note: ʒ is pronounced as a rolling J (*jsh*), as in the name "Jacques"

| | |
|---|---|
| Adonis | A-duh-nis |
| Alvena | al-VEE-nuh |
| Cahsari | CAH-suh-ree |
| Catervi | CAH-ter-vahy |
| Daiki | DAHY-kee |
| Darcarus | dahr-CAHR-uhs |
| Darival | DAIR-i-vawl |
| El'adorium | el-uh-DOHR-ee-uhm |
| Elarium | el-AHR-ee-uhm |
| Elvorium | el-VOHR-ee-uhm |
| Emal'drathar | e-MAL-druh-thahr |
| Ephraim | EF-reym |
| Erallus | e-RAWL-luhs |
| Eraydon | e-REY-duhn |
| Esera | EH-sur-uh |
| Fildor | FIL-dohr |
| Hadoream | ɦAH-dawr-uhm |
| Hairem | ɦEY-rem |
| Hashauel | HAH-shoo-el |
| Heshellon | he-shel-LON |
| Ilrae | IL-ruh |
| Ilsevel | IL-se-vel |
| Itirel | AHY-ti-rel |
| Jekum | ʒEH-koom |
| Jikun | ʒEE-koon |
| Kaivervi | KEY-ver-vahy |
| Kasan | kah-SAHN |
| Kisacaela | ki-suh-CEYL-uh |
| Laethile | LEYTH-ahyl |
| Laikum | LEY-koom |
| Lardol | LAHR-duhl |
| Liadeltris | lee-uh-DEL-tris |
| Lithriella | lith-ree-EL-luh |
| Madorana | muh-doh-RAH-nah |
| Malranus | mal-RAW-nuhs |
| Merkan | MEER-kahn |
| Mikanum | mee-KAH-nuhm |
| Mirwen | MEER-wen |
| Mistarel | MIS-tuh-rel |
| Navon | nuh-VON |
| Noc'olari | no-koh-LAH-ree |
| Nulaves | noo-LAH-ves |
| Ralaris | ruh-LAH-ris |
| Reivel | rey-VEL |
| Rulan | ROO-lahn |
| Ryekarayn | RAHY-kair-en |
| Saebellus | sey-BEL-luhs |
| Sairel | SEY-rel |
| Secora | se-COH-ruh |
| Sel'ari | sel-AH-ree |
| Seladar | SIL-uh-der |
| Sellemar | SEL-le-mahr |
| Sevrigel | SEV-ri-gel |
| Taemrin | TEYM-reen |
| Thakish | THAH-kish |
| Tiras | TAHY-ruhs |
| Turmazel | TOOR-muh-zel |
| Tuserine | too-su-REEN |
| Valdor | VAL-dohr |

# Race Glossary

| | |
|---|---|
| Darivalian | dair-i-VAWL-ee-en |
| Eph'ven | EF-ven |
| Eph'vi | EF-vahy |
| Faraven | FAIR-uh-ven |
| Faravi | FAIR-uh-vahy |
| Galwen | GAHL-wen |
| Galweni | GAHL-wen-ee |
| Helvari | hel-VAH-ree |
| Helven | HEL-ven |
| Lithri | LITH-ree |
| Malraven | mal-RAH-ven |
| Malravi | mal-RAH-vee |
| Noc'olarian | no-koh-LAH-ree-en |
| Ruljen | ROOL-jen |
| Ruljenari | rool-je-NAH-ree |
| Sel'ven | SEL-ven |
| Sel'vi | SEL-vahy |
| Vetri | VE-tree |
| Vetri'an | ve-TREE-en |

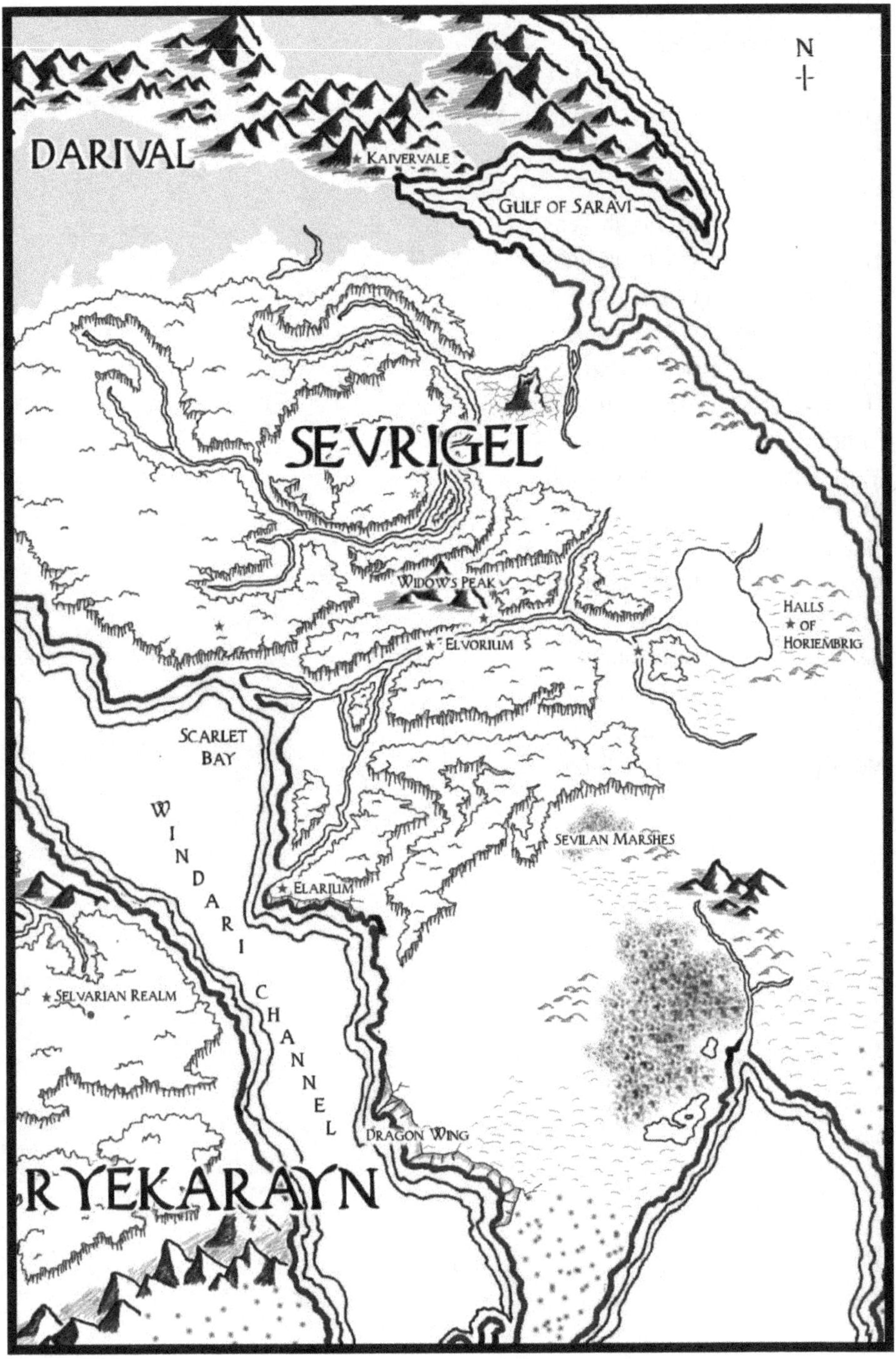
N
DARIVAL
Kaivervale
Gulf of Saravi
SEVRIGEL
Widow's Peak
Elvorium
Halls of Horiembrig
Scarlet Bay
Windari Channel
Sevilan Marshes
Elarium
Selvarian Realm
Dragon Wing
RYEKARAYN

*32 Felserine 8694 P.E.*

*Let the history record the truth of our departure from Sevrigel.*

*What year this corruption began, I cannot say, but my father and his father alike strived with great determination to quell the arrogance of the Council of Elves. Despite all efforts, their wanton destruction will not be ceased. My deepest desire has been to forcefully remove such evil from positions of power; however, elven tradition has long decreed that the people will elect a council to represent their needs, and no ruler may supplant its will.*

*Lest any elf be tempted to forgo tradition for force as I was, recall that Tradition is the foundation of elven society. Through keeping our traditions laid down by our founders and the goddess Sel'ari herself, the elves have remained above the carnage of the lesser races. It is truly one of the greatest virtues of our people. As such, I will not demolish the elven tradition of these lands by forcefully removing this corruption and usurping the will of the people. To do so would be to introduce tyranny into our land.*

*So it is with great sorrow that I have reached a similar outcome as my forefathers: failure.*

*In my last meeting with the Council of Elves, I presented an ultimatum: they may vote for their own resignation, or for my dismissal from this country. As expected, the council remains entrenched in its determination to hold power and thus my consequence has come to pass. I will not subvert the will of the population of Sevrigel.*

*Nevertheless, I will not permit those subjugated by this corruption to continue to suffer. I shall embark for the Homeland of Ryekarayn, where our kind once dwelled in harmony with the humankind. I shall establish a new Realm and return to our old traditions, and all who wish to begin again will be welcomed with open arms.*

*Until such time as Sevrigel turns from its path of self-destruction, the Realm of the True Bloods shall have no political association with its Council or its future royal line. May Sel'ari bless and guide us all.*

*King Silandrus*
*4th of the line of Ranwen since the Second Age*

# PROLOGUE

A fierce howl of wind tore in from the north, bringing with it a fleeting chill. The rain pelted against the armor of the soldiers scattered across the earth below as thunder cracked and bellowed in Aersadore's evening sky. The two armies stumbled and sank into the muddy ground of the canyon floor, voices and weapons lost in the tumult of the raging storm.

Jikun swung his blade around swiftly and plunged it into the soldier behind him, throwing his weight away to spin back into the teeming mass of enemy troops.

"General, Saebellus is retreating!!"

Jikun rounded toward his captain's shout, seeing the soldier stumble from the fray. His captain lurched to the side, black hair plastered to the sides of his pale face as one hand groped for balance on the face of the canyon wall. The captain tore the clasp from the drenched cloak about his neck, letting it fall to the mud beneath his feet. Relieved of its weight, he pushed free of the canyon's face and shoved Jikun aside, his blade whistling through the air as he swung high to decapitate the soldier behind him.

"I know, damn it!" Jikun shouted in return, eyes narrowing against the onslaught of rain. It bit into his flesh like shards of ice, but in the midst of battle, he was hardly aware of the pain. He stepped forward, willing the meager distance to grant him vision through the torrent of rain. Vision of the enemy that lay ahead. A tremble coursed through the earth as thunder cracked once more. A bolt of lightning lit the towering walls of the surrounding canyon, capturing the deep shadows in the jagged stones and the sunken faces of his weathered troops. "Don't let him escape!" he bellowed to his soldiers, fighting to be heard above the wind, his throat raw. He shoved forward, leaping over the body of a dying soldier, kicking the grasping arm away from him.

He could see *him* now.

Saebellus.

The throng of fleeing enemy troops had parted, just long enough for Jikun to glimpse him twisting through the grey. The warlord shoved his blade through one of Jikun's soldiers, grabbing the elf by the hair and wrenching his blade free as the body slumped to the mud. He glanced up abruptly, as though aware of someone's gaze, and his eyes caught Jikun's in a moment of calm, cold solidarity: an acknowledgement of each of their roles in the war. Then he turned, raising his hand high. The throng of soldiers closed behind him, fighting to defend the backlines as he and his army fled toward the north.

For a moment, the image of those emotionless, black voids had stilled Jikun. Then he found his voice, bursting forth louder and stronger in his anger. "Move! MOVE! Don't let them escape!!" he shouted, a rumble of thunder following his screams with equal fury.

There came another rumble, resounding almost immediately after the last. It had come too soon.

Jikun paused, jerking his head upwards along the walls of the canyon, searching the length of sky for the source of the unnatural sound. There was another flash of light from ahead, but this one came red and hot, erupting from the midst of Saebellus' army. It struck the canyon wall with a ferocious crack that sent a tremor through the earth about them.

Jikun's eyes widened in horror. "AVALANCHE!!!" he roared. He stumbled backward, raising an arm above his head. A thick dome of water swept upward from the mud at his feet, freezing as it grew, forming at once into a thick shield of ice that protected him and his surrounding soldiers.

He could hear the crashing of stones as they plummeted down the mountain face, smashing through the troops and horses before him, plowing through the line of soldiers behind him. They slammed into the side of his icy barricade, hurling him backwards into the far wall.

And then there was silence.

Jikun looked up, raising a hand against the ice to let it fall once more to mere water about his body.

Saebellus and his army were gone.

# CHAPTER ONE

Seven hundred forty-five hard fought days and seven hundred forty-four miserable nights they had borne to return to this place. Now the sun that arose from the horizon was more vivid and welcoming than any sunrise Jikun had seen on any day before. The sky was golden, radiating a warmth of color that cut through the cold spring morning fog like a blade. The ancient trees that lined the wide dirt road and covered the surrounding landscape shook off little drops of water as a fragrant breeze gently wove toward the elves' greatest city on Sevrigel: Elvorium, the seat of the Council of Elves.

"Forgive my cliché, but isn't that a sight for sore eyes?" grinned his captain. "The gods certainly know how to remind you of what you are fighting for, do they not, General?"

"That they do, Navon," Jikun inhaled deeply. Even the stench of blood and rotting leather from one hundred fifty thousand soldiers could not conceal the pleasant aromas twisting their way toward him from across the canyon: at long last, through the final trees skirting the edge of the forest behind him, Jikun's eyes could see the breadth of the Sel'varian city, plainly visible in the center of the cliff side that jutted out into a "V" shape over the canyon. At the end of the precipice, settled between two rivers that cascaded over the edge of the cliff, was the palace of the king.

A roar of relief and excitement arose from behind the general and his captain. Several helmets dared sail past the two, ringing as they bounced off the stone bridge before them to drop like stones into the canyon below.

"Hold onto your possessions!" General Jikun roared, turning in his saddle. "The next elf who acts like a god damn human will be stripped naked and paraded through the streets with the horses!"

The clamor quieted and Jikun turned back to Navon with a thin smile etched across his lips.

Although it was a far cry from home, he had to admit that he too was glad to return to the capital.

"Don't make indecent threats lightly; the troops take you quite seriously," his captain rebuked him with all the airs of a typical Sel'ven. Jikun considered it ill-suiting, as the captain had not a drop of Sel'varian blood in his body. Which was a relief for him amongst his troops.

"I was entirely serious, Navon."

Jikun nudged his horse forward across the stone bridge that stretched over the vast ravine. The structure was a marvel of Sel'varian engineering, architecture, and magic, hardly comparable to the other elven races' ability to design. Extending at a great expanse, the bridge was held in place by curved stone pillars mounted to the cliff side and supported by magic. The columned archway and railing across the bridge were intricately detailed, but more than being merely an adornment, they helped to shield travelers from the sudden canyon gusts that could catch a passerby off-guard.

Jikun had, on more than one occasion, imagined himself lurching over the side to an inescapable death and now found himself wondering if the archway and railing had been part of the original concept, or if they had been added later after some visiting merchant had met his doom. But of course, the Sel'vi would never admit to such a design mistake. Perhaps this was why a score of houses still spotted the canyon face below the palace where they would one day, inevitably, fall away beneath the erosion of the stone and send their poor, but foolish, inhabitants several leagues downward. During which they would hopefully have sufficient time to contemplate their poor life choices.

Jikun stiffened and edged his horse to the center of the bridge. This bridge, like the one on the opposite end of the canyon, led into the south and north ends of the city respectively. With the east end of the city banked by an enormous lake, the bridges were the primary entry points into the city. And all the elven magic in Aersadore could not comfort him when marching several hundred thousand bodies across its lengthy structure.

The horses whinnied faintly as though sharing mutually in Jikun's dislike for this final stretch of their journey. He reached forward, patting his mare softly on the neck. Perhaps even she recognized the sight up ahead. At the bend in the bridge just before them, he could see the city's gateway swung open wide and hear a roar of triumph and praise erupt from the guards at their posts. The salutary trumpet blasts seemed to have already been announced and Jikun imagined the waiting elves had let them loose when the watch had first seen his army rising across the west bank's hillsides. Jikun pulled to the center of the bridge as Navon respectfully withdrew behind him.

*'What I wouldn't give to skip this drivel of politics and charades and take a damn* hot *bath,'* Jikun muttered to himself as the bridge seemed to lengthen around the bend. He glanced once over the marble side—it had been over two years since he had last seen its depths; it still made his stomach drop like a stone. Far below them was a large forest, heavily shrouded in the center by the thick rolls of mist running off from the waterfalls pouring toward a lake below. From this lake, a thin river, banked on either side by a narrow field, wound its way into the distance, away to the Noc'olari or Ruljen ethnicities in the northeast.

Jikun's head snapped back up in unease and he directed his attention instead to the first male at the gate.

"Congratulations, General, on yet another victory!" the captain of the city guard greeted as Jikun passed underneath the archway and onto the safety of the cobbled streets of the city. "His Majesty awaits you at the palace."

Jikun nodded his head once toward the guard and pressed onward, eyes sweeping the streets of Elvorium. The gold-slated rooftops glimmered in the light of dawn and the long shadows across Mehuim Way crept up the cream faces of the buildings tinted with an orange glow. All along the street sides and hanging from windows were countless elves tossing flowers, shouting praise, and glowing with smiles. Despite having been awoken before the dawn by the welcoming trumpet calls that had saluted his troops' approach, the Sel'vi were beaming with neatly braided hair and broadening smiles, as though they had long been awaiting this day.

But Jikun imagined they didn't even remember what he was fighting for. It was simply the "victory" itself that had driven them to patriotism.

The street curved gently toward the entrance of the palace. Even as Jikun was lavished with shouts of praise and welcome, it seemed but a short march down its way before he and his soldiers passed beneath a flower-laden archway and stepped into the presence of several scores of elves.

Here, the mood shifted palpably. The elves waiting before the palace were taciturn and silent, bestowing no salute or praise onto the defenders of Sevrigel. Their lack of response was contagious, spreading like the Cadorian Plague through the troops and into the city beyond. Jikun's face grew stoic, the joyous welcome forgotten. Even the naivety of praise and victory was preferred over the stiff bastards that delayed his hot bath now.

These males before him were guards, council members, and a large portion of the nobility. However, despite the conspicuous splendor of the surrounding elves, the most prominent figure stood at the forefront: Hairem, Prince of Elvorium and the Sel'vi, second of non-royal blood since the Royal Schism.

As the army fanned out behind Jikun, the crowd before him, with the exception of the prince, went down to one knee.

This gesture was a long-established practice, and Jikun doubted that he and his army would have been shown the same respect were not the Sel'vi pedants for tradition. Pedant was, without a doubt, the most accurate and all-encompassing word he could ascribe to that breed of elves. The council members were pridefully stiff in their bows, eyes never fully lowering to the earth. Their guards, though more sincere in their respect, were nonetheless all too quick to their feet.

*'I'd like to see* you *leave your homes to lead a war. Then we'd see how your respect rises,'* Jikun reflected sourly in response, though his expression remained carefully detached.

He was not a Sel'ven and it was perhaps this fact that led him to regard their actions with an extra tinge of cynicism. He was from the far north—the frozen lands of Darival, land of the Lithri and Darivalians. Though his army was diverse in the race of elves it had deployed, now in Elvorium he felt out of place, as his appearance clearly spoke that he was a foreigner. His hair was a blue tinted silver, like the mountains that framed Darival. His skin was a grey-white, like shadows banking the snow. And although he was tall and slender like his Sel'varian brethren, his facial features were stronger and sharper—like a sculpture chiseled from ice.

Jikun knew there was one other of his kind amongst the group before him, but he could not spot the council member's presence amongst the crowd. He wove his hand once into the air and heard his fellow riders obediently dismount to the smooth cobbled stones. He swung himself lightly from the saddle and dropped the reins at his side.

There was a sudden eruption of murmuring from the council members. When he twisted from his horse to look, surprise rooted him in place. Hairem, prince of the Sel'vi, knelt on one knee before the army, his symbolic sword scraping carelessly across the ground beside him as though he was blind to all but the triumphant troops.

Non-royal blood or not, the gesture caught Jikun by surprise as well. Though he had not lived amongst the Sel'vi for long, he imagined that in the history of their proud nation, no ruler had gone on bended knee before any male or female of lower rank. And for all purposes of tradition, as far as the elves were concerned, Hairem was as royal as the True Bloods of The Royal Schism three centuries before. Attesting to this were the wide-eyed council members, mouths agape between murmurs as they stared in shock toward the scandalous behavior.

*'Now what am I supposed to do?'* Jikun regarded Hairem with a knit brow and slightly parted lips, then glanced in the direction of his Helvarian captain, hoping Navon would have a notion of the most appropriate response.

His captain responded with an equally bewildered look and glanced about himself, seeming to hope the answer would materialize from the crowd.

*'He has no idea...'*

Yet Navon's eyes flicked back to the prince and he seemed to gather himself enough to move; he slowly went down to a knee before the male. In a wave, the army followed.

Jikun placed a hand to his breast and bowed low, eyes never leaving Hairem. He had been on his knees for the prince's father for two and a half years: a bow was more than sufficient.

It was only when the army had returned the gesture of respect did the prince stand, raising his head sharply and drawing himself up before the army. He was young, but his blue eyes were cold and hard. His long, golden hair was loosely braided back and thin strands buffeted his face in the sharp gusts of wind coming in from the east. Raising his hands in welcome, Prince Hairem spoke formally, "Sevrigel owes you her gratitude for yet another successful war against Saebellus. Without doubt, you and your army are road weary, but I must detain you for a moment longer. Come, General, we have matters to discuss." And with that, he turned in a sweeping motion, his golden cape billowing out and catching the wind, and stepped away to the palace beyond the crowd.

Jikun heaved an inward sigh, though a report to the king was expected. *'Gods I just want a damn* bath.*'* He handed the reins of his horse to Navon and his captain passed him as subtle a rebuke as he could manage.

Was his impatience that apparent?

No, Navon just knew him too well.

Jikun left his army behind as he followed Hairem through the parting cluster of council members and guards. He could see their lips move slightly as they leaned in to one another, losing no time to gossip about what had taken place. Jikun focused back ahead in time to catch the end of the prince's cape vanishing around the corner. He quickened his pace and strode free of the crowd, mindfully aware of the seething mass of hypocritical politicians he had just stepped through. At least it was to King Liadeltris that he reported.

"Keep up, General Taemrin," the prince beckoned as he swept around another bend and stepped in through a side door of the palace.

Jikun glanced once behind him and his brow knit. Was this the usual way toward the king? It had been a few years since he had set foot inside the palace. They moved down a steeply sloped, mildly ornate hallway to a large, arched doorway.

Here the prince stopped, propping the door open with his foot, and leaned in toward a nearby shelf.

It took Jikun a moment to gather his surroundings: soft blue light from the orb bobbing near the ceiling, gleaming rows of mildly dusty glass, wooden racks that tucked their contents snuggly in carefully carved bowels. He looked about the cellar in bewilderment. Surely the prince was not above calling upon servants to do these tasks.

"Your Highness, would you like—" Jikun began.

"No, almost have it," the prince grunted. "Ah, there we go. Is Eastern Glades a satisfactory vintage? Well, I certainly hope so as it appears to be the best bottle in here." He patted the dust from the side with a cough.

Jikun held the door open as the prince tucked the bottle beneath his arm in order to pick up and examine two glasses. Appearing satisfied, he passed the Darivalian without so much as a glance and staunchly strode back up the way they had come. And further still, up a staircase divided by many levels of open rooms, all of which were empty and lit only for the sake of appearance. Here, the palace's grandeur reached the obscene—it was as though all the gold and jewels of the kingdom had been inlaid into every facet of every surface. The highest room, and one of two private council chambers of the king, was their final destination.

This room, unlike many of the others, was designed to give the appearance of a vast and heavily used study, but the dust about the room was almost tangible—as though the place had not been touched since the Royal Schism.

Prince Hairem set the glasses and bottle casually in the center of the desk, striding toward the king's chair.

"Will His Majesty be joining us this morning?" Jikun inquired as he gave the lavish room a quick, distasteful glance. He heard the guards outside close the door softly behind them. Jikun's brow knit as he eyed the wine that the prince uncorked.

"Your failure to receive our dove makes me wonder who did." Hairem paused a moment, staring briefly—blankly—at the glass bottle. "My father passed away thirteen days ago of an illness."

Jikun's eyes met those of the prince in shock. His lips parted, but he knew not what words he sought. *'Liadeltris is dead...?'*

As though reading his mind, the prince waved a slight hand as he pulled his heavy chair back with his free hand. "I need no words of your deepest sorrows to remind me of mine. I have seen one elf die in the last century and you have undoubtedly seen the passing of thousands in the last few weeks alone. To which of us goes the greater sorrow, I have no doubt. I have had the consolation of my city. I instead offer you my deepest condolences on your recent battles." As he waited for Jikun to sit, the general could feel the king's eyes searching his face for emotion.

He gave him none: neither for the late king nor his soldiers. He had indeed seen thousands die in the last weeks alone. And thousands before that. There was a certain numbness that was necessary to survive in times of war—Jikun had long since acquired it. "Thank you for your condolences. I shall pass your words along to my army."

"And how *are* your soldiers?" the king inquired, taking a glass and filling it. He leaned forward and offered it to the general.

"...Thank you." Jikun accepted it, swirling it with a gentle twist of his wrist. "My army is gratified to be serving its king," he replied, trying to infuse some semblance of emotion into his voice. But that too had gotten lost beneath his mask.

The corners of Hairem's lips twitched. "Jikun, I am not—may the gods grant him safe passage—my father. I intend to run this kingdom differently. First and foremost, I would request that, in matters of conversation, you treat me as your equal. It benefits neither of us to bear your polite cynicism."

Jikun leaned back, taking a long sip of wine. He had to admit—he was intrigued by Hairem's approach. That was twice today that the king had suggested that he was not like other nobility. "As you wish, Your Majesty," he spoke after a moment's hesitation, noting that Hairem shifted slightly at the retained title. "We are fatigued, but their spirits are high. Saebellus is a fierce opponent; his army fights with conviction and skill. Our victories have been hard fought and we have paid steeply. I return home with fifty thousand fewer soldiers than I set out with. Saebellus' forces are wounded, but hardly defeated. And while we spill our blood for the sake of the kingdom, we hear rumors of unrest amongst the politicians… Some say that a peace treaty draws near."

Hairem tilted his fair head back and laughed once, loudly and almost mockingly at the content of Jikun's words. "A *peace* treaty? Let those that suggest it be branded as traitors. I assure you that the kingdom will never settle terms with Saebellus, General. You do not bleed in vain." He stroked the corner of the desk, eyes hardening as though reflecting on his resolve.

Jikun wondered how strong it was. "Every battle we've engaged in has been in Saebellus' favor. He knows we have the upper hand in numbers and so territory has been his strategy. He never allows us to engage him unless he has a way to flee after a defeat—and when he flees, he and his army simply vanish. And it's not teleportation magic—no portals at all. Such magic leaves behind a distinct residue and none of my mages have ever found such a trace. Neither, would it seem, is Saebellus capable of using the magic to appear—I would imagine such an ability would have been used countless times for surprise attacks or motions to surround us in. We're simply grabbing the lizard's tail for now. But let me assure you, Your Majesty, that Saebellus will be defeated. Even the advantage of territory has won him no battles."

Hairem nodded his admiration and gave a faint smile. With a slight raise of his glass, he spoke as though still attempting to reassure Jikun of the city's tenacity. "You are an excellent general, Jikun. No doubt you and your army shall put an end to this war soon enough. Many in the city other than myself believe this as well."

Jikun nodded his head, knowing it was with overconfidence that the elves placed their trust in Elvorium's army. Yes, Saebellus had won no battles, but he was by no means defeated. "Saebellus still retains control of the Beast…" he trailed off, grimacing at the shadow that loomed just outside his mind. These were the hardest words yet. Simply in speaking them, he felt he trod on the darker matters, taunting them to reveal themselves. Even after so many battles, its shape felt faint and distant—surreal in the midst of war. But how real it *was*. "We have had several battles with the creature and no magic or weapon seems capable of taking its life."

Jikun saw Hairem's lips purse into a hard, thin line as his fingers interlocked, but his eyes wavered. Perhaps it was fear that moved them.

As it should.

"Is there anything I can offer you that my father had not already given?" Hairem spoke after a moment's deliberation.

Jikun exhaled. "Nothing that myself, my captain, or my lieutenants cannot conjure up on our own. I will let you know if matters change. We intend to stay in the city until we hear of Saebellus' movement again. Those that have homes within the city shall go to them. The rest shall make an encampment outside the city to the north. The soldiers need to refresh their bodies as well as their minds. As for myself," Jikun continued, leaning back into his chair, "I intend to return to Darival."

Jikun could see Hairem's lips part in hesitation, and then his eyes softened. He nodded his head once toward him. "I imagine it is about time you see your home again."

"It's been three years," Jikun replied with a faint smile. "I would imagine so."

Hairem set his glass down and absentmindedly straightened a stack of unruly papers beside his elbow. Jikun could judge, by the dates smudged along the upper corners, that they were far past their creators' expected response time. "I was not privy to the extensive military campaign you have led against the rebel warlord. Your last battle was…?"

"Fifteen leagues north of Widows' Peak. Saebellus fled into the mountains. He has several sorcerers in his ranks—one of which sent an avalanche behind him. We spent two weeks digging out our dead. I do not know where he plans to go from there. …I'm afraid there is little to tell. No cities have been conquered or besieged. Just dead elves and dead horses." He raised his glass and again swirled the wine inside, ignoring the piece of dust floating at the top. He took a sip. "I assume under your reign my campaign against Saebellus may continue unchanged?"

Hairem nodded. "Yes, General. With, I hope, more fortune in the future." He paused briefly. "What is your goal, General?"

Jikun blinked, his rigid composure thrown by the question. "My goal…? To fight the war. To *win* the war, of course."

Hairem shook his head. "No, I meant after the war, when Saebellus is defeated—what is your ambition?"

Jikun felt the barriers inside himself rise; his face returned to its frigid countenance as memories of disconnected battles scattered the edges of his vision. He scowled inwardly, finding Hairem's presumption offensively naïve. "You are assuming I live through it."

Hairem opened his mouth and closed it, clearly discomforted by Jikun's straightforward, if pessimistic, approach. "I am certain Sel'ari shall protect you for your loyalty and devotion to her people."

Jikun raised his glass. "Indeed," was the only monotonous response he could trust himself to offer. He took another sip before transitioning to the next "necessary" words in their political game. "What has taken place in the city while we were gone?" The words rolled off his tongue rather forcefully. It was difficult to put whatever bickering or vices the city suffered at any level of concern in his mind when placed in the perspective of his wars. But he nevertheless lowered his glass and met the eyes of the king with respectful attention.

"At home the council is scattering. When my father assumed kingship after the Royal Schism, it was due to his previous position as El'adorium that granted him the power and hold over the council. I, of course, have had no such experience. My father's death has left them grasping for new loyalties and I'm afraid I will not be keeping all of them. I may need your help in the coming months."

Jikun's expression blanked for a moment even as his gut unsettled. "Help with what…?"

"I need to know that I have the support and protection of our military. It is not easy to pick up where my father left off and not expect things to change. I will have to upset the balance."

Jikun felt uneasy at the suggestion, but he replied with no semblance of hesitation. "Of course, Your Majesty. The military's first duty is to the king."

"Thank you, General." Hairem paused for a moment, face growing grim. "One of my most loyal council… Just three days before your arrival, the assassin struck within the city again…"

"Who was taken?" Jikun asked, leaning forward with unfiltered intrigue, his leather armor creaking softly in the heavy silence that had suddenly settled over the room.

"Lord Leisum Na'Hemel of Nostoran. Stabbed repeatedly in his bed while he slept. Only the maggots knew for the first two days."

Jikun's stomach lurched. Both hands tightened on the arms of his chair. Not at the thought of the mangled body or the feast of insects upon it, but at the thought of the Beast that reawakened at the back of his mind. *Hairem had seen nothing of death. Of true slaughter.* "How is this assassin being dealt with?" Jikun forced his mind back to the topic at hand. "City Guard? Night's Watch? Mercenaries?"

"All of the above," Hairem heaved a sigh. "It is the same killer—he leaves his victims' arms crossed across their chests, like the worshipers of Asmodius do. Perhaps they are cultist killings..." He trailed off and Jikun scoffed to himself.

Cultist killings that only targeted council members? No. And he had no doubt the king knew better.

"But let us put this matter aside," Hairem's voice rose forcefully, snapping his attention to Jikun. "A great victory has been won against the rebel. You are a hero yet again, Jikun Taemrin. May Sel'ari and all the gods bless you in all of your future battles. For now, drink and rest."

Jikun raised his glass in a due gesture of formality. "All glory and honor to your greatness."

*

"Navon, my reins," Jikun demanded as he neared his captain, the last figure that lingered by the palace's side gates. He grabbed the saddle of his mare and hoisted himself up, jerking his horse around stiffly. "The king is dead, Navon."

He knew the words would unsettle Navon as much as they unsettled himself and he could see the flicker of concern cross his captain's face. "How?"

Jikun hesitated. Hairem had said it had been an illness, but in light of the recent string of assassinations he was not as ready to sentence the king to such a swift and sudden conclusion. And yet he buried his suspicions and replied, "Illness. It must have come rather suddenly." His voice was stoic, but he knew Navon could read beneath his apathy.

Liadeltris had been a fierce king and opponent to Saebellus. It was common knowledge that Saebellus had been dishonorably discharged while serving as captain in the last war with the sirens, but no one knew why. Jikun had long since let the prodding curiosity subside when even Liadeltris had refused to shed light on the matter. But whatever the reason, it hardly mattered now. Saebellus had taken those loyal to him and turned on the elves' empire.

Navon seemed to share his concern, but his tone revealed little else. "And the prince... king... what are your thoughts on him?"

"What?" Jikun looked up, still managing to catch the skepticism across the male's face through his distraction. "I believe what he said. There will be no peace terms with Saebellus. In fact, I believe his eyes are open to the corruption of the council. And I think he has the stupidity to oppose it."

"...but you are still concerned."

Jikun's brow knit. "Hairem is young. For all Liadeltris'—"

"May the gods grant him peace—"

"—experience, he still bent to the council's pressure. Three hundred years as king, a dozen centuries as the El'adorium before that, and Liadeltris could not resist them. Once Hairem learns how the damn politics in this country go, I wonder just how strong he will remain."

Navon gave a nod of reluctant agreement, eyes staring stoically ahead.

"Here is more news from home whilst we were away—"

"Something in your tone brings me to believe that I am not going to like what you are about to say..." Navon frowned, eyes flicking toward the general attentively.

"You remember the murders before we left? Another council member was assassinated."

Navon's eyes flashed in recognition, but the rest of his face remained apathetic. "He struck again?" He gave a heavy sigh, as though the capital should have done better to prevent such an atrocity. "No doubt the Night's Watch will be far more numerous for some time now. It is unprecedented that an assassin has committed so many murders on high officials—within an elven capital, especially." He paused to give a slight smile, churning out optimism from the news as he usually did. "I suppose there are some benefits to being out of the comfort of this city." His eyes shifted across the nearest alley as he spoke, almost with a certain daring curiosity.

Jikun watched Navon for a moment and then cleared his throat loudly. "Gods, I could use a drink!" he barked. "How about a good drink and a fine woman to share it with?"

The darkness in Navon's eyes faded and he surveyed his general in a reprimanding fashion. "General." He pulled his horse to a stop, interrupting Jikun before he could continue. "Let us pause this conversation. Sel'ari's temple. We should stop and thank the gods before we retire for the evening."

In Jikun's absorption with his news, he had somehow missed the building's slithering approach. His eyes lifted to the golden dome rising up toward the heavens, the white doves nestled at her base, and the pillars that made the elves below seem small and insignificant—as they undoubtedly were. He could hear the echoes of soft singing in the distant marble halls and the pure chime of bells, calling the elves to worship. He turned his head and laughed. "I'll thank the gods when I see the gods at work. When we are in the right and Saebellus in the wrong, I can only spit on their names every time they let one of my soldiers die for Saebellus' damn cause. We sleep in shit and spill our blood so some damn elf can rise in the morning to sing praise to their righteous asses. We are just their pawns. No. No, gods for me today, Navon. Give me a good drink and a fine woman—those are all the gods *I* need."

Navon gave Jikun another distasteful and reprimanding glare before he stiffly dismounted, the offense apparently affecting his gait. "Then can you keep a hold of these for me, General?" he asked tartly, tossing Jikun the reins to his bay horse. "*Someone* has to give Sel'ari thanks that you are still breathing."

Jikun leaned to the side sharply in order to the catch the reins. His horse whinnied in protest and the general quickly righted himself. "When I was a boy in Darival, a priest of Sel'ari came through. A group of youths beat him dead for the single coin in his pocket. I don't think Sel'ari cares about any of us, Navon, more than she'd care about one of her priests. And if she did not see fit to save him, then we're all going to the grave, god or no god."

Navon leaned forward, squinting in a reflective manner. "They are not absent from us, Jikun. And I have a story to counter your own. Years ago on my way to Sevrigel, I saw a stowaway cry out in Sel'ari's name for protection. Everyone who tried to lay a hand on him perished in an instant. Sel'ari always has her reasons, Jikun," Navon replied with a simple smile. "Sometimes they just do not fit into our expectations. Religion is a virtue …and one of the only reasons Sel'ari hasn't sent this country to Ramul." He turned toward the temple, as though his words were a monument of inspiration and the general should immediately reflect upon their wisdom.

Jikun shook his head distastefully. "While you are in there, put in a good word for me for lovely company tonight," he called after with a smirk. "The more 'virtuous,' the better. I'd take a cleric!"

Navon gave only a dismissive wave of resigned acknowledgement.

Jikun's smirk broadened in amusement and he leaned back idly in the saddle. He watched the lean, dark male vanish through one of the double golden doors. For just a moment he glimpsed the white marble interior, gleaming from the countless candles within. And the face of Sel'ari. He felt himself recoil slightly, perhaps more out of shame than disgust. Even in the form of a statue, the goddess' eyes were coldly perceptive, piercing through his veil of disbelief like a dagger. He nudged his horse lightly in the flank, urging it away from the doors and further along the street until he came to the shade of a low balcony.

Away from the temple, he found himself once more at ease. He leaned an arm against his horse's neck, watching the bustle of elves moving about through the sunny street. They acknowledged him with polite nods of their heads or wide smiles, but Jikun found little reason to smile in return. Why should he? What had they done today to equal his last two years of warring for their sake? Ate and danced and pleasured themselves. He knew not all males could serve in the army. And yet, that did not stop his resentment at every able bodied male he saw enjoying himself in the comfort of the city's walls while Saebellus waged war outside.

Perhaps his inner thoughts had revealed themselves on his expression as he noted several responding elves regard him with unease and confusion. He wiped his face of expression and instead let his eyes trail up along the towering buildings with their many windows, pillars, and gleaming rooftops, still further up the hill of the street and into the distance. Elvorium was not his home, but even so, it was better than any place he had been since he had left Darival.

Except, perhaps, for the whore houses of Roshenhyde.

"That was pleasant to see her again," Navon's voice came from behind him.

Jikun straightened and turned, eyeing the peaceful smile stamped across his captain's lips. He tossed him the reins, watching Navon leap with some faint form of grace onto his horse.

"So, where to, General?" Navon queried. His voice had livened from his perceived notion of Sel'ari's mewling praise, afforded to him by his recent prayers. "To the camp?"

Jikun laughed, pulling his horse away from the egress of the city. "No, let the soldiers relax without your reprimanding eyes. They deserve a little freedom and rashness. To my estate, Navon. And we will stop along the way to pick up some gods of my own."

# CHAPTER TWO

The morning rays filtered through the cracks in the sheer curtains, mixing with the thin layer of smoke that still clung to the air of the bedroom. Jikun groaned and pulled his pillow over his face.

Two years since he had had such comfort and now the sun dared wake him.

He grumbled to himself, his mind resisting his body's urge to sleep longer. He reached out a hand, but the woman who had lain with him was gone. He sighed disappointedly, sitting up with a grunt and drawing forward a knee on which to rest his head. The sweet taste of Elvorium wine still hung on his lips. Or was that the woman?

There was a bellow of laughter several floors below him, startling him from where he had begun to doze. He determinedly swung his legs out of bed, running his tongue along his lower lip, and picked up his shirt from the glassy marble floor.

"How do you manage?" he muttered to himself as her undergarments fell from its folds. The women around Elvorium almost seemed to do it with deliberate frequency. He picked them up and tossed them casually into the smoldering fire. It flicked to life, lustfully spreading its flames over the silken red fabric.

Jikun pulled his shirt on, stretching his arms above his head and twisting his waist. He inhaled heavily. The thick aroma of flowers that slowly became apparent to his senses was pleasantly calming—such a stark difference to the usual stench of wet leather and the forest floor.

The marble was cool against his feet as he padded to the open chest beneath the window. He reached up, pulling the curtains back sharply and flinching slightly at the light that burst into the room. It was shortly after dawn and the glare of the sun reflecting off the gold-slated rooftops of the city below him was not unlike armor in a midmorning's march. He possessed a certain level of disdain and affection for that. He held a hand out against the glare and cast his eyes across the city.

He was mildly disappointed to find his first morning in Elvorium as he expected: peaceful, serene, and wholly uneventful; he could see Elvorium's citizens far below him, walking along the cobbled streets of the city, milling through the market he could just glimpse between the towers of a nearby mansion. The Sel'vi were often up with the sun, their day beginning and ending with its cycle. How difficult it had been to get them to march in the evening! A throng of them gathered beneath the long shadow of a nearby pavilion, eating breakfast in the fresh spring air. Their music was far too cheerful for that time of day. He withdrew into the smoky room behind him to crouch at the chest at his feet.

*'Home to Darival...'* he thought to himself with a faint smile as the bright light and bustling city faded. It had been three years since he had seen his home. The Sel'vi's warm, sickly polite facade had quite worn on him. He reached down and lifted free his chainmail, clean and unmarred, from the stack. The repairs had been perfect.

However, the rest of his gear was not as fortunate. He frowned as he lifted up his breastplate and leather. Gods, why hadn't he thrown that away? He dropped the leather at his feet carelessly as he ran a hand meticulously across the dented surface of his armor. His fingers stopped upon reaching the deep gashes set into the side. Elven craftsmanship and armor: no doubt second only to the mountain dwarves on Ryekarayn. And yet the Beast had torn right through them. The sheer strength of his arm had crushed it inward. He flinched as he remembered the blow, the wind around his ears, the force of his body colliding with the earth.

There was a dull knock against the white frame of the open door and Jikun started.

"You're not going to wear that home, are you?" Navon berated him as he stepped into the room, eyeing the breastplate with an amused shake of his head. "Sevrigel's general should be a *little* better dressed during his homecoming than *that* twisted heap of metal." He raised a hand in an afterthought of greeting.

Jikun dropped the breastplate into the chest, giving it a hard kick. The lid fell down and bounced once in a tetchy protest. "Of course not," he replied with a scoff. He picked up the leather and tossed it to his captain. "Take care of it. Why do I still have that? Gods, am I sick of that smell."

Navon lifted it to his face and recoiled with a gag. "Too many wet spring days and nights, I suspect. I'll have a replacement in hand for when you return."

Jikun pulled his chainmail over his undershirt and his shirt over that. "Don't bother. I'll pick up something in Darival. I'm tired of this damn cow hide."

Navon gave an agreeable nod and paused. "When *do* you return?" he questioned. Jikun could see him eyeing the trunk of armor thoughtfully, his azure eyes flicking across the metal bolt. It was moments like this that Jikun felt the wild Helvarian blood in the captain stir.

He *knew* what his captain was thinking. His eyes flashed. "Navon, I expect that I can return home without worry that you will meddle in affairs you *should not touch.*" He threw his cloak over his shoulders, fastening his general's emblem to his chest. "Whatever this beast is, it's the libraries for you and nothing else. Do you understand me?"

He could see Navon's eyes roll in protest, his thin lips purse. How swiftly Navon's behavior changed off the battlefield in the privacy of each other's company. Sometimes, Jikun found that tolerating Navon's cavalier responses was difficult even after their years of companionship on the field. He watched Navon sweep a hand through his long, raven hair, silent to his general's rebuke.

"I will be gone for six weeks, I imagine. Elvorium's portal will emerge in a destination about two weeks outside of Kaivervale," Jikun carried on in response, grabbing his sack from the floor beside his chest. He looked in with a frown. "Did you clean this out?"

Navon shrugged, waving a slender hand dismissively. "I don't remember. Maybe? Sometimes I feel like a squire rather than a captain. Anyways, I already prepared one for you downstairs. Food and water. And your horse is equipped as well. You just need spare clothes and you will be ready." He paused, a sly smile crossing his lips. "*Oh.* And *this*." He held up a finger as he reached for his back pocket. "I never took you for one to keep a journal."

Jikun stiffened as his eyes landed on the familiar and tattered object clutched triumphantly in the male's hands. It was old, over-used, and had seen too many wet springs. Nor had matters been helped when a groggy, bleary-eyed soldier had, in a sad attempt to find a stump, pissed on his leather-bound sack late one night last winter. His gaze narrowed. "Navon, give that back."

His captain held the leather-bound book behind him, keeping it safely out of his general's furious reach. "The latter stuff was boring—after you joined the military. War, war, war. But the *early* stuff…"

"*Navon!*"

"The *early* stuff is downright delightful. Take this: 23 Felserine 8682:—That's before the True Bloods left, isn't it? Anyways—"

"Navon, give that back," Jikun growled sternly.

Navon retreated another step for additional safety before clearing his throat. He then continued his tirade in a voice pitched high and feminine,

"As clear as ice
And white with glow
Her complexion like the tundra's snow
Flowing, twisting, silks and furs
From southern markets ripe with heat—"

"Navon, I'm warning you one more time."

"—She moves across the frozen land
On silent or whispering hurried feet.
The walls cannot stop her;
The wind carries her
Over and into the city of ice—"

"My patience is waning, *Captain.*"

"Ever oblivious the watchtower sits,
To the rise of the White Queen,
In Tuserine's presence."

Jikun flushed, feeling the heat rising to his cheeks in discomfiture. "Are you quite done?" He attempted to appear somewhat collected—his rise about the journal could only make the mocking worse.

Navon clicked his tongue as he flicked a yellowed page. "No, there are countless treasures in here. Give me a moment, I think I lost the folded corner to the next piece of—"

Jikun darted forward suddenly but the Helven twisted away once more, suddenly and superiorly agile. *'You prying bastard…!'*

"Ah, here it is. I like this one. A*hem.*

"A soldier's life
Working
Sleeping
Eating
Working.
Hands raw
Bodies burned.
Drinking until it doesn't hurt."

Jikun stepped swiftly aside the trunk, making a straight dash for the captain. He caught the end of Navon's sleeve, but the Helven simply snapped his arm free and escaped to the empty center of the room.

"No, no, I want to read you another one—"

Jikun scrambled after the male, snagging the end of his sleeve and jerking his arm toward him. "I don't need you to read them to me, you bastard. I know what they say."

"Wait, I have to— You *have* to hear this next gem—"

"Tch!" Jikun clenched his teeth, patience finally reaching the end of its abilities; it was replaced with a far more final method of dealing with the insistent child before him. He swept his hand downward, fixing his attention on the ground behind Navon's evasive feet. A small sheet of ice covered the marble floor, and as Navon retreated one step farther, his foot met the icy trap, slipping out beneath him. Jikun lunged forward and caught Navon by the arm, wrestling the journal out of the Helven's clenched fingers. Then he shoved him away, straightening in an attempt to regain some dignity. "Are we done here?" he spoke sternly.

"Yes," Navon replied casually, seeming unfazed by his defeat. "Well actually, I do have just one question…"

Jikun narrowed his eyes in warning.

"Are these poems… rough drafts? Because by the *gods* are they awf—"

Jikun lashed out his arm, cuffing Navon squarely in the ear with the palm of his hand. Navon choked off the rest of his words, raising a hand to his ear in indignation. He appeared ready to protest the violence, but a threatening glare from Jikun ended that notion as well. He instead stiffly smoothed down the front of his shirt, but Jikun could see the internal laughter raging behind those unabashedly curious azure eyes.

Jikun placed all the menace of Sevrigel's general into his tone before speaking. "Don't empty my sack again." He stepped away, patting himself down subconsciously. "Ah, my sword," he muttered, turning from his captain and back to the chest. He raised the lid, which gave a joyful squeak to once more breathe a fresh breath of air, and paused, eyes falling again to the torn breastplate and the blow that had smashed the chest inward. He knew those azure eyes were following him intensely now. And just as intrusively.

He paused. "…This creature could be demonic, Navon." He pushed the torn metal aside, knowing his words fell on deaf ears. Navon already knew that the creature could be demonic. It was that fact that drove his curiosity. He reached down to the sword lying below, its hilt carved as though from Darival's ice and embellished with the mountains' countless gems. He pulled it out and fastened it to the belt at his side.

Navon was ready immediately with a counterargument. "Suppose it is demonic, Jikun. What old traditions are of value anymore? This country has been changing since Eraydon's time. Necromancy is just a step further down this road of progress. We discussed this the last time we spoke of the beast." Navon did not need to remind him—Jikun remembered every time the word necromancy had been breathed. And yet, his captain's tone seemed to prod Jikun further along as though, by the general's words, he had opened the conversation. "And I have been thinking… reading, as it were. Demonic entities will not fall to our magic or weapons and—"

Jikun turned sharply before his captain could continue further. Gods, why did he insist on provoking him?! "NO." His voice was raised and sharp, echoing across the stone walls around them and vanishing into the vaulted ceiling above.

Navon fell silent once more, his teeth snapping back together with an audible *clack*. Jikun could see the muscles tense along the jaw line, incensed once more from the rebuke.

Jikun walked briskly past him, brushing against his captain's shoulder as he made no move to step out of the way. "Let's try this again," he breathed slowly. "Demonic entities…" He paused, waiting for his captain to continue their oft-repeated conversation.

"*May* be susceptible to obsidian. But the only elves on Sevrigel who possess that material are the Malravi. And obsidian is simply not a practical weapon in battle against those wielding steel or elsteral blades… or armor. If Eraydon let *Tiras*—"

"You are not Tiras and I am not Eraydon. Libraries *only* for you," Jikun replied firmly, straightening from his boots and feeling that he had given him more than a fair chance to express his stance. "Do you understand me? If you dare touch..." he hesitated, forcing the word out with almost fear-filled venom, "*necromancy*, so help me Navon..."

Navon protested, turning back toward him. "This is the *problem* with this damn country, Jikun! Tradition upheld in one realm is wholly dismissed in another. The lines are just a blur now, even in you! The Sel'vi are notorious for upholding virtue when they fear progress and abandoning those same customs when it benefits them. Banning necromancy is just another one of their conjured 'traditions'—it holds no historical weight! More importantly, it's our best chance at fighting a demonic entity!"

"If tradition is a virtue and the lines are too blurred now, I'd rather err on the side of the Sel'vi on this one," Jikun replied stiffly. This was the *one* area he could agree with those arrogantly naïve bastards. The elves of the mountains had been dabbling in the dark magics with terrifying consequences long enough for tradition to mark *that* with due negativity.

Yet Navon persisted. "History defines what traditions *are* virtuous: it separates the old traditions from these new *frivolous* ones. The ban on necromancy is just some new 'tradition' created out of fear, *not* an old tradition that upheld the framework of the just society under Sel'ari where—"

"Well, soon this history will create the 'virtuous tradition' of banning necromancy as well. We'll find another way to fight this 'demonic entity.' *If* that is what it is," Jikun replied calmly.

"*Very likely that it is.*"

"Possibly."

"Probably."

"No." Jikun spun back suddenly and grabbed Navon sharply by the front of his shirt, his anger rising, his icy eyes meeting the Helven's coldly. "You keep your eyes open while I'm gone and you do not *touch*... that cursed magic. Do I make myself clear? This is general's orders... *not* just the law of Sevrigel."

He saw Navon cast his eyes to the side, the stubbornness fading even beneath the resentment at the command. Gods could Navon be a fool! A stubborn, *persistent* fool! "Yes, General," he muttered stiffly.

Jikun dropped his hand and smoothed down the ruffled fabric. He gave Navon a hard smack on the chest, forcing himself to smile. "Now, I'll be back in a few weeks. Relax. Enjoy yourself. Bed a woman. Dream of Sel'ari.

Whatever it is you do in your free time." He tucked a few spare clothes beneath his arm and journal. "I'm off for home."

He saw Navon smile despite himself, his eyes flicking pointedly to the leather-bound book. "Just go. And stop your worrying. Somehow I'll manage without your overbearing eyes for a few weeks." His smile broadened. "But no more than that."

# Chapter Three

Hairem slouched in his seat, groaning, his arms hanging limply over the sides of the chair. "Why must the gods hate me so?" he moaned.

The girl brushing his hair folded her hands against her abdomen patiently as his hair disappeared beneath the back of the chair, not bothering to hide her exaggerated eye roll. He was *such* a sloucher. His father had been one, too. Even now, over the din of her own thoughts and Hairem's complaints, the handmaid could hear the late king's hypocritical rebuke toward his son. "Sit up straight. Shoulders back. You're a prince, not a pauper."

She eyed the ceiling, attention flicking from the chipping gold paint to the webbed center of the dome. She would need a very tall ladder to reach that one. Perhaps there was one in the cellar. She glanced once more toward the king, who seemed to have slipped further down the chair.

"I will tell you that this is the worst. The worst—no, no, I take that back… that damn council is the worst… but *this* is damn close. You understand how these things work, do you not?" He tipped his head back and she saw his brow knit as he found the web at the center of the dome. "Ah… forgive my language, Alvena… You are not a male, you are a gir—a lady." He gripped the sides of the chair and pulled himself straight, flicking his hair behind his head again. "Carry on."

His fit paused, the girl raised the brush again and worked it through the now static ends of his hair. A *lady*. Ha! If she was a *lady* she would not be a handmaid. She pulled a little on his hair absentmindedly. She had just begun to bleed two years ago and that, in the eyes of the elves, hardly made her more than a child and certainly not a lady… but she liked when he used that word. She stood a little taller.

"I will have to sit there with a sweetly sickening smile the entirety of the time," he suddenly groaned. He turned his head, hair yanking from her hand, the brush still caught in the ends. "Does this smile look false to you?"

The girl nodded.

"Maybe I shall simply *not* smile."

She shrugged.

The king slumped back into the chair and she pried the brush from his hair. He had a lot of hair. Not as much as his father, but it was so frizzy now!

"I know… It is just that… Nilanis has the greatest influence over the council. If I sit through a dinner with him, perhaps I can create a more amiable atmosphere at the council… which is something I desperately need if those meetings are to go anywhere at all." He was quiet a moment. "Are you almost done? It certainly is taking you a while this morning."

* * * * *

The carriage ride to the estate of the El'adorium was long, rolling gently along the winding roads of the city. When Hairem's mood was agreeable, he would call it scenic—when his patience ran thin, it was superfluous. Nilanis' home was located on the west side of the city, along the bank of the lake, which was located in the exact opposite direction of the palace. Yes, this ride was superfluous.

*'And,'* Hairem mused, *'what an ironic reflection of the supposed close relationship that the El'adorium holds with the king.'*

For all the expectations that the El'adorium was supposed to work closely with the king, Hairem actually knew very little about Nilanis' life. Personally, that was. Economically, it was impossible to *not* know the male. Nilanis seemed to own the Port of Targados and the lake itself: it was usually his ships and his trade that came in to port. The male had acquired most of his fortune off of the trade that both came *and* left the capital, and subsequently his power derived from the wealth and control of the majority of Elvorium's commerce. Stripped of his powers as the El'adorium, Nilanis would *still* hold a potent influence. His reach could be felt as far north as Darival and as far south as even the coastline of Dragon Wing. Even before he had become the El'adorium three centuries before, a lord of his status and economic influence had been in no short supply of power.

Even the True Blood King Silandrus had struggled with the non-royal regime…

The carriage bounced suddenly and Hairem's face smacked against the side of the carriage wall, drawing him sharply from his thoughts. *'Ouch! What in Ramul are you doing out there?'* he muttered internally as he rubbed his brow. *'Excellent. That's a mark.'*

The carriage drew to a stop and the door swung open, an apologetic carriage driver leaning sheepishly to the side.

"What did we do, hit someone?" Hairem jested, though he half expected something to be lying behind on the road after that jolt. He stepped out onto the cobbled steps of the estate grounds, eyeing the street behind them.

"No, Your Majesty!" the carriage driver quickly exclaimed. "Just a toy some children threw into the road. Erallus has reprimanded them—"

"And warned them of the dangers, I hope," Hairem interrupted. "Lucky it was their toy and not one of them." *'And now I sound like my father... Gods know how many times* I *played in the streets...'*

He saw a tall, heavily armed male wrap around from the back of the carriage, on queue to respond. He drew up stiffly to the king's side and offered a half-bow. "Of course, Your Majesty. They have been warned and sent away. Is there anything else you require? Or shall we wait for you here?"

Hairem's eyes abandoned the sparsely occupied road and flicked to the estate grounds where the cobbled path led to a set of intricately-carved mahogany doors. "Here will do," he replied slowly to his personal guard, letting the carriage door swing closed. "And pray that this dinner goes quickly," he added with a mutter below his breath.

"What was that, My Lord?"

Hairem patted the guard affectionately on the shoulder. "I will see you shortly, Erallus," he dismissed before taking several brisk steps up toward the estate. Before he had progressed farther than that, the doors swung wide and two thin servants pressed back against them, as though trying to make themselves invisible.

And it was hardly a difficult task, for there between them, framed in the opulent doorway, was Nilanis.

"Good evening, Your Majesty," the Voice of the Elves greeted boisterously, sweeping his elegant bow low before the king. Nilanis straightened beneath the glowing light of a lantern swaying gently above him. "No escort this evening?"

Hairem offered a soft smile and nodded his head in greeting, wondering if the evening light around them was enough to render the mark on his head visible. "Good evening, Nilanis," he replied as he reached the top of the steps.

He glanced back once, longingly, to the comfort of the carriage. "I do not need an escort to see a dear friend," he spoke as he faced his host, lips twitching into a practiced smile.

Nilanis smiled in return, broader and far better versed in deceit than Hairem could ever hope to manage. "Welcome to my humble home. I hope we can serve you most adequately this evening." The elf turned and led him into the estate, his long, gold-hemmed robes dragging across the polished wood. His clothing seemed all too warm to be worn in the mid spring, but Hairem imagined that it was a gesture of his wealth and status to be so heavily—and luxuriously—clad in the silks, velvet, and gold of the offshore elven cities.

Hairem found himself looking rather drab beside him. He subconsciously ran his hand down his chest to smooth his shirt.

"Our dining room is just over this way," Nilanis was saying. He must have said something prior to this statement, but Hairem found himself now overly focused on the strange statue of a naked female arched back against a large tree. With one hand on her inner thigh, she taunted males to stare. Hairem felt it was in rather poor taste, especially for a Sel'ven of Nilanis' class.

Nilanis paused his steps to glance at the statue. "My wife—may she be at peace—was rather fond of that work. It was one of the surviving pieces found in the Farvian Realms after the Cataclysm. I feel it defines quite well the risqué nature of their elven people… But I cannot bear to remove such a nostalgic symbol of her memory." He sighed briefly, almost, Hairem thought, longingly.

He grimaced slightly as the carved female took on a more personal tone.

"And that chandelier is from Eraydon City—a new design, actually. Exquisite, is it not? No doubt you have a dozen such chandeliers in your palace."

Hairem turned, his grimace growing. He, in fact, had none. Not simply because he knew nothing about such décor, but because it would inevitably look gaudy in any elven room. As it did here. He stopped beside where Nilanis had paused, looking up at the golden chandelier dangling from the ceiling of the dining hall, light from the candles reflecting off of its countless crystals. "Exquisite," Hairem replied, attempting to weave interest into his tone. Fearing he had failed, he flashed a sickly sweet smile.

A servant hurried forward from the shadows at their right, bowed low, and drew out the head chair for the king.

Hairem sat, giving his thanks as Nilanis carried on about some specially carved maiden etched into the chair in which he now sat. He only stopped to beckon the servant away after being seated himself.

"*How* are you, as of late?" Hairem interrupted before Nilanis could continue.

The elf tapped the table and a servant hurriedly returned. "There has been minor pillaging of ships bound for my ports by southern human pirate scum... but I knew this was inevitable, what with the news of the famine spreading across Ryekarayn... This winter will be brutal for them. They're lucky to have such generous allies as ourselves or no doubt they would never survive." He sniffed and stroked the rim of his golden goblet.

Hairem muffled a snort. *'Generous? I would never go so far as to call* you *generous...'*

Nilanis seemed not to notice and merely raised his empty wine glass to eye it reproachfully, as though it ought to fill itself. "And a male has begun residence in the estate to my left. He has two children as wild as Faravi who have unfortunately been cluttering the street outside with their toys. They like to lay siege to the wall around my estate, it seems. Ah, but I can't complain. No, I can't complain. His wife is gone to the same illness that took my wife and your mother. Pity on the poor males who must raise their offspring without the guidance of their wiser half."

Hairem's brow knit faintly. He liked to think he had turned out fair even without his mother's assistance.

Nilanis paused, briefly studying Hairem's face as though attempting to gather his nonverbal response. When Hairem offered nothing, he reluctantly abandoned his search. "So overall, quite well, Your Majesty. Fortunately, a male of my trade profits even in times of war. I certainly am not suited to the life of a pauper." He gave a private laugh and then spoke quietly to the servant. "I apologize, My Lord, for my daughter's late arrival."

Hairem's brows rose in confusion and for the briefest moment, he wondered if he had missed something earlier. "Your daughter...?"

Once again there was a flurry of movement as a servant rushed from the room, his departure then heralding the entrance of a dozen males bearing large silver platters of delicate foods and wines. For a moment, Hairem's bemusement overshadowed his confusion at Nilanis' comment, and he wondered if the El'adorium realized that his servants' frenzied activity conveyed more agitation than grace.

"Yes, my daugh—ah, finally!" No sooner had the table been laden with luxurious foods than the door was once more thrown open, and Hairem had to repress a sigh as he turned to greet the new arrival.

In the doorway stood a lady, her dress shimmering softly in the candlelight as each delicate strand of silk vied for attention on her lean form. And to Hairem's surprise he found his tension ebbing as his muscles relaxed, the bustle of the servants all but fading from his mind.

All elves were fair. This, no person could argue. But even amongst elves, this female was enchantingly beautiful. She entered timidly, as her class found proper, with hands folded in front of her. Hairem had never met Nilanis' wife, but given his daughter's radiance, it seemed at least, to Hairem, that she certainly did not take after her father. Most pleasantly, her demeanor exhibited all the elegance and unobtrusive grace that the rest of the household lacked.

"Your Majesty, this is my daughter, Ilsevel," Nilanis spoke, taking her hand and passing it to the king.

Hairem stood, aware of his unblinking stare, and yet, he couldn't manage to take his eyes off of her. He watched as her lean form bent into a graceful curtsy and he raised her pale hand, kissing her smooth and unmarred skin. "My lady," he spoke with a faint smile, nodding his head in acknowledgement.

She looked up shyly, green eyes flashing with a flicker of interest. "Your Majesty."

Hairem released her hand, reseating himself and watching as she took the seat at his left. She jostled her thick, golden hair slightly from her shoulders, adjusted the sleeves of her almost shamefully-flattering dress, and picked up her fork. Hairem glanced at Nilanis as though to be certain that the lady before him was in fact related to the weather-beaten face of the councilmember. And the king's smile abruptly faded.

Nilanis was looking *quite* satisfied with his level of interest.

*'Of* course *that is what he wants,'* Hairem thought irritably, picking up his fork and quickly resubmitting his smile of polite company. He forced his eyes to return to the grandiose meal—as though it could hold any interest after her appearance—and reprimanded himself for his shameless gawking. Even worse, her presence closed off the topic of politics.

And so it was, as Hairem expected, a long dinner. There was mostly the clanking of the silverware, the flickering of far too many candles, and the pitter patter of the constant comings and goings of servants at Nilanis' beckoning. He made sure to use them at every opportunity, as though to demonstrate his authority and wealth.

"How is the kingship treating you, Your Majesty?" Nilanis inquired as he reached for a thin slice of venison. "I can only imagine your father's sudden death thrust upon you quite the burden."

Hairem's expression remained resolute as his eyes met with the El'adorium's. "Indeed it has been quite the change," he agreed. "But I watched my father closely for years. And I had my close associations with the True Blood princes to learn from… No male was better suited than my father and so I had no better male to learn from."

The left corner of Nilanis' thin lips raised slightly before he replied, with some form of a twisted and almost unsettling smile, "Only three centuries to learn the politics of kings, but your father was a brilliant male."

"Yes, he was. I have had both his triumphs… and his mistakes… to learn from." Hairem looked up and smiled in return—a slow, pointed smile.

Nilanis' ease faltered. Hairem liked the way the El'adorium pondered the possibility of a personal touch in the response. "And what mistakes might those be, Your Majesty?"

Hairem raised his wine glass in a dismissive manner. "I don't believe that this is a topic worthy of such lovely company." He nodded his head toward Ilsevel with a faint, apologetic twitch of his lips that he hoped resembled a smile. "I would certainly not wish to depart on such a weighty topic without the proper time to fully defend my late father's decisions. Perhaps another time?"

Nilanis smoothed over his tensed jaw line in a swift, broad smile. He seemed to operate on a standard of shifting and carefully controlled expressions. "Why of *course*, Your Majesty." He paused a moment to take a sip of his wine and to allow a proper break in the conversation before changing topics. "You had your first meeting with the general the other day, did you not? How did you take to him?"

As much as Hairem had liked to see Nilanis momentarily discomforted, he groaned inwardly at the change. *'I suppose the general is not* technically *politics…'* He slid his fork across his plate absentmindedly as he recalled the Darivalian male's rigid composure and apathetic mannerisms. "He was… very difficult to connect with. A bit abrasive and distant. Cold, I suppose I'd describe him as." He shrugged offhandedly. "*Honest*, at least." He had truly not given the general much thought since their meeting. In a way, Jikun Taemrin still seemed like his late father's business, even after his passing: a Darivalian male with whom he had artificial authority over and even less in common. And furthermore, with the general's stoic and cold approach, he had been remarkably easy to forget.

A self-satisfied smile spread across Nilanis' lips and Hairem felt his mood sour further. No doubt the El'adorium would savor displaying the knowledge he possessed—the knowledge of a topic that extended long before Hairem's reign. Indeed, Nilanis seemed to relish in his superiority for a moment, drawing out a long pause before he responded with all the airs of familiarity on the matter, "Ah, I expected as much," he breathed with a faint tsk. "It's the Darivalians in general. They are such a *difficult* people to find amicable. Entirely unambiguous, really. They say exactly what it is they are thinking and possess not a bit of character or depth below the surface. Emotionally, I'd say, what you see is exactly how they feel. It is, of course, why they make such excellent soldiers. They couldn't engage in subterfuge if their lives were entirely dependent on it. It is why we appointed him, especially after that unspeakable mess with Saebellus. Get a dog to do a dog's work."

Hairem pursed his lips in distaste. "Surely the general has a commanding mind of his own."

Nilanis laughed once. "I certainly hope not!" He raised his glass and took a sip, chuckling to himself again as he set it down. "But let us speak no more of the general or the war. The council meetings are a more appropriate time for such trivialities." He continued even as Hairem's eyes widened in disbelief. "I have something of, no doubt, *far* more interest to your exquisite tastes. *Ilsevel* was the most accomplished student of her tutor in art and poetry," Nilanis offered as he cut the remainder of his meat.

Ilsevel pushed her food across her plate and laughed. "Oh, Father."

*'...Far more interest to my exquisite tastes...? Gods, if ever there was a stretch for a topical transition.'* It was difficult for Hairem to even *feign* interest in this political game. "That is... wonderful. You must be proud." He could hear his voice coming out flat, but he was past the point of bothering to change it now.

Nilanis gave a nod. He didn't seem to notice. "And Ilsevel plays the lyre most beautifully, a talent she no doubt received from her mother. If Your Majesty wishes to hear her play..." he added, trailing off as he scraped the last contents from his plate.

Ilsevel smiled and looked down, her cheeks growing pink. "I am certain King Hairem has heard far better from his palace musicians."

Hairem gave an internal sigh. Every part of him fled inwardly toward the door, but he smiled nonetheless and politely requested, "Why, I must hear you play, Ilsevel." This, at least, came out with a *little* more tonal variety.

She nodded sheepishly and stood, as though his words had been a direct command, and left her chair behind for the servant to push in. "My lyre is in the Great Room, if you will just follow me." She gave no emotion behind her words, but merely glanced back once to see if he was following. Then she turned her pretty face away and vanished into the hallway.

Hairem regrettably left his wine and paused at the edge of the room. He sent Nilanis a quizzical glance when the lord made no attempt to pursue. "Will you be joining us…?"

"Oh, go on ahead," the lord encouraged in a tone fit for the reply to a merely rhetorical question. "I have some dessert preparations to discuss with the servants."

With resignation, Hairem contemplated the situation as Ilsevel glided on ahead of him.

"I suppose you have many Great Rooms," Ilsevel began slowly as she led him into a vast, marble-tiled room. The wall directly ahead of them was made of painted glass, but the night was too dark to allow more than the faintest colors through. The lady moved to a round seat beside the fireplace and picked up the gold-plated lyre, stroking it once as color fell across her fair skin from the windows behind her. She waited patiently for Hairem to sit across from her.

Whether Nilanis had ever heard his daughter play was doubtful. Much like a sword on stone, she grated through two pieces of musical genius that at once became barely recognizable. Her redeeming quality, however, was her voice. Enchantingly soft, she wove the lyrics over the music until the king almost forgot where he was—and what he was listening to.

"Truly, you are quite gifted," Hairem complimented her as she finished. He could not deny that her voice had impressed him far more than any musicians at court. Her body language while playing had been quite enticing as well—fluid and elegant, despite her inability to pluck a single tune.

Yet for that reason alone, he'd have strongly recommended she never pick up the instrument again.

Ilsevel set the lyre beside her and brushed her golden hair behind her shoulders. "Surely you jest, My Lord," she blushed timidly.

Hairem stood, returning no further comment on the matter. Lying, even politely, did not sit overly well with him. "Your father has probably finished.

Let us rejoin him." He held out his arm and the lady took it in her small, fragile hand.

The absence of Nilanis was immediately noted as Hairem reentered the dining hall. Before he could speak, a servant bowed low before him. "Nilanis has been called away on urgent business. He understands how greatly this disrupts your evening. He sends his deepest apologies and hopes you will forgive him."

Hairem forced a thin smile. He should have expected as much. "Of course."

"He wishes that you do not leave without enjoying the dessert he had prepared for you."

The king glanced toward the mahogany doors, praying inwardly that some "urgent" business would arise for him as well and he could escape back to the comfort of his rooms.

"I am certain that His Majesty has more pressing matters to attend to than to stay here," came Ilsevel's voice suddenly from beside him. "I apologize for my father's absence." She bowed her head and stepped aside, folding her hands before her abdomen.

After a brief moment of surprise, Hairem quickly donned a smile, partially genuine this time. He was relieved that she avoided her father's games. "Since your father is no longer here, I am afraid that there are other matters that warrant my attention. Good evening, my lady. I wish your father well, in whatever business matters have arisen. I hope that he and I shall soon be able to meet again under such agreeable circumstances."

* * * * *

Hairem returned to the palace scarcely a few short hours after his departure. Alvena was surprised to see such a quick return—his late father had spent many an hour deep into the evening on political matters, especially with figures as wealthy and notable as Nilanis. *'I wonder if things went poorly...'*

She leaned against the railing of the wide marble staircase as the king shook the rain from his strong shoulders. She forgot her duty for a moment, simply captivated by watching the sheen of the candlelight dancing off his golden hair. Hairem had taken after his mother in appearance, she had long since determined. His father's sharp and harsh features were captured in his eyes, but the gentle curve of his cheekbones and jaw—those were his late mother's. *'So handsome...'* She ogled him shamelessly.

"You are drenched, Your Majesty. Let me get you something to drink," Delaewen was saying, fussing over the way the king's shirt had plastered to his chest.

*'And so strong...'* The girl watched the older elf unfasten the cloak from his shoulders and drape it over one of her spindly arms.

She quickly snapped to. *'The king is wet! Pay attention, Alvena!'* She hurried down the stairs, noting for the first time the distant rolls of thunder.

"Oh, I will be fine. It is just a little rain," the king insisted, waving the fussing servant away. "If you do not mind drying the floor so someone does not—"

And quite to her embarrassment, Alvena caught the edge of the puddle forming at his feet and went sailing past him to land hard on her rump.

"...slip..." Hairem finished slowly. "You just wanted to capture the moment, didn't you?" he chuckled as he extended his hand toward her. "Are you alright?"

The handmaid subconsciously took his hand, letting the king pull her to her feet. Then she quickly recoiled, shaking her head in speechless apology.

"What? Oh, come now," Hairem rebuked. "Let me tease you."

Alvena gave a quick curtsy and tiptoed carefully around the water before dashing up the stairs in horror.

*'How embarrassing!'* Gods! And then she had let the king help her? She sighed, reprimanding herself. *'Oh well! Hairem won't really remember it. He has been so absentminded as of late.'* She felt a little bad even as she thought it. No doubt the war and his father's death were taking their toll. At least she would make certain he had some dry clothes set out and a hot bath going. She knocked on Lardol's door and shifted impatiently from foot to foot as she heard the male inside scurrying for the door.

"Oh. It is just you," the male frowned, crossing his arms. He eyed her reproachfully. "This had better be about His Grace and not another thing like the *sap* in your hair."

She glared at him. That had been important! She couldn't walk about the castle with her hair all clumped together with sap! And if he had just put the bird back in the nest like she had asked, she would not have had to get all—

"Well? Get on with it," he barked.

The girl pointed out his window, gesturing to the rain, and then gestured to her head and shivered.

"The king is wet and cold? I will get a hot bath going for him," Lardol replied, beckoning for her to leave. "And I will find him warm clothes. You should just stay out of his way. Go retrieve something for him to eat and leave it outside the door."

The girl glared and hurried off. *Stay out of his way*. She scowled at the wall statue outside the kitchen for good measure. *'Boot-licking Lardol* always *having to do everything himself!'*

"Oh, Sel'ari bless you," Madorana, the nicest of the palace's cooks, sighed in greeting as soon as the girl entered the room. "You would think the king is on his death bed with the way we are all running this way and that to tend to him. His Majesty does so hate being fussed over." She raised the spoon from his soup to her lips and gave it a noisy sip. "Prince Hadoream was the same way. Whenever he would come in late—and gods know if he came in late he was with his brother—Darcarus it was, not Sairel—Sairel was ever the studious one and he was never late. Darcarus was the trouble maker. Oh gods he was a trouble maker. You would think he had a streak of gnome in him. Ever getting into our hair and causing mischief. But oh, he was such a charmer…" She blushed and paused briefly, as though she had forgotten where her thoughts had been leading her. "Oh yes, Prince Hadoream was just like Hairem: we would all gather around him and he would try his best to escape." She laughed. "Oh, Lardol remembers those days. He used to curse the old princes off, you know. The mouth on that male!" She pushed a tray into the girl's arms, and she was relieved that Madorana's tangent was significantly shorter than usual. "Take this to His Grace. I certainly do not want to be the one responsible for him catching ill!"

The girl sighed and turned right back around. Madorana was right—Hairem *did* hate being fussed over and that was *exactly* what everyone was doing. No doubt he would go lock himself up in his room to cease their constant worrying. Perhaps it was because of the recent death of his well-beloved father that endeared the servants, at least partially, to the male. And yet, she had heard many stories, even as a youth, of Hairem's kindness toward them. Just a few years ago he had been caught sneaking off with a handful of servants. She always wondered what sort of mischief the young prince had been up to, but she had long been told he had acquired his cavalier ways from his close association with the True Blood princes. But they were across the ocean now. It was just Hairem left.

The girl stopped outside the king's door and set the tray to the right. She could hear Lardol's muffled speech from inside and she leaned a little closer in an attempt to catch what he was saying.

"Well, I am certainly in no hurry, Lardol. But thank you for your concern," she caught Hairem's reply.

"I simply do not wish to see the kingdom without an heir should—and gods forbid—anything happen to you, My Lord," the male servant replied reproachfully. The girl was surprised with the frankness with which he spoke with the king, but then, Lardol had been serving Hairem's family line for three hundred years and the True Bloods before that. She supposed there was a certain familiarity that came to breed such candor with that length of service. "Marriage to Lady Ilsevel would ensure you the loyalty of her father and his substantial financial support. The crown will soon bend beneath the weight of Saebellus' war and the recent schism. When Silandrus left with his sons, he took thirty thousand subjects and enough wealth to pay for a full transition to Ryekarayn. Now his eldest son rules his thirty thousand elves with more wealth and control than you do *yours*, I'm afraid. Your enemies know this. They also know of King Sairel's influence, even from a continent away. You have neither his wealth nor power."

She heard only silence for a minute. When Hairem replied, his voice sounded heavy. "I know you mean well, Lardol, but I do not want to follow in the footsteps of the kings before me. I would like to marry a lady for more reasons than the gold that lines her father's pockets. Maybe that is half the reason our kingdom is the way it is."

"And what way is that, My Lord?"

"Corrupt… Manipulative… Using others for wealth and control…"

"I believe that the reason the kingdom is in its current state is due to rich and powerful males like Nilanis *not* being under the control of good males like you. And if his daughter is the key to political stability, then perhaps—"

"I know… I just… You are probably right, Lardol," she heard Hairem interrupt the old elf. "You have been around for many centuries. You have seen what has gone on in these halls far longer than I have. I suppose it is wishful thinking to imagine that I might genuinely *love* the lady I marry."

Alvena could sense a level of bitterness in the king's last words, and imagined Lardol had caught on to the same resentment. "You have every right to wish it as well as demand it, Your Grace. You are the king, after all. I simply ask that you consider the political weight of your decisions. No doubt if Silandrus had remained on Sevrigel with his sons, Sairel would have been betrothed to Ilsevel instead. You will not find a better political position than with Ilsevel by your side." There was a brief silence before Lardol continued.

"Enjoy your bath. If there is anything else you need, do not hesitate to call for me."

The girl leapt back, surprised with how quickly Lardol had reached the door. She scurried off down the hallway before he could catch her eavesdropping. Hairem might not punish her, but that foul-tempered boot-licker certainly would!

* * * * *

Hairem sank into the warm water as his door closed, exhaling in a long, deep sigh. He could still hear the servants bustling about outside his door as though he would—as though he had *ever*—summon them while he was trying to relax. Lardol's insistent approach toward marriage had not helped to unwind him, either. He rubbed his face, leaning his head against the rim of the tub. All this fuss for an heir! But then… if the line broke a second time…

He had heard stories of the chaos that had ensued after The Royal Schism, but he had not understood the full weight of what had happened politically those centuries before. A great deal of this was owed to his father, who had swiftly shielded him from the questions and anger aimed at him due to his friendship with the princes. If the line ended with him merely three centuries after the True Bloods' departure, he imagined that the elven nation would once again struggle through a significant political upheaval and, inwardly, he felt the darker tug of a greater concern: if Saebellus was not defeated by then, perhaps their government would not survive.

And somehow, Nilanis had the audacity to call the war trivial.

He dunked himself under the warm water for a moment. When he raised his head, he let out a soft smile as a peaceful sound came to his ears; somewhere in the courtyard he could hear the cheerful and dramatic, yet soft, melody of the palace musicians, playing in the rain as though they hadn't a care in all of Aersadore. He briefly recalled Ilsevel's feeble attempts and a soft chuckle broke loose.

Yes, there was yet time for marriage and heirs.

He closed his eyes, tapping his fingers softly along the side of the tub.

Sel'ari would design his fate. There was plenty of time.

The music twisted its way upward, guided by the breeze to weave outside the window behind him. It was familiar by the first few notes and he found himself singing the lyrics quietly to himself, concerns washed away by sentimental familiarity.

"Why count your blessings when men before
Have lost what they thought they had?
Or number your allies in times prewar,
When loyalties are not yet bled?
Know that the man who stands at your side,
Costs more than the score to be,
And the count of trials one man provides,
Are more than the waves of a sea.

Once, the ancient man walked with his kin,
The owl from Noctem's shore;
The golden lion from the dreamer's spin,
The raven from Æntara's core.
The Earth, she gave her one elven son,
Beside him did walk the moon,
And behind them slithered the darker one,
The serpent of forest's ruin.

With blood they fought the trials north,
And with blood they fought to flee,
'Til all the dust had settled forth,
And seven were left to be.

"Onward!" Did beckon the ancient man
And through mountains they did climb;
After black waters from the raven's clan,
Toledoth did drown them in less time.
In dark they fought Malranus' pride,
The light new allies did ring,
But home had the head of lion's love died,
And the dreamer was made the king.

With blood they fought the trials west,
And with blood they fought to flee,
'Til meaning of their trial's quest,
The seven were left to see.

"To the horsemen of the eastern shore!"
The ancient man tried in vain,
Though there Malranus cried defeat's first roar,
When the Pride's mighty kin was slain.
One by one the items, they were lost,
Through the mountain, plain, and tree,
While serpent paid a paradoxal cost,
A clever wicked one was he.

With blood they fought the trials east,
And with blood they fought to flee,
'Til vanquished all bad man and beast,
The seven victorious free.

"Here comes the end," the ancient man cried,
"With this one last war to fight!"
At dark, the serpent forced the moon to hide,
And put the Earth's elf son alight.
The lion roared and owl took wing,
The blind raven fought to see,
But it was ancient man that took their place,
And gave to them victory.

With blood they fought the trials south,
And with blood they fought to flee,
'Til silence came from every mouth,
For but spared from death were three."

The ancient words were familiar from his youngest years—the great *Ballad of the Seven*. He chuckled to himself: Hadoream was *always* singing that tune, to the great annoyance of both of his older brothers: Darcarus, who was not particularly fond of history, and Sairel, who had never been particularly fond of "fun."

Yet, Hairem found its familiarity comforting. Heroes. A Golden Age. The thwarting of the revival of Malranus and his dragon horde…! *'Sel'ari, the world sounded so much better back then…'* Or perhaps in the face of familiarity, the tale had lost some of its darker meaning.

Yet Hairem smiled to himself. He liked to think that perhaps, in the ballad of Saebellus' defeat one day, maybe he would get a mention or two. Certainly not like *Eraydon*, but an Ephraim or Riphath status would do.

Additionally, he would prefer to take after the hero's companions and live *through* the war.

He chuckled to himself again, flicking a little mountain of bubbles over the side of the marble walls of his tub.

It was perhaps childish and somewhat prideful to imagine such a notion, but already Silandrus had acquired a *score* of songs from his actions in the Royal Schism. If he could survive a few more dinners with Nilanis, even *he* would have the fortitude to accomplish anything. A Golden Age? After suffering Nilanis, that would be child's play.

Hairem felt his muscles loosen and he closed his eyes to the drifting sounds of the palace musicians.

# Chapter Four

The wind howled through the frozen tundra of Darival, entrapping Jikun's cloak in the thick white swirls of snow sweeping up from the earth around him. The general watched them with affection as they twisted into the air and then showered in small flurries back across the now-still earth. His fist tightened on the base of his hood, drawing the thick white fur closer about his face. His strides were long in the thick layer of icy snow, his feet leaving no trace of his passage; driftwalking, as the northerners called it, was the only reason they had been able to thrive on such difficult terrain.

He smiled as he cast his eyes to the left where he could see a few faint, familiar, gentle slopes—so different from the towering hillsides of the south. His gaze trailed up into the sky behind them. When the sun emerged from her heavy blanket of clouds, the landscape would return the glare with brilliance, but for now, the shadows across the snow were a comfortable and familiar grey-white.

He inhaled heavily, holding his breath to savor the scent of the frozen world.

Still, as much as Jikun cherished the north, he was not entirely immune to its bite. His head turned down sharply as another wind swept viciously across the tundra, carrying with it the little frozen shards of snow from as far east as the Merktine Peaks. When it once more paused to rest, he raised his head to survey the landscape before him: the heavy gusts of snow had cleared somewhat, leaving the expanse before him crisp and clear.

The world had not changed since he had been there last. Before him stood the Turmazel Mountains, so named for the blue, green, and purple crystals found in abundance throughout the region. During the millennia, the mountains themselves had become renowned for the size of the crystals they had birthed; in all his travels, Jikun had never encountered another place like it. Even the Kisacaela gemstones glittering from Elvorium's canyon walls paled in comparison.

And another, albeit less noted, positive was that the humans were far too cautious and weak to dare to mine the northern landscape.

And so it was that only two races occupied the vast expanse of the north: the Lithri, who bore no noteworthy mention, and Jikun's own kind: the Darivalians.

The city of the Darivalians had once stood at the base of those mountains, but it had long since moved into the safety of their fold. Their city was Kaivervale, and it stood as a guardian to the mountain's riches, unmatched in strength, abounding with the unique powers of the Darivalian people. He narrowed his eyes against the pockets of shadows spreading across the mountain's surface, but the flurry of snow had hidden the city's icy walls from view.

However, even in the cloudy mid-afternoon, the vast chasm to the left of his gaze gleamed like a beacon in the night—even now, a blue glow emanated from its depths to color the face of the surrounding mountain. From the unseen heart of the fissure in the mountain stone, a steady stream of cerulean light flowed out, its rays fading and vanishing far into the sky. The birthplace of Darivalian magic, legend had it. He remembered being led out of the city and down the narrow, steep staircase by his parents, behind a train of priests and family. He had hardly lived past his seventh year of life when he had stood at the edge of that great chasm for the first time. His fist had clenched in anxiety and his stomach had dropped as he had gazed down into the endless blue abyss at his feet. He had stretched both hands out into the light as Lithriella's priests chanted stridently.

He had teetered on the edge of the supernatural.

Days later, late at night when the elders had retired and the guards on watch had slumbered away at their posts, he had crept from the city and travelled once again to that otherworldly breach. He had stood there in that chilling presence, whispering into the dark, conversing with Lithriella as though he and she had formed an inseparable bond at that religious ritual days before. He had whispered his fears of failure, his dreams of glory, his aspirations of success—all the vague things a Darivalian child of his age would clutch deep within himself: the paths of the Darivalian elves were limited. Hunter? Weaponsmith? Miner?—Surely the gods had destined him for something much greater.

And in the midst of his fervent prayers, just for a moment, he had thought he heard a keening sound deep below, a faint echo in that cerulean light. Perhaps that had been what had held his religious fervor for longer than rationality should have allowed.

Even now, hundreds of years later, the significance of the moment had not left his mind—it was as crisp and fresh in his memory as the icy wind that, once more, buffeted his bare flesh. Tuserine, they called it: the Heart of the Goddess. And even with Kaivervale before him, he could not help but pause briefly in awe.

He did not stop again until he had reached the base of the mountain and the slick sheet of ice that sloped steadily up its face. In the distance, the gate of the city, now visible, stood closed. Jikun raised his left hand and swept it upward, watching with satisfaction as the ice before him turned to water, cascading down the side of the stairs revealed underneath. With his right hand he raised the water upward, freezing it into a thin railing, which he then used to steady himself against the gusts of tundra wind as he climbed.

Even this dangerous trek up the mountain face was infinitely preferable to the Sel'varian bridges that spanned Elvorium's canyon.

To his right was a mass of boulders and a small ridge of the mountain where an ancient watchtower stood as one with the stone underneath it—as though it had formed from the stone itself. Thin sheets of ice served as panels of glass in the windows, glowing a faint blue from the light emanating within. It was more stunning than any watchtower designed in the south—simplistic, sturdy, and yet breathtakingly beautiful. And it was not his sentiment forming this opinion: any objective elf would have to admit the same.

What a stark contrast to Elvorium. In the city of the Sel'vi, the first building one could see from any direction was the palace—its elegance and comfort. Its assurance of safety—all the while glittering on the edge of a cliff. Here, in the north, the watchtower was a stark reminder of how his people had a far firmer grasp on reality.

But the building he sought lay behind the tower. He strained his eyes, but his position below the ridge allowed him no glimpse of even its rooftop.

He looked instead to the tower's right, his eyes lingering on the massive, frozen waterfall pressed against the face of the mountain. Its icy falls twisted across the surface and split over a great stone. Both branches fell away on either side, one significantly smaller than the other, but both shimmered with equal intensity, gleaming with thick, white icicles. And they both vanished in stillness beneath the snow at the mountains' base.

At one time, it would have formed a river for Jikun's ancestors of the valley. But he and his kin could only remember the frozen age of Darival.

He ascended the first slope of the path and paused briefly to adjust the hood of his cloak before advancing once more. Ahead of him, the city walls stood in magnificent welcoming. The gate of the city was made of a solid sheet of thick ice, smooth and unmarred, simplistic compared to the elegant carvings and ornate work of the Sel'vi. There were no hinges, no handles or holes. The gate could not open, inward or outward, by any traditional means. On either side of the enormous door, the ice-made walls of the city flowed into the mountainside, colossal jagged spikes jutting from the spine in an unsystematic manner. Where the walls met the stone of the mountain on the right, the watchtower rose higher still. Jikun stopped before the doors, finding himself a small mark compared to the vast expanse of the city defenses. Perhaps others would see the cold simplicity as shunning, but to Jikun, three years away had only enhanced its allure and his breast swelled in respect at the unchanged grandeur.

Only two ornate, towering statues broke the simplistic realism and sturdy design of the wall: on the right side off the gate was Koriun, founder of the Darivalian city; to his left was the goddess of the Darivalians, Lithriella. Their arms extended over Jikun high above, and where their hands clasped, blue-white flecks swirled like ice and snow, shimmering in an unseen source of light.

He scoffed, reminded of his disappointment that even his people still clung to their mythic roots like the Sel'vi he had just shaken from his back.

He tore his eyes away in aversion and approached the gate.

"Hail, traveler," one of two guards greeted in a voice struggling to rise above the howling wind. He raised his spear in a firm salute, though he made no attempt to open the gate. He was thin, lanky, and held a faintly chiseled face. He looked like an unfortunate ice-sculpture—one misshapen and battered by wind and ice.

Jikun lowered his head, drawing his face so deep within the fur of the hood that he all but vanished. "Hail," Jikun replied, tucking his arm against the general's medallion on his chest. "I seek rest within Kaivervale for a few days."

He could see the feet of the second soldier shift, perhaps in thought. The boots were ill-kept—the kind that a southern soldier would berate the male harshly for. "What is your name and origin? What brings you to Kaivervale?" the second soldier inquired in a husky voice.

Jikun glanced up slightly, enough to glimpse the soldier's inquisitive gaze. "Elstirel from Elvorium. On business for the general."

Jikun heard the first soldier shift as well. The two males were silent a moment before the first soldier stepped forward, the heavy furs of his cloak dragging across the damp ground behind him. *We don't get many visitors*, he expected him to carry on cautiously, but the male instead halted a short ways before Jikun and narrowed his eyes. He was searching within the darkness of his hood for some semblance of familiarity to ease his caution.

And to Jikun's dismay, even the shadows could not protect him at that proximity.

"By Lithriella…! Captain Jikun—er that's General Jikun now, is it not?! Rulan, it's—!"

Jikun lifted his head, raising a hand quickly. "Daiki, Rulan," he cut the soldiers off as they exchanged broad smiles of recognition—almost a look of triumph as though they had solved a grand mystery. "I only have a short time to visit before I must return to Elvorium. No ruckus. No big celebration. I have been on the road for years and I only wish to—"

"Oh, of *course* not," Rulan piped up before Jikun could finish, his smile growing even broader. It was wide, crooked, and only mildly reassuring. "Let the tundra only hear my silence!"

"Gods know any male who spends three years from home deserves a quiet family reunion," Daiki continued in swift agreement, giving a brief flick of his silvery blue mane of hair; it only helped to emphasize the gangly-ness of the host below.

Jikun drew his face back into his hood, giving each a firm and commanding glare. When they fashioned him only understanding smiles in return, he gestured at the gates. "…So may I?"

"Of course, General," Daiki spoke, spinning around and returning to his position of watch. "Enter, our wayward Lord of the South."

Jikun ignored Daiki's quip and strode between them to the doors, placing his hand against the smooth, cold surface. "Not a word," he cautioned them as a small, door-sized hole formed in its surface. He stepped through, straightening as the refreezing crackle of ice sounded behind him and the excited murmurs of the two soldiers vanished behind the thick wall at his back.

Before him, the wind had died away, unable to find its way from its low berth to climb over the rocks and ice that surrounded Kaivervale. Snow covered the rooftops and ground, nestling on the sills of windows and balancing on the edges of the petals of flowers.

Here, everything was resilient. Here, everything had learned to survive.

He stepped forward, his first footstep deliberately firm, forcing a mark into the icy snow at his feet.

He was truly home.

His eyes immediately swept across the city, hungry for the familiarity. The garrison rose up on his right—octagonal in shape—and the barracks opposite it towered on his left while its southwestern corner molded into the mountain wall itself. Behind the barracks he could hear the soft barks and howls of the winter wolves, the Darivalians' primary hunting force.

He passed between the military front of the city and advanced into the street. "Street" was a loose term, not at all meant to testify to the land where he walked, but rather the use of it. There was no cart-driven road, no cobbled path. The buildings of Kaivervale were not set in neat little rows with flowers sprouting between their walls and vast, tree-filled orchards for idleness; rather, the buildings were spotted across the snowy, sloping landscape in an unsystematic fashion, creating gaps and walkways between them. The widest of these led from the gate, curved right into the large expanse of a snowy field where Jikun had spent many a day training, and then back onto a narrow trail between houses. Its final stretch extended up the slope of the mountain to the open grounds before the palace.

Like each race of elves, the Darivalians had not given up their own royal line. He imagined it was some semblance of caution in the event that the Sel'varian rule finally ruined itself. And in Darival, like so many other elven places, most Sel'varian customs and laws were quietly disregarded. Even the Darivalians' own council member pretended not to know of his race's insolence toward the capital—although Jikun had been lectured extensively in private upon his appointment.

But he had not come to reflect on them. He instead took the widest path, glancing once at the long banquet hall beyond the field where he had eaten his last meal in Kaivervale. He looked away just in time, narrowly dodging the corner of a building in his distracted state. *'At least* rows *of houses prevent* that.'

He turned to his right then, away from the main street, and wove his way through the snowy pathways between houses. He remained just on the edge of the business portion of the city where half the city's populace made their livelihood. Jikun could not help but compare it to his recent time in Elvorium: Darival was so unlike the city of the Sel'vi, bustling with their foreign merchants and countless city-dwellers. For being the main economic force of the city, the business district here was quiet and calm, and even as Jikun glanced down between the buildings, he saw only a handful of elves drifting between the shops.

He was grateful for this as he turned down the street, his hood still drawn well over his face. Before he went home, before the city knew he had arrived, there was someone he had to see.

At the end of the path he had taken, a jagged staircase cut into the stone of a mountain ridge, leading up to where the watchtower sat. This was the path he desired and his destination lay just beyond the peak. He pressed his hand against the stone, forming another makeshift railing to steady himself against the icy rock.

At the crest, nestled into the stone behind the watchtower, was a small cottage.

Jikun hesitated there. He could scarcely recall Murios' face, and yet, there was a sense of unease about the place that he was not accustomed to feeling in Darival. A darkness of presence: that same feeling that enveloped him when Navon spoke about necromancy. He wondered if it was his own caution that gave rise to such feelings, or if there was a naturally sinister aura surrounding the matter. He grimaced at the strange runic markings carved into the stone face of the home and the faint, red-orange light glowing in the windows.

The inscrutability of it all certainly did not help. He swallowed audibly, his fists tightening on his hood. *'Don't be a coward,'* he growled internally.

"General Jikun, welcome," came a sudden voice behind him.

Jikun started, slipping on the ice and nearly tumbling back down the stairs. A hand caught him under the arm, steadying him.

"Ah, I'm sorry. I thought you sensed me coming," the voice lamented.

*'Sensed you? I didn't even* hear *you,'* Jikun thought, turning to regard the male, who carried on walking past him once his balance was reestablished.

He was lean, tall, and ageless. The blue of his hair had faded so that only the deepest white remained. He looked, in fact, remarkably like the Lithri, though his strongly chiseled face revealed his true origin. Although he was the oldest elf Jikun had heard of, he moved with grace and ease, stopping in a stoically composed manner before his cottage door.

"Are you going to stare at me until Darival melts, or are you going to come in?" the elf demanded as he waved a hand at his opened door.

Jikun hurried swiftly up the last few steps, across the snow-covered ridge, and stepped quickly through the male's door. He glanced over his shoulder as the male followed him inside. "How did you know that it was me?" he frowned curiously, brows knit as the door closed behind them.

The elf chuckled as he set a basket down beside the fire and bent his lean, old body toward it with a little huff, as though a breath of warmth would inspire the flames to burn with a bit more radiance. "With age comes perception, General Taemrin."

*'Well, I suppose this is useless then...'* Jikun thought as he drew his hood back.

"But," the elf continued, straightening the vase of flowers on his table, "the emblem on your chest helped."

Jikun looked down at his left breast. Right. He glanced back up, eyes sweeping the cluttered home briefly. It was devoid of color and life—a dry, simple mess of old books and scrolls, with those chilling runic markings beginning across parchment and finishing on another surface—as though one material was inseparable from another in the mage's fervent scrawlings.

"I can perceive, however, that you are troubled," the elf continued as he faced the fire, prodding at it once with an iron rod.

A shower of sparks danced up the chimney and Jikun followed their path, wishing they would linger longer within the home. His brow knit. "I show that I am troubled?"

"Why else would you come to see me?"

Jikun's eyes turned away and narrowed. "I'm starting to doubt this whole 'perception with age.'"

At that the elf looked up, leaning the metal prod beside the chimney, and smiled. The lines around his eyes creased and for a moment, age gripped him. "Sit, please," he beckoned, gesturing to a chair beside the flames. "You did not write to me. This must be a truly personal matter indeed."

Jikun felt his chest tighten anxiously. *A truly personal matter indeed...*That much was true. He settled into the chair, sinking deep into the under-stuffed cushion. He rested his hands on the mahogany arms and returned his attention to the elf, keeping his face as passive as he could manage as the topic loomed darkly overhead. "Murios, I am sorry to trouble you," he began as the elf walked to a shelf of books. Jikun frowned. "I can see that you are quite busy... but I travelled all the way from Elvorium for this matter—"

"For your family."

Jikun blinked. "...Yes... To see my family as well."

The elf rounded, a black, leather-bound book gripped tightly in his hand. He settled into a chair across from Jikun and dropped the book onto the table between them. It landed with a heavy thud, far greater than a book its size should make. "For your family," the elf repeated. "Navon, your brother-in-arms."

Jikun looked down at the book sharply. The edges of its leather jacket were tattered and stiff, curling back from the tarnished metal beneath. He could see that the edges of the pages were worn and brown, appearing so flaky that a mere touch might turn them to dust. "What is that?" he demanded stiffly, leaning slightly away.

Murios pressed a single, long finger into the center of the book, and the tome itself seemed to groan softly. "My father acquired this. And my father's father before him. And his father. And his father's father. And now I. It is a tome which once belonged to Tiras."

Jikun's eyes widened in a flicker of fear. No title was needed. No last name. No origin. Even though he knew of whom he spoke, he found himself demanding clarification, as though grasping for some last ray of light in the darkening room. "*The* Tiras?"

"The only."

Jikun found himself recoiling from the tome before him. "Is that… *necromancy?*"

The elf chuckled and Jikun felt his skin crawl. There was nothing humorous about the situation. "My fifth father was an apprentice to Tiras in his younger years, before Tiras quested with Eraydon. This was a book of spells that Tiras taught to him."

Jikun shook his head firmly, daring to push the book away. "Murios, I have come with questions concerning Saebellus' Beast," he spoke stiffly, forcing the topic down his chosen path. He continued before Murios could direct it otherwise. "It's an enormous creature—seven feet tall or so, very muscular, brown-skinned, auburn of hair. Two black horns curve backward from its head. Yellow eyes. It has these two tattered leather wings… like dragon wings… but I have never seen it fly. It fights in melee combat using long talons and unnatural, overpowering strength. It seems immune to injury. We've shot it, stabbed it, bludgeoned it, burned it… and it returns just as fierce. Murios, it has slain countless soldiers. *Countless*. You are the wisest elf I know."

"You mean the *oldest*. Somehow, age is akin to wisdom." The elf leaned back, regarding Jikun thoughtfully, his pale eyes shifting across Jikun's face in an unnaturally scrutinizing stare. He revealed nothing about himself and yet Jikun could feel his layers of defense peeled back by the intensity of the male's gaze. "I have not heard of a beast like yours. His looks sound of a man with demonic qualities. Cambions rarely retain the large form of their demonic parent, but perhaps that is what you are dealing with. Although this is no typical demonic entity. Immunities to weapons… that, I have not heard of in mere cambions. And yet, High City Demons are inescapably grey-skinned. Ramulean—well, if it was Ramulean, you would all be dead." He paused then, as though giving Jikun the opportunity to end the conversation. When Jikun offered no reaction, he continued, his voice softening, "There is one magic that deals with demons. And this is what you fear." He leaned forward toward the tome.

"With good reason," Jikun retorted, keeping his body pressed away. "I fear that in Navon's desperation to stop the Beast, he will use necromancy. And whether it is successful or not, I fear what it will do to him—due to its own nature—and what retribution Elvorium will invoke." He paused, closing his eyes tightly as Navon's suggestions in Elvorium rushed back to him. He took a deep breath. "Am I wrong to fear necromancy?"

When he opened his eyes, Murios' face had grown grave.

"No," the male replied solidly. "You are not wrong to fear it. Tiras lost his wife and child to his practice of necromancy and he himself eventually became blind as a result of its use. The Helvari on Ryekarayn have long allowed the use of necromancy, but even they are wise and fear the magic. The river that runs beside their mountains is teeming with the souls of those killed *for* the magic… or *by* the magic. And it is a terrible place of suffering and torture. Necromancy, even used for good, as Tiras used it, is a dark magic. Souls subjected to necromancy are often souls which were safe within the Realms of the Dead. When they are wrenched once more to this earth, they become weakened, tattered, and confused. And to utilize such power, the necromancer himself often must travel to the Realms with his own soul. The Realms are not a place for mortal men—and souls do not freely leave it. For a necromancer to travel to the realms and attempt to leave in entirety, the risk is great. A necromancer can be very great indeed, but if he cannot leave the realms, his magic is useless. As such, necromantic magic is often destructive to the user's own soul or body. And with the loss of the soul comes the loss of self. Sel'vi have good reason to loathe necromancy. And you are wise to fear it. Your comrade is a Helven. He should know the stories of necromancy from his people."

Jikun heaved a deep sigh. "I thought as much. And it doesn't bring me comfort. Navon sees the devastation the Beast wreaks in battle and it only spurs on his deep lust for necromancy, turning it into one of 'justified' motivation. Is there nothing good that can come of it?"

Murios hesitated. "Tiras was one of the greatest mages of his age. And without his assistance, The Six would have never succeeded in their quest. Malranus would rule this world and you and I would be cowering deep within the mountains for fear of dragons. Back then, it was the cost of the revival of Malranus' dragons weighed against Tiras' soul. You tell me… is the Beast worth Navon's?"

Jikun stood slowly, his eyes hardening. "Thank you, Murios. That's all I wanted to know."

*

Weaving down from Murios' home and travelling north across Kaivervale, Jikun came to the great lip of a cave. It towered high above him, casting a third of the city in its shadow in the morning and half that as evening fell. The turmazel stalactites jutted from the ceiling in enormous shards of purple often streaked with lines and waves of cerulean blue. Smaller, green crystals had formed near their bases and eagerly attempted to extend as far. But their efforts for growth were often halted by their odd directions. Before they had grown too far, they collided with one another and formed a sort of web of luminescent, green crystal-rays above him.

He took several more steps into the shadow of the cave and the snow beneath his feet gradually thinned until only a dusting encroached upon the base of his mansion. The home of the general was made of both ice and stone, although it was primarily ice that extended across the exterior. He took the stairs up to the front of his home and opened the unlocked doors, throwing his hood back as he stepped into the great hall, his boots echoing softly in the high vaulted ceiling.

The hall was cold and empty, and perhaps its chill was amplified by the heaviness that weighed on his mind. Was Navon obeying him, or was he even, at this moment, throwing himself deeper into the confines of necromancy?

Jikun shook the dark magic firmly from his mind, forcing his eyes to sweep the clean interior; the residence had been well-kept in his absence, and yet somehow he found it oddly unwelcoming. For a brief moment he stood there, a stranger in his own home, and reflected that he would rather wake up from a thousand nights on the ground of a fur-sprawled tent, surrounded by his soldiers, than alone in this drafty, empty house—there was something far more final about its loneliness.

And why *was* it so empty? He passed underneath the turmazel chandelier hanging still above him, between the columns of ice sculptures, and swept from room to room… But aside from his furnishings and belongings, the place was vacant.

Jikun dropped his sack beside his bed of thick, white furs and left his mansion. His gaze turned toward the falling sun and he strode with deliberate steps to the west. He noticed nothing but the market as he passed, and even that was now still—the lights in the buildings had gone out and the city was oddly dark and silent.

He glanced around with the caution he had grown accustomed to in the army, but there was not a soul in sight. He paused briefly at the edge of the street. *'Odd…'* he wondered, before finally turning away.

His quickened footsteps—perhaps finding greater speed as the emptiness of the night unsettled him—led him to a stop at the door to a small, square, stone home. An ice sculpture of Lithriella was displayed in the midst of a garden of purple and white hyaline flowers, whose petals had begun to close for the evening. He reached out for the door, knocking solidly and swiftly, and with a hint of frustration, against the stone.

Here, the sign of life came in a muffled hum of voices and the quiet padding of feet. He stepped back once and the door swung open.

The male who stood in the stone hallway before Jikun was a few inches taller, sturdier, older, and dressed in thick grey and brown furs. Yet there was an uncanny similarity to their chiseled features.

For a moment, the two males just looked at each other.

"Why—" Jikun began in a slightly exasperated tone.

But the male extended his arms and grabbed Jikun firmly by the shoulders. "Catervi, Jikun has come home!"

It was almost instantaneous that a female's head bobbed into view over his shoulder, eyes wide, and shoved her husband out of the way. "Jikun! My dear, dear Jikun!" She grabbed him by the front of his shirt and jerked him in. "Close the door, Nulaves!" she barked to the male as she dragged her son forward. "Oh, stop for a moment and let me look at you."

"Why—" Jikun tried again, feeling her hand on the front of his shirt push back against his body to force him to a halt.

"By Lithriella, you look underfed!" she lamented, shaking her head ruefully. "Do they not feed you in the army?" She released his shirt and clasped her petite hands together, smiling broadly. "I was just setting dinner out! Come. Eat." She paused for a moment and then threw her arms about him tightly, burying her face into his chest. "I prayed to the goddess every day for your safe return," she breathed, struggling to keep her voice steady.

Before Jikun could offer his mother words of reassurance, his father had stepped up beside them and dropped a strong hand on their shoulders. "Let us move this into the dining room," he insisted with a gentle push. He was getting hungry and even the reunion of mother and son could not stand between his father and his meal.

Catervi stood back and quickly wiped a tear from her eye. She was a bit more emotional than her mate. "Why, yes. Of course. Come, this way," she beckoned, stepping quickly down the hallway and turning into a small dining room. A fire roared in the hearth on the far wall and a pot simmered gently above it.

"*Why*," Jikun finally breathed as he slowly took a seat, "are you still here? My mansion is countless times larger than this. I insisted that you stay there. This house is no place for the parents of Sevrigel's general."

They laughed, Nulaves chuckling heavily as he set a plate and bowl before himself onto the worn wood of the ancient table. He would have left the others to fend for their own dining wares were his mother not in possession of the soup ladle. "Oh, I'm sure the Sel'vi won't make it this far just to scrutinize your parentage."

"Indeed," Catervi huffed, brushing a strand of blue-tinted hair from her face. "And your home is *lovely*, Jikun. But it's far too big and drafty for just the two of us. We didn't know what to do with ourselves! This place is far more suited to our lifestyle. But we have kept your mansion well for you—so that you would have a nice place to come home to."

Jikun looked about the small dining room. The shelves in the stone were still cluttered with neat rows of little knickknacks Jikun had made for his parents as a child, and the rug beneath the table was still faintly stained with the blood of Jikun's first military training injury. Like the ice and snow of Darival, the people of the city never changed. Not even his parents. And yet he wondered if, by leaving Kaivervale, he *had*.

The affection for the simplicity about him had dimmed somewhat beneath the wealth and grandeur of Elvorium. The loving grasp his parents had on his youth seemed unprofitable and rather puerile.

Internally, he started at the thought—he had never had reason to complain about Darival in the past—let alone his own blood. Indeed, the status of general had weakened his character and he attempted to shake such corruption violently from his head. "I just do not want to see you uncomfortable," he drew his focus back to the loving couple before him.

He paused, his previous thoughts of his solitary walk through the city returning to him. "Where, by the way, is everyone…?"

His father placed a hand on Jikun's shoulder as he sat down beside him. "Jikun, may I give you some advice?" He paused, meeting his eyes steadily. "Pull out the stick the Sel'vi have shoved up your ass, and *relax*."

Jikun reclined in his chair and inhaled deeply. His father was right. He *had* changed. He stood, walking stiffly to the pot of stew simmering above the fire. Lingering there for a moment, he inhaled the rich smells of the soup until they had drawn him in and his shoulders relaxed. He attempted to lift a floating piece from its surface. "Is that rabbit?"

"Yes," his mother replied, smacking his hand with a spoon and turning with a wink. "Do they not teach you manners in the army? Nulaves, hand me the bowls." She jostled Jikun aside until he had retreated to the table and was sitting as impatiently as his father. When dinner had been laid out across the table, his mother sat down on his other side, bright-eyed and expectant.

"Tell us about the war and Elvorium," his father began, raising a spoonful of soup to his lips. He blew on it softly as his eyes rested attentively on his son.

Jikun reached out and placed a slice of bread on his plate. Back south, it was only Navon he could confide in. But here, in his hometown, he knew every word he said, every action he took, would never leave the frozen tundra. A genuinely tranquil smile crept across his lips. "Elvorium is as haughty as ever. But Liadeltris has died and his son has taken the throne. Based on my conversation with him when I returned to the city, I believe that things may change—he seems to have the courage to defy the corrupted politics of his council."

"Oh? Liadeltris seemed like such a respectable ruler," his mother lamented, though Jikun was aware that she knew nothing of his time on the throne. "May the gods grant him safe passage."

Jikun paused to sip his wine, noting that Darival had still not received news of the death of the king. He felt it demonstrated just how removed from the Sel'vi they had become. Even their own council member, Mikanum, had not prioritized the information to his people, perhaps thinking it better to distance himself even further from his wild brethren of the north.

Jikun continued, keeping his voice as dismissive as he could. He knew that it was his mother's nature to worry excessively. His father, on the other hand, had at least half of his attention on fishing out bits of rabbit from the soup. "As for Saebellus, he has not been defeated. I cannot stay in Kaivervale for long—I have responsibilities to the army in Elvorium." He straightened his shoulders. Of course, what he said and did may remain in Kaivervale, but with nothing new leaving or coming, the city was ripe with gossip. It was best to tell his parents firsthand that he had seen the mage. "I came here first and foremost to see Murios."

His mother looked up and he could see her brows knit in concern. "Murios? Why Murios?"

"Is something wrong?" his father demanded, leaning forward sharply. His soup lay forgotten.

Jikun sipped his wine calmly and set the glass down. Still southern wine, even for the north. He remained silent for a moment, tapping a piece of the dried bread along the edge of his plate. "It's just a little issue with one of Saebellus'… soldiers. A private matter. I simply sought Murios' wisdom. I cannot stay long."

His father nodded understandingly, even as his mother sighed in disappointment. She tapped the table once as though in thought, and then suddenly clasped his hand, seemingly desperate to change the topic. "I just remembered—eat more bread, you look famished—Laikum's son killed a white thakish the other day. *By himself.*"

Jikun raised a brow, glad as well for the change in topic. "A white thakish by himself? Was it fully grown—eyes fully set in and everything?"

His mother nodded excitedly. "Brought back three, fully developed eyes to prove it! What a soldier he will make!"

Jikun chuckled, admittedly impressed. "Indeed." He remembered the hunts shortly before his deployment to Elvorium—they were always a rush of adrenaline. But he had never known any elf crazy enough to hunt alone—in fact, no hunt was even *allowed* with less than four soldiers.

"What about you, dear?" his mother broke in. "Do you still hunt frequently? With your new southern friends, I suppose?"

His father laughed. "It must seem like child's play to hunt the passive creatures of the south!"

Jikun's lips twisted in resignation at the question—unfortunately, he didn't know whether he was now displaying a smile or a grimace. "I don't hunt. I have no time."

His mother's fingers slipped from her cup in offended disbelief and she raised a brow. "Well, they *must* give you time to yourself," she said reasonably. When Jikun offered nothing more, she pried further, suddenly grinning and eyeing him expectantly. "What about your poetry, then? Are you winning any hearts in the military?"

Jikun trailed his spoon through his soup as he flatly met her gaze. "There are no females in the king's army. And even if there were, I haven't written poetry since I moved to the capital."

"What?" his mother exclaimed in dismay. "But you used to write all the time. I still have the poem you wrote about Lithriella—the one where you said that her world uses so *many* colors that, to mere mortals, it appears white. I thought that it was so lovely and clever."

Jikun pursed his lips at the mention of the goddess' name. "I don't have time for such luxuries working for the capital." He was a general now—not some green soldier. Things were different in the south.

But unfortunately it was his father he was sitting with, and the male who had raised him was scrutinizing him with a piercing gaze. Nothing could get past him, even with half of his mind on food. "…Do the other males still give you a hard time about your religion?" he finally grimaced.

"No," Jikun replied shortly. His eyes flicked down in subconscious shame before he realized his action. *'Damn it.'* There was no avoiding the conversation now.

"What do you mean 'no'?" his father pried. "You wrote to us after you were first transferred and said that the military is quite cynical about the practice of foreign religions. You're telling me that the soldiers simply dropped the matter all together?"

"Yes, as *you* should," Jikun replied stiffly.

His father narrowed his eyes. "You're worshipping Sel'ari now, aren't you?"

Jikun laughed outright, shaking his head once in anger. "No. For your information, I am not groveling to *anyone* right now."

His mother let out a little gasp and her eyes flicked to his father as though demanding he repair the situation.

"Jikun Taemrin, you should be far wiser than that! A lack of devout worship is only complete arrogance to—"

Jikun raised his finger and pointed it sharply to the ceiling. *Gods* could they not drop the subject?! "You think she cares?" he demanded in exasperation. "The fact that I walk out of every battle without so much as a *scratch* and some of my most devout Sel'ari-*grovelers* are cut down *screaming* proves otherwise. She *doesn't* care who abases himself to her and who does *not*."

His father stiffened. "I would think your safety and success proves she *does* care for you."

Jikun snorted once. "I have seen thousands upon thousands of adoring followers die in ways you can't even *imagine*. Gods. Don't. Care. Not one of them," he snapped, numb to the frustration and pain at the core of his attack.

"Jikun, you are a—"

His mother smacked the table desperately. "Boys! Boys!" she raised her voice sharply in desperation. "I get to see my son once every few years and I will not have this home turned into another battleground. That's enough. You two can write angry letters back and forth about this, but you will not carry on in my home. Nulaves, *silence*."

Jikun's expression softened as his mother bit her lip, eyeing him as though he was an icicle just waiting to fall loose and shatter. He sighed and forced a smile onto his face, nodding to his father respectfully.

"Lais just got a new winter wolf pup," his mother spoke after a moment of silence, continuing the thread of their previous conversation as though the fight had never occurred. "His was killed on a hunt a few months ago. The poor boy. The garrison let him have first pick from the newest litter."

"...A good, large pup," his father ceded. He scraped the remaining contents from his bowl and dabbed his lips with the cloth on his right. His expression had become passive once more, but Jikun suspected that fury, indignation, and concern still roiled beneath the ice.

He sighed, wishing he had better-concealed his disdain for the gods. The gods' folly was no fault of theirs, and it was not his desire to break down their lifelong faith.

"And I was thinking," his mother continued, "When it gets cold in the south, you could bring Nazra with you to Elvorium. She would certainly be an aid in battle. How she misses you!"

Jikun smiled faintly, but shook his head. His mother already knew the answer to that. "I would not put her at such risk. Animals make it back far less often than even my *best* soldiers."

His mother patted his hand as she refilled his bowl, as though to comfort him. But Jikun knew it was she that needed reassurance. "The life of a soldier is rough..." she trailed off quietly.

Jikun drew his hand away and met her gaze steadily. "It is what I want."

His mother sat back down, taking a long sip of wine before she spoke again. "Merkan and Nalaen got married," she carried on. She waved a finger at his bowl sharply. "*Eat more*." She paused and exchanged a look with his father, a subtle attempt Jikun caught only from the corner of his icy blue eyes.

He looked up and narrowed them cautiously. "Oh please—"

"Jikun," his father began reproachfully.

"Kaivervi has grown up to be *beautiful and strong*," his mother spoke in almost a reprimanding tone, and yet she giggled—a sound far more youthful than her age.

"The point being," his father added, waving a hand at his wife. "With your reputation, you could have *any* of these ladies. How do you think I won such a lady as your mother? A good soldier is a desired spouse. An excellent soldier, more so. Don't squander it!"

Jikun opened his mouth to respond, but a loud knock interrupted his cynical reply.

"I wonder who that is… Nulaves, the door," his mother barked her orders again. As he vanished from the room his mother leaned in, dropping her voice to a soft whisper. "While you are here, you *will* see her, won't you?"

Jikun had begun to protest when a tumult of voices erupted from the front door.

"Nulaves!" A chorus of males shouted their boisterous greetings.

"We heard Jikun is back in the city! Where are you hiding him?!" a voice jested loudly in a charismatic ring.

Jikun heard his father chuckle. He leaned forward, glaring reproachfully at his mother. "No—I wanted a peaceful—" he began in irritation to her, but no sooner had he begun his sentence than a dozen faces crowded into the doorway of the dining room, grinning broadly.

"Jikun Taemrin!" one bellowed, some throwing in an afterthought of "general" or "captain" behind it.

Jikun leaned back in his chair and waved a hand. He could see tattered boots poking out from the feet amassed before him and a silvery mane of hair bobbing behind a shoulder; Rulan and Daiki peered up sheepishly from the back of the throng.

"This is no hero's welcome!" Jekum waved a hand from the front, as though brushing Jikun's parents aside. "No offense, Catervi."

"Jikun, up! Come!"

Before he could respond, hands grabbed his arms and dragged him forward, down the hallway, and toward the door as though he was entirely weightless and his protests were mute.

"Have a good evening!" his mother called after them.

Jikun found himself half-carried through the streets despite his continued protests. The temperature in Darival had fallen with the sun, who had also, it seemed, taken her blanket of clouds with her. The sky was a show of glittering stars and moonlight, as light as dawn with the white rays reflecting off of the snow. In the distance, he briefly glimpsed the turmazel crystals glittering from the mountain's face.

He was finally deposited at the north end of the banquet hall. Whereas the rest of the city lay dark and quiet, the torches outside this building were lit and a tumult of muffled noise sounded from within. "I—" he began, not certain what he was going to say after that, but he didn't have to finish. The doors flew open and a gust of warm air laced with grease and ale swept over him. He was released and pushed into the long room in the final endeavor to raise him to social interaction.

"I—" he began reproachfully once more as the males squeezed in behind him. But he stopped at the sight of the hundreds of elves crowding the room, raising their mugs in anticipation for his arrival. A slight smile crept across his face despite himself and his cheeks flushed. It was one thing to be honored before his own soldiers. But he knew every one of these faces. "Thank you," he spoke humbly after the eruption died just long enough for those two words. Perhaps, in a more sober state, they would have even demanded a speech.

Fortunately, that had passed.

"Our table is over here," Merkan began as the ruckus once more filled the room. He smiled his slightly crooked smile, a match with his brother, Rulan, and pranced half clumsily toward the west end of the room.

"There is enough ale to fill all the dwarves in the Black Hills!" Daiki piped in as he hurried after him. "As you may be able to tell, *some* of us have already dipped in."

*'I would have never guessed,'* Jikun thought in amusement. He walked between their escort to the long table along the wall, eyes scanning the familiar faces across the hall. He inhaled heavily as he went, sucking in the sweet scent of sugar baked into something along the far wall. In the south, the scent was as common as the gold, but here in the north, sugar *was* gold.

He dropped himself down on the thick stone bench. They had spared no expense in celebrating his return.

"You walk so rigidly… the commanding nature of a general, I suppose?" came a quiet voice behind him the moment he had settled. A lean body bent over his right shoulder, pressing a slender hand against his.

"Kaivervi…?" Jikun began, his chest tightening, but she drew away before his words had left his tongue, dragged swiftly away by Nalaen toward the south end of the table. Damn Nalaen!

"You don't mind if I take this seat here, do you?" Rulan asked as he dropped himself heavily down beside Jikun, unclasping his cloak and kicking it under the table. "Damn, what a long watch today. Can bones freeze?" He breathed into his hands and swiftly rubbed them together.

Jikun narrowed one eye at him, turning away from Kaivervi reluctantly. "I told you not to tell anyone."

"Oh, I didn't. Not a word. Not a soul," Rulan protested the accusation. "Daiki did."

Jikun kept his face stoically reprimanding for another moment, making sure to catch Daiki's eye, and then his face broke into a broad smile. His muscles relaxed. This was home. These were his friends and family. This was the Darival he remembered: before he had even finished his dinner the entire city was aware that he had come home. How many nights had he spent in these halls as a child, a page, a soldier, a captain? He had fished beside the great ice falls in the summer, froze fish in the autumn, and prepared stews in the winter. He had hunted and trained his way up from the digging of excrement trenches to the mansion he now possessed. There was nowhere else he'd rather be—not even Roshenhyde.

And that was a damn good place.

"What are you waiting for? Give me my first ale!"

And they did. The first. The second. The third. The fourth. Things gradually became more humorous. His responsibilities faded. And the weight of his military title fell somewhere into the bottom of his third mug.

Laikum had settled in across from him, his youthful face riveted to Jikun in adoration. They were close in age and had trained together in the academy, and yet, the years had been far kinder to the broad-shouldered male before him—he had hardly aged a day in the last two centuries: he had the body of a male and the face of a child. "How many soldiers have you slain in battle?" Laikum asked excitedly, leaning forward from across the table. "Twenty? Thirty?"

Jikun blinked. "Twenty? Thirty…? Gods. You know I've been fighting for *years*, right?"

"So then eighty?"

Jikun waved his hand. "Two."

"Eighty two?"

Jikun rubbed a hand over his face. "Eighty two what?"

"Soldiers. Dead."

"Where?"

Laikum paused for a moment thoughtfully. "I don't remember. What are we talking about?"

There was a sudden rumble through the mountain that rose even above the din and the hall fell into a deathly silence.

Jikun's mind cleared somewhat and he raised his head from Laikum's plastered smile. "What... was that?" His hand moved on instinct to the hilt of his sword.

"A white thakish," Daiki replied with a shake of his head, leaning in from the other side as a wave of whispers swept the room. "They have been particularly vicious this spring."

Jikun frowned thoughtfully, wondering if that would mean something to him in a more sober state. But the noise in the room was rising once more and the words seemed even less important.

"Ladies! Tell about the females in the army!" Jekum breathed excitedly, waving away the white thakish, leaning forward and knocking an unclaimed ale across a half-eaten plate of food. Jikun watched with a grimace as Lais picked up a piece of food from within the pool and popped it into his mouth.

"Females..." Jikun looked up, catching Kaivervi's eye down the table as she glanced away from Nalaen and Merkan. She smiled at him and he could see her cheeks redden.

He found himself smiling back, his cheeks a little hotter, his heart a little faster.

Jekum followed his gaze and leaned forward, his long, silvery hair trailing into the food before him. "You know," he whispered conspiratorially. "She still loves you."

Jikun started, forcing his eyes away from Kaivervi. Was it obvious? Or was he theorizing? "Your hair..."

Jekum sat back, wiping the ends on the sleeve of Lais beside him. They were apparently still very close. Lais merely swallowed the food he had found and wiped his sleeve back on Jekum's shirt.

"A song!" Rulan suddenly shouted out from his conversation with Daiki, interrupting Jikun's thoughts to matters of a less interesting nature. "Daiki was just reminding me of your ceremony out of Darival. Gods, did you sing! The army must be full of songs! Sing us one!"

Jikun laughed. Perhaps more sober he would have frowned on the request. But ale had loosened his lips and spirit and he found himself standing to oblige.

"Valiant and daring,
Light Ones, they fight,
To push back the Dark God's growing night,
Far away, far away.
Sel'ari bring them home!

Quick and fleeting,
Spirits they run,
Over the hills to the setting sun,
Far away, far away.
Sel'ari bring them home!

Sad and weeping,
Their kin they rest,
In the bosom of the Light God's breast,
Far away, far away.
Sel'ari bring them home!"

The words were not exactly rippling with cheer, but the melody made up for that. He raised his mug at the last line and the ground attempted to scamper out from under his feet. He toppled backwards through roars of laughter.

A face appeared suddenly above his, blue-grey eyes creased with a smile. "Why don't I help you home? If you keep drinking like that there won't be enough for the rest of this room, let alone the dwarves of the Black Hills."

"Kaivervi…!" he let the mug fall from his hand and roll across the floor as she helped him to his feet—somehow managing to assist despite how unsteady she was herself.

She turned to the rest of the room, her hand tightening on his arm. "I believe our general has had enough for this night, my friends. Bid him goodnight! I'm sure we shall see more of him in the coming days!"

There was a clamor of boisterous and genuine honor as the room erupted with farewells. But their faces had become merely a blur of greys and blues.

Kaivervi put a strong arm underneath his, balancing him against her sturdy frame. “They love you, don’t they?” she commented with a smile as she pushed the banquet hall’s door open.

The comment sent a rush through his chest and words left his lips before he could catch himself, “Do you?” The door snapped shut at their heels and the sounds of laughter and music became muffled.

Kaivervi laughed and stumbled slightly as she took the first step. “Oh my. I don’t think I’m very much more… much more… damn it… I don’t think I am any much more… *ANY MORE* sober than you are.”

Jikun blinked as his mind tried to process her sentence. Was there an answer in there? “Do you remember where I live?” he asked finally.

She chuckled. “How could I not?”

Their feet trudged through the snow for several minutes as they talked about the food and alcohol they had just consumed: trivial chatter, but it was about as much as Jikun could muster.

“Does your army really sing those songs? Do you sing with them?” Kaivervi asked as she turned him around a building to follow the narrow street.

Jikun nodded his head as he took an unsteady step to the right. “You think I remember a song about *Sel’ari* without it being drilled into my sub…conscious through years of war? They are Sel’vi. They don’t stop singing. I listen. I… have an appearance to maintain… I’m a general after all… A general has… certain obligatoriations to maintain…”

She grimaced. “Obligatories…”

“Right. A general has certain obligatories to maintain.”

She nodded and then giggled.

“What?” he asked, finding that it was now he that had to catch her balance as they stumbled past another building.

“I have no idea!” she replied. “It’s the ale. I mean, obviously it’s the ale.”

“Obviously,” he agreed with a nod. “I asked you a question earlier…” It was suddenly coming back to him now. “I asked…”

“Are there females in the Sel’varian army?” she interrupted, diverting his path to avoid a row of close-budded flowers.

“Not in the Sel’varian army,” Jikun replied with a shake of his head, his mind losing the trail of his previous thought. He hopelessly abandoned retrieving it. “I have to get all my women with money,” he grieved.

Kaivervi turned her head sharply, her surprise utterly plain, even through the ale. “Prostitution? Gods, there is a death penalty for that!” She seemed mildly sobered at those words and her smile vanished.

Jikun laughed dismissively and waved a hand. “You sound like my captain. There is only a death penalty *if you get caught.*” He narrowed his brow. Something sounded ridiculous in his response, but his mind was too foggy to pinpoint what that was.

Kaivervi shook her head. “You never were very good at doing what you didn’t want to do…”

“You were never good at being the thing that I didn’t want to… that I wanted to…” he trailed off. “I don’t know what I was going to say.”

She chuckled once more, the lines on her face easing. Gods, was his mother right… she *was* beautiful… Blue-tinted hair. Cerulean eyes. Cheek bones that jutted fiercely from her alabaster skin. “I don’t know either!”

Jikun shook his head, determined to clear it somewhat. “What are you doing now?”

Kaivervi cocked her head. “Walking you—Oh. I’m a hunter. Lais, Nalaen, Jekum, and I. We’ve been tracking the behavior of the white thakish since last fall.”

Jikun looked back at her again. A hunter… She had filled out—sturdier than the Sel’varian females he was used to seeing these last few years. Maybe as supple as some of the human women he had bedded… Tall, lean, and muscular. He found his eyes had landed on her breasts.

Kaivervi took a large step, forcing him to look away in order to not trip. “I see where your eyes are,” she spoke with reproach, but he saw the corner of her mouth twitch slightly. “We are here. Welcome home, General.”

Jikun put a hand out against his door frame and stepped away from her support. He looked at her slight smile for a moment, thoughtfully considering her. She gazed back at him, silent and… expectant? “…You should stay,” he spoke softly, his mind feeling clearer than it had been since he had started drinking.

Kaivervi took his jaw in her hand and kissed his cheek. “No thank you, Jikun. I would like to imagine our reunion as more substantial than that. You get some sleep.” Her hand dropped away and she turned, stepping swiftly down his steps.

Jikun opened his door with a heavy exhale, not sure if it was the door or him who sighed more loudly.

Kaivervi paused at the last step and glanced once over her shoulder. “Would you like to go on the hunt with us in a few days?”

Jikun felt his chest lighten and his smile returned. "Gods know you'll have to remind me of this conversation tomorrow… But yes. I would like that, Kaivervi."

# CHAPTER FIVE

Elvorium: the seat of The Council of Elves, around which the politics of Sevrigel revolved. Hairem noted the fitting composition of the city, with its seven uniquely designed mansions circling the center of the city in arrays of color and design, yet closed off to the world around them. And his palace—balanced on the edge of a cliff. No great beauty in its majestically pearlescent and golden structure could allow Hairem to see beyond this fitting arrangement.

The largest structure in the center of the city was the Council's Hall. The building was enormous, with creamy white walls and plated gold along the roof. Eight columns supported a long archway over a steep staircase leading from the cobbled street to the carved, double ivory doors. In the shadows of the overcast sky, it presented a rather formidable atmosphere. Hairem knew that the building was far larger than the council members could ever make use of, but rather than allow it for public use, the unused rooms sat empty and useless, collecting dust, webs, and whatever city critters saw fit to utilize the taxpayers' coin.

On the left of the Council's Hall was the second home of Nilanis. He did not use this home for himself, but it was a testament to his wealth and power. While his wife had been alive, she had used it for lavish entertainment with the high nobility of the city. Now, Hairem believed it primarily housed his guests and merchant captains when they came into port. As such, it was perhaps the busiest and gaudiest home in the city.

The house to the left of Nilanis was that of Yulairm, the speaker for the nocturnal elves, the Noc'olari. His title, Nocalarum, was owed to the Noc'olarian worship of Noctem—a practice every bit as unseemly as the rest of their culture. They were unabashedly scandalous individuals, with a deep fascination for the humanoid body and other living creatures. Rumors would occasionally surface of research conducted by the Noc'olari that would be sacrilegious to a follower of Sel'ari, but the secretive nature of the race had prevented any proof from surfacing. Here, the line of Noc'olarian council members had seen fit to ensure no one forgot their risqué tendencies: the porch columns were naked dancing maidens, and the arches they upheld were crescent carvings of the night sky. It was, even by Noc'olarian standards, verging on shocking.

To his left was Mikanum's estate. Mikanum was, in addition to Yulairm, one of Hairem's most consistent supporters. Mikanum was the speaker for the Darivalians and General Jikun had been his strongly recommended appointment—and as General Jikun had yet to lose a battle, this had helped to endear him further to the king. The home for the speaker had always been a rather jagged, incongruous mansion, taking after, Hairem imagined, the plain and simple tendencies of the Darivalians. Fortunately, recent renovations, on which Mikanum and his wife had spent their personal fortune, had toned the building out to a far less garish and more elegant palace. At night, it would shimmer like carved ice and perhaps could be named the fairest building in the city.

Beside Mikanum was the speaker for the seafaring Galweni. The architecture of Fildor's home reflected the ocean—the roof swept downward like a crashing wave and the pillars seemed to remain untouched beneath it. Having Fildor on the council was fittingly like a day at sea—one moment he was calm and the next he was a raging storm. Hairem pursed his lips; walking past the house gave him a sour feeling. Unwed and generally disliked, it was purely by the request of the Galweni that Fildor had found a place on the council at all.

Then there was the home of Cahsari, the Kasan, or speaker of the Helvari. His home was made entirely of white stone and the entrance to his mansion was like that of a cave. Though the number of Helvari on Sevrigel was scarce—most of the elves of the mountains choosing to reside on Ryekarayn—Cahsari had slithered his way in with the right people—as had the Helvarian council members before him. He was, without a doubt, one of the fiercest opponents Hairem had had the displeasure of working with.

The Eph'ven speaker's home, now occupied by Heshellon, was perhaps the least appealing in its bland, sandy architecture, but the mere knowledge that one of his few supporters lived within somehow made the home seem remarkably agreeable. There were times when Hairem had heard his father's bitter complaints about the Eph'ven need for outsiders to "prove themselves" in order to gain an Eph'ven's cooperation, but Hairem had not seen this desert cultural insistence at work for himself. In addition, Heshellon had only been in his seat of power since Gilden had been murdered by the assassin two years prior. Yet, he had wasted no time in staunchly reverting to the Eph'ven cause previously aligned with the True Blood tendencies toward politics. To Hairem, this seemed perfectly agreeable.

The last home was the smallest of the seven, making an impression like ripples on the water—which Hairem thought fitting considering it was their race that held and traversed Sevrigel's inner waterways. It had been the home of Leisum. Hairem paused briefly outside of it, bowing his head in respect, eyes flicking across the flowers still strewn about outside of it. He knew that within days of hearing of Leisum's murder, the Ruljenari had appointed a new speaker. Ilrae, as he was known. With Hairem's coronation having yet to be completed at Leisum's death, Hairem had had no say in the appointment. He wondered what sort of male this new Ruljarian speaker would be.

Along with the Council's Hall, the seven other buildings created a circle around a cobbled courtyard and the statue planted at the center. As was his custom acquired from the True Blood prince Hadoream, Hairem made his final stop before it, bowing his head in respect to the memory of the six ancient warriors.

Yet his pause was longer than usual that day.

*'Put in a word for me to Sel'ari,'* he prayed. *'...That Ilrae is half the male... even* half *the male that Leisum was, and I shall build an even grander temple in your honor.'*

It was a rather lofty promise and he didn't pause long to think whether he would *actually* tear down the temple for a larger one, but he imagined she would accept the essence of his words.

Of the six stony faces, only one gazed back at him. Hairem felt self-conscious then, averting his eyes and giving another brief bow. He stepped past them, across the cobbled way, and up the wide stairs.

"Welcome, Your Majesty," his personal guards greeted before the door.

But Hairem's anxieties had drawn him inward and their voices fell deafly upon his ears. He glanced down at himself once, debating his particular color choice of such a passive white and gold. Red would have been better. Fiercer. Or perhaps it could be too closely associated with Malranus. Yes, bad choice. He probably should have worn a blue. Something darker. More—

"Er... Haire—Your Majesty," Erallus' voice cut off his thoughts. "The council is waiting for you."

Hairem looked up sharply, realizing the doors had been thrown wide to his arrival and the hall had fallen into expectant silence.

The seven eyed the door inquisitively.

"Greetings, Your Majesty," Nilanis finally spoke loudly, causing the males about him to scramble swiftly to their feet and fall into deep and respectful bows.

Hairem's eyes flicked from face to face and his brow raised faintly. *'I thought I was early…'* Yet every member was already present. "Greetings, Nilanis," Hairem finally replied, nodding his head toward the speaker in a strong, curt motion, attempting to project complete control over his expectations.

Half of the game of politics was maintaining the appearance of control. He had been given this advice countless times by Sairel, but the eldest of the princes had never seemed to lack genuine power at all. Attempting to imbue himself with the male's personality, he glanced stoically about the well-lit room as his feet padded softly across the marble floor. He took the stairs up to his desk and stopped before his chair. Even with his back toward them, he could feel all eyes boring into him, narrowed and scrutinizing, searching for the slightest suggestion that his countenance was anything less than assured.

Hairem turned about to the males waiting for him to take his seat first. *'Gods grant me patience.'* And he sat.

"My lord," Nilanis began before the other council members had even pulled their chairs in toward their carved desks. "This is Ilrae. He is the new speaker for the Ruljenari since Leisum—may Sel'ari grant him solace—is no longer with us."

The unfamiliar face to the left of Mikanum offered an otherwise expressionless half-smile, bowing his head toward the king. He seemed slightly older than the other elves in the room, with faint lines at the corners of his mouth and eyes suggesting he had climbed well into his years. His silvery blue hair was braided back sharply, pulling his eyes slightly at an angle and accentuating the sharp rise of his cheekbones. Hairem squinted, his muscles subconsciously sympathizing with the poor elf's taut composure. "It is my great honor to join you on the council, My King," Ilrae spoke softly, stormy eyes rising in expressionless affixation. There was something unsettling about the intensity of the gaze and Hairem found himself incapable of more than a mere nod in return.

He drew himself up. *'Half of the game of politics is maintaining the appearance of control,'* Sairel's words rushed back to him suddenly. Hairem stiffened. “Welcome, Ilrae.” He rubbed his jaw, making sure to study the Ruljen with unabashed frankness. He knew little about the male and so far, Ilrae had given him no more than a cold gaze to work with. His face shifted expressions as though on etiquette’s queue, but his eyes had remained unsettlingly emotionless.

*‘I suppose time will have to tell...’* Hairem gestured for Nilanis to seat himself as he prepared to conduct their meeting.

The El’adorium opened his mouth to speak further, but changed his mind, pulling his seat up in exact proximity to the desk as the others had done. He straightened the already straight emblem on his chest, as though reminding Hairem of his position.

Hairem regarded them all silently, blue eyes flicking from one expressionless, attentive face to the next. There was the twist of anxiety in his stomach, but his composure was deliberately relaxed. *‘I let them see only who I want them to see,’* he recalled Sairel’s stoically commanding words. If ever a male had been born to be king, Sairel was that elf.

Hairem drew himself up against the back of his chair, tapping his finger once on the solid wood of his desk. “I see here there is a list of matters that we need to address… ”

Several pairs of eyes regarded him cynically and several bodies shifted impatiently, as though his failure was somehow, already, unsalvageable.

Hairem set the parchment down, leaning back with an inward sigh. The council would have no patience with his lead. Not at this time. It was true: he hardly knew what he was doing. Revealing the extent of this fact would perhaps be more detrimental than just… “Nilanis, if you would?”

The speaker for the Sel’vi stood swiftly, moving around the circle of desks to stand in the middle of the room as though he had been waiting for Hairem to turn over command. And yet, Hairem could not help but be impressed as he noted the way the male walked—strong, brisk, and remarkably commanding. His experience was unchallenged. He stood silently for a moment, tension building. Finally he spoke.

“Yes, my fellow council members. Today is the day that we must finally address the proposition by our Noc’olarian brethren: term limits on the council positions. Since this matter is clearly a primary concern for our Nocalarum, Yulairm, we shall let him express to us his people’s concern.” The tone he used was, without contest, passively aggressive and Hairem was taken aback by the unabashed bias with which he had already addressed the matter.

Yet his inner emotions remained closed behind an outward composure of silent observation. He rested his chin on the back of his hand. No sooner than a few score words and the internal conflict of the council had begun. Or perhaps he had not accorded them enough credit—his mere entrance in the Council's Hall seemed to have created a rather chilly atmosphere.

Yulairm stood, grey eyes regarding Nilanis with open contempt. He transferred his attention toward Hairem. "My Lord, the Noc'olari wish to see term limits placed on the council members. Their concern is that there are members of the council who, once they have gained power, can, without repercussions, ignore the will of the people and pass laws applying to their own personal benefit. Let me remind you of 3514 P.E. when the council passed a yearly income increase of fifteen percent when there was no financial reason to do so—all council members were already earning ten percent more than the average elven home, entirely excluding their personal financial ventures. If a term limit—or a vote to renew the term—could be established, corrupt council members could no longer remain on the council for—" and here he paused to deliberately eye Nilanis, "three hundred years or more."

His eyes returned to Hairem as though he knew that a term limit was exactly what the king had been advocating to Heshellon for the last few weeks. Had Heshellon opened his mouth? Damn it!—this was too soon to bring it before the rest of the council for a vote! What had prompted the Nocalarum's impatience? Did he fear that Hairem would become corrupted by the other council members? His father had certainly lost his sway over the council over time…

Lost his sway to people like Nilanis. Leisum had been a respectable council member, but he had retained his position for one thousand five hundred years. And Nilanis was nothing like Leisum. Additionally, he likely had well over two thousand years left. It helped that the elven people were intelligent enough to appoint older elves as council members—to allow shorter terms by impending death—but when a younger elf like Nilanis slithered his way in, there was no extricating him. Especially when half the city's commerce went through his docks.

Hairem leaned forward on his hand, inclining his head to encourage Yulairm to continue. He would have to make the most of this unexpected timing. He knew his eyes were reproachful, however, rebuking Yulairm for bringing the topic to council without his foreknowledge.

Still, the Nocalarum was fearless as he pressed forward. His lean body drew up sharply, as straight and tall and scraggly as a weathered tree, but his eyes were grey, deep, and fierce. "I have been advocating shorter terms on the council for over fifty years, Your Majesty. And every year the council votes against it. Three centuries ago, the former royal bloodline abandoned Sevrigel for Ryekarayn because of the corrupted state of our council. Silandrus went so far as to abolish any such council on Ryekarayn and now his son Sairel rules as sole voice for his people: King *as well as* El'adorium. I challenge any council member here to come forth with a reason as to why a term limit—or even vote of renewal—would be a negative addition to our laws. If the True Bloods deemed our shortcomings to be such a detriment to the people we serve, then perhaps we should find a way to—"

Cahsari snorted and Hairem felt a rise of hatred toward the Helven at the interruption. "Of *course* the Noc'olari would propose this." He rubbed the narrow ridge of his pale nose and then threw his hand outward in a broad, animated sweep. "With the shortest average lifespans of our peoples, one can hardly see a reason *not* to. And a term limit certainly does not affect Yulairm either. You have had your seat for what… sixty years? Seventy years? What sort of term limit are you proposing? Two hundred? Three hundred? It must be nice for you to see the rest of us removed while you retain power. Fresh, inexperienced blood for you to take control of when the rest of us are disposed. We all know Silandrus was a power hungry savage who shared your ideals. He allowed our elves to fall beneath the clutches of the sirens. Saebellus is a testament to what sort of prodigy he left behind with *his* ideas and affinities. I daresay such ideas even border on being treasonous! Like Silandrus, Saebellus would also see us all removed—except that he possesses the madness to follow through with his sword. He would take our heads first, the king not being withheld from the same fate."

Yulairm narrowed his icy eyes threateningly. "Silandrus was not only a *True Blood*, but a very well-respected king amongst the Sel'vi in Elvorium *and* the other elven cities throughout Sevrigel. That is your first offense. The second… How *dare* you suggest that I am as corrupt and manipulative as you, Cahsari. If I was, let me assure you that you would long since have been *removed*."

Cahsari stood, blue eyes flashing. "Is that a threat on my life? Last I recall, you saw Leisum last before he died. Perhaps you did not appreciate his traditional stance on the seat terms. I—"

"ENOUGH," Hairem spoke forcibly. He narrowed his eyes at both elves, noting how they hesitated to immediately comply with his order. "Sit. *Both* of you." His voice rose in force, wresting control over the room.

Cahsari sat back slowly as Yulairm muttered an apology.

"First, I will not hear ill spoken of the True Bloods. Keep it to yourself in my presence, Cahsari. *Now*, it seems to me that the Noc'olari's proposition is quite reasonable. If the council was to be renewed by vote every two hundred years, that would help to maintain a will of the people. In order to prevent a benefit on the timing for this proposition, council terms could be voted on for renewal next year and proceed to a two hundred year cycle thereafter."

Mikanum raised a hand slightly, gesturing to himself. "If I may, Your Majesty."

Hairem leaned back, smiling slightly. Mikanum would no doubt have a far more elegant method of persuasion on his behalf. "Speak."

The heads turned as Mikanum stood and pulled himself up to a straight, regal stance. Standing before his chair in the stiff composure of command, he appeared to Hairem as a far older version of the general. And his first meeting with the general had been a relief from the façade of polite politics. He was lean, pale, and even from the great expanse across the room, Hairem felt as though he could feel a chill emanating from his icy exterior. "Thank you, Your Majesty. No doubt every one of us is a strong elf of tradition. I would like to remind each of us of the council's tradition that even the True Blood king Silandrus would not usurp or alter—"

"Your self-importance knows no bounds," Yulairm spat. "Silandrus didn't uphold tradition because he respected the council, he upheld tradition because he respected that the *people* elected you here. The same *people* whom you now exploit and ignore."

"Enough," Mikanum retorted, his visage of venerability fading as irritation began to surface. "*Now*, in theory, the proposition for which Yulairm and his people so staunchly argue for seems in the best interest of the people—*when* regarded in first light." Hairem could feel his smile quickly fading. "But has not *tradition* always been the best interest of our people?—A virtue *necessary* to the fabric of our society. If we do not have our tradition, than who are we but *humans* or *dwarves?* When the other races fled Eraydon's side, who there remained but our elven brethren? It is our tradition that separates us from the lesser races: our tradition of racial bonds, of history, of gestures, of gods... of morality. And there is no tradition older than that of our council.

"When our races first united on Sevrigel after The Last War, a Sel'ven was appointed king of all the elven people in honor of Ephraim and Eraydon's heritage. When the True Bloods abandoned the throne three centuries ago, a Sel'ven was appointed to replace him. To this day, a Sel'ven has always been the king of all elven people—just king or unjust. You, Hairem, are a figure of tradition. Although you are not of traditional royal blood, your father's Sel'varian heritage and his position as the El'adorium made him the next king without contest. Would you give up your position—tradition—to allow the people to *vote* for who they wished to be made king? Do you believe that the people know best? Or do *you*, Your Majesty, know best?" He paused here briefly, challenging Hairem to consider.

Hairem did consider. Of course he believed he knew best. Did not every elf? And the idea of giving up power to a vote…? The thought was comical at best.

"The council is like our king. Yulairm is the king of the Noc'olari. Cahsari is the king of the Helvari. Fildor is the king of the—"

Yulairm shook his head sternly as his voice sharply interrupted the Darivalian from continuing. "If we are like the kings to our respective peoples and not Sevrigel as a whole, then why are, say, the Lithri not represented?—the Lithri may live near Mikanum's people, but the Darivalians had never feigned camaraderie with their kind. We are required to be so much more than the representatives of our races and we have an obligation to serve *all* of Sevrigel. Reducing our time ensures less risk of corruption in serving our own interests, *or* those solely pertaining to our own kind—"

Cahsari laughed, a burst of sound so sharp that it projected as though it had been long contained through Yulairm's speech. Hairem grimaced once more. Gods, did he ever let anyone finish? "The *Lithri?!* No one gives a damn about the *Lithri.*"

"And let's be honest," Fildor joined in with a soft tone that the room hushed to hear, "Murios once prophesized one of their kind would wrest the throne from beneath the king and slay his followers by the hundreds. The further they are from this capital, the better."

"A Lithri born of Lithri blood but not of Lithri parentage?" Yulairm repeated in disbelief. "It doesn't even make *sense*. That prophecy is millennia old and Murios is nothing but a mad—Wait, by *Noctem* this is an entirely diverging topic! My *point* was that too much power is being attested to our positions and our races when—"

Mikanum raised his hand, even as Hairem leaned forward in interest. The reason for excluding the Lithri from the council was rarely spoken of, and yet this prophecy was regarded as unquestionable truth. And that it had come from a suggested necromancer had not weakened its weight of fear over past kings. "I'm sorry to interrupt you as you so *rudely* interrupted me, Nocalarum,"

Mikanum spoke, taking hold once more of the conversation, "but I'm afraid I was not finished in making my point. As I was saying, we *have* been appointed to represent our respective peoples. What is good for our people is good for the Lithri and those alike—surely they are not above our needs. And each of us kings stand in the shadow of our one king—King Hairem of Sevrigel." He turned away from Yulairm to focus his gaze upon Hairem. "We are appointed by vote to take on the responsibilities of a ruler—a king like yourself, Your Majesty. Just or unjust. And like a vote cannot strip you of your position, neither should a vote strip us of ours. The tradition of elves dictates your position as it dictates ours. As such, I must stand with Nilanis in refusing to grant the Noc'olari their proposition."

Hairem was quiet a moment. It was difficult to refute the tradition. No, impossible. Mikanum was accurate on all accounts. It was even tradition itself that had long since barred the Lithri from sitting on the council—even if the prophecy extended another millennium, the Lithri would never join them. But there were traditions of virtue that had been present since Sel'ari... and those traditions that the elves had created themselves. And the council was... "Well spoken, Mikanum." Hairem stood, finding it difficult to follow Mikanum's disappointedly elegant opposition. "Let us not forget that even we make mistakes. And that tradition not defined by Sel'ari is *not* above change. The Noc'olari's proposition is not unjust. Nor does it change that every council member would still be appointed by vote. And unlike myself, none of you are truly kings. What this proposition accomplishes is checking the seat's stance against that of the will of the people. You are appointed to uphold their will, are you not? Tradition first appointed you to do *that*." He could see Cahsari's scowl and Heshellon's smile of approval as he shifted his eyes to the new male. Heshellon rarely spoke at the council meetings, making it difficult to find verbal support on matters. But perhaps this Ruljen... His spirit rose as he reflected on his earlier prayer request to Sel'ari. "Ilrae, what is your view on this matter?"

Ilrae stood, stormy eyes shifting as he met Hairem's. His lips, which had drawn as tight as his eyes, loosened. "I stand with Nilanis, Mikanum, and Cahsari. I am not a king in name. But it is what I was appointed to act as. If the elves wanted the council to be voted upon, they would have declared so at the formation. I am not about to change a nine thousand year-old tradition for the sake of some nocturnal savages who still live in canopies and run about half-nude."

Yulairm leapt to his feet. "You *dare* insult my people, you river rat? While your people were still living in tents my people cured the Amondos Plague. While your people were shitting in the same water others drank, my people made the year and the day and the stars to navigate by."

"Oh? Your people made *stars*, did they?"

Hairem put a hand to his forehead and rubbed his brow as Ilrae lashed back. *'Thank you for nothing. I asked for only* half *the male Leisum had been.'* "Council," Hairem raised his voice in exasperation, but Heshellon and Cahsari had entered the argument as well. "Council! COUNCIL!"

They quieted, turning towards him slowly as though challenging him to come up with a reason as to why they should remain silent.

He could not afford to lose them further on the matter. It pained him to have to adjourn the topic when it was so solidly a loss. "*Clearly* the discussion of this matter has come to a close. Nilanis, if you would take the vote." Things would change, he reassured himself. The council was smugly comfortable right now. Let them think so. He would shake things up soon.

Nilanis bowed, the silence in the room remaining so at the king's command. "Of course, Your Majesty." He moved from council member to council member, allowing them to sign their names in support of the new proposition. He stopped last before Hairem, setting the parchment onto the wooden desk.

The king sighed. Only Yulairm and Heshellon had signed the Noc'olari proposition. Even with his signature counting for two of theirs, the vote still rested in the opposition's favor. He picked up his quill and signed regardless, an overwhelming sense of discouragement settling in. It had been one thing to know the proposition would fail—another to see it happen. This proposition had arisen so quickly after his father's death. He had had no time to win the council outside these aggressive meetings! He had been far too naïve…

Nilanis held the parchment up then, turning slowly so that each elf might see the signatures—as though the action was at all necessary—and spoke with a rather satisfied smile, "The Noc'olari proposition has been opposed. My regrets to your people, Yulairm."

"Better luck next year," Cahsari sneered under his breath. "Maybe your people will invent some poison we can test on you before then so we do not have to endure this yet *again*."

Yulairm shot him a venomous scowl behind his fierce, gray eyes and remained silent.

"Now onto our second vote," Nilanis prefaced, smiling broadly as though the first topic was solidly behind him. He patted down the red silk of his shirt as though un-ruffling from the last tension. "No doubt this topic is something we can *all* find agreement on. The celestial phoenixes' territory is being encroached upon again. As most of you know, this creature is almost extinct and now only inhabits the southern end of Sevrigel, specifically in the Sevilan Marshes. This happens to be the same territory where the centaurs have their savage little ancient burial grounds. Over fifty graves have encroached farther in the last 10 years. The burial grounds can be moved. The phoenix cannot."

Hairem held up his hand and Nilanis fell silent. "You will have to forgive me—no doubt this topic has been a matter of importance while my father was still on the throne—but what exactly is being proposed here…?"

"Forgive me, Your Majesty," Nilanis spoke with the faintest impatient undertone. "Firstly, money for their conservation. Secondly, and most importantly, moving the centaurs."

Hairem blinked, his mind refusing to grasp the proposition. "Excuse me? *Moving* the centaurs? Exactly how do you propose that they are moved? Drop a saddle on their asses and ride them out?" The thought caused him a laugh, inappropriately so.

Nilanis observed him seriously, and yet could not mask his discomfort in the king's response. "Of course not, Your Majesty," he replied calmly.

"Gods, put that proposition *away*," Hairem ordered, smile vanishing. What in the realm of the gods were they thinking?!

Nilanis remained calm, his eye contact steady. "I apologize, Your Majesty. I understand that the council is a new position for you to partake in, but the proposition can only be 'put away' when a vote has been finalized."

"Who speaks for the centaurs?"

Nilanis raised a brow. "I do not understand what you mean. One of us? None of us speak for the centaurs…"

Hairem threw a hand up in the air. "No one here speaks for the centaurs? Are you proposing you move them without any representation on their part?"

"Why don't *you* represent them, Your Majesty," Fildor suggested. He twisted a murky strand of hair about his claw-like finger and sneered wryly. Challengingly.

Hairem turned his head toward the Galwen, regarding his polite, thin-lipped smile as a challenge. "…I shall," Hairem replied, standing. "First off, we are fighting a war right now. A *war*. Seeing as how you have all been voting on the money being sent out to fight it, you should all have some concept of just how much this is costing us. And the *last* thing I am supporting is sending our much needed and limited supply of money to some asinine celestial phoenix conservation when we have a damn brilliant warlord on our doorstep! *PUT THE DAMN PROPOSITION AWAY.*"

Nilanis did not lose his calm stance. In fact, his apathetic expression did not change. "Is there anything else you would like to say on behalf of the centaurs?"

Hairem raised both of his hands in frustration, trying to keep his temper from flaring further. "They are ancient burial grounds. It is *their* tradition. The celestial phoenix is, I am well aware, a symbol of Sel'ari and I respect that as much as any of you. But if we uphold our tradition so highly, what gives us the right to spit on theirs? Leave the phoenix. *Leave the centaurs.*"

"What if," Mikanum began thoughtfully, running a thumb down across his icy face to pause on the sharp point of his chin, "we simply send Jikun down that way. Saebellus just lost a decisive battle—he won't be ready to lose another one immediately. Jikun's army is large enough to simply scare the centaurs west or east—wherever they wish to go. *Extinction is permanent.* The centaurs refuse to be concerned with their effects on the creature of our goddess. Our religion versus theirs. Hardly an extreme to push them to move their burial grounds another direction. Just order the general to not use lethal force. The phoenix is saved. The centaurs have their burial grounds somewhere else. For but a little discomfort, everyone will ultimately be satisfied."

Heshellon was shaking his head, his sandy blond hair shifting back and forth across his narrow shoulders. "This is simply *mad.* Jikun should be nearby, not in the southern wastelands moving horses for the sake of some blue *pigeon—which,* for the council's record, does not return the protection in kind. Gods know Leisum was saved from this idiotic discussion!"

Nilanis' eyes widened slightly. "Heshellon! Sel'ari may not be the goddess of your people but *she is ours.* That is reason enough to '*deserve*' our assistance! Watch your tongue!" He straightened himself, patting down the silk of his shirt once more. "Jikun is not here now. And if he is off romping about in the northern tundra, *clearly* we can spare him."

"Him, yes. But we *cannot* spare his soldiers," Hairem replied angrily.

"*By the gods*, just vote," Fildor groaned, leaning back in his chair. He gave the twist of muddy hair a jerk in release and threw his hand into the air. "Just move the fucking horses already. Then this whole cursed issue is at a rest. We have to talk about this every damn month. Get it *over with.*"

Nilanis turned to Hairem questioningly.

Hairem hesitated. It was truly mad to even consider sending Jikun down south to deal with the centaurs—Saebellus wounded or not. If Saebellus found the strength to strike while Jikun was away, the repercussions would be devastating. Could he take the city…? Perhaps not Elvorium, but the capital was hardly the only city on Sevrigel.

He looked from one council member to the next, trying to think of something else to say. What else *was* there to say? The entire proposition was so poorly timed that words escaped him! "If you want the centaurs to move, I will make it happen… just wait until the war is over. *Wait until the war is over*, and I will comply. Take the vote," Hairem sighed. He watched the parchment make its rounds, growing increasingly concerned at each signature added. When it reached him, his jaw slacked. "The vote passes? You have voted to use our general to move the centaurs *now?! ARE YOU MAD?!*"

There came a soft, gurgled chuckle as the elf that had omitted it had been unable to swallow first. "There are, you will understand, issues at home that must be dealt with, even in times of war. The centaurs are not going to store their rotting dead while waiting for us to move them," Ilrae spoke softly. "As a matter of fact, My Lord, as unfortunate a fact as it may be, the people overall will profit from the sale of military equipment and goods to do this bloodless operation. A war like this will certainly help to refill our coffers."

"I know *who* will profit," Hairem spoke harshly. Nilanis would—his ships would take to port a large number of necessary goods. Cahsari would—his people were the primary suppliers of weapons. Fildor's people—they controlled the ports Nilanis would ultimately have to pass through at the coast near Elarium. Mikanum would—his reputation increased every time General Jikun gained another victory. And Ilrae's people had primary control of the river and ground trade from shore to shore. And every one of their signatures was on the proposition.

"Last, but not least, there is a matter here right at home that we must address," Nilanis began slowly, as though giving Hairem the opportunity to contend further. The king held his tongue. He was furious to realize that he had no power on matters where the council was concerned—even on something as grave as the war for Sevrigel herself. They needed but five votes to pass—or not pass—what they saw fit. His vote worth two was nothing more than a mockery of how little power he truly had.

He had once asked for assurance in Jikun's military support... His chest tightened at the thoughts wiggling free from the deepest crevices of his mind... He could... *refuse*... to order Jikun to move the centaurs...

The thought frightened him suddenly. He had few allies and Jikun was as far north as one could go. He had all the appearances of wealth and power, but these males... the males that voted against him held the *true* wealth and power in the country. He was nothing more than a pawn.

*Their pawn.*

"Your Majesty?"

Hairem snapped back, regarding the tanned face of the Eph'ven before him blankly.

"About the cotton, Your Majesty," Heshellon nudged.

Hairem tried to recall what he had gathered subconsciously from Nilanis' most recent statements. "...I apologize. Will you repeat the last thing you said?"

"...About the silk or the cotton or the tax...?" Nilanis asked.

Hairem sat up straighter, trying to look authoritative. He would *not* be their pawn. "*All* of it."

"Yes, Your Majesty. This is a proposition by some of our people. Some would like to see an increase of imported cotton from Ryekarayn as well as a lowering of its tax. The argument, of course, is against silk's relatively expensive cost."

"Continue."

"...And that is a summary of what I said last."

Hairem nodded matter-of-factly. "And what are the consequences of this proposition?" *'Aside from your personal income,'* he added to himself wryly.

"Sevrigel is known for her silk. We hurt our people at home by bringing in—"

"Competition?"

"...Cotton, Your Majesty. Cotton is a cheap, simple fabric. The price of silk simply cannot compete with it. If we bring in cotton, every maker and seller of silk will financially suffer."

"But the majority of people shall benefit from the option of a cheaper fabric?" It was a rhetorical question, but he liked to see the council squirm a little. Every one of them, with the exception of Heshellon, Mikanum, and Yulairm—whose people did not wear silk—were heavily invested in the silk market. "How would *you* suffer, Nilanis? You control the majority of trade for this city. If you were bringing in more cotton, would that not benefit your market? Why would other merchants not benefit the same?"

"...I do not have connections in the cotton trade, Your Majesty. As it is hardly a fabric of high demand, there are not many of our merchants that do."

"So get connections."

Ilrae leaned forward, his dark eyes narrowing to become mere slits from the tightness of his hair. "Sevrigel is the largest center for silk in the world. If the demand in our nation decreases, our creators suffer. They have to cut the number of workers they employ. The *people* suffer."

"Then they can make cotton instead. I do not see how this will negatively—especially since cotton, as you stated, *is so cheap to make and buy*—affect anyone except those who are *personally* invested in the silk market."

"Hear hear," Yulairm spoke half-heartedly. He appeared quite worn out, slouched slightly in his chair. His eyes met with Hairem's and his unspoken words were very clear:

*You are fighting a losing battle.*

"...Let us take the vote."

*

Fury and hopelessness accompanied Hairem like newfound friends as he left the Council's Hall. *'No wonder the True Bloods didn't establish another council when they got to Ryekarayn!'* His perception of the difficulty that lay ahead of him had grown infinitely.

In his distress, he did not perceive the female standing beside the first column of the stairway, nor did he notice her hurry after him until she had caught his arm and tugged him to a halt.

"I apologize, Your Majesty," she said quickly, dropping her hand. "I just—you could not hear me so I—"

Hairem regarded her blankly for a moment, staring at her face as his mind struggled to return from its thoughts. "Ah, Lady Ilsevel. I'm afraid I was distracted." He raised his hands at the guards on either side of him whose hands rested at their weapons' sides. "It is alright. Give us some space." He had not immediately recognized her, so far from his thoughts had she fallen. He attempted to force a smile.

"The meeting went quite poorly, didn't it?"

Hairem could see her eyes searching his face for his own emotion. She was already aware of his failure in the meeting. He could tell by her tone—apologetic and… sympathetic? His emotions, no doubt, were written plainly across his face. "*Poorly?!* There are hardly enough negative words in the elven tongue to describe just how 'poorly' it went. I'll have three new propositions on my desk in a few days, *none* of which I think are in the best interest of the people as a whole!" He found himself continuing, pouring his aggravation out onto her. "Today I lost the majority of the vote all three times and one of the males from whom I expected the greatest support was one of my most adamant opponents. I do not know how my father did it—or any king for that matter. The True Bloods may have been onto something—getting away from here!"

"It is difficult when the council is so… venal."

"Yes! Ex—" he stopped and looked at her again. He had not expected that opinion from the daughter of the El'adorium. She had to know that her father voted—or did not vote—on almost every twistedly-selfish policy that came through the doors. With that sentence, the timid female he perceived her to be was gone. There was no hesitation to her words, no fear. She was soft spoken, but there was a fire in her eyes that he had glimpsed only for a moment when he had seen her last. Something he had perhaps mistaken for embarrassment.

"I am sorry for my father's decisions. I wish there was something I could do. I do try to talk to him, believe me," she continued as though not noticing Hairem's surprise. "But you know, he is a *very* difficult male." She shook her head wishfully. "And… I wanted to apologize for the other night. It must have been wholly exasperating to have my father, well… trying to introduce us." She laughed then, rocking back on her heels. "I do not envy your position. I suppose every lord with a daughter in the city is trying to have you present for dinner."

Hairem frowned, surveying her for a second time. He was not certain what to make of her. She did not seem to be the shy girl from dinner. And he was not sure how to reply to her unabashedly straightforward comments.

She seemed to detect this and continued without breaking stride. "Oh, I apologize. You were ranting about the council. Gods know you need to."

Hairem smiled slightly then—an ever so slight, genuine smile. "I did not mean to unburden myself on you. That was rude of me. The council is what it is, and I can hardly expect to change it in a few weeks. *But* I am a very patient male."

The female slid a bit closer, intensely focused on his words, as though they were sharing a secret. "Did the council lower the taxes on the cotton imports?"

Hairem pursed his lips for a moment. "*No*. I'm afraid quite the opposite."

"*Truly?* But what about Mikanum? No doubt Yulairm and Heshellon voted with you, but why would Mikanum vote against you? His people have no interest in the silk market."

"Mikanum's *people* do not, but *Mikanum* is another matter entirely."

"The gall of him!"

The door to the Council Hall swung open then and the lady fell silent, casting her eyes aside as the council filed out. Hairem stepped to the side, waiting for them to pass.

"Ilsevel," Nilanis called to her as he paused before the council's steps. He bowed his head briefly to the king, dismissive to his presence as though his mind lay on far superior matters. Like his three most recent victories.

The lady gestured for her father to wait and turned back toward the king, seemingly apologetic once more. "Have a good evening, Your Majesty. I wish you more fortune tomorrow." She hurried after her father in swift, pattering strides, long blond braid bobbing softly behind her.

Hairem stood wholly perplexed. She had, no doubt, intrigued him.

# Chapter Six

A faint crunch sounded under each of Jikun's footsteps as he stepped heavily across Kaivervale's fresh layer of snow—it would be many months in the south before he would even glimpse a dusting. Dawn was just rising now, casting long shadows across the city. The sun was hidden deep behind the Telsuel Peaks in the east, but the cloudless sky was still filled with her light.

Jikun glanced to his right at the soft sound of crunching snow not his own. A stone home stood quiet and dark except for a small, heavily clothed child creeping from the doorway.

"F-fair day, General Taemrin," the girl greeted with a start as she stepped outside. She closed the door carefully behind her, leaning her face close to the crack as she did so, as though helping to soften the door against the frame.

Jikun paused, regarding the child reproachfully. "Do your parents know you are out?"

The child shifted sheepishly, eyes lingering on her feet. "Of course they do," she replied, pulling the basket she carried tighter to her side.

Jikun narrowed one eye. She was dressed in heavy boots and a thick cloak. A handmade scarf wound tightly about her head, but little tuffs of white hair poked out from beneath it. He could catch a glimpse of the end of bread protruding from the opening of the basket. "Where are you off to?"

The child took a long step past him. "To the market, General. So glad to see you home! Lithriella's many blessings be upo—" she choked on the last words as Jikun caught her by the hood of her cloak and jerked her to a solid stop.

Children these days! Hardly different than the rabble of soldiers he had had to nurse for the last several years. "Hold up there," he insisted with a tone he reasoned was at least mildly intimidating. "Where did you say you were going?"

He saw the girl flinch. She hesitated for a moment, and then her jaw set. She turned, attempting to yank the cloak out of his hand. "To the market."

Jikun released her. "To the market," he repeated steadily. He could see the girl's eyes waver as he narrowed his gaze. "...Well, off with you then," he gave a sudden, off-putting smile.

The girl retreated several steps away and then fled down the street toward the business district. He saw her glance over her shoulder twice before she vanished behind a building and was lost.

He remained where he was standing thoughtfully. What trouble had he gotten into as a child? ...Gods, he was a terrible example. Still, the city was small and close-knit, with practically every member of the community looking out for one another's family—what could she possibly be doing, running off without permission, that wouldn't eventually be discovered?

He finally turned away and slipped behind the barracks. Yes, she couldn't do worse than he had: icing over doors, freezing the snow underneath unsuspecting elven feet, tossing a few rocks through the Watchtower's windows... The military had certainly curbed the miscreant out of him.

*'Prostitution? Anti-religious reprobate?'* He could almost hear Navon's stern reproach from a thousand leagues away.

Jikun scoffed. *Most* of the miscreant, anyways.

He stopped, eyeing the great field of white mounds stretched out before him. He placed his hands against the fence of ice that encircled the land and strode in without pausing, passing through the opening that he had formed in the ice. It closed behind with a soft, crackling refreeze.

"Nazra!" he called.

The field before him shifted. The mounds of snow raised their heads, grey noses sniffing the air, ears perking up. From his left, a wolf leapt to its feet, shaking the snow dust from her fur, tail beating rapidly against the face of a companion just behind her.

"Nazra!" he called again, a broad smile sweeping across his face. "Come."

The winter wolf pushed off the earth and bounded across the snow in long, rapid strides, skidding to a stop in front of him and coming to sit in a great wiggling mass of impatience and affection. Jikun crouched down before her large form and reached out a hand to stroke the long, thick, white fur of her chest.

"Good girl," he purred in response, tapping his knee softly. She leapt from her sitting position, licked his face once, and tore off to the fence of ice from which he had entered. He chuckled slightly. "Impatient, aren't we? I didn't say we were going on a hunt."

Nazra froze, her ears becoming stiff and attentive, her eyes round, blue reflections of the sky. Her tail hung still.

Jikun walked up behind her and unfroze the fence, passing through the newly made gap and gesturing to Nazra to follow. He closed the hole behind them. A hunt *was* the intention. But first... Jikun's eyes flickered back toward the market. Curiosity: the curse of the elves. Damn it.

"Nazra, come," he muttered below his breath, retracing his steps to the doorway where he had encountered the child. Her footsteps were invisible in the snow, so light and small. But Nazra's eyes dilated as she sniffed around the doorway. "Find the girl," he ordered, pointing toward the market.

Nazra bounded off, vanishing behind a few buildings every so often and reappearing eagerly to ensure her master had not lost her trail. But Jikun could see her massive paw-prints embedded in the snow. Unlike the child, the wolf had not driftwalked her bounding march across town.

Jikun's brows knit in amusement as they turned toward the north end of the city: away from the market. "As I suspected," he mused. After so many years in the strict regimen of the army, being involved in such a frivolous task seemed relaxing.

Was it worth the hassle just to tell the child off?

Absolutely. And perhaps he would march the misbehaving girl home to her worried mother, who would be undoubtedly grateful for the assistance...

Though it would hardly make amends for the terror he had caused the city in his youth.

"Nazra, good girl," he praised as she wound them between the frost-covered buildings and through the gardens of flowers that were just beginning to pry open their icy petals. They passed beside the Temple of Lithriella, a crescent-shaped building glittering at its towered peaks as sunlight filtered through her structure of solid ice.

"*Further?*" Jikun inquired, his amusement fading to raw curiosity. Beyond the temple grounds flowed the expanse of a field and the grounds of the palace. The former was flat and sprinkled with patches of purple flowers. The latter was towering against the mountain face, made entirely of ice and turmazel crystals, glittering in purples, blues, greens, and whites—silent, dark, and still in the early dawn.

Yet there was no sign of the child. If *he* had been as gifted at drift-walking at her age, he may have staved off a good flogging or two.

Nazra had moved out into the field, her nose lowered to the earth, raising her head thoughtfully as she looked on ahead. She had turned slightly to the right of the palace, to a thick icefall that crashed into a frozen lake and vanished under the earth. There, to the right of the fall, Nazra concluded her hunt, sitting down before it and waiting patiently for Jikun to reveal the secret beyond.

Jikun studied the scenery. There was a small pool of ice in the snow, pressed against the face of the mountain where a long-since frozen waterfall cascaded into its depths. It was still. Unmoving. The face of the mountain was solid and unmarred, just a frozen fall against stone. Jikun stepped forward and rubbed his chin, running his hand down the side of the ice where a poor repair job had been fashioned after obvious deconstruction.

Someone had broken the fall. Why?

He let the ice melt before his hand until a hole formed large enough for him and Nazra to pass through: a hole that led right through the falls and into a cavern of the mountain beyond.

"Lithriella wing me!" he heard a surprised voice exclaim from shortly ahead.

Jikun hardly absorbed the blasphemous curse as his eyes quickly adjusted to the sight before him.

Three children sat in front of the back wall of the shallow cave, their bodies half turned, their eyes wide. But Jikun hardly noticed them. What they had gathered around, Jikun had never seen the like of in all his travels throughout Sevrigel.

"What is that?" he demanded, finding that his voice came out strong and fierce in the small cavern. It revealed nothing of his unsettled nature or caution.

Nothing of his fear.

Before the three children was a small hole in the earth—no more than a foot wide in either direction. Like the chasm before Kaivervale, this hole emitted rays of blue light which lit the cavern fully around them. Where he had expected stone at the back wall, a thin layer of ice shimmered softly.

And behind the ice wall…

A great eye. Over a meter wide and nearly as tall—nearly the size of each child crouched before it. It stared unseeing back at them from beyond the layer of ice. Frozen. Still. Unmoving.

And yet, so animate.

Nazra let out a low growl, her lips curled against her bared teeth.

The three children spun fully around, wide-eyed and frightened. The girl dropped the stone she had clutched in her hand and it rolled to her right with a soft grate against the ice. "How did you find us?!"

Jikun's eyes flicked downward at the broken silence and he pushed his fear away. The aura in the room was almost tangible. Something of fear and death. He stepped forward, coldly knocking the girl aside and picking up the stone.

He raised it in his white-knuckled grip while he ran his free hand across the ice covering the eye... The ice that had been recklessly chipped.

Behind him, the children were silent, frozen beneath his stern movement.

"How did you find this?" Jikun suddenly snarled, rounding on them. "What were you doing?!"

The three responded at once, blaming someone else accordingly as they made a scrambling, terrified retreat toward the icefall. Nazra blocked their flight with a resounding snap of her jaws.

"One of you," Jikun barked. "How did you find this?!"

One of the boys stopped, biting his lip. "I found it, General Taemrin, sir," he swallowed. "You always find a cave behind the falls, don't you know? And we thought it would be our secret place... Like in *The Tales of Rukalain* or *Twin Nights*..."

Jikun dropped the stone into the chasm at his feet, disregarding, in his focus, its chilling similarity to the Tuserine outside the city walls. "Do you know what this *is?*" he demanded, pointing at the eye behind him.

The three children exchanged glances. "A dragon?"

"The Mother of the Thakish?"

"A demon?"

"Worse," Jikun hissed in reply. "If you free it, it will rip you from limb to limb and drop your bones into this hole. And no one will ever know what became of you. Do you understand me? Do not *ever* return here! Do not breathe a *word* of this. *It will remember who awakened it.*" He snapped his fingers and Nazra stepped to the side to let the children run, screaming and crying, from the cavern.

Jikun turned back to the wall, no sympathies given, and rested a hand tensely on his wolf's head. "*Gods* only know what that thing is," he breathed nervously. A dragon? The Mother of the Thakish? A demon? Emal'drathar grant them protection from any of those beasts.

Nazra bared her teeth at it once more.

"Come. There is nothing more to do here..."

Jikun turned from the pale yellow eye and stepped out from the cavern.

"Jikun, what are you doing?"

Jikun straightened abruptly as his eyes readjusted to the morning light now peering up over the Turmazel peaks. "Kaivervi. Jekum. Lais. Nalaen," Jikun greeted them in turn.

Lais cocked his head in unison with his wolf as he gazed at the hole in the falls, piercing grey eyes alighting with curiosity. "Yes, what *were* you doing?"

"We almost left without you," Nalaen continued reproachfully, huffing out of her plump frown. "I did tell Merkan I would be back before dinner."

Jikun glanced at Nazra as her composure relaxed and she ran to join the four other wolves. He exhaled heavily and gestured silently behind him.

"What?" Kaivervi's brow knit as she studied his face. Silently, she stepped past him and ducked into the hole in the falls.

"By the goddess of Darival," he heard her voice echo in horror from within.

The other three immediately shoved past him and vanished through the hole.

"Jikun! How did you find this!" he heard Nalaen's high voice gasp.

"What in Ramul *is* it?" Lais breathed.

Jikun remained where he was. Saebellus' beast had unnerved him. Frightened him even, as it should. But this creature, even in death, was comparable in the aura it produced. "I don't know what it was; it was discovered by a handful of children," Jikun responded. "I have felt something like this before in my war with Saebellus. But nothing of this size. Only the gods know how long it has been there."

"Perhaps since Izre froze Darival?" Jekum theorized, reappearing from the cavern, somewhat paler than usual, even given his alabaster complexion.

Jikun turned in stern admonition for the ridiculous theory. "That's mythology, Jekum. There are no gods."

Jekum scowled. "Keep your skepticism to yourself. That's not important right now. I *mean* hundreds of thousands of years."

Lais, Nalaen, and Kaivervi appeared behind him shortly after, Nalaen closing the hole in the falls with the artistic perfection not achieved by the children in their attempt to protect their secret. "Whatever it is, it's better off left where it is." She shivered, tossing her light blue hair across her broad shoulders. "To think it's been there *that* long and no one knew…" A shiver ran up her stocky body, but it was not the cold that made her shake.

"We're not going to tell anyone?" Lais frowned, his thin lips drawn slightly in anxiety.

Jikun regarded him coolly. Even having been away from home for the last three years, he knew better than to suggest such a notion. "Do you really want to have people poking around that… *whatever* it is? Gods know someone's curiosity will win over his reason. And if not us, the Sel'vi will hear of it. And they *will* come and they *will* explore it. You know the stories of the Black Iron Dwarves."

He saw the four of them glance at each other nervously. Jekum and Lais grimaced as one.

"Dig far enough and you will not like what you find," Kaivervi responded with a curt nod, as though for a moment any one of them could forget the lesson. "Whatever it is, it's buried beneath this mountain. Lithriella's blessing that you found this before the children caused trouble. Better we leave it there. We'll make sure no one finds it."

"Well, currently, your challenge is keeping the mouths of three children shut," Jikun replied, smacking his thigh to get Nazra's attention. "And I suspect that is challenge enough." He stepped away from the fall, Nazra leaping several feet ahead. "Are we going on the hunt?"

He watched the four of them draw their eyes away from the falls.

"The thakish have been unnaturally vicious as of late," Nalaen nodded as she focused in on his words. "We'd better get to it. Better to cull their numbers quickly before matters become much worse."

Jikun fell into step between them as they moved away from the falls, but he found that his mind had wandered once more from the hunt, shifting past the great eye to the Beast. Was this the curiosity Navon felt when he delved into necromancy? Was this why he pursued his questions so persistently?

Did he not also feel the foreboding that lay in their answers?

*

Jikun tightened his grip on the scruff of Nazra's neck as he lowered his body down over hers. He could feel her muscles tense beneath him.

"Do you see it?" Kaivervi whispered beside him from the back of Husakai. Her cerulean eyes were intense, her high cheeks purple in the cold.

Jikun pulled the focus off of her proximity and followed the narrowed gaze of her wolf out across the vivid white glare of the tundra. The world was silent and still—not even the wind dared breathe across her surface.

"I don't see this one…" Nalaen murmured from his other side, her breath rising in a soft, white cloud above her thick lips as she gave a soft exhale.

Jikun studied the snow before him. The white thakish were skilled hunters, digging themselves into the tundra with their four powerful front legs and burying themselves back in with a handful of flexible finger-like structures on their backs. Their fur was as white as the snow itself, so even a failed bury was difficult to spot. And a successful hide was nearly impossible: just the tip of the thakish's white nose and solid white eyes would remain above the surface.

And they were infinitely patient.

Jikun's eyes slowed across a slight dip in the landscape.

"Ten meters, slightly to your left," Kaivervi continued.

Jikun could see Lais and Jekum nod as one. "I see it," they replied in unison.

Jikun's eyes swept the tundra at her description and paused. Yes, there—nearly impossible to distinguish in the landscape. It stared directly at them in perfect stillness, waiting for one of them to wander close enough to its fanged jaws.

"I've gotten quite poor at this," Jikun muttered shamefully. Gods, just as his father had said, southern hunting was embarrassingly easy compared to this. "That would definitely be a dead elf and wolf on my part."

"That's why you never hunt alone," Jekum replied with a smile, raising his spear slightly. "Lais. Nalaen."

Jikun watched as the two formed a wide circle around the thakish, coming to stop a good breadth behind it.

"Get ready," Jekum ordered.

Kaivervi moved forward, nudging Husakai toward the waiting beast.

"You just freeze it, don't you?" Jikun inquired, confused by the unfamiliarity of the hunters' movement.

"We try to," Jekum replied. "But lately it hasn't been enough. You should see how they've changed over the last few months…"

Jikun's brow knit. What drove the thakish's new aggression? He watched as Kaivervi halted five meters from the beast and raised her hand before her fur-bound chest. In instant response to her command, the snow around the creature's body liquefied and began to refreeze.

No sooner did this begin than the tundra around them shook.

Nazra had seen this many times before, but still, she reeled back cautiously, snapping her jaws and shaking her great head. Jikun's body tensed as one with hers.

The thakish burst from the icy water in a single, high leap, sending snow and ice from its thick fur to shower across the tundra, letting out a shrill cry of fury as it landed beside Kaivervi.

Jikun's eyes widened at the distance it had covered. *'What in Aersadore…?!'*

As though of one mind, the wolves of Nalaen and Lais dashed forward in response, their riders' hands clenching the fur at their scruffs, legs pressed into their sides.

Jekum raised a wall of ice before Kaivervi to give her a moment's retreat, but as though it had been made of glass, the beast smashed through it with the single force of its weight, sending wolf and rider tumbling away.

"*Kaivervi!*"

Jikun watched as the two spears of Nalaen and Lais buried themselves deep into the haunches of the beast. It let out a shrill roar of fury, but to Jikun's horror, it did not turn to the two elves behind it, as Jikun remembered their behavior's usual predictability. Instead, it leapt forward, front legs crashing into the earth beside Kaivervi, crushing Husakai beneath its front left leg as easily as the snow beneath its right.

"*HUSAKAI!!*" Kaivervi let out a cry of anguish and terror that resounded across the tundra like a crash of thunder. She scrambled backward, throwing up a desperate wall of ice before her as she reached back toward some semblance of fleeting safety.

"Nazra, go!" Jikun ordered abruptly. He heard a shout of protest from Jekum as he lurched forward, tearing across the tundra toward the thakish. He loosed his spear, embedding it into the skull of the beast above the eye, causing it to toss its head in pain. It shifted its body away from Kaivervi long enough to identify its new attacker.

"Jikun!" he heard Jekum bellow again in desperate command. "Don't!!"

Jikun stopped beside Kaivervi, leaping from Nazra's back and scooping up her spear in a single, fluid motion. He launched it into the creature's middle eye. A series of walls formed before him as Nalaen and Lais circled back toward the front.

For a moment, the thakish was lost behind the façade of safety. "Are you alright?" Jikun asked as he pulled Kaivervi to her feet, eyes scanning her body swiftly for injury.

He could see her lips tremble as they parted for a response, her body balancing against him as her mind reeled from what had just occurred.

Her eyes scanned the ice behind him in desperation.

"He's gone," Jikun interrupted her harshly, pushing her toward Nazra with a disconnect he willed would snap her instincts to return. "Go!"

Kaivervi climbed onto Nazra's back, jerking her scruff to the left, and turned back toward Jikun. "Come," she ordered, extending her hand.

"Nazra, go!" he barked before Kaivervi had a chance to protest. He saw her face flicker in surprise as the wolf tore away on command.

But Jikun knew: Nazra couldn't carry the both of them. She was not as large as Jekum's or Lais' companion. He swept his hand near the snow at his feet, a lance of ice forming in his right hand as he moved. He felt the earth around him tremble as the thakish slammed through a wall of ice layered before the next. He saw the taloned toes of the beast grip the top of the final wall before him, and the silhouette of the creature slid away from the earth.

Jikun stepped backward swiftly, raising the spear at the ready.

"Jikun!" Lais shouted from his right, his deep voice twisted high in terror and desperation. "Gods, what are you doing?! You're going to get yourself killed!"

Jikun glanced over his shoulder where Nazra had stopped beside Jekum. Kaivervi had climbed from her back and the wolf regarded him expectantly.

"Come, Nazra," Jikun shouted as he darted to the left. A shadow formed suddenly above him. He didn't look up, but threw himself forward, tumbling across the snow and falling to his side. He let the snow around him turn to water, his body dropping into the icy cold like a stone.

A heavy thud sounded from where he had been and he raised his head above the surface in a painful sputter for air. He saw the thakish raise its body upward, unfazed by the volley of icy spears that had once again lodged into its body. It shook its head angrily, kicking its back legs against the snow and sending a shower of cold across the elves behind it.

Its eye met Jikun in hatred as its lips curled to reveal yellowed fangs. *'This is not the beast I remember…!'*

Jikun dug a hand against the side of the pool of water, holding himself up from sinking further into its depths. Wet. Cold. And entirely vulnerable.

It hunkered down and leapt, crashing through a desperate wall of ice cast by one of the hunters behind it. Its jaws opened to consume Jikun in a single, crushing blow.

As its face came over the water, Jikun raised a hand in defense. He watched as the water before him shot up in an instant, hardening and piercing through the skull of the thakish in a large, solid stalagmite. At once, the beast flailed and went limp, dangling from the point by its head.

"Wing me and all things holy… *By Lithriella*," Jekum blasphemed as the elves ran toward him. Like a shadow, Lais was directly at his heels, leaving Nalaen to trail behind with Kaivervi.

Jikun climbed from the icy water, putting a hand to his chest as he did so. With a deliberately casual sweep of his hand, the water was pulled from his clothes and dropped back into the pool.

The four jerked to a halt at his side, dubious to his cursory motion.

"Completely dry?" Nalaen demanded, grabbing him by the front of his shirt and jerking him toward her wolf. She gave his hair a sharp tug.

Jikun pushed her thick hands away, freeing his head with a glare.

"Your control over water is so… fast," Lais breathed in awe as he dismounted his wolf in a slow stumble of astonishment. Beneath his mass of silver hair, he blinked his gray eyes balefully, once toward the thakish hanging limp above them in a final salute to its failure.

Jikun watched as those large, grey eyes shifted to regard him as the others did. Jikun disregarded their admiration and instead gestured toward Nazra. "Kaivervi, go ahead. I will walk."

Kaivervi remounted Nazra with a faltering gaze as she glanced past them. Jikun felt a twinge of pain in his chest as he followed her thoughts.

"Husakai was a good wolf," Jekum lamented, struggling to break the silence. He looked to Lais for some words of support, but his friend, for once, seemed at a loss to assist.

Jikun recalled that his mother had said Lais had recently lost his wolf in a hunt several months before. Years ago, such a thing was hardly heard of. He glanced once more to the thakish as the group departed, then his eyes pulled away toward Kaivervale. At their distance, its great wall was merely a shadow against the mountain face.

The thakish *had* become excessively aggressive, just as he had been warned at the banquet several nights before, when that howl had torn through their celebration with furious rage.

Thakish… throwing their own wellbeing aside in the lust for food…? But the tundra had not changed. …Had it?

His eyes scanned in wary caution with the others as they travelled back across the frozen earth.

*What*, then, drove their hunger?

"I don't remember you having such control before you left," Jekum commented, snapping Jikun back to the elves about him. "What else can you do?"

Jikun's eyes flicked back to the single face that had dared to take its eyes from the landscape and smiled slightly, remembering the marveling reaction of his soldiers when he had first cast in battle. "Freeze water from anywhere. Even the unseen. As long as there is water in the air, I have something to manipulate."

And if he had not been there, what would have happened to Kaivervi, let alone the others?

Nalaen's wolf loped several steps ahead and she pulled him to a sudden stop in front of the general. "Teach us!" she begged. "Show me. With that power, we could beat the thakish! You know damn well we would have been in a far worse state if you had not just been with us on that hunt. Things only continue to worsen!"

Jikun raised his hand out from his side and pulled the water from the air around them until he had formed a perfect sphere of ice. He tossed it to her and watched her eyes widen in amazement.

"I can't teach it," he replied. "I don't know how I do it or what, exactly, it is that I do. It's thoughtless. Like a reflex..."

Nalaen tossed the sphere to Lais with an extra flick of frustration. Her shoulders straightened and she drew her stocky body up. "Nonsense. There must be something you can teach. Something you have learned!"

Jikun shook his head bitterly. "There is not, Nalaen. I haven't given it much thought and hardly more practice. I'm a *general.* My own magical potential is fairly irrelevant when I have a warlord to fight for Sevrigel." And *damn* that warlord. Kaivervale needed him.

Nalaen drew her wolf aside to let him pass, but he could see her disappointment reflected in all of their gazes.

Back south, his ability was nothing more than a trivial annoyance to Saebellus and his beast.

There was a sudden series of shrill cries at their backs that split the moment of silence like a blade. Jekum spun round on Susai; his knuckles grew white. His mouth parted but no words left it. His eyes were torn wide in horror.

Nalaen looked up in a mesmerized gaze of equal terror. "...RUN!" her high voice cracked across the tundra.

Jikun turned long enough to catch sight of the pack of white thakish in the distance, tearing through the tundra rapidly as their six legs propelled them across the flat plane.

"A pack?!" Kaivervi cried in disbelief. "Jikun, you must get on a wolf!"

Jekum's hand was already outstretched and Jikun mindlessly took hold of it, swinging himself up behind the largest of the wolves.

Their minds had all centered on one thought, Jikun knew: *Thakish did not move in packs, let alone hunt together.*

Their wolves fled to the west, running along the base of the Turmazel, the shrill cries of the thakish rapidly growing louder. Jikun turned slightly, throwing up a field of ice-made stalagmites behind them, causing the thakish to break to the left in a wide circle. The wind at his face was bitter, numbing his senses, cutting through the furs on his body like sharp blades. Still closer the thakish came and Jikun could feel an unsettling exhaustion gaining on him as more ice formed at his command. He caught Jekum's shoulder to balance himself.

"Jikun, are you alright?"

Another shrill cry echoed across the tundra, hardly one hundred feet behind them. *The beasts were undaunted!* He did not bother to utter a response but reset his focus on the ice at his fingertips—he knew his strength was waning now—hardly a fragment of its former self. He let the snow behind their wolves turn to water, the ground giving out beneath the feet of the first thakish. He refroze it instantly and the beasts' movement terminated as only their back legs protruded, kicking viciously, from the frozen surface.

And with that, Jikun's strength all but vanished. The world abruptly spun and Jikun's grip loosed from Jekum's shoulder. He felt a sharp pain shoot through his body as he collided with the earth and tumbled across the hard snow. He heard cries of alarm from ahead and the rapid sounds of feet returning to him.

"Jikun!" Kaivervi screamed as her feet landed beside him. "Get up! Get up!"

He heard ice shatter to his left and raised his head in time to see a thakish burst through the quickly formed wall Nalaen and Jekum had created. It leapt forward, jaws snapping short of Jekum's arm, ripping the blade from his hand and tossing it carelessly aside.

Jikun struggled greatly, digging what meager strength he could find within himself to form a solid wall before them. But it had taken everything he had left. He collapsed against the earth just as a distant trumpet call rang out from the north. His mind struggled to clarify the sound.

"Up ahead!" Lais shouted. "Hunters! They must have heard the thakish!!"

Jikun could see the beasts hesitate and withdraw slightly as the sounds of snarling wolves grew closer. This was not just the sound of one or two hunting groups, and the tumult of noise led Jikun to believe that there were at least a dozen such contingents approaching.

The thakish seemed to conclude the same. He saw the creatures turn, tucking their short tails between their hind legs, and flee to the east.

*'Damn it...'* he muttered wearily to himself and his eyes slid closed beneath heavy lids.

"General Jikun," came a voice from above him moments later. It was foggy—muffled by the cloud that hung across his mind.

He felt hands pull him up.

"General Jikun has expended himself, I'm afraid," came Kaivervi's reply.

"Did you see the thakish, Captain Resul?" Lais demanded. "A damn pack of thakish!"

There was silence for a moment, then a bitter reply, "I saw them. Are you all alright?"

Jikun blearily opened his eyes in silent response.

"More or less." Nalaen rose merely to Jikun's breast, but still, she helped him forward, wrapping a firm arm around his chest. "Can you stand?"

Jikun shook his head once, humiliated to have to express his weakness so plainly before Kaivervale's new captain. "No, I don't think so…" he muttered.

"Let's get the general back to the city," Captain Resul spoke up, as though Jikun's state was inconsequential. "Daiki, Sesul, take the general to his home."

*

By the time Jikun was assisted into his mansion, his strength had returned somewhat—albeit pitifully—but it was enough to allow him a somewhat dignified stumble to the living room. He sank into the couch beside the fireplace, wearily resting his head against the cushions. As Daiki and Sesul left, Kaivervi vanished into the kitchen.

Captain Resul lingered in the doorway, his lips parted as though aching to speak. Yet he merely watched Nalaen, Jekum, and Lais settle in beside the general.

"Can I help you, Captain?" Jikun muttered, closing his eyes.

Captain Resul cleared his throat. "I apologize for this untimely summons, but Elvorium has demanded your immediate return to the capital. It seems you are wanted on the warfront."

Jikun raised his head sharply, feeling a wave of nausea rush over him. "What news? Has Saebellus moved?"

Resul stepped forward, extending a parchment toward Jikun. "The letter did not say."

Jikun let Nalaen accept it for him as his arm faltered its extension. She unfolded the parchment, holding it level to his eyes to allow him to scan it.

Resul hesitated to interrupt his reading. "Good evening, General. May Lithriella bless your recovery. You saved their lives today."

Jikun nodded his thank-you curtly, his mood growing sour as the captain's footsteps faded down the hall.

"Here, Jikun. Eat. Drink." Kaivervi had reappeared from the dining hall and laid a tray across his lap. "Did I hear that right? You are to return to Elvorium already? You've hardly been here four days."

Jikun reached down and raised the cup of hot tea unsteadily to his lips, aware of its proximity to his groin, and shifted his arms to the side in the event that his grip faltered. He could hear the concern in Kaivervi's voice as she came to stop beside him. "Yes."

Lais crouched back as the fire started in the hearth. He pushed off his knees as he stood, dropping the iron rod against the stone wall. "Is there anything else you need, Jikun?" he asked after a moment of silence.

Jikun shook his head wearily, wishing the fire would rise more quickly. What he wouldn't trade for the fiery magic of the Malravi instead.

"Well then, Nalaen, Jekum, and I will give you a tundra's length. I will take Nazra back to rest, if you like."

Jikun shook his head solidly, setting his cup aside. "Leave Nazra," he commanded quietly.

Nalaen strode to the edge of the room in her short, solid strides, and paused in the doorway. "Thank you," she spoke softly. "The thakish would have surely taken us."

Jikun flinched slightly at the praise. *Damn Saebellus!* He should be in Darival for at *least* weeks longer to help his own people! He raised a hand slightly to stop them. "When I return to Elvorium, I shall send what I can to assist Darival in the purging of the thakish. You can expect significant aid within a few weeks. Elvorium cannot let this matter go unchecked."

He saw the four of them exchange smiles.

"Come, Kaivervi," Jekum nodded toward her as he stepped through the doorway. "Let the general—"

Jikun caught Kaivervi's hand as she stepped away. "Wait."

Kaivervi hesitated, her eyes meeting his anxiously. She turned her head slightly to the side to call after them, though her eyes remained locked with his. "Go on ahead. I will catch up."

Jikun dropped her hand and waited until he heard the soft tap of the door against the icy frame. He raised the cup once more to his lips and sipped the tea silently for a moment.

"What—"

"Nazra needs a master. The battlefront is no place for her." He looked up, catching the tears forming in her eyes.

She looked away sharply, determined to hide her anguish.

"I would be honored if you were that master."

He could see her swallow, as though taking her tears with it. She turned back, forcing a smile across her dark lips. "Thank you. I would be honored to be hers…" She wiped a hand quickly across her cheek and shook her head fiercely. "I'm sorry. Husakai and I were together since The Wailing. You start to grow invincible, you know? After you have seen that much, you start to think you and he will just continue on and time will just… slide past you."

Jikun smiled weakly. No, he did not know what she meant. War had taught him that life was fleeting and time was a cruel master. He sipped the tea as she turned to watch the flicker of flames in the hearth before them. For a long time, they sat in silence.

"I suppose I should get home. Are you alright now? You seem stronger." She stood, moving the tray from his lap to the table.

"Stay." He caught her hand again, softly this time.

Kaivervi smiled faintly. "If I stay, does that mean you will return to Elvorium and paid women will be forgotten? If I stay, will I become the lady of single importance to you?"

Jikun released her hand, his smile faltering.

Her eyes met his, piercing through his barriers with the ease of long familiarity. "You *will* return home. *I know what you are thinking.* But that does not mean that I wish to wait here loyally for you while you squander your affections on other females. You can't expect me to wait here for you when you don't wait out there for me."

Jikun remained silent, his face hard and emotionless, pushing her insight away. He would not let her see him vulnerable.

"Are you afraid?" she suddenly whispered, moving to sit beside him, leaning forward and resting a hand against his chest as though she was reaching past his mask. “Even when the thakish bore down on you, I saw no fear in your eyes. What drives your fear now?”

Jikun scoffed, setting his cup on the table and pushing her hand away.

She caught his wrist, squeezing it firmly. “What drives your fear now, General Taemrin?”

Jikun pursed his lips tightly in silence.

“Are you afraid that you will leave this place and spend your years in fervent loyalty to me, only to die and have it all be wasted?”

“Dying benefits us nothing,” Jikun muttered.

He saw her eyes flash, her grip tightening on his wrist. “Does loving me prevent you from living?”

Jikun opened his mouth but she leaned forward sharply, locking lips with his, drawing her body tightly against his and pressing her breasts against his chest. And for the briefest moment, they were inseparable.

“Or do I help you live?”

Jikun tried to kiss her back, but she pulled away just as fiercely, standing in resolution.

She laughed. “I know what the answer is, Jikun. You do not need to tell me. You would be willing to die for any of your soldiers. And for your country. But… you cannot live for me.” She smiled and turned. “Good evening, Jikun. May your journey to Elvorium be blessed by the goddess.”

And to Jikun’s shame, he said nothing, and the door to his estate closed with a hollow snap.

# Chapter Seven

Jikun tossed his head, shifting slightly. His eyes opened into thin slits for a moment, confused as to why he would be awake so early after last night's escapades. It *felt* early, at least.

He lay there a moment, blearily, before he settled once more into his bed, closing his eyes with a grunt.

There was a sudden knock on the room door, causing him to jerk sharply. "General? Are you awake? I have a message from the king."

Damn Hairem. Jikun groaned in protest and opened his eyes.

There was a knock once again. "General?"

"Yes, I—" He cleared his throat as his voice cracked. "Yes, I am awake. Slip it under the door."

"Yes, General," the servant replied.

Jikun sat up slowly, drawing his legs up so that he could rest an arm across his knees. He rubbed his eyes with his free hand and tried to shake the grogginess from his head. Damn Sel'varian wines. Even after his welcoming in Darival, he had not awoken with such a heavy cloud over his mind.

"Why are you awake, My Lord?" came a sultry voice beside him. Jikun felt a slender hand slide up his inner thigh.

The rays of morning light shone through a crack in the chiffon curtains and came to rest on the exposed breasts of the woman lying beside him. He saw her smile as his eyes landed on her.

"Duty calls," Jikun replied with another groan as he swung his legs over the side of the bed, reluctantly pulling her hand aside. He pushed off his knees and sauntered to the folded slip of parchment lying just inside the door.

"What is it?" the woman asked as he unfolded the note, attempting a soft and alluring tone as she settled once more into the bed.

Jikun rolled his shoulders back, eyes flicking across the page. "The king summons me." And about time! He had arrived in Elvorium early the day before and had heard nothing from the king or council since. And here he had hurried his ass straight across the tundra with hardly a cautious glance either way for thakish. Not even Navon had been made aware of the reason for his prompt command to return to the capital.

He turned back toward the prostitute and inhaled sharply. She had thrown the covers aside and was lying with her legs spread, stroking her own inner thighs.

"Come here, General. Let me give you your money's worth," she purred and patted the bed beside her enticingly.

"Five minutes," Jikun warned.

*

"I will pretend I don't know what happened in there last night."

Jikun let the door to his room fall shut behind him, passing a silent smirk toward his captain.

"It is *not* humorous, General," Navon rebuked him sharply. "Need I remind you what Sel'vi do to whores and those who bed them?"

What a rhetorical nag. Jikun rolled his eyes in annoyance, raising his hand to signal the elf to fall silent. "She will be back on her ship, returning to Ryekarayn, in a week. With the way the council draws everything out gods *know* she'd have years here before anything ever happened to her." He heard Navon push off the wall and fall into step beside him. "Have you heard anything new about the content of the summons?"

Navon shook his head, blue eyes shifting toward the door with what Jikun perceived as the faintest trace of lust. Amusing. He hadn't seen that look on the male in years. He supposed even Navon could not be above the desires of the body, despite his whoring tendency toward Sel'ari and her absurd tenants. "No," the Helven replied. "But the king's carriage is waiting for you outside. Taking that into consideration, the matter must be of some significance."

Jikun's brow knit in caution. "The king's carriage?" he spoke aloud, eyes shifting warily to the side view of the estate outside. Liadeltris had never sent for him in such a manner. He felt his gut unsettle.

"Wait, where do you think you are going? You need to eat," Navon abruptly reprimanded him in his usual, grating manner, pointing sternly toward the dining hall.

"I already ate."

Navon paused a moment and then his lips pursed into a tight line. "That was crude."

Without acknowledgement to his captain's incredulity, Jikun pulled open the door of the mansion and leaned out. The carriage before the steps glistened in the gentle drizzle of rain. "Come, Navon," he barked.

*

The guards crawling through the city had little impact on the two elves as the carriage bounced along the cobbled streets. As it had been over two years since either of them had set foot inside Elvorium's extensive residential district, the abnormality of it did not immediately register. Instead, Jikun noted the poor weather, the dark clouds in the south, and the weight of his sword across his lap. The sky was soft—a gentle blue-grey speckled with clouds and shimmers of sunlight. The rain had released the rich smells of the flowers in the city and they hung like a heavy veil across the rooftops. Such a contrast from Darival, it was a difference he had admittedly missed.

"Do you miss it?" Navon asked across from him.

Jikun started. Was it that obvious where his mind lay? "Darival? Always." But he shook his head to clear it, reverting to his mask of command, as all Darivalians had mastered by nature in the tundra. His emotions were obsolete—Saebellus was his concern now.

It was not until they passed beneath the ivy archway of the palace courtyard that Jikun was struck by the unnatural lack of civilians milling about through the marble pillars and carefully maintained greenery. Here, it was merely a mass of glinting silver.

The number of guards was stifling. There was an air of fear—almost tangible—as the door to the carriage opened.

"What is going on here, soldier?" Jikun demanded of the nearest male, wiping the droplets of water from his face with a swift gesture, as though even they must not interfere with his indifferent inquisition.

"Lord Yulairm was murdered by the assassin last night, sir," the soldier replied. "The guards you see here number first in the legion of the palace guard—security has been dually increased for His Majesty."

Jikun's eyes trailed along the shadowed faces beneath their helmets. Even in the brilliant light of dawn glinting down in shafts through the clouds, cutting across the golden slated pillars of the palace in some unnaturally serene beauty, not a single face had become lax. But the guards' concentration was no surprise to Jikun. *This assassin...*

He leaned his head slightly to the right as he saw Navon open his mouth to speak.

"Yulairm? Leisum's body has hardly cooled," Navon whispered. "That's the fourth council member…"

The verbal connection was unnecessary, but Jikun understood his implication. His brow knit. Four council members? And for the briefest moment, he wondered too how Liadeltris had died. "Damn…" he trailed off as King Hairem appeared expectantly in the doorway. "Wait here for me," he ordered Navon, picking up his pace to come to stand before the king.

"Your Majesty," he spoke with a low bow, a little deeper than his usual respect, possibly transferring a suggestion of unspoken sympathy into his movement.

Hairem raised his head toward Navon and acknowledged him with a slight nod, but Jikun could not read the king's face—his fine features were strangely calm and withdrawn. A true accomplishment for a Sel'ven. "I hope Darival found you well. I apologize for the swift recall. Jikun, come with me," he spoke in an even, unrevealing tone.

The general straightened and caught the faintest glimpse of caution on the king's face as he strode toward his council chambers. He noted the lack of confidence now, that confidence that had surrounded Hairem when the two of them had last spoken. What had transpired while he was away? *'Damn, I can't take my eyes off this place for five minutes!'*

The king was silent as he ascended the stairs to the chamber. Once at the door, he beckoned Jikun in with a stiff, formal nod and then shut the door behind them.

As soon as it closed, Hairem leaned back against it, a rush of emotions washing over his face. His eyes closed and he raised his head, palms pressed against the door. Jikun found himself unnerved by the sudden change in the king's countenance.

He was staring at a boy struggling to be an adult.

"I apologize, General," he breathed, pushing away from the door and wearily walking to his desk. He sank into the old yew chair and rubbed his temple, as though forcing the tension from it. "It has been a long, long night. I do not know if you have received the news, but last night, Lord Yulairm was murdered in his sleep. His wife is in shock—she seems to have seen the murderer, but… her tongue was cut out and her eyes gouged… and she is completely incoherent… This man… this *creature*… is psychotic."

Jikun slowly sat across from him, regarding him uncertainly. Tongue and eyes…? "Why did the murderer simply not kill her…?"

Hairem's hands withdrew tightly together. "I do not know." He exhaled heavily and shook his head in a mixture of frustration and sorrow.

"Everyone is a suspect, General, but I have highest suspicions that this assassin is foreign. Nilanis often makes trade with humans from Ryekarayn. I've assigned him the task of finding out if this man perhaps entered through his port. The ship logs should give us some indication."

Jikun's brow knit. Nilanis… the El'adorium who had replaced Hairem's father.

He had always looked like such a snake.

"Is Nilanis not suspect himself?"

"Of course he is," Hairem replied, in a tone that suggested Jikun's question was unwelcome. "But there is no one else with possession of the ships' incoming and outgoing logs."

*'Then you steal them,* boy,' Jikun scoffed. "The assassin must be taking orders from someone." Again, his statement was obviously true, but he could not resist the tone that came with it.

And perhaps even Hairem had detected his cynicism about the handling of the matter. The king's eyes flashed reproachfully. He ran a thumb across his lips, seeming to force his rebuke aside. "This has come so recently after Leisum. Four council members in the last few years…" Hairem trailed off and Jikun cocked his head slightly, trying to grasp the emotions across his face—the mask was entirely dissolved. There was something of fear and plainly an essence of hopelessness. But those fierce blue eyes were solid and strong—even as the rest of his face reeled back from the blow of the murder, his gaze pressed forward. Maybe he *was* stronger than he first appeared.

"May I ask what it is you wish of me, Your Majesty?" Jikun asked slowly. He rubbed his lower lip hesitantly. Granted the assassin was a curse upon the city, but he could not see how this related to him. Gods knew he had better things to do than prowl about looking for some human or elf of bloodlust. Politics was a job better left to kings and their pawns.

Hairem focused on him then, seeming to silently consider his possibilities. The boy was gone. Age seemed to sweep over him and Jikun could see his thoughts twisting through his expressions. He looked like his late father, burdened beneath those politics. Did he *want* him to discuss the murder? He had his thoughts, but it did not benefit to have the king elope with his conspiracy theories. Four council members—four council members that had opposed key issues that the majority of the council had pressed—now dead. Was the council murdering its own brothers?

No, not brothers—its political, racial rivals. Hairem had to suspect this.

Suddenly, Hairem exhaled heavily. "How was your journey to Darival?" he finally spoke. His gaze shifted away, as though this was not the topic that weighed down on him but rather the pause he needed in order to find the courage to address what was to come next.

Jikun hesitated. The great eye. The thakish. He had promised to send Kaivervale aid, but something told him that he would not receive the answer he sought: something in the king's countenance reflected remorse—but not for Yulairm alone. "Darival is in dire need of assistance. The white thakish—the plague on that land—have grown significantly in number and ferocity since the fall. Hunters and wolves are falling where we have never lost them before. I request the allowance to send aid to Kaivervale: a few hundred soldiers to help purge the area of the thakish."

Hairem's lips pursed, as though he regretted having asked him. "I'm afraid, General, that I have some grave news for you as well. This matter of the assassin—this is not your trouble and I shall not make it so. General, I have orders from the council."

Jikun narrowed his eyes, attempting to wrest control of himself lest his temper escape. His request had *not* been rhetorical and yet, Hairem had avoided his requests for Darival entirely. And furthermore, Jikun could tell quite plainly that he was not about to like what he was going to hear.

Hairem continued, pushing through his orders in a hasty, almost regretful way. "You are to move out against the centaur tribes of the south. Their encroachment on the territory of Sel'ari's Celestial Phoenix is pressing the beast to extinction."

Jikun's face blanched. "What about Darival…?" were the only words he managed to find as his anger began to rise.

Hairem shook his head slightly. "I will bring the matter before the council, but what with your army to be split between Elvorium and the south, I cannot see—"

Jikun could feel his lips part slightly, his eyes stare blindly ahead. "You will have to forgive my pertinence, but is the council dabbling in Ulasum's Tooth? What in *all the demon realms of Ramul* are they thinking?!" he demanded, his voice rising, his composure shattering as his anger burst forth.

There was no containing it now. "I have one hundred fifty thousand soldiers to drive back Saebellus and to protect our people, not to chase damn horses across old gravesites!" He slammed his fist down on the desk, causing the papers at the end to shudder fearfully. "This is a *mockery* of my position!"

"Jikun, calm yourself," Hairem rebuked sharply, a fierce strength holding even as the Darivalian male bore down on him. "I understand your anger, but orders are orders. The council passed the vote and I can no more refuse them than yourself."

Jikun pushed back his chair, standing, determined to drive the insanity from the king's proposal. It clattered into the marble behind them, but its echo was lost beneath his cry. "Refuse them? You are the *king*, Your Majesty. The *KING*. Refuse their demands on behalf of this *nation!*"

Hairem's lips pursed. He seemed torn. His long fingers locked together as he closed his eyes and inhaled deeply. Now his calm composure was nothing but *sickening*. "General Jikun Taemrin, you are to move against the centaurs with as many males as you deem fit. You are to push them away from the phoenix using non-lethal force. You are to take Julum, a guide from the south, who will be able to assist you in the territory. These are the council's orders. You are to fulfill your vows to this country and *obey*."

Jikun gritted his teeth, feeling the anger rising violently at the stress on the king's last word. *Obey*. That was what he was paid to do. Not to win the war, but to *obey*.

"*Yes, Your MAJESTY*," he hissed. What a fool he had been! Hairem was just another pawn of the council. And thus, so was he. Instead of defending the capital from the warlord Saebellus, he would be trudging through the grounds of dead horsemen. "Is there—"

"Jikun, I am truly sorry to put you in this position," Hairem continued in a useless attempt at humility. He raised his head. "This decision by the council disgusts me as well. But neither of us are above the will of the people. I will bring your concerns for Darival before the council."

"Is that all, Your Majesty?" Jikun growled softly, refusing to be swayed by his pathetic attempts at pacification. What else could he say? Arguing with this *boy* was foolish.

Hairem ran a hand down his face. "Yes, General. May the grace of the gods go with you."

Jikun did not return the blessing. He whirled sharply and stormed from the room, letting the door slam back against the frame with a resounding echo. "Gods grant you an early grave," he snarled below his breath. The personal guard outside the door flinched slightly, recoiling from the raging storm that swept past him.

How dare the council make a fool of him! Empires fell on decisions such as the one the council now made. Defy them, and they would simply behead him as a *traitor*.

"Jikun? ...Jikun!"

Jikun had hardly caught Navon's call the second time as he exited the palace. His eyes snapped up, still burning fiercely. "They are shitting on us," he growled. "The entire council is shitting on us." He continued storming forward, knocking away the outstretched hand of the carriage driver.

"What is happening?"

"My request to assist Darival is as good as denied. And worse: we are to cease defense of this city and move south. Immediately. Where we shall promptly move the centaurs—non-lethally—to the east and west."

Navon coughed in his perplexed response, momentarily choking on his words. "South? By the gods, what is south?"

"*The centaurs, Navon. The centaurs.*"

Navon tried to grasp the ridiculous concept being thrown at him so frankly. "The centaurs? We are to move the centaurs? Pray tell, *why?*"

Jikun's lips were moving in rapid speech, muttering inaudible curses at the king in the Darivalian tongue. The drizzle seemed forgotten, even as his hair began to cling to the side of his hollow cheeks. "The council has voted to protect Sel'ari's emblem—a *phoenix*—over this city. *Sel'ari*, Navon. Do you understand? I'm supposed to march my army to the beat of some damn goddess while our homes are left empty. It is like the gods love to spite me just because I won't bend."

Navon wiped a strand of hair from his face, searching Jikun's eyes for some emotion other than anger. Jikun gave him none. "...That is just adding to your anger—not the cause of it."

Jikun turned, eyes meeting Navon's scrutinizing gaze briefly in contempt, before he turned away to stare blankly at the glistening street. "Moving south at this time, for this matter unrelated to the war... that is the *cause* of my anger. And you should know this."

Navon nodded understandingly, but his face had suddenly grown passive. "But the council ordered it, General. They have determined that this is in the best interest of the people."

Jikun hated when Navon disagreed with him when trying to calm him down. Jikun damn well knew that his captain felt the same on the matter as he did. What a façade of unquestioning obedience! "…Hairem does not."

Navon's brow creased. "What?"

"Hairem does not think this is in the best interest of the people. And no doubt it is not. Saebellus was just defeated, but he is not beaten—we *all* know that. Hairem is *weak*. Hairem is a damn weak king, just like his father. Gods grant me kingship and I would shove a sword through every damn council member's throat. There would be no more of this *shit*."

Navon sighed in inward contemplation and Jikun knew he could feel the tension pouring off of him. It was not even as much his concern for the triviality of the task as it was the condition of his road-weary soldiers. They had hardly been home in years and now… now to march to *this?!* And meanwhile, Darival would be left to fend for itself!

But Navon knew that. And in his usual, patient tone he spoke, "General, your army will make short work of this task. No doubt we will be home before we even realize that we have left."

Yet again, Navon had won in his infinite patience. Rationality once more surfaced from within Jikun. Yes, Darival's troubles and Saebellus' troops would still amass while he was in the south, and yet, there was something begrudgingly pacifying about Navon's persistently calm demeanor. Perhaps it was the last words alone that allowed him to push his temper down just enough to return to a reasonable tone: his captain was right—his troops would make swift work of the task. Perhaps it would be no more than a brief—albeit foolish—aggravation. "Navon, you are an optimistic fool. A damn, optimistic fool."

But he allowed himself the slightest smile.

# CHAPTER EIGHT

Hairem had watched the general and his army depart with a nausea that seemed to sit in the pit of his stomach like a stone. For two weeks, the city had been bustling to supply sixty thousand soldiers with the supplies necessary to engage the southern centaurs. And then, in a silent, almost shamed procession, they were gone at daybreak from Elvorium.

And Hairem had done nothing. He rationalized it, of course. Reasoned that he needed more time to smooth the council to his desires. To his plan. But the tightness in his gut suggested his true motivations were far less noble.

The council itself had treated the whole affair with mild disinterest, enveloping the following meeting with their primary concern—their own personal finances. Unlike the palace treasury, those of the council members were filling up like a halfling's pockets in a treasure trove. They bickered primarily about who should send the supply caravans south to resupply the general during his mission. When it was finally determined that Ilrae should assume the responsibility, Nilanis stood with a satisfied, thin-lipped smile on his tightly drawn face.

"And lastly, I have been informed that the inquisitors have discovered yet another shredded body."

The council grew still, the air snapping immediately to become formidably stifling. Hairem glanced across their knitted brows and white knuckles. "That makes seven now. One citizen every other day since Yulairm's passing—may Sel'ari grant him solace," Hairem spoke. "Seven elves murdered by—what we can only assume—is an assassin. *The* assassin."

Nilanis waved his hand dismissively. "Or a mimic. Perhaps there is an elf in this city who is using the murders of the council as a cover for his heinous crimes. Or perhaps, more likely, even a human. We receive human ships in from Ryekarayn from time to time. Why, one just came in last week. It's due to leave in a few more—we should have it inspected before it departs. However, I have discovered nothing yet in my ship logs. Current investigations do not indicate any particular human as a primary suspect, but I shall endeavor to reach the truth of this matter."

The council murmured agreement as Hairem sat back stiffly and wondered who before him was involved. He remembered the general's face when he had mentioned the reappearance of the assassin. And Yulairm's murder. The deaths that had followed the council member's... Hairem's lips pursed. Could it be a mimic? *Two* such criminals? He frowned skeptically. He found it hard to believe any mortal was capable of such atrocities, let alone two. More likely, it was a weak attempt to cover the murder's true intentions:

Hairem's loyal council.

"The Night's Watch should be doubled again," Hairem decided.

"Again?" Cahsari snorted. "Or replaced? You would think with how many there are roaming the streets, one of them would have seen *something*. It's not like the murderer has even been committing his crimes entirely behind closed doors. Two nights ago, one of the guards was killed right in the street."

Heshellon broke in, coming to immediate defense for the soldiers. "One can hardly blame the Night's Watch for being incapable of managing something like this. This murderer is exceptionally skilled. Back in Tavash, the city guard and night watch are trained for the usual beasts of the desert. Even our most experienced males once struggled to catch our city's greatest assassin."

Mikanum nodded. "I must agree with Heshellon. This is unprecedented on Sevrigel. Never before have our people been subject to such vicious and consistent murders. No doubt this can only be a human at work. What seemed like deliberate and ordered attacks now has transitioned into a vicious rampage. The question is, why the change?"

Nilanis paused for a moment in consideration, finally seeming ready to join the more probable theory. "It must be to draw off suspicion. Or perhaps he has merely become emboldened. It is futile to speculate why matters have diverged. Humans are, as we know, difficult creatures to understand."

Hairem rubbed his temple as the tension only grew. He couldn't possibly blame a council member without more proof than he was ever likely to get his hands on. How did the king of Ryekarayn handle such horrific crimes in his own land, where such atrocities were so commonplace? "Nothing but money has ever been taken from the homes."

"That's not entirely true," Fildor ventured. "Last night a vase was taken."

Hairem regarded Fildor's weak attempt to sound more informed with a sour purse of his lips.

"…It was made entirely of gold…"

Hairem continued with a vexed exhale. "Right, so nothing but money has ever been taken. All we can hope for now is that doubling the Night's Watch will produce some sort of tangible lead," Hairem sighed. Was it true?—A *human* was capable of out maneuvering the entirety of his Night's Watch?

Cahsari raised his hand slightly, his chin tilting into a haughty pose of superiority on the matter—Hairem was getting numbingly used to such a predictable tone. "This is something that should be taken to a vote. Doubling the Night's Watch is no cheap expense. In addition, we don't even have enough elves to double it. We'd have to pull males from the city guard and place them on the Night's Watch."

Hairem's eyes hardened at the haughty suggestion. "*This* is not a matter of vote. The Night's Watch will be doubled. I will take care of the details."

He could see for the first time the council regard him more cautiously, and perhaps, somewhat, with respect. Not to be mistaken with affection. The mere rejection of their vote left all of them, even Heshellon, with a gleam of contempt in their eyes.

"Your Majesty, a vote must be taken on a matter as large as this one," Nilanis smiled at him. It was the type of smile that made Hairem stiffen, coated in false amiability and arrogance.

In a wave of fury, Hairem opened his mouth to retort, but he was interrupted before he could begin.

"His Majesty is right," Mikanum ventured, to the clear surprise of the others. Even Hairem had begun to expect consistent disagreement from the Darivalian. "This is an unprecedented matter requiring military-level action. We cannot allow this murderer to roam our streets another night. This is a personal matter of Elvorium's safety and is not a matter of vote. He is the king, after all."

Hairem glanced across the room at Cahsari, noting the pursed lips and hardened eyes of incredulity. Nilanis, however, gave a slow nod of agreement, casting his gaze to the side as though being pacified by some internal reflection. "Yes… of course…" Then, his gaze shifted toward Cahsari and Hairem struggled to interpret the meaning of his flickering gaze. No sooner did he feel he was just grasping the speaker's true emotion than Nilanis turned to him and Hairem's glimpse past the mask was broken. "If that is all, my brothers, Your Majesty? This matter should be taken care of immediately."

"And I shall take care of the shipments to General Jikun's forces," Ilrae spoke for the first time, his almost bored expression fading with the expectation of immediate release.

The council stood as well.

A face flicked briefly to mind: cold and furious. No longer so easily forgotten. "Wait," Hairem spoke up, raising his hand. He felt the eyes in the room regard him cynically as he took command once more. "There is one other matter. A personal request from the general. While in Darival, General Jikun stated that the people there are besieged by white thakish in unnatural numbers. He requested that several hundred soldiers be sent to aid them. I shall do so."

Ilrae laughed softly and Hairem felt the air thicken with menace. "Now this, Your Majesty, is a matter for vote. The day the king uses the military for his own uses is a dark day indeed."

"These are hardly—"

"No, Ilrae is most certainly correct," Cahsari joined in with a sneer. "Gods know you would never use the military for your personal reasons. Even in your desire to help the general. An honest mistake, no doubt."

Hairem's lips hardened at their twisted phrases and he stood. "Cease the tone, Cahsari," he replied solidly, hoping his young voice matched the severity of the far older Helven. "The matter may be voted on once I finish informing this council of the situation. Since the fall of the year last, the white thakish have killed Kaivervale's hunters and wolves. This number is growing and they have no reprieve in sight. Our general has earned such an honest request. The Darivalian people are our responsibility as well. Mikanum, I would think such a matter would weigh heavily on your mind—I have not seen the likes of one myself, but the general's countenance suggested a reasonable respect for the beast."

Mikanum nodded curtly, his reply strangely short and vague. "I have heard the rumors."

Hairem's brow knit in confusion, certain he was missing something through the Darivalian's stoic composure. "Does this not concern you?"

Mikanum hesitated, glancing at the solid gazes of Cahsari, Nilanis, and Fildor, almost as though for permission. "...While it *does* concern me, Your Majesty, the matter does not seem to warrant military assistance from the capital, especially from Jikun's few troops remaining guard of Elvorium. I'm afraid, with Saebellus not yet defeated, such a decision would be in poor timing."

"But the centaurs were not," Hairem replied flatly.

Mikanum smiled weakly.

"You all will vote on this," Hairem ordered, pulling out the parchment from his desk and briefly writing Jikun's request. *'He is the king, after all,'* Mikanum had just said—but Hairem knew enough now to be aware that the king was merely a pawn. Still, he would not be moved easily. He passed his request to the right, but not a single vote but his own scratched the parchment.

"The council draws to a close. May the gods alight our future days with wisdom," Nilanis spoke in calm triumph as Hairem coldly retrieved the paper. He stepped to the side and bowed low as Hairem moved to pass before him.

*May the gods alight our future days with wisdom.* Hairem laughed scornfully to himself. "You should be ashamed of yourselves," he spoke softly. The gods must be looking down upon what the great nation of Sevrigel had become, shaking their heads in pity. There was something to be said about the short lives of men—such established corruption was as swift to come as it was to overthrow. Ilrae had reminded him of their selfishness and corruption as rapidly as the discussion of the murderer had made it flee.

*'Sel'ari, I need your help!'* he heaved in inward exasperation as he stopped outside the doors of the council's hall. His attention shifted as a shimmer of silk caught his eye. To the side of the council's entryway was a female, standing quietly beneath the shadows of the columns, her upper back leaning against the stone, long blond hair pulled tightly behind her head in a half braid that fell over her left shoulder.

Hairem bowed his head. "Lady Ilsevel," he greeted. He had expected her there—she was often present, waiting for her father to emerge. He made a mental note to appear more pleasant and refined than he had on their last verbal encounter.

His controlled attempts over his emotions seemed to be efficient. She smiled a politely sweet smile and curtseyed low before him. "Your Majesty," she replied, allowing him to take up her hand with a swift kiss. "If I may dare to say, the council seems to have taken greater strides toward the positive this day?"

Hairem gave a forced smile. "There are few council meetings that will impact me as heavily as did the first." He released her hand, letting her fold it against her abdomen in that strangely passive stance he could only assume was a mask for her father.

"Has Yulairm been replaced yet?" she inquired. Hairem noted in amusement how, even while her tone remained calmly inquisitive, she attempted to catch sight of the others still left in the hall by leaning slightly around him to peer through the crack in the ajar door.

Nevertheless, he inhaled the sweet air with a heavy breath and regarded her question with a grave tone. It was, after all, yet another vexing matter of the council. "I'm afraid that the Noc'olari propose a number of candidates, all of whom the council—" He paused. This was certainly not a discussion he desired to have so close to the members' ears. And perhaps… His eyes flicked daringly over her lean figure. "Ilsevel, would you like to join me for dinner? I would be more than happy to unburden these matters on you, but only if I can somehow return the favor." He flashed what he dared suspect was a rather charming smile.

The lady faltered in composure, a hue of red rushing to her cheeks. "Y-yes. Certainly, Your Majesty."

*

As the two elves strolled toward the business district, there was little concern in Hairem's mind about his association with Nilanis' daughter. Whether the Sel'varian Speaker heard—or did not hear—what honesty he had to say about the council, there was little Nilanis could do. He was tired of playing the council's game and if Nilanis' daughter herself would listen to his vexations, then he felt some semblance of progress, as false as it was.

The business district was, as usual, a teeming mass of elves, but without the chaos and tumult of noise the True Blood princes had told him lay across the sea in Ryekarayn's human cities. The elven race seemed unhurried and casual, stopping to greet familiar faces and converse with acquaintances. The sight of their confidently carefree movement was somewhat inspiring, Hairem had to admit. Whatever happened within the Council's Hall, the elves outside carried on seemingly unaffected. He felt the weight on his shoulders ease at the sight of their smiles and laughter—it was easy to forget that this side of the city *would* carry on, happily naïve to the council's corrupt decisions.

The guards that escorted them maintained their distance ahead and behind at a respectable and reasonable berth, allowing the two to speak idly to one another along the way. But as elves, of course, Hairem was fully aware of their ability to hear the pair despite the generous distance.

Hairem enveloped himself in her words, losing sight of the crowd that melted respectfully about him and pressed into the walls of the nearby buildings to gawk shamelessly at the royalty passing in their midst. He was not a True Blood, but a recent successor such as himself had only made them more fascinated with his unnatural presence.

Ilsevel herself spoke lightly, casually, all the while with eyes flicking with recognizable emotion in response to Hairem's words: her verbal opinion she retained for herself. She too seemed to see nothing but the male before her, attentive, entirely, to his every word. And Hairem had to admit, such devoted attention was yet another respite from the arrogance of the council.

*'He is the king, after all.'* The thought of Mikanum's words made him scoff. His decision for the Night's Watch—that had been his first and only taste of power since he had ascended the throne. And the feeling that came with it… was that what the council felt every time they raised their chins? Rebuked him? Mocked him? Flicked their signature across a proposal he clearly disdained?

Then how easy it was to understand how power could corrupt. Such a taste had only made him more wary of them. And himself.

"Hair—Er, Your Majesty," Erallus stumbled to attach a swift title to his candor, pulling Hairem from his thoughts. "You're here."

Hairem blinked. Here? Oh, *right*. He straightened, pressing his hand more firmly across Ilsevel's placement on his arm, reassuring her he had been listening to her most recent conversation—though he wasn't actually sure if she had been talking at all.

He paused to let his personal guards open the doors and then, with a staunch, commanding gait, led the lady inside the quiet establishment.

"My father used to take me here when I was a child," Hairem explained as the guards led him through the vast marble halls to a lone table situated on a balcony overlooking the building's courtyard. "He told me it was my mother's favorite place."

Ilsevel leaned over the railing slightly, eyeing the green, flower-sprung courtyard with a gentle and understanding smile to his sentiment. Several elves moved about below, their voices and laughter soft. "I believe our mothers passed within a few days of one another… At least, that's what my father said. I can't say I knew mine well, either. That was a dark year for this city." Her fingers curled around the railing and she swung herself away with a growing smile. "I do the same thing—visit the places she loved. Sing the songs she sang. And this. This is a lovely little alcove," she replied. She turned, moving smoothly to the chair he had pulled back, sweeping her dress neatly beneath her before she sat. "Thank you, Your Majesty."

Hairem took his own seat and leaned to the side to give his command. "You may leave us, Erallus." He waited for the bodyguard's footsteps to fade before he straightened himself and returned attention to Ilsevel. He was silent for a moment, uncertain whether or not it was more appropriate to ask her questions about herself or whether he should answer the questions about the council that led them there to begin with. Gods, when was the last time he had had time to see a female? His eyes widened. Was he really *that* absorbed with work?

Ilsevel looked aside and coughed, as though trying to fill the silence as he drew once more into his own thoughts. "Thank you," she spoke, raising her wine glass elegantly to the servant who entered through the curtain. "So…"

Hairem rebuked himself sharply for his shameful lack of focus. Work had not only dictated his recent social life, but he found his mind cluttered with more ideas than he had time to address. "I was speaking of Yulairm's replacement, wasn't I?" He raised his glass to the side as he spoke, allowing the servant to refill the drink before leaving the two alone. "I suppose the politics of your father are not a lady's affair?"

"My father has no sons," Ilsevel replied slowly, eye contact faltering as she spoke those words. "Not anymore. My brother died in the war with the sirens and since then, my father has pressed ever more urgently for me to be a lady for courting and nothing more. What I gather from the council is, perhaps, little more than the commoners do." She hurriedly added, "But believe me, Your Majesty, the matters are of sincere interest to me."

Hairem felt a smile twitch at the corner of his lips. "I certainly do not wish to overstep my bounds where your father is concerned," Hairem began slowly, tauntingly. Truly, he did not care if Nilanis tried to shelter his daughter from the world of politics. The lady clearly had a mind of her own. He knew she could tell that he was provoking her with the information—she was watching his every gesture with undivided attention. And he lapped it up with an ostentatiously broadening smile.

Ilsevel leaned forward, bright eyes urging him silently, full lips parted slightly.

"Ah, what a look," Hairem smiled, tossing up a hand. "As you wish, my lady." He sipped his wine and set the glass aside with a soft tap, drawing her attention to his fingers as he extended them before her. "The Noc'olari have proposed five males for the council to choose from. One of the males—who appeared on all accounts as honorable, albeit revolutionary—became investigated shortly after raising his fury about the general's mission to the south."

"Investigated about what?" Ilsevel asked, raising her brows in curious inquiry.

"Accused of supplying arms to a rebellious faction of Noc'olarian outcasts about twenty-five years ago. Of course, with no survivors from the rebellion, it is a lengthy and difficult matter to pin on him. The council, of course, states that he cannot be appointed while under investigation."

"Sounds like an illegitimate investigation to remove him as an option?"

"Aye," Hairem nodded gravely, even as her thirst for knowledge drew him into her excitement. "Three of the elves are of dismal character and, not surprisingly, are under strong recommendation by the council. I believe one of them has recently been pressing the ridiculous notion of drawing and quartering as a form of criminal punishment! But the council loves him for his groveling regard for their political wisdom."

Ilsevel's eyes widened in shock. "By Sel'ari!" she spoke with a little gasp of repulsion.

Hairem continued with an inwardly amused smile. "The last male is very young, but had earned great fame as a soldier of the Droth Guard before a facial wound left him half-blind. He was discharged from the military. The council has refused to give him any consideration. It appears that his political beliefs are not aligned well with theirs, but as his record is unquestionably unblemished, they can't truly 'eliminate' him."

"The council votes on who they wish to appoint, is that correct?" Ilsevel inquired in a rhetorical tone. "So the first and latter of the council members are not truly options?"

"I believe any male whom I recommend will not be an option," Hairem grieved.

Ilsevel reclined in her chair, thoughtfully running her finger along the rim of the glass. "Is it a *law* that the council must vote upon the new council member?" she tested.

Hairem's brow knit. She must know the answer to that, at least. Such a thing was common knowledge. Hairem cocked his head subconsciously. "It is a long standing tradition not to be undermined." Tradition… yet again the word left his lips. But was this Sel'ari's tradition or was this the mortals'…?

She leaned forward as though to draw him in. "If I may be so bold, My Lord…" she began slowly. Hairem started, eyes flicking back to her face at the change to the much more personal address. He found himself listening more attentively, as though such a thing was possible. "You should appoint to the position the male who is best suited for the duties. I believe you have a strong opinion of who that should be."

Hairem concealed the surprise he felt—and the inner elation at her sudden intimacy. Clearly she *was* sheltered from the politics of her father. Oppose the council? Refuse to acknowledge their vote and appoint his own council member?

And yet the thought tempted him.

*'Why not?'* he prodded himself. If change was to be effected, he would have to be the initiator. The traditions of his brethren must be pushed. Gods willing, if he succeeded, Sevrigel would remember him well for it. He had suggested the notion of being like one of The Seven: if he expected to achieve such a standard, then sitting passively by while the council trod over him was not an option.

"Yes," he replied, his voice growing in confidence. *Gods willing.* "Lord Valdor—the ex-Droth Guard."

"You—" she stopped, looking down at her wine glass coyly, dark lashes brushing her cheeks. "I must apologize, My Lord. It is not my business to intrude on your matters of state. I certainly overstepped my bounds. You wished simply to unburden yourself on me. Please, speak."

Hairem regarded her with silent consideration. She grew more fascinating with every opinion she expressed. She was so unlike her father. There was a fire in her eyes, a passion for the political world that her father had shunned her from that was as tangible as the wine they sipped. He hesitated to encourage her behavior, feeling a certain level of caution against the opinions of a noble lady unfamiliar with the core of his world. "Your opinion is not below my consideration," he ceded finally. "Although I would caution your rashness. Such spirit is not welcome where you wish to tread."

Ilsevel nodded her head silently, as though humbling herself. Still, he knew the fire was there. She had learned to tolerate her father well.

"Lord Valdor shall make a worthy council member," he continued slowly with a smile.

She looked up then, relaxed, and smiled.

Hairem leaned back and laughed. "By the gods, what did you do *before* your father became El'adorium?"

Ilsevel flushed. "I... I... I play the lyre and sing and write and dance and ride and sew...!" she stammered.

Hairem shook his head and took a moment to swallow. “It was a serious question,” he chuckled. “I am sure you possess all the qualities of an elven lady—I simply wish to know what encompassed the area that politics now fills.”

Ilsevel’s gaze fell and she let out a long exhale as though it was difficult to speak what came next. Hairem felt the light conversation grow heavy even before the words left her mouth and he regretted having trod so unabashedly forward. “My brother, My Lord. He was always around, getting me into trouble and teaching me how to get out of it…” She smiled. “And he taught me how to ride and how to dance. And perhaps a few un-ladylike qualities as well. …He tried to teach me how to wield a blade and how to hunt, though I never did have time to become well-versed in either. Since my mother died when I was very young, I do not remember her. Admittedly, my brother played that role for me. My father… well, my father is not that sort of male.”

Hairem’s brow knit. He yearned to ask her details, question her relationships further, to delve deeper into her story, but he held back his prying curiosity. Already the tone had grown far more serious than he had intended and he doubted further travel down the road would yield more cheerful results.

Ilsevel met his gaze and shook her head, as though reading his mind.

“A few hundred years ago, when Saebellus was ordered by the council to war against the sirens, my brother was one of his lieutenants. When Saebellus rebelled, my brother tried to resist him and bring him before the council for trial… but Saebellus was stronger than him. My brother was bested… and Saebellus had him executed.”

Hairem felt the pain etched across her face as her gaze lingered wistfully on the distance, grasping at some distant memory. “I am sorry to hear that. Your brother served his country well.”

Ilsevel smiled strongly—proudly. “Yes.”

Hairem forced a smile in return, though he spoke apologetically. “Well, this certainly is not what I expected when I asked about what you did before politics. Let us talk about something lighter…” He paused briefly, attempting to recall the list she had strewn to him of her activities at home. “Tell me of your writing,” he finally concluded.

“My writing?” Ilsevel turned her head aside, blushing. And Hairem wondered how much more terrible she could be at writing—that she should reveal embarrassment—when she had not had the sanity to refuse to allow him to hear her play that god-awful tune on the lyre several weeks previous. “Oh, I am no great writer, My Lord. But… I am fascinated with it—the historical literature is my weakness." She looked back, smiling. "The Legends, you know? The tales of Shalah, Eraydon and his company… Those days when our traditions and religious virtue defined us! What it would be like to go back to those days—when we *first* came to Sevrigel! *The Ballad of the Seven* has been my favorite musical piece since I was a child. When the door to this continent truly opened to us. The possibilities for our growth seemed endless."

Hairem gave a nod, trying not to smile at her over-enthusiastic excitement. "I know it only too well," he agreed, recalling the tune his palace musicians had played just weeks before. "I cannot tell you how many hours I was forced to spend pouring over the ancient works. The True Bloods were obsessed with them—Darcarus perhaps not so much, but Sairel and Hadoream most certainly. And even when I was not at study, they would often bombard me with such tales—though I suspect with a level of embellishment to some of their stories." He chuckled. "You know, Hadoream once told me that the entirety of Eraydon's group scaled the mountain face of the Yislaval in the Æntara Mountains with nothing but their bare hands. …But I agree—there is nothing like the heroism and adventure in their tales."

"It is the spirit of it all," she carried on, almost as though he had added nothing at all. "The fierceness of the warriors to resist fate—they defied every reasonable outcome. There are not heroes like that anymore. Sometimes, I doubt that *they* were even like that …"

Hairem had thought of this often when he passed their vigilant statues in Eraydon's Square, wondering how, in ten thousand years, it was Eraydon's group alone that had impacted those millennia. "I believe that every hero is exaggerated to a degree. But what they did… what they accomplished, even in the face of unprecedented adversity… That alone is legendary enough."

Ilsevel eyed him with a subtle smile behind her wine glass, "Like what you do now."

Hairem laughed, feeling a wave of embarrassment rush to his cheeks. He attempted to regain composure as she giggled almost silently at his flush. "Gods, no. I am nothing like them. I wish I was, but I assure you, I am nothing like them."

"Oh, do not be so modest. You have many years of false traditions to fight against… and males who are so entrenched in their positions that force is required to remove them. Maybe it is not as grand as slaying dragons or fighting against Malranus' servants, but I think, My Lord, that you are not just another pawn. You may be Sevrigel's first real king."

Hairem felt his smile falter as his mind whisked him back to General Jikun's request for Darival—that bold confidence he had assumed with which Hairem could grant his request… if he had the courage to do so.

He *was* the king. Not just over Elvorium, but *all* of Sevrigel.

The council… The council may have voted against his decision, but Darival *would* see assistance: it was his responsibility. His duty. Even if he had to use his own personal guards to do so, Sel'ari help him, Darival would receive aid.

And *that* was just the start.

# CHAPTER NINE

Nilanis raised a hand in order to shield his eyes from the harsh sunlight reflecting from the glassy surface of the lake before him. In the distance, white sails glared in the sunlight, engulfing the ship beneath them in their brilliance. He lowered his hand in consternation and turned to the nearest ship resting in his Port of Targados, watching as it rocked back and forth gently in the water that lapped against the wooden docks.

He frowned. It was getting late, but just a short while longer and he could return home to dinner with Ilsevel.

He glanced back out into the waters. Damn. *Or* he would be late. His eyes flicked optimistically down the docks. Perhaps his ship of interest had already made port without his knowledge…?

But only an endless line of rocking vessels returned to him, causing his stomach to twist anxiously.

"My lord, here is a record of the cargo from *Her Mirelidontris*," a man spoke up loudly beside him, attempting to be heard over the noise that surrounded the crowds moving on and off the ships. He shoved a scroll into Nilanis' outstretched hand, sniffing and wiping a hand down his dirty cotton pant leg.

Nilanis stiffened as the rough surface of the scroll drew his attention back to the matter at hand. He turned away from the distant ship and regarded the human down the bridge of his sharp nose. "Hm," was the only acknowledgement he gave as he snapped the scroll open and scanned the contents with swift dissatisfaction. "And this is it?" He closed the scroll, pointing it knowingly at the man's sun-burnt chest. "We simply cannot do business if you… *lie* to me, do you understand?"

To Nilanis' dismay, the human took a step closer. He lowered his voice to become barely audible over the ruckus. "And Ulasum's Tooth, of course. But you know we can't have that written on parchment." He gave a horrendously eye-scarring grin with his row of blackened, crooked, half-present teeth.

Nilanis recoiled at the offensive sight, pressing the end of the scroll against the man's chest rather vigorously, forcing him to take a step back. It was a small triumph. "I expect the payment for this… *oversight* to reach my mansion this evening. If you fail to do so, you can expect that this is the last time your ship will berth here."

"Of course, of course." The human rolled his watery eyes, sniffed again, and reclaimed the parchment. He waved it carelessly behind him as he sauntered toward his ship. "UNLOAD!" he bellowed victoriously.

Nilanis turned away, walking briskly toward a newly docking ship across the docks and straightened the fabric draped over his arm as he went. He found his stomach twist again as his eyes searched the side of the hull for the ship's name. *The Sea …tch.* He frowned. The paint was heavily faded and he could not distinguish the last word. He cocked his head as he turned over the possible words in the Common Tongue. Tch… What probable words ended in 'tch'?

"My lord!" his thoughts were interrupted as a young elf hurried up to his side, bursting from the crowd in a shout. The youth paused for a moment to rest his hands on his knees, panting heavily—like one of those raggedy dogs from overseas that the sailors brought in an attempt to fill his docks with fleas. "May I see Ilsevel today?" the boy breathed as he straightened, wiping aside his thin blond hair as he attempted to appear dignified.

It was painfully futile.

Nilanis snatched a roll of parchment from a passing merchant and strove to appear busy. "How did you find me?" he muttered below his breath, daring to glance sidelong at the boy just long enough to gather his wide-eyed, giddy gaze of barely contained excitement.

The boy darted to Nilanis' other side, attempting to rise above the edge of the weathered parchment. "You're always here," the boy responded, confused. He looked around, perhaps at the mass of crowds around him, stretching across the leagues of port along the east side of Elvorium. Was he searching for *his* daughter amongst this drabble? Hah!

Nilanis raised the parchment farther over his face, hoping that it would dissuade the boy from continuing. He was dismayed as the parchment was snatched back and the victimized merchant muttered a curse below his breath.

The El'adorium found himself faced regrettably with the wide-eyed youth. *'Persistent child.'* Nilanis attempted to make his expression as bored as possible. "*Who* are you, again?"

The boy glanced around in dismay, this time clearly searching for sympathy in the bustling herd around them. "Me? Why I'm Relais, My Lord. I come here every—" He broke off as he made to fall into Nilanis' quickly fleeing steps. "I'm not giving up, My Lord. I shall ask you every day until you let me see her."

Nilanis heaved an annoyed sigh and stopped. "Be gone with you. You may see her when you become a male of high regard and wealthy standings. Until then, we shall play this out again tomorrow, I suppose." He pointed away from him. "Now go before I have the guards drag you off again."

"My Lord!" came a sudden shout from his left.

Nilanis watched the boy strut off out of the corner of his eyes. Good gods. Finally. "Yes?" he called out in return, focusing his attention back to his work.

His brow knit. No one.

"MY LORD!"

Nilanis turned again. And looked down. Ah, a gnome. Of course. How easy it was to forget their existence.

"Lord Nilanis, I presume?" the gnome demanded after the elf lord, with his scowl of dismay, gave no attempt to respond.

"Are you the captain of *The Sea* ..." Nilanis trailed off. "This ship?" He gestured pointedly to his right and wondered, briefly, if the abhorrent human scum had once written *bitch* across her hull. What unsavory creatures.

"First Mate...The captain can't come on account of his being already occupied by... a someone else..." the beastly little creature trailed off awkwardly and shifted his weight to his left.

"Prostitution is not allowed in Elvorium," Nilanis growled, glaring and forgetting, for a moment, his interest in the ship.

The gnome immediately adopted an air of indignation, strutting around his legs with convincingly wounded pride. He pounded his fat little chest once. "Why I never heard such a low assumption about my captain in all my days! To think, here we dock at the famed Port of Targados only to be jabbed at! The Sel'vi and their hospitality...! What a myth! I—"

Nilanis cut him off before he could carry on further in his charade of offense. "Be silent, creature," he barked. "Why have you docked here?"

The gnome paused a moment to smooth down his falsely wounded pride and then leaned forward. "Fo..." he whispered.

Nilanis crouched down lower. “What?” he asked, acutely aware of the visible tangle in the gnome’s grey beard. If he could just… cut the knot out…

“Four.”

Nilanis straightened and the gnome whirled swiftly about and began to bob away toward the ship. *‘Four…?’* he repeated to himself blankly. His eyes widened then. “Wait! Did a man get off your ship?!”

The gnome turned and waved. “Have a good night, My Lord!”

Nilanis opened his mouth to call out again, but quickly let his jaw snap shut. Such a vague response… was it a gnome’s childish sense of humor or the location of his mercenary? He pursed his lips. Why hadn’t the damn creature just whispered what he needed to know?! *Four!* It’s not like anyone could hear a damn word going on in the ruckus around them! He looked back toward the gnome and hurried after it, ignoring a sailor’s attempt to shove another cargo list before him.

He caught the gnome by the shoulders and spun him around, which was unsurprisingly easy to do. “What does ‘four’ mean?” he demanded.

The gnome’s brows knit as he regarded the elf disdainfully. His fat little fingers pried Nilanis’ smooth hands away. “I don’t know. I had a weird fellow on the ship this time and he said to find you and say *four.* Weird fellow. One of them. Four. Now if you’ll be excusing me.” And with that, he stiffly strutted away, as though it was *the elf’s* presence that had offended him.

Nilanis straightened indignantly. What did *he* have to be so worked up about? He was just a gnome! He eyed the ship in the distance, his interest in it rapidly dwindling.

*Four.* …So he had returned.

His desired information in hand, a great part of him wished to depart for home—no doubt he would be late for dinner with Ilsevel if he waited for the last ship. And yet, he could not help but let business detain him. *‘Damn humans. Never punctual!’* He lowered his hands and restlessly watched as the last ship came to port.

*

The smell of roasted lamb, baked and slathered with freshly churned butter, hung heavy in the air as Nilanis stepped through the wide, grand doors of his estate. He raised his nose and smiled affectionately. Ah, what a succulent scent. How Ilsevel spoiled him!

"My Lord," the servant behind him began as he closed the door to the flowery scent of the city outside. Much better—it clashed something terrible with the imminent meal. "Lady Esera is waiting for you in the dining hall."

In slow confusion, Nilanis raised a brow as he unfastened the clasp from his neck. "Lady Esera. Who…?"

Veletris took his cloak and brushed a bit of dust from his chest.

*'Ugh, probably from that foul human…'* Nilanis thought disdainfully as he recalled the man's horrendous smile and audacious proximity.

"Lady Esera is the widow of the late Lord Ceulris. Ilsevel asked her here on your behalf." The male looked up expectantly, wiry frame stiff and attentive for his next command. When the El'adorium gave him none, he stepped back beside the door, vanishing into the shadows as though he had never been.

Which was precisely what he was hired for.

Nilanis raised a brow as he turned. *'Ah… a proposed courtship…'* he thought to himself, amused at his daughter's interest in his status. At least Ilsevel would be there as well. He had little interest in females since the death of his wife. Even with as many centuries as had gone by, her passing still felt rather near. He looked fondly at the old architecture from the Farvian ruins as he passed by on his entrance into the dining hall.

The table in the center of the grand room had been lavished with fine foods and wines, but Nilanis was dismayed to note that Ilsevel's seat was empty. Not of just herself, but of all semblance of dining ware. *'What is this…?'* His eyes landed on the female sitting awkwardly across from his own chair, hands folded into her lap as she waited for *someone* to arrive.

Nilanis' cheeks flushed in embarrassment and he hurried to his seat. "*Forgive* me," he grieved, pausing before his seat and taking a moment to straighten the gold buttons of his shirt, presuming his slow and stately movement was a sign of his importance and authority. Perhaps it was a good reparation of the situation. "My business at the Port of Targados was quite substantial today." He sat down slowly and folded the silken cloth across his lap. "Lady Esera, it is a pleasure to meet you." He had passed by the usual courtesies of hand kissing and eyelid batting—he did not want to lead the lady on further than she already had been. "Has Ilsevel left the table…?" he questioned, even as he noted once more that there was no indication that any place had ever been set for her.

The blond-haired lady smiled forcefully, the same sort of sickly sweet smile Hairem had worn the entirety of his dinner not that long before. "I'm afraid your daughter said that she will be unable to join us. She said that urgent business has called her away."

Urgent business… Nilanis could not help but chuckle softly to himself. *'Ah, Ilsevel.* That *is your point, is it?'* She had said little to him after he had left her alone with Hairem, but he imagined that this was her concocted form of revenge. He shook his head with a slightly amused smile. What a difficult queen she would have made!

Lady Esera picked up her wine glass. "Oh, no, it is quite alright, My Lord."

There was discomfited silence between them for a moment as the servants filled their plates with food and Nilanis attempted to remember what her response was in reply to.

"These chandeliers are from Ryekarayn," he offered after a moment, noticing the lady's eyes glance upward. "Exquisite, are they not? No doubt there are a dozen such chandeliers in the king's palace."

The lady regarded the numerous crystals of the chandelier with greater interest. "Do you think?"

Nilanis raised his wine glass and sipped it slowly, puffing out his chest in due pride. "Why, of course. I am quite close to the king, as you would imagine."

The lady nodded her head expectantly. Of course she must already think this. He *was* the El'adorium, after all.

Nilanis set his glass down, seizing further advantage of his proximity to the king. "Why, just recently Hairem asked himself over to dine with Ilsevel and myself and stayed afterwards just to hear Ilsevel play the lyre. No doubt she must have impressed him with her exceptional abilities. And to think, he has all of those palace musicians to compare her to…" He trailed off, watching the lady cock her head slightly to the side, as though thoughtful.

"I—"

"Of course, I am not one to boast," Nilanis continued swiftly, sniffing. "She most certainly acquired such talents from her mother." He took a small bite of lamb so as to not disrupt his stride. "No doubt you are a magnificent singer as well—a female of your high standing."

"Well—"

"But then I just waste your time with such rhetoric. How do your estates fair? Do you oversee the business now?"

The lady had just taken a bite of food and Nilanis took this as a queue for him to continue to carry their meeting.

"I have had to hire a *legion* of workers to help me manage the ports. There is, of course, my personal selection of guards, the ship's cargo logs, their origin books, the captains to meet, and news to keep myself informed of… No doubt a lady of your standing is quite well informed."

The lady smiled weakly and opened her mouth half-heartedly to respond. Nilanis frowned slightly. She was certainly a quiet female. *This* was Ilsevel's choice?

Ah well, he'd have to sustain them further. "The latest news from Ryekarayn is, of course, the famine. They are just in the beginnings of it, but the pirates have already begun to prepare by laying siege in the continent's far south, starting with, perhaps, even the Eph'ven, I imagine. They have even made bold attempts against several of Sevrigel's prestigious ports. In vain, of course."

The lady smiled once again. Is that all she could do?

He fell silent for a moment, turning his mind over for some question that might interest him about her. He could think of none.

"Lord Nilanis," the lady began hesitantly, "what is four?"

Nilanis stiffened. "Four…?"

The lady pointed with her knife toward his plate. "Yes…"

He looked down, raising his brows in surprise. He had scratched "four" into the remainder of his food. Was his mind that preoccupied with the assassin? He pursed his lips, swiping it away with the fork. "Business," he replied curtly. "What businesses are you involved with…?"

"Cotton trade," she replied, looking up from his plate. "I have been advocating the increased importation of cotton and the lowering of its tax…"

Nilanis dabbed off his lips. What time did his mercenary expect him? It must be nearly seven. Had he expected him at four? No. His room number, perhaps?

The lady cleared her throat. "I have a son of two hundred. Close to your daughter's age, if I am not mistaken. Perhaps we should introduce them one day?"

But how would the mercenary know his room number before he had even arrived at the inn? Nilanis frowned. He had a good idea of *where* he was staying, at least. There was only one inn which would admit the likes of him.

"…Is she already betrothed…?"

Nilanis looked up, sliding out his chair as he considered leaving promptly. No, that would be terribly suspicious… "I'm afraid business distracts me. You were saying?"

The lady's smile faltered. "About your daughter…"

*

Nilanis escorted Lady Esera from his mansion after dessert. As the door opened and the lady stepped out into the warm summer evening, Nilanis could see the moon had risen high into the night sky, the stars glittering around its soft yellow glow. It was a good evening to see *him*. Though it had grown rather late for one to be about the streets.

Ah, it could not be helped now.

"Have a pleasant evening, Lady Esera."

The lady nodded once before she hurried away down the steps, dully silent even at their farewell.

He tsked his head incredulously. Never mind that. He had work to do. But first, he supposed he had an apology to give. He retreated into his estate and made for the living quarters, straightening as he went. "Ilsevel, you have made your point," he spoke to himself, smiling fondly. She had such a fierce spirit, no doubt a trait she had acquired from him.

He stopped before her door and knocked softly on the jagged edges of its sharply ornate design. "My dear, I shall not embarrass you like that again," he began, wondering briefly why they did not have more hospitable doors. He shook his hand out as he waited for a response.

"Are you asleep? Ilsevel?" he tried again. But only silence greeted him.

Ah, it was late. Ilsevel was likely already in bed. He would have to speak to her in the morning. "Goodnight, my dear," he whispered tenderly as he turned.

*Now finally*, there was business to attend to.

The door opened suddenly before he had even fully turned away. Ilsevel's fair face peered out through the crack, sheepish in its gaze as it drew him back to her. "Are you mad?" she asked slowly.

Nilanis chuckled slightly, turning about and smiling fondly at his lovely daughter. "Mad? No, my dear."

Ilsevel's nose wrinkled once as though joining in his amusement, and smiled beneath closed lips. How like her mother she looked! And that expression!

He leaned forward and kissed her lovingly on the forehead. "Goodnight," he spoke softly. He stepped back, adjusting one of his golden buttons subconsciously, and turned about.

"You're going out, aren't you." Nilanis could almost hear her head cock in question.

He paused. Her perception was unnerving at times. He wondered what had given it away. He had been rather short in his response. Or perhaps his fuss of his appearance—he always found his mind subconsciously drawn to such subtleties before going into the public. "Just for a little while," he smoothly replied. Such lies were second nature to him now. He turned his head back enough to see her from the corner of his eye.

"What for?" she persisted, drawing her robes around herself as she opened the door fully. She eyed him expectantly, crossing her arms before her chest.

Nilanis shook his head once, sternly this time, no longer taken by her sweetly coy charm. "This is something you may not know, Ilsevel. I cannot tell you everything."

"Sometimes," she responded, putting a hand on the side of the door, "I feel like you tell me nothing." She closed it with a quiet, but definite, snap.

Nilanis turned with a sigh. Well that had gone short and rather poorly. But it could not be helped: the matter of the assassin he would take to his grave.

*

*'Is* this *where the man is staying?'* Nilanis wrinkled his nose in disgust. To think a building so rundown and miserable could reside in such a fair city! He drew his hood low over his face as a large human squeezed past him in the hallway. Gods, he could let no one see him in such repulsive squalor!

There was no Poverty Den in Elvorium. No Thieves' Nest. No paupers, beggars, or Skint District—certainly not in a Sel'varian city and *especially* not in Elvorium. There was, however, a shady district of sorts. After all, it was the small section of the city where humans and other non-elves resided while docked in the Port of Targados. Unlike the rest of the city, here the buildings showed a degree of wear and age.

The establishment he had just entered was a particularly sad estate. In its glory days it had been the home of the previous port master, but had since been remodeled as an inn for non-natives. The outside had given way to grime and faded paints, and the inside was worse: walls and floors begged for mercy as the spiders danced along their glinting, silky strands strung across the ceiling.

*'Disgusting...!'* was his understatement of the century.

As he traveled down the hallway, the door to room four opened ahead, suddenly and perceptively, just wide enough for a mop of hair to poke through.

The dark eyes narrowed. "Ah, Nilanis, my friend," the man cooed quietly. He stood back, throwing the door wide and sweeping a low bow before the elf lord.

Mockery was what Nilanis sensed, and he wondered if the man had been waiting all this while just to greet him in such a grotty manner. He stiffened and entered, picking up his robes ever so slightly to avoid the pile of clothes strewn near the door.

He dropped his robes as he reached the center of the room and turned to face the man he had called upon, subconsciously wiping the front of his silks where they had brushed the frame of the entryway. He waited for the grimy, old door to close behind them before he dared to speak. Had this place *ever* been cleaned?

The human turned and sauntered to the edge of his tangled sheets where a woman lay in deep sleep, her naked back exposed.

Nilanis pursed his lips, attempting to avert his eyes from the scandal. He was not sure exactly what he had expected, but somehow, even in expecting nothing new, the human had disillusioned him. He was still an unkempt low-breed with as much charisma as a dwarf and far less muscle, even after all the coin he had been given. "Prostitution is not allowed in Elvorium…"

The human laughed once—cold and dismissive. "Neither is murder, but I believe we are past all that, are we not?" He leaned over the side of the bed and picked up his shirt, pulling it over his slightly perspiring chest.

The room was hot and muggy, like a windless summer day. Nilanis ached to remove his robe, but he dared not let his face be shown in the event that the woman awoke. Instead, he bore the humidity with futile attempts to circulate air with his hand.

"Why did you call me back, elf lord? Is my student not fulfilling what I promised?"

Nilanis scoffed as the full reminder of his fury returned to him. He dropped his hand in swift frustration. "Your student has made a mess of things. He has left the council confused, but equally as skeptical. His rampage has continued ceaselessly since you left. I told you that a few occasional murders after you were gone would be satisfactory, but instead there are a dozen elves dead within this city and no end in sight. I want your student dismissed. Send him back to that shithole you call Ryekarayn."

The man's smile faded slightly, his jowl quivering once. "Now, now, Nilanis. There is no need for such venomous attacks. I will send my student home." He lifted a small, empty bottle from the nightstand and examined it absentmindedly. His long, claw-like fingers curled around the vial and a faint grin eased back the scars that slithered up across his dark-tanned cheeks. "But surely that is not all you have for me. Another council member for me to dispose of, I hope?"

Nilanis glanced toward the drawn curtains of the room and almost requested that the window be let open. He found his clothes beneath the robe now clinging to his lean frame. He refocused on the man. "No. Something else this time. I have received news from a recent ship from—well that's really none of your concern—that the True Bloods have sent someone to Elvorium. I do not know who or why, but no matter his purpose: I want him dead. But first I need to know what the True Bloods are scheming. I need you to find out who he… or she… is and what that person is doing here. Once you acquire that knowledge, report the information back to me *first*, and if I have what I require, then I shall need you to kill him."

The assassin grinned again, his right hand twitching slightly as he set the bottle of Ulasum's Tooth back down with a soft clink. His toned muscles rippled with the rush of adrenaline at Nilanis' voiced commands and the scars on his face seemed to pop in the candlelight. "Absolutely, my lord," he replied as his lips peeled back to form a broadened sneer. "Consider it done."

# CHAPTER TEN

In the last week, a political occurrence had stirred the kingdom of Sevrigel. Elvorium was bustling with delegates from cities across the continent and the council was livid. What the girl gathered from the other servants was vague and, as she could not ask for the details, she had nothing to make assumptions about. Hairem had done it, whatever *it* was. No sooner had *it* occurred than the king took to ignoring the consequences. He would not see the delegates and appeared in public only long enough to attend the council's meetings.

"My Lord, Marsiol is here on behalf of the Northern Halls of Shil'von," Hasiar was saying. "He requests a meeting with you within the coming week." He was scratching away with his quill as he spoke, looking up just long enough to catch the king's expression. He was a slender, young Sel'ven, with a dimpled jaw and a pleasant smile. But he rarely smiled. And today, certainly, he would not.

The girl raised the hand-painted jug carefully and added a little more spiced wine to Hairem's glass. Wine always eased a stressful day. Or in this case, week.

The king muttered his thanks as his brow knit. "No. I told you no. No more of these ridiculous requests. I have announced what I intend to do and it will be so. There are no questions to be had—no use in attempting to change my mind. Please stop bringing me these useless delegations." He heaved a sigh and lifted his glass. "And by the gods, what are you still writing? What *is* there to write?"

The girl watched as the glass was quickly emptied.

"…I am sorry, Your Majesty. I was just making a note next to those useless requests… so as not to make the mistake of bringing them to your attention again…"

Hairem set his glass down and rubbed his nose in what the girl took to be a shameful way. "Hasiar, my apologies. You are doing a fine job." His hand flicked forward, beckoning him to continue. "What is next?"

Hasiar's eyes scanned past the list of what, she could only imagine, were more delegates. If she was just a *little* bit taller she might have known for sure. But as it was, the page was tilted a little too high for her to discern the youthful scribe's scrawlings. "Lord Elisum's ship sunk off the coast in Lord Dajnal's waters. Lord Dajnal refuses to allow anyone into his waters. Lord Elisum would like permission to retrieve his goods."

The girl watched as the king's brow knit with perplexity and she wondered what treasures had sunk to the bottom of the water. "Tell Lord Elisum that he may not retrieve his goods if Lord Dajnal refuses to allow him to do so. And if Lord Dajnal *does* allow it, Elisum is to pay tribute of half their worth to Lord Dajnal for violating the privacy of his land—waters." He rubbed the ridge of his nose again. "I need a rest. Do you mind if we continue this later in the evening?"

Hasiar quickly rolled his parchment up and offered a swift bow, perhaps as relieved as Hairem on the matter. "Whatever you desire, Your Majesty. Forgive me."

The girl wondered why Hasiar bothered to reply to a clearly rhetorical question. She watched the young male walk briskly from the room and raised the jug to fill the king's glass once again.

"Oh no, I have had quite enough," Hairem laughed, moving his glass and nearly causing the girl to spill across his lap. He stretched and stood with a grunt, seemingly unaware of his action. "Have you been outside yet this day, Alvena?" he asked as she set the jar aside. "There is something I have been meaning to do for the last few days, but simply have not had the time."

Or did he mean opportunity? She was simply dying to know what the king had done that had suddenly made him such a demanding figure to speak with! She wiggled restlessly. What a curse it was sometimes to not be able to speak exactly what was on one's mind!

"Is that a no?"

There she had gone and completely forgotten that he had asked her a question to begin with! She quickly shook her head. Or wait, maybe in shaking her head she said no to something else the king had asked. She frowned and then raised a finger with a weak smile.

Hairem chuckled. "You are always such an innocent thing. I wish I was in your place sometimes... but I certainly would not want to curse you with mine!"

The girl blushed. Queen? Oh the thought! She allowed herself to giggle.

Hairem's brows rose swiftly in response. "What a pleasant sound! You should do that more often... though I suppose I would have to give you more reason to laugh then..." He smiled charmingly and the girl felt her smile broaden. She quickly tried to wipe it away, feeling rather foolish for being so taken by the king's charm, but it was not as easily done as she would have thought.

"So you have not been outside today yet," the king carried on, turning toward the doors of the courtyard. "Come. I have a favor to ask, if I may."

The girl quickly took step behind him, wondering what she could possibly do for the king outside. *'Hopefully it's not to pull weeds. I hate pulling weeds...'* She gave a little hop to step alongside his long, regal strides.

"Let me tell you a secret," he began with a little smile. "There may be a lady whom I have taken a liking to... Don't look at me like that! I am telling you because I trust you not to tell a—wait, that sounds terribly unfair. I mean that I trust you. *Certainly* do not tell Lardol. Gods know I will *never* hear the end of it!"

The girl felt a little disappointed even as she grew excited by sharing in the king's secret.

...Why should she be disappointed? But... she supposed that every female must have a little private fantasy of being Hairem's queen one day.

"I would like to send her flowers, but I certainly do not know a lady's taste. Would you like to assist in selecting the bouquet?"

The girl had hardly offered a nod before Hairem grinned broadly.

"Excellent! Come."

"My Lord, I apologize," came Lardol's curt voice from the stairway. "Alvena, go help the females in the dining hall and leave His Majesty alone."

Hairem looked up and waved a hand. "I asked her to accompany me, Lardol. If the females need assistance in the dining hall, you have my permission to take her place."

Lardol flushed and instantly vanished from view. Alvena could not help but giggle again.

She liked to see the old elf flustered.

"I swear, if he does not give me a moment's peace..." Hairem was muttering as he pushed the doors of the courtyard open.

Alvena stepped out and inhaled deeply as she was flooded with the scent of thousands of flowers. The center courtyard was awash in the vibrant colors of summer and the fresh fountains of water that flowed from Sel'ari's open hands. She loved coming out to the privacy of the place and getting lost somewhere within its wilderness. What adventures she had! She had once found a nest of tawny mice and had rescued them from the ravaging of the garden's cantankerous caretaker by putting them into a little sack and releasing them to the grand safety of the mysterious, old Rilden Estate on the south side of the city.

Her eyes lit up at the latest request. And now, to make a bouquet fit for a king!

"A bouquet of charm and interest, but not formality," Hairem was saying as he walked toward the flower of the yellow maiden's hair. "What are your thoughts?"

Alvena hopped lightly to the blue spinner's thread, snapping a few of its thin, long, silky blooms into her left hand.

"Bold, aren't we?" Hairem commented, handing her three of the maiden's hairs. "Pink? Red? What? Green?"

Alvena nodded and crouched down to the little, round, green blooms of the galientris, plucking several of them as well.

Hairem then seemed to resign himself simply to watching, as though she was acting with a skill that he could no longer compete with. She liked that—catching glimpses of the king's impressed smile and intrigued eyes. *'What a florist she would make!'* she imagined for his thoughts.

When she finally presented the finished bouquet, the king nodded agreeably.

"My lady, you have a fine talent for this." He raised the flowers up and gave another nod of approval. "And look at you—accenting the smells." He winked and handed it back. "Now I have another favor, if I may be so bold as to request one more."

Alvena found herself nodding eagerly.

"Will you take this to Lord Nilanis' daughter, Ilsevel? With this…" He reached into the pocket of his vest and handed her a small, folded piece of parchment.

Alvena accepted it and nodded again. Yes, My Lord, she wanted to say, but could only smile. She clutched the bouquet to her chest and waited attentively for his next movement.

Unfortunately, his time in the courtyard for such frivolity seemed to have expired. "You have my utmost gratitude," Hairem spoke, opening the doors leading them back into the palace.

Alvena felt quite appalled to once again let him do such an action for her, but quickly scurried through nonetheless.

"And when you have finished, take the rest of the evening off. Enjoy yourself."

Alvena quickly curtseyed her thanks and hurried off to the estate of the El'adorium. The king was so kind—Lardol would *never* let her take the night off. She raised the flowers to her nose as she passed out of the palace gates, inhaling deeply. She *had* done a fine job, hadn't she?

"Alvena, where are you off to?" one of the guards called.

Alvena ignored him, picking up her pace. He knew damn well she could not answer him.

It was only a short walk to the bustling stone streets of the city and she found herself quickly enveloped into a crowd of elves as they passed by the countless shops lining themselves down Mehuim Way to the northern bridge. Nearing the city's marketplace, she quickly forgot her irritation and broke away into the center of the streets where the crowd was thinnest. A flurry of scents bombarded her—juicy meats and sugary pastries, bitter herbs and sweet spices—but all the while the excellent aroma of her bouquet surpassed them all.

She pressed the flowers against her breasts, shielding them from the bustle of the city around her. With new delegates and their entourages in the city, Elvorium's calm streets had become a churning mass of chaos. Keh, *foreigners!*

Her left hand tightened around the envelope. This lady Hairem was infatuated with… If *she* had had the ability to speak, would there have been a chance anyway? Sometimes she liked to think so, that maybe her charm and beauty would sweep the king off his feet like one of those enchanting siren maidens of lore. But… there was a higher probability of her marrying Lardol than anyone of noble birth. It was a cringe-worthy thought, but it still made her laugh and shake her head.

With a start, she collided solidly with another figure, nearly falling back onto the street.

The male caught her arm. "Look where you are walking," he barked, releasing her with a reprimanding glare.

*'And where were* you *looking?'* she thought hotly, shooting the male a dirty look that held all the non-spoken reproach she could muster.

The male dusted a few beads of pollen stiffly from his shirt. "The least you could do is to apologize," he snapped arrogantly. "*I* could have let you fall."

She rolled her eyes. *'I didn't* ask *for you to catch me.'* Her gaze widened as she thought suddenly of her task. She looked down at her flowers in dismay. They looked like they had been crunched… between two people…

"Please, hold your tongue. You have said too much already," the male spoke with an exasperated sigh. "Are those yours? Or are they for someone?"

Alvena pointed to herself and shook her head.

"It would be easier for the both of us if you used words instead of acting like some dumb human. Gods. Let me—" he began.

Alvena felt her fierce composure waver. *'Dumb human…'*

It must have become visible then even to the male, because his mouth closed suddenly and he regarded her with instant compassion. His emerald eyes flickered beneath dark, thin brows. "I did not mean—"

Alvena retreated and made to move swiftly around him. He was faster and she nearly collided with him again. 'GO' she mouthed angrily, pointing away from her. She stomped her foot fiercely.

"Let us not make a scene. Wait. *Wait.*" He sidestepped in front of her again.

Alvena scowled, regarding him coolly. She did not want his sympathy.

"Let me at least replace those flowers. They are truly not worthy of being given to anyone at this point. Let me just replace them." He raised his hands slightly, unfolding them as though offering them to her. "Please?"

Alvena looked back down at the flowers. If it was not for Hairem, she would have shaken her head. But he had asked a favor of her… and giving these to the El'adorium's daughter would be more of a punishment to Hairem than herself. She sighed and held the flowers out. She pointed at them and gave him a stern glare.

"Exactly like this?" the male replied. "But—"

She waved them pointedly at this face. *'EXACTLY.'*

He took the flowers, regarding them with mild contempt. "I am afraid I am new to Elvorium, so you will have to at least show me where to go." He stepped aside.

Alvena glanced back at him a moment, then turned to the shops along the street. She had never been to a florist before—the palace had more flowers than she could imagine were in any one—or dozen—shops.

She tapped her bottom lip lightly in thought and then started down the street. She could hear the unpleasant male following her. He looked new, now that she thought about it—his clothes were cotton, yet somehow regal in appearance. He wore light armor and she could hear the soft jingle of chainmail beneath it. She would have named him for a mercenary except that the blade at his side was uncharacteristically adorned for anyone in their trade. Perhaps he was a Sel'ven from overseas—though rare it was to find a Sel'ven of any kind on Ryekarayn or from Ryekarayn. The True Bloods and their followers were not welcome back on Sevrigel after the Schism and kept primarily to themselves.

He asked her no questions as they walked. In fact, he made no attempt at any conversation—she was mute after all. She supposed that it was awkward for him. To him, as to everyone else, she was now a poor invalid in need of assistance. Gods, did she wish she could speak! Rebuke them for their pity. Curse them for their ignorance.

"Wait, lady," the male called. "What about here?"

Alvena paused. She had walked straight past a florist in her thoughts. She retreated to him, allowing him to open the door for her to pass through. Unlike with Hairem, here she had earned it.

Inside, the white walls held large panes of glass. The dome above was likewise made of many panels of clear glass, allowing the sun to filter in on the rows of flowers below. The building smelled damp and fresh, accented by the scents of flowers and a variety of soils.

"Exactly like this," she heard the male requesting from the counter to her left as she absorbed the sight around them. She turned to watch him set the flowers gingerly down on the counter and produce a small leather bag. "Two silver coins? Those are rather expensive flowers," he muttered as he laid the coins out in front of the shopkeeper.

Alvena smiled satisfactorily. Yes, they were.

"New to Elvorium?" the florist asked, taking the ruined bouquet into one hand as she examined Alvena's exquisite array. She looked up when he delayed his response.

"Yes," came his short reply.

The florist nodded. "Your accent is foreign. Ryekarayn, I presume?"

"Yes."

"What brings you to Sevrigel? Mercenary work?"

"No," he again answered shortly. Alvena had expected that by now and was surprised that the florist was so slow to catch on.

The florist glanced up once in question. "I will have these finished shortly," she spoke finally, turning to the rows of flowers behind her.

As the male leaned back on the counter, eyes flicking up to the panes of glass above him, Alvena paused. Her eyes widened. There was something familiar about this male. His face was slender and finely chiseled. His chin was narrow, his jawline well-defined and strong, despite his delicate elven features. He looked back toward her.

The statue in Eraydon's Square. The one directly to the right of Eraydon: of the hero Ephraim. The hair was different—unnaturally short for a Sel'ven—mere inches at its straightest points. Ephraim's was much longer—past his shoulders and regally braided. But that was not important. It was the face that captivated her. So stunningly similar were the male's features, she felt a little breathless looking at him. The lion, the king of the Ryekarian Sel'vi almost nine thousand years ago.

The elf raised a brow. "What is it?"

She opened her mouth in excitement and raised her hands to gesture. Then stopped. Her face fell. Lardol was right. She could be a foolish girl. *'This is not a great adventure. You're delivering flowers. Grow out of your fantasies,'* she thought to herself in his rebuking tone. She sighed. *'Oh, Alvena.'*

The florist returned, the bouquet as perfect as the one before. She handed it to the male, taking the coin and depositing it behind the counter. "Are these for the lovely lady over there?" she smiled, nodding her head in Alvena's direction.

The male laughed.

Alvena flushed.

He quickly choked back the sound. "No," he replied. "I am helping the lady out, is all."

The florist nodded. "Sel'ari bless you. Come by again."

*'No wonder he doesn't speak much,'* Alvena thought with a huff. *'Every time he opens his mouth he reveals what a jerk he is. King Ephraim had certainly never been so uncivil.* No *king would be!'*

They exited the shop into the street outside. The male closed the door with a quiet snap behind him.

Alvena turned and stiffly held out her hand.

The male handed her the flowers. "I… apologize for the delay," he spoke forcefully and slightly below his breath, as though the words had gotten caught in his throat along the way. Or he had never apologized before.

Still, Alvena turned the bouquet in her hands, satisfied. She nodded her head once in acknowledgement and turned.

"I am Sellemar," the male offered her. His eyes shifted to the side, still seeming to feel guilty over his offending laugh. "I doubt you would need anything, but if you do, I will be at The Whistling Glade on the east end of town."

She paused, glancing back at him. He was a bit arrogant, but… She smiled and nodded her head.

Then she spun round and quickly allowed herself to be enveloped into the crowd before something more could happen to her flowers.

*

The mansion of the El'adorium was grander than she had imagined. She had heard tell that Nilanis was the wealthiest male in the city, with perhaps the exception of the king, and yet the grandeur still surprised her. She stopped before the gates of the sprawling estate and held out the letter, but her eyes were cast away to the great marble walls beyond them.

One of the guards took the parchment and examined the seal briefly. "Enter," he beckoned, pulling the gate open and snapping his fingers to draw her focus back.

Alvena took the envelope absentmindedly and passed through the silver gate to the base of a gently sloping hill. It was covered in dark green grass dotted with thin wildflowers that were orange, pink, and yellow in hue. Centered on the hill was a narrow pathway of white stone steps which led up to the double doors of the estate. She began the ascent carefully, holding her bouquet protectively that she might not ruin Hairem's gift a second time—or rather, protectively so that someone *else* might not ruin Hairem's gift a second time. Her mind flicked back briefly to the tall foreigner, but as she came to the top of the steps and extended her fist, his regal visage left her.

Her knuckles had hardly scraped the door when it swung open and two spindly elves stood before her. Did Nilanis have a pair of servants ordered to just hover about his estate's doors? He must be obscenely wealthy indeed!

She held out the letter as she ogled the scrawny males intensely.

"Go straight into the dining hall and then turn right," one of the males stated after examining the script. He shifted slightly as his gaze remained unbroken. "...Lady Ilsevel is in the Grand Hall."

Alvena padded between them with a backwards glance and then turned her attention to the further luxury held by the El'adorium. *'As rich as a king!'* she marveled. The wealth was scattered across the estate as far as she could see in a clutter of gold and marble and jade and some-weird-orange-material...! Alvena's footsteps slowed and she turned about, shamelessly ogling the garish decorations in every direction.

But if *she* ever became as wealthy, she would have it better organized.

She passed down the long hallways into the dining hall. Here she could catch the faint whisper of voices from the right, in the direction of the Grand Hall, raised, but still indistinguishable at her distance. She skirted beneath the stone archway leading into a narrow hallway. It was made of grey stone and fixed with many arched glass windows revealing the lush greenery of the estate's courtyard outside. A beautifully splendid chandelier hung from the middle of the hall and glittered with light from the countless crystals dangling from its holders. The light that leapt from their faceted surfaces scattered in a rainbow of colors across the hall and her fair flesh. She raised her arm in wonder. Why didn't Hairem invest in such an exquisite object?!

"—et it be!"

Alvena paused, straining her ears, lowering her arm in attention. The voices were becoming more audible now. The Grand Hall was just beyond her.

"...you ask... impossible!"

"*TRUST*... Necessary!"

Alvena halted before the doors, feeling small beneath their majesty, and raised her small fist seeking a smooth place with which to safely knock.

"This... Lord Valdor... He is going to be under the king's thumb. We all know it, Ilsevel!"

"*Father*. He is young. You are far more experienced. What could Lord Valdor possibly say that would surpass your knowledge and experience?"

"And what about sending soldiers to Darival?! Hairem went against the explicit vote of the council!"

"They *were* from his personal guard, were they not? And is Hairem not allowed to use the personal guard in any way for his defense?"

Alvena's fist remained frozen in the air and she leaned attentively forward.

"Well, yes, but Darival is not for his—"

"Perhaps, Hairem felt that the dangers in Darival affected his own safety."

"Ilsevel that is ludicrous."

"Perhaps, Hairem felt the thakish may take their aggression southward."

"Ilsevel now you are just pushing for—"

'You *don't know what Hairem was thinking!'* Alvena thought resentfully toward the male voice.

"Father."

It was silent for a moment. "Ilsevel…"

"Please, Father."

There was silence again and Alvena desperately leaned closer. Was she missing something? Finally the male spoke, his voice soft, even at their proximity. "I will do this for you and Hairem, but that is all. You stretch even *my* limits thin."

"Thank you, Father."

Without even realizing it, there she had gone eavesdropping again! Alvena quickly knocked and stepped back. She didn't know what sort of punishment she would receive outside the palace, but if Lardol had caught her, she would have felt the sting for weeks.

"I will get that," Ilsevel offered. The door opened a moment later and Alvena found herself faced with an older, and inarguably far more beautiful, female.

*'So this is her…'* Alvena looked down at the flowers regretfully for a moment before she donned a forced smile and held them out with the letter. She bowed her head. *'Hairem's lady…'*

The lady took them with a wide smile. "Thank you, my dear." She pulled up the wax of the parchment and unfolded the letter slowly.

Alvena straightened. Should she wait? The lady hadn't dismissed her… Alvena fidgeted impatiently as the lady paced back and forth as she read. It was an unfortunately long letter. How much did Hairem have to say?!

Ilsevel's smile grew the farther down the page her eyes trailed. She looked back up after she had finished and a hint of pink rose to her cheeks. "Tell His Majesty that it is perfect and I shall see him then."

Alvena felt a little hollow as she responded with a stiff curtsy.

And with that, she left. She traced her path back through the elaborate halls and out into the warm relief of the sun.

*'Ah, Alvena…'* She finally heaved a sigh to herself and gave a private shrug. Well, the lady *was* prettier. And she could talk. Nothing surprising, really, but her childish fantasy wilted a little.

She put a fist in her hand in a smack of self-rebuke. Nothing to do about it! She would go back and tell the king. *'Lady Ilsevel better treat him well,'* she thought to herself defensively. Back through the streets, winding and weaving she went, until she finally returned to the cool halls of the palace and stood before the door to the king's chambers.

She gave a light knock. The surface of this door was far more agreeable.

"Lardol, *go away.*"

She raised a brow. Surely Lardol did not hesitate to give the door a good pounding. She knocked lightly again.

Hairem sighed, as though the weakness of it all had pacified him. "Come in."

Alvena opened the door a crack and popped her head into the room with, what she hoped, was a reassuring smile. *'No Lardol here!'*

The king was seated on a chair outside the balcony—it was a wonder he had heard her knock at all. "Oh, Alvena, come in! Welcome back." He smiled and beckoned her in, his exasperated expression quickly switching to one of eager anticipation, but Alvena liked to imagine that it was merely because he was as excited to be free of Lardol as she was.

She closed the door behind her and moved to stand before him, admittedly eager to share her success in his request.

"So, what did Ilsevel do? Did she like them?"

Alvena sniffed her invisible bouquet and smiled.

"Wonderful!" the king alighted, much like an excited child. "And what did she say?"

Alvena found herself rolling her eyes at his behavior before she could stop herself. The king looked surprised.

"What? No? Or she didn't like the letter? Do you think she liked the letter?" He leaned forward in the chair, eyes gazing at her face intensely.

Alvena blushed a little and shook her head. Then she nodded. Then nodded a second time, just for good measure.

"She liked it?"

She smiled and nodded again. Gods, were *all* males so insecure about a female's affections? She would have found it even more amusing… if it weren't Hairem who was portraying it.

"And she agreed to meet, I hope?"

Alvena nodded once more.

Hairem beamed with satisfaction. "Let me tell you another little secret." He leaned forward and Alvena grew giddy at the proximity. "This lady is the one. Now don't go telling anyone. Nothing is official yet. I have yet to make my proposition to her father, and there is still plenty of time for all that. But I must say, regrettably, that for all Lardol's insufferable nagging, I will have to thank him. He nudged me into this—insisted I consider her."

Alvena gave a smile, mimicking his elation.

Another thing she could hate Lardol for.

# CHAPTER ELEVEN

"SHIELDS UP!" Jikun bellowed as he ducked down, his head low to the sour stench of the muddy ground. The ends of his hair dipped below the surface of the swamp and a persistent buzzing hung near his ears. A rain of arrows cascaded around him, bouncing off the soldiers' raised shields.

"General. General!"

Jikun jerked his head around, but the male calling for him was indistinguishable in the chaos: fifty-five thousand soldiers and a swamp as far as the eye could see.

Five thousand were gone. They had fallen in the first week. Some of them would fight again. Others…

"GENERAL!"

A male fell to his left, an arrow protruding from his spasming neck.

Jikun stood and, as soon as he had twisted about, found the edge of a shield slammed into the side of his face. His feet flew out from under him and he splashed heavily into the thick muck around him.

"Jikun, gods damn you!" Navon growled, lowering his shield. "You almost had a shaft of wood through your skull!"

The soldiers around them knitted close together in order to protect their general as he lay in a blank daze. He could feel his cheek throbbing and a warm trickle slip down to the edge of his lips. Navon reached out, firmly yanking Jikun back to his feet.

"Thank you," Jikun muttered, feeling the wet mud slide down his back, unnervingly aware that his concentration in the humidity was fractured by the delusions brought by the heat. He was not built like the creatures of the south.

He wiped the back of his hand across his mouth to clear the blood away and steadied himself on his captain. "How far ahead are they?"

"About a furlong," Navon replied with a cough, wiping his plastered hair from his face. A bead of sweat rolled down his temple in a slow, meandering trail. Jikun noticed how his eyes focused slowly on the distance ahead of them. Perhaps the heat was getting to him as well. It was so god damn humid!

"We will never catch them in this damn swamp…" Jikun grunted as he trudged forward. The grey sludge filled his boots and weighed his legs like chains. For every foot they advanced, the centaurs pulled ahead several. Catching them off guard had been for naught—with their long legs, they kicked themselves free of the swamp's pull and escaped through the foreign terrain in a way the elves were simply not built for. They were vastly more familiar with the land. "Madness is what this is," Jikun growled. "SHIELDS UP!!"

Another wave of arrows fell about them, taking several soldiers with them.

"Our orders are to move them out of the phoenix's territory… And they are moving," Navon assured him, stumbling and falling forward. He was slow to put his hands out and landed with a splash.

"Watch yourself," Jikun barked, his annoyance at his captain's usual optimism abated by the fall. He pulled him sharply to his feet. "I will lose every one of my soldiers if this continues as it has been! How much farther does the swamp go on?"

"I just spoke with Julum a little while ago—another league in almost all directions," Navon replied as he coughed hard again. He jerked slightly, recoiling from a shiver.

Jikun tried to focus his responsibility on the events around him: there were soldiers falling all about them—Navon would have to care for himself. "We will stop on the edge of the swamp for the night. Send word for the caravan to rendezvous with us there."

"Yes, my lord," the captain replied.

"SHIELDS UP!" Jikun bellowed. He could not hear Navon's whispered magic over the shouts and screams of the soldiers around him, but he could see the elf's pale lips moving rapidly. And then, with a little flash of light, a raven shot from his hands in wisps of black smoke that vanished into the sparse canopy overhead—a messenger spell, and the only one Jikun knew his captain possessed that did *not* have ties to necromancy.

"GENERAL!" came the shout yet again. But this time the fierce cry was aided with a hand on Jikun's arm, jerking him to a halt before the scout. "General Jikun," panted the elf, waiting until Jikun had turned his full attention to the male before continuing. "The cavalry has gone a day ahead.

They say they can cut the centaurs off from the front. If we can continue to push them forward, they say that the horsemen will be surrounded by the morrow."

Jikun withheld his own anticipation and calmly replied, "Tell them to—" But he was drowned out by the shouts of his captain:

"SHIELDS UP!"

"Tell them to—"

"Captain!"

Jikun turned sharply at the frantic tone of a soldier behind him, letting his words fall short.

Navon was doubled over, retching violently.

Jikun placed a hand on the Helven's shoulder, his brow knitting sharply. He tried to maintain his calm mask even as alarm roiled inside him. He caught an archer beside him by the shoulder plate and twisted him about to face them. "Take the captain to the back lines. See that he is kept safe," he commanded.

"No—" Navon gagged. "No, I will be fine…"

Jikun steadied him as he lurched in a pathetic attempt to move forward. "That is an order, captain," he growled sternly.

The archer moved forward and took Navon by the arm, tugging at him gently. "Come, my lord," he beckoned.

"I—"

"NAVON GET YOUR ASS TO THE BACK LINES," Jikun bellowed. "NOW."

He heard the captain fall silent instantly, his clammy jaw snapping closed.

"SHIELDS UP!" Jikun roared.

*

By the end of the week, half of the army lay retching in the plains of the centaurian horde. By the end of the following week, half of those soldiers were dead. The disease swept through Jikun's army like a swift and terrible retribution from the gods.

*Gods*. Here the elves fought for the honor of one and she allowed her people to retch until their insides poured from their mouths.

Jikun paused, his hand resting on the entrance to the tent flap before him. He could hear the sounds of coughing all around him, weak and constant. A muddy scout drifted from his rest to return to his post in the fields outside the troops' encampment, his legs dragging as he walked. In the distance, Jikun could see the horse lords moving about in the expanse beyond the army's hill, just waiting for the elves' will to break.

He shifted his hand on his blade. He did not want to see Navon go like the others had. Not to die retching in the foreign land of the horse beasts…

"Is that you, General?" came a hoarse voice from inside.

Jikun started and quickly composed his face to one of unnatural calmness. He pushed the curtain aside and ducked beneath the low top. "Captain," he greeted stoically as he stepped across the muddy earth and settled onto the stool on the right side of the bed made of furs and thin cotton sheets.

"Good to see you, General," Navon whispered. The elf could barely talk—a few days ago, not at all. He watched Jikun situate himself with bloodshot, glazed eyes and a small, parted-lip smile.

"And you, Navon," Jikun replied, leaning forward to squeeze the elf's shoulder in comfort. In the humidity of the tiny enclosure, the air reeked of urine from the pits at the edge of the hill. "That stench just holds up in here, doesn't it?" he muttered regrettably. "But you are looking better."

The sick all had—before they had been seized one night by such violent retching that—

"You think so?" his friend laughed slightly, a frail, pitiful sort of laugh that made Jikun's stomach twist. "I ate today. Just a little—but that is some improvement." He rolled his head to the side to look directly at the tent flap. Sometimes, the breeze would catch it and, just for a moment, he could perhaps see the world outside. It was difficult to tell—the focus in his eyes seemed weak at best. "Tell me—what is going on with the battle?"

Battle? Or was it war now? They had met the centaurs now on numerous occasions outside the swamps. Jikun's army had barricaded itself in on a steep hill just a league from the worst of the swamp lands. The position allowed them a clear view of the plains around them and the centaurs milling below. But the number of battles had decreased as more soldiers took ill. For a week now, there had been nothing but utter silence.

"Things are bleak," he replied honestly. "I believe it is safe to say that we are on the defensive. With half of the army ill, I cannot move to find better ground and I do not have enough soldiers to fight them. As long as we are up here, however, the centaurs do not seem eager to make the dangerous trek uphill into our arrows." *'What few arrows that we have left…'* he added cynically to himself.

Navon's eyes closed for a moment and Jikun started. He reached out frantically toward the Helven's wrist, but jerked back as his eyes opened again. "Did you write to the council?"

Jikun nodded stiffly, quickly hiding his concern beneath his venom. "Gods pray they listen, Navon." They *had* to listen. The centaurs would not move—not without a fight that Jikun could not give them.

"Maybe we will be called home soon," Navon whispered with a distant, optimistic smile. "I must admit, this feels like the longest battle I have endured. Three weeks and I have not slain a single enemy, and yet, I feel as though I have never fought so hard."

"Death has never been so close," Jikun replied softly.

Navon's smile faded slightly at those words and a glimmer of fear because visible in his faltering gaze. "I don't want to die out here… not for this war."

Jikun felt the anger rise in him and he tried vehemently to push it down. How *dare* the council ask him to do this?! To die such a miserable death unrelated to the warlord Saebellus or even the safety of the realm? Navon deserved far better. *Every one of his soldiers deserved far better.* "You are not going to die of illness. I will not let that be your fate…"

Navon's body jerked slightly and he flailed a hand. Jikun took it sharply in his and gave it a firm grip for reassurance.

Even his captain's hand was like fire.

"If I could ask," Navon began with a gasp, "for you to pray to Sel'ari on my behalf."

Jikun's lips pursed, but he willed himself to reply evenly. "Of course," he lied.

"So… hot," Navon muttered. He closed his eyes and his head nodded to the side.

Jikun's grip on his hand tightened. "Did I ever tell you about the gardens in Darival?"

Navon started again, eyes struggling back open. "No… I don't think so," he whispered.

Jikun leaned forward, resting his other hand on top of theirs. "Imagine snow and ice as far as the eyes can see. Palaces and houses built of ice and stone."

Navon smiled weakly as he gazed off, far outside the physical world around him. "That sounds nice…"

"It is. More beautiful than a mortal has the right to see. The gardens are filled with sculptures of ice and the walls are sprinkled with a dusting of light snow. In the morning, the light glints off the city and dances across the streets and snow banks. Then the flowers that closed their heads at night unfurl—blues, purples, and whites—tiny, glass-like flowers covered in ice. No matter how cold it gets, no matter how much snow covers the land, the little flowers persist on."

"Almost poetic," Navon commented wistfully. "Not like you… to speak that way…" His eyes closed heavily. "It… feels colder already…"

Jikun clenched his teeth as his stomach tightened painfully. *'Damn you, Sel'ari!'*

# CHAPTER TWELVE

It was dawn on Sevrigel's eastern coast, along the white shoals far below the jagged cliffsides that spanned the cloudless, summer sky. All across the peaceful countryside, the elven cities were stirring awake. They would pray and drink and eat and grovel to their corrupted politicians: until night came to place a temporary pause in the endless cycle.

Not far to the west, the first carts of the stable, eastern economy were beginning their march to the next city for trade and gossip. And still further west, boats were setting sail to their respective destinations to cheat the humans of their valuable goods in trade for overpriced wares numbering in silks and golds.

What a picture he could paint of his once glorious lands.

The orange rays of sun warmed the backs of the hillsides as they spotted their way into the east. And somewhere in the foothills to the north, the trilling of a flock of blue elhars could be heard on the edges of the strong gusts that swept in and through the encampment about him.

But here, in the shade of the Roan Forest, night had not seemed to pass.

Saebellus stood on the forest line, concealed from the foothills by the shadows of the broad canopy above him. The great Roan trees towered high, spreading their vast branches like a blanket over the forest floor.

His black eyes had not shifted from their scrutiny of the golden plains stretched before him.

"General," came a voice behind him.

Saebellus reached his hand behind his shoulders without turning. He felt the parchment at his fingertips and drew it forward with a flick. The trilling grew softer for a moment and he allowed his eyes to scan the page as the male behind him continued speaking.

"Our scouts have returned from the south. Jikun is still engaged with the centaurs. It appears that his troops are currently laden with disease. Adonis says that there are so many bodies that they have a fire on their hill that burns all day and all night. Sometimes they just throw half-burned, or even still raw, corpses down the hill. They have not fought for several days… They are in no position to fight at all."

Saebellus raised the parchment to his mouth and exhaled softly upon it. Slowly, but with growing intensity, blue-black flames sprang from the center of the parchment and devoured it. Saebellus let the smoldering remains drop from his long, pale fingers into the dry grass at his feet. "The Vetri may know we are here," he spoke, nodding toward the foothills of the elves of the valley, his face impassive. "Come, Vale. If King Hairem and General Jikun think they have time to war with the horselords, then we will march on the elves' Halls of Horiembrig. Let them know that we are to be taken seriously."

As they moved into the darkness of the forest, they left the blue-black flames to rekindle on the dried grasses of the Vetri'an plains: there was no tolerance for the council's sympathizers.

# CHAPTER THIRTEEN

"Too formal? Or not formal enough?" the king fretted, tugging at the end of his silk sleeve.

Alvena crossed her arms, leaning back thoughtfully and feigning deep consideration for his plight. The king had been fretting often as of late. It was different than his complaints about the lords of the city trying to entice him to wed their daughters or his stress about the corruption of the council. No, *this* fretting always sent him into frenzies of appearance-based concerns and constant inquires as to the hour of the day. She rubbed her chin a few times as he turned toward the mirror.

"On second thought, this is just not… subtle enough. Too bold. Too bold? Yes… Too bold."

And there he was, off talking to himself again. *'Too bold for what?'* she wondered. She picked up a few shirts that had been tossed to the side and began to fold them neatly into their prior states. She could hear Hairem sifting through his chest, a pile of undesirables growing on his left.

"Here, nonono," the king insisted, waving a hand at her. "I will clean this up when I return home this evening."

The girl reluctantly set the clothes back on the floor, giving Hairem a steely glare. She knew what that meant. Tomorrow it would be just as shambolic as they left it tonight.

The king gave a laugh of denial. "I will. Upon my honor or a curse upon me." He raised a hand in a pledging fashion.

Alvena smiled, though doubtful, and pointed to a shirt he had dropped onto the pile.

"Ah, this?" Hairem held it up, turning it around several times as though it would manifest itself more desirable at different angles. "This…? Hm. I think you may be right."

The girl waited for Hairem to change, turning awkwardly to reach for the shirts on the floor again.

"Noctem above, I am late, aren't I?!" Hairem suddenly cursed. He nearly tripped over her—as she was reaching for another shirt—and dashed madly for the door, his shirt only half buttoned.

Alvena stumbled out of his path, blinking wide-eyed in surprise.

Hairem's head popped back into view and he waved a finger at her. "And put those down, Alvena!"

* * * * *

"Erallus, this is far enough. You and your guard may turn back," Hairem spoke as they entered into the quiet, cobbled streets of the western end of the city.

"There are humans in port this week, My Lord," his guard replied solidly, eyes flitting about the alleyways and nearby rooftops. "And the assassin could be roaming anywhere in this city."

Hairem gestured toward the west incredulously. "If—"

"Perhaps if My Lord had chosen to take a carriage, I would be more inclined to leave you alone in the open streets."

Hairem scoffed at his rebuking tone. A carriage! He certainly did not require a carriage to travel from *his* palace to Nilanis' *estate*. There was something about recent events that made the lifestyle of the nobility sickening to him.

Not just *something*. *Everything*.

He glanced fondly at the relatively simply adorned homes of the common elves on his right, with their white marbled walls and golden domed rooftops—simple, yet richly elegant nonetheless. He felt more at ease beside them now and wondered if it was by choice or a realization in his lack of power that made their kind seem more akin to himself.

Still, as simple and harmless as the city appeared, Erallus' point could not be ignored. "Carry on, Erallus," he caved, allowing his guards to escort him for the remainder of his journey, through the winding streets to the little wall that encircled the El'adorium's estate.

"Here you are, My Lord. We shall await you here," Erallus spoke as he took his place near Nilanis' gates. He leaned slightly out into the street, reproachfully eyeing the jumble of children's toys from their station of siege outside the wall.

Hairem smiled faintly at the little line of cavalry, swords stuck into their wooden hands as they prepared to decimate Nilanis' estate wall. Ah, to be a child again! He stepped over them carefully as he passed into the grounds and hopped briskly to the estate's doors. As though hovering on the other side for his arrival, the servants swung them wide before he had extended his hand.

"Your Excellency," the male began with a fluent bow that threatened to topple him forward. "I will inform Lord Nilanis of your arrival."

Hairem watched the wiry male hurry away and stepped inside, finding himself alone in the grand entry hall. His eyes flicked across the countless paintings that stretched up the length of the wall, swam across the blue-tiled ceiling, and dropped down to the gaudy atrocity that was the Ryekarian chandelier. Aside from its own yellow glow, a redder essence seemed to paint its gentle curves. He glanced once behind him, out the towering windows to the blood red flush of the horizon.

On a day of horrendous loss, the gods of death had long since painted the rising and falling of the sun in blood. He clenched his jaw.

"My king," came a pleasant voice, pulling him sharply from his thoughts. "I thought I heard you arrive."

Hairem turned around in time to see Ilsevel straightening from a curtsy. She tilted her head in a charming smile and set the half-sewn needlework in her hands down on a statue behind her—that awful naked maiden statue that Nilanis had kept as a reminder of his wife. It offered a relieving, albeit somewhat meager, covering of her breasts.

Hairem shifted his gaze back to the lady and smiled in mutual affection. Gods, was she as radiant as ever. Her appearance was a distraction from what was to come.

She gestured toward a door to her right. "Would you join me in the dining hall? My father will be here shortly." She smiled warmly, extending a hand from the flowing sleeves of her evening gown, beckoning him to come closer before she could dare continue in a hushed voice, "He is in a pleasant mood this evening. Now is a very good time for us to talk to him about General Taemrin." She pinched him sharply. "Hairem, focus, dear! You wanted my father to host you tonight, so you had better look happy! And I'm here, so you have all the more reason to be so."

Hairem found himself smiling easily in return, despite the thoughts still lingering at the back of his mind. "Lead on, my lady," he commanded with the offering of his arm. As the doors closed the blood red of the sunset was lost and the sweet and succulent scent of food was replacing its memory.

The dining hall was brightly lit by half a dozen atrocious chandeliers and a pleasant fire yawning in the hearth on the north side of the room. The long table in the center of the room was neatly set near the head chair, prepared at length for the arrival of its notable guest.

"Your Majesty. There you are," came a graciously polite voice. Nilanis swept in briskly from behind them and paused, ever so briefly, to flourish a half-bow.

*'Where did* he *come from?'* Hairem thought as he watched the male straighten, wondering at Nilanis' ability to slither in or out of any situation he chose. Quite an enviable talent.

The El'adorium did not seem to note Hairem's mild regard of surprise and strolled away to the head of the table. "You will have to forgive my detainment—there were a few personal matters that called on my attention. Please, sit."

There was a moment of uncomfortable silence as they took their seats and the servants filtered in on wordless commands to fill the wine glasses and spread the food across the table. Hairem attempted to break the silence with mindless comments about the enticing appearance of the food, but Nilanis' mind still seemed detained on distant matters.

And *that* intrigued Hairem, finally piquing his interest about the El'adorium's life. He wondered what could be more important to Nilanis than the possibility of the king's interest in his daughter. After all, he had pushed *that* rather clearly the last time they had sat before this table.

Ilsevel did not seem put off by her father's distance and merely slid her venison across her plate impatiently. She gave Hairem a sharp nod of encouragement. *'Go on!'* it insisted.

Hairem hesitated, chewing deliberately as he watched Nilanis swirl the wine in his glass. The lord had hardly even looked toward the two of them. Hairem felt the surge of curiosity swell even greater and he leaned forward with clear intent. "Is there some way I can be of assistance, Lord Nilanis?" he found himself inquiring.

Nilanis started, as though he had genuinely forgotten that the king was there. "What? Ah, I am afraid not. You *must* forgive me, Your Majesty," he insisted, smiling thinly. He set his wine glass down and leaned forward with a suggestive smile. "There are no doubt things you wish to discuss with me."

Hairem gave a forceful smile in return. *There* was the sly snake he had expected—half attentive and all façade. "Lord Nilanis, there is, in fact, a matter of severity that I wish to discuss."

Perhaps the male could read his forced smile, or perhaps he simply knew what the matter was. In either regard, he sat back, thin smile fading. "Go on, Your Majesty."

"I would like you to call for an urgent council meeting on the morrow."

"I assume this is in regards to the general's raven?"

"Avoiding the matter at the council will not save you from addressing it, Nilanis. This is not a situation to be taken lightly—"

"And I do not," Nilanis snapped suddenly, cutting him off, "take the matter lightly." His dark brows had knitted together so tightly in irritation that they nearly bound together. "Your Majesty, the general has only been combating the centaurs for a month—"

"Combating the centaurs…? The only thing the general is 'combating' is the plague."

"Well then gods forbid he brings it back to the city."

The king's mouth fell agape. He felt an ache in his hand and loosened the iron grip he had taken on his knife. What madness drove his stubborn response?!

"Father," Ilsevel's eyes flicked away from Hairem's whitened knuckles and she spoke up quickly in an attempt to salvage the conversation, "His Majesty has come to dine tonight that you might listen to his reasoning with an open mind." She reached out and rested a small hand on her father's, patting it once as though to confer patience on the male.

Nilanis' face smoothed out slowly and he picked up his wine glass once again, allowing his other hand to remain in hers. "My daughter is right to rebuke me. Forgive me, Your Majesty. Speak your mind."

Hairem felt considerable affection for Ilsevel as she smiled back at him, once again encouraging him to continue. "The general stated that his army is incapable of continuing to fight. They are—and this is not an opinion—defeated. If they remain on the hill, without proper food, water, or medical attention, they will likely *all* perish. Saebellus already took the Halls of Horiembrig but two days ago. Additionally, the plains of the Vetri have turned into a raging wildfire of some strange and unquenchable black magic, forcing them to abandon their positions across the southeast. Chaos is ensuing, Nilanis. Elvorium has never been in more danger. If you leave the one male who might be able to defend it rotting in the south, you can dismiss the number of your ships and wealth as it is only a matter of time—a *short* matter of time—before Saebellus lays siege to Elvorium. And you, along with everyone else, will lose *everything*."

The words hung heavily in the sudden silence of the room. Nilanis stared into his wine glass for a long moment, eyes lingering on some unknown image to which his mind had whisked him away. He did not speak for some time and Hairem found his expression unnaturally composed. "As the lords of the council stated yesterday, why concern our citizens with the outlying cities when we have other important issues that must be addressed? We simply cannot ignore all other matters while Saebellus continues to drag this war out for the next century or two. He is as far east as one can go—what more can we ask for? The Halls of Horiembrig have long since ceased to be of cultural or economic importance. It is but a small victory for him. We cannot scatter our small supply of soldiers to every corner of this vast country in defense. We must protect that which is most important."

"You mean that which is of *single* importance to you?" Hairem suggested steely, surprised by his own boldness. "We know where he lies now. Let Jikun and his army return home, recover, and meet Saebellus again."

"And send our troops as far east as they can go as well? What defense do you leave us with, then?"

"What *other* enemy do we have to defend against?" Hairem shot back. "Jikun is not here now, so what does it matter to you if he is east or north or south? This is a matter of principle. If we let Saebellus maintain the eastern capital, then we say to him that the east is his. We must show him that every city—every space of this country—is ours. Let Saebellus meet defeat again."

"Hairem is right," Ilsevel vocalized sudden agreement, her voice rising with a flame of emboldened heroism. "Would Eraydon have let Maryk take even the *least* of Ryekarayn's cities without paying the highest cost? The council can only appear weak by turning a blind eye to his rebellion."

Nilanis laughed, setting his glass down rather forcefully at her words, cutting the visage of The Seven swiftly from their minds. "Both of you wish for me to oppose the will of the rest of the council?"

Hairem's voice grew in strength as he replied with a fierce shake of his head as he pressed his persuasion forward. "Not to *oppose*. To speak for Sevrigel. To sway them. You are the speaker for the Sel'vi *and* the council. You can sway them to see that even the Halls of Horiembrig must be defended."

Nilanis sat back then, sharp eyes flicking from his daughter to Hairem. He rubbed the ridge of his nose and tapped the table for a moment. "… I will call for the urgent meeting you requested on the morrow. I will speak on your behalf. *But—*" he continued before Hairem could respond, "I make *no* promises."

"*Thank you*, Nilanis," Hairem smiled, shoving the elation of his triumph down. His eyes fell on Ilsevel, nodding slightly to give her the queue to swiftly change the topic—before her father could change his mind.

"Oh! Father! I just remembered," she began flawlessly. "I wrote a new piece of musical literature about The War of Dragons."

"Your daughter is," Hairem said with genuine sincerity, "brilliant at writing ballads. I want my palace musicians to put it to song. Then perhaps she could play it for us one night."

Nilanis' mouth twitched into a forced smile, even as he seemed to grasp for the first time that it was a couple that sat beside him. "That is a generous offer. I am grateful for it."

It was not easy to find topics to flow into from there, Hairem discovered. Mostly he focused on his relationship with Ilsevel. Of all the topics he could offer, he knew this was the only one for which he and Nilanis could share similar elation. When the food grew cold and their wine glasses emptied, Hairem stood.

"Thank you for dinner, Nilanis. I will see you at the council tomorrow," he said, offering his hand to Ilsevel.

Nilanis got to his feet stiffly and bowed his head. "Yes, Your Majesty." Hairem could tell by the hardness of his eyes and the pursing of his lips that he was still irate—the mood had only been temporarily masked.

Ilsevel stood as well and slid her chair back. "I will see His Grace out, father." At least that burden was taken from him.

Hairem was glad for her company out of the dining hall—it saved him from the awkwardness he would have felt to leave Nilanis staring bitterly after him.

He held out his hand and turned with her, moving from the dining room to the empty hallway. Ilsevel walked lightly beside him, her back straight. He could not help but steal surreptitious glances at her figure. Gods, she was beautiful. How had that twisted, ugly, old male made a female as agreeable as she?

"I must thank you for keeping your father's temper at bay, my lady," Hairem spoke finally, raising her hand and kissing it affectionately. "I am certain that, with the history your father and I have, we would have been at an impasse without you."

Ilsevel smiled, looking slightly embarrassed at the praise. "Surely your charm could earn even my father's regard."

Hairem laughed lightly, his broad smile easing away the creases that the stress of the last month had burdened him with. There was hope now, thanks to her. "You flatter me."

She smiled and shied away from his hand. "Well… I am glad that I could be of assistance to you."

Hairem's smile faded slightly at her words and he felt the creases at his eyes smooth. "Ilsevel, I believe you blur the lines between my political desires and… my desires for you. I did not come simply to talk with your father tonight, but to be with you." He pulled her hand back toward him, suddenly, fiercely.

He felt her breath catch.

"Surely you can tell that my affection for you has grown in the recent time we have spent together."

Ilsevel seemed surprised by his boldness. He had shown it to her privately in politics, but he had ever maintained a very calm and delicate balance of affection toward her.

The contrast now to her was… *intoxicating.*

"I… yes. And… I as well, My Lord," she stammered in breathless admiration.

Hairem released her as quickly as he had drawn her in and gave her a sweeping bow. "Then I hope to see you tomorrow, my lady."

"Of course, My Lord," she whispered.

And with that, Hairem stepped out onto the stairs of the estate, his guards falling into immediate step beside him. Gods, the night was beautiful!

"You seem most pleased, My Lord," Erallus spoke with a subtle smile just visible beneath his helmet.

Hairem smiled broadly in return, the visage of Ilsevel still swaying before his eyes. But he feigned focus on the streets about them. "It is a *most* pleasant evening," he replied, sucking in the fresh air with a deep breath. "Come."

They wound their way back through the wide streets, buildings glistening in the moonlight, trees swaying in the breeze, and Hairem forgot his battle with the council just long enough to enjoy it. When they arrived at the palace, Hairem dismissed Taelarel.

"If you could stay just a moment, Erallus," he requested, watching his other bodyguard vanish through the double doors. "Could you do me a little favor?"

"Of course, My Lord," Erallus replied, stepping forward in attentive obedience.

"Could you tell the servants that I am 'sneaking in through the back'? I'd like to go upstairs in peace tonight."

Erallus smiled, his composure relaxing. "Of course, My Lord. I heard Prince Hadoream was known for that. I wonder where *you* acquired such a notion. Give them half a minute to scramble for you and you'll be free to enter."

Hairem smiled shamelessly. "I don't know what you are speaking of. Hadoream had only the best of influences on me."

It was as Erallus said—Hairem made his way unseen to his chambers and locked the door for good measure. He could just imagine Lardol's fury when he discovered the ruse. Ha! He chuckled to himself and turned toward the room.

The floor was clean—the pile of clothes he had left before dinner was gone, undoubtedly folded and tucked neatly back inside his chest.

"Ah, Alvena," he said to himself, shaking his head affectionately.

# Chapter Fourteen

The fog hung heavily across the swamplands, thick and yellowed, glowing with the western light. The sun had sunk toward the horizon and it now remained as no more than a faint yellow flame in the sky. Jikun batted his shirt against his chest as he gazed across the hot and muggy world. He felt a bead of sweat roll down from his hairline, across his temple, and slide down his neck to rest against his damp collar.

In the distance, across the emptiness of the Sevilan Marshes, he could discern a small, lone figure trudging through the muck to the base of the army's hill. Even the centaurs had retired from the heat, vanishing into the shade of the sparse trees in the east. But this figure dutifully carried on. Jikun watched as he stumbled and fell, dropping into the slush at his feet, but he reemerged once more and dragged himself further up the hill. Finally, his face became distinctive, the crest on his armor visible, and he stopped at the end of Jikun's tattered boots.

"General," the elf breathed. "The centaurs have not moved. There is nothing new to report."

Jikun's face remained impassive as he looked down at the weary, crouching scout, careful to appear confidently expectant in the news. He bent down, slipping a hand underneath the male's arm, and pulled him to his feet. "Good work. That is good news." But he could tell his words had not inspired the hope he sought for the soldier. "Go—clean up and rest."

The centaurs had not moved. And so, neither could Jikun.

The soldier nodded once, his eyes dull as they shifted toward the camp. He gave a faint salute and staggered away, drifting into a heavier slump the farther into the tents he moved.

"Gods," Jikun muttered, watching the scout vanish into a large tent. There was no water for him to clean up with—he knew it. The soldier did, too. At the start of the plague, there had been a large basin for bathing the ill and one for the well, but as the number of ill increased, the army had been forced to use both to fight the sickness.

And as the sickly state of the army progressed and the clean water dwindled, the basins had been entirely cast aside. They now stood empty halfway down the hill, caught beside a body lodged against a stump.

Jikun tore his eyes away and turned stiffly to his own quarters. His footsteps remained unbroken as he passed the tent where the scout had entered; he could see several males emerging, carrying the soldier's limp body between them. Their gait was solemn as they moved toward the roaring fire at the outskirts of the encampment.

Jikun ducked beneath the flap of his own tent and let it fall closed behind him. His hand slid against the pole in the center for balance, and he rested his head against his forearm. For a moment, he remained wearily still.

Somewhere in the encampment, he could hear the familiar sound of flames crackling and recoiling from liquid, and the familiar scent of freshly burning flesh reawakened him—it was only when a new body joined the fire that his immunity to the smell weakened. As much as the dead had been burned for their own sake and to combat the illness, Jikun knew, at the same time, they needed the dead to keep their fire going… and to cook what food they had left.

In a slow, solemn lament, Jikun could hear the voices of his soldiers rise in mourning for the dead. Over the years, he had heard many songs from his soldiers. But the *Ballad of the Dragon Wars* had been the persistent piece of their new trial. No matter how many fell, they sang it again and again, as though it was the last tie holding them to the living world.

"Sel'ari watch us in our dawn,
For many have already gone,
Bitter, weak, and cold we are,
And though some souls do travel far,
Resisting death we have carried on.

The heat of dawn's first summer brought,
The beasts of fire; death they wrought,
Plain and forest, bird and tree,
A blaze of red and agony,
And warriors to resist them naught.

When Noctem rose above the sky,
Banner-men came down from on high,
Blue of eye and golden hair,
The elven-kind's most fairest fair,
To give the lands' first assembling cry.

The elven lord and mighty king,
Gave the beasts a great offering,
Countless gems and endless gold,
Writings of their most ancient hold,
Of all the vast wealth they had to bring.

For dragon kind mere peace was feigned,
For when the king turned he was slain,
His skin and hair, bone and blood,
A chasm of red in the mud,
And all the elves cried out for his reign.

Sel'ari watch us in our dawn,
For many have already gone,
Bitter, weak, and cold we are,
And though some souls do travel far,
Resisting death we have carried on.

With son and heir their new high lord,
A rally rose with one accord,
Through the peaks and over seas,
An echo of beasts' travesty,
To bring all the elves as one in sword.

In the dawn of Sel'ari's light,
Dragon and elfkind met to fight,
Steel bit and fire shed,
So not a single one not bled,
With a battle raging through the night.

The victory brought no great mirth,
As beast fled to the depths of earth,

Tears and blood, a solemn hymn,
The casualties of war were grim,
For so great a cost was freedom worth.

A journey to the eastern brome,
To rest the dead in the catacombs,
Grief and gloom, hurt and pale,
Even those who lived were frail,
Before they departed for their home.

Sel'ari watch us in our dawn,
For many have already gone,
Bitter, weak, and cold we are,
And though some souls do travel far,
Defeating death we have carried on."

Jikun heaved a deep sigh as the song ended. He knew that, even now, despite *everything*, his soldiers' spirits rose at the words. "Defeating death, we have carried on," he spoke the words, testing the feel of them on his lips. They merely left him feeling hollow.

"General," a voice came from outside.

Jikun started, straightening himself and quickly recollecting his composure. "Enter," he commanded stiffly.

The tent flap moved aside and a thin, frail Sel'ven stepped through. His badge of position had long since been lost and he shifted before Jikun in a desperate attempt to appear somewhat commanding.

"Lieutenant Reivel," Jikun greeted with a solemn nod of his head.

Reivel hesitated for a moment, his blue eyes flicking across Jikun's face in visible concern. "Are you alright, General?"

Jikun waved a dismissive hand, drawing himself up and shifting his weight casually. "Of course. What is it?"

Reivel cleared his throat, pushing down his skepticism. "I'm afraid our worst fears are about to come to pass... We have a week's worth of clean water left... At best. And that is not taking into consideration that the ill suffer from severe dehydration already."

Jikun felt the wall that surrounded his emotions finally begin to crumble. "Thank you for the information, Reivel. Do not let the army know this. Try to ration the water amongst the healthy. You are dismissed." He could see

Reivel's brows knit as Jikun hurried through his response, but the lieutenant nevertheless took the hint and departed swiftly through the tent flat.

It fell closed, leaving the general once more in solitude.

A week of water. Jikun pressed his hands against the small, round table beside him. A week of water. *Gods* did the council not understand that they had lost?! With sudden fury, he heaved the table to the side, sending a vase to bounce and roll across the ground. He sank against a large wooden chest. *Gods*, they were all as good as dead! He raised his hand before his face, staring at it cynically, recalling the amazement with which Nalaen, Jekum, Lais, and Kaivervi had regarded him for his magic.

"Damn me!" he cursed, kicking the nightstand angrily and sending it crashing to its side. If he had spent more time focusing on that talent rather than sleeping and drinking, would their fate be different now? He raised a hand, pulling the thick water from the air around him and freezing it into a small sphere. He stared into it, his chest tightening.

The male who looked back at him was disheveled and pale. There was no dignity in his composure. No radiance of command. He was just another weary soldier.

His fingers closed tightly around the pathetic sphere. That was *it?!*

His mind wandered back to Darival: the frozen tundra beneath his feet, the cool wind at his face.

What he would not give to be there now.

His brow knit and he stood, pushing off his knees. *'Damn it, Jikun. Get a hold of yourself,'* he growled internally. *'You've done better than this before!'*

He reached down, stiffly picking up the vase at his feet and straightening both tables. He set the vase onto the last, dropping the sphere inside. He heard the little clink, the tap against the side, the little whisper of encouragement as ice tapped stone.

He closed his eyes, feeling the thick air around him, remembering the icy tundra, the watery pool in which he had fallen before the thakish, and the solid wall he had formed as protection. A sharp pain tore suddenly through his ankle.

"DAMN IT!" he swore, leaping away from where a stalagmite had formed at his feet. He reached down and tried to pick it up, but its roots ran deep into the earth. "Fool. You have no idea what in Ramul you are doing," he berated himself. Without clearly seeing the water as he had in Darival, he found his magic difficult to predict and still harder to control. And a single stalagmite had taken a toll on his already waning strength.

Still, he grasped his sword and slammed the hilt against it in a frustrated rise of determination until his pounding broke it away from the earth.

Enough water in the ice for one male for a day. It was a start.

# Chapter Fifteen

Between the towering white walls of two buildings, bathed in the cool shade of the evening's shadow, was a narrow, cobbled alleyway. From the entrance to a garden of a nearby building, a slight male wrapped in dark clothes crouched behind the vine-twisted archway. He could glimpse a few weeds between the stones—evidence that the respective buildings were somewhat less privileged than the other regions of the city. This was the eastern end of Elvorium, not far off from the city's crude inn that housed the ship-bearing foreigners.

*Humans*, in particular.

Although out of sight himself, he could still see a thin, wiry man leaning against the wall of one of the buildings, resting his hand on a barrel where a mug and lyre lay. His clothes were simple cotton, but the jewelry on his body and the golden band in his oiled hair spoke of a comfortable wealth. The human had attempted to weave his image as a harmless idler, but the watcher perceived beyond this guise.

Shifting to obtain a better view of the alley, the watcher narrowed his eyes. As the human in the alley raised his mug, his sleeve fell back to reveal a small tattoo on his wrist. It branded him as a dealer of his ship's goods, a travelling merchant of sorts. And who he was selling to this time…

"Gaestoran, my friend!" came a Sevrigelian-accented tongue in common. Another male had appeared from around the bend in the building and stepped into the faint light of the alleyway, arms open and fair face beaming as though his presence was to be expected. A Helven, by all appearances: black hair, blue eyes, pale skin. The watcher could recognize his kind easily. The newcomer glided across the cobbled stones, his silk clothes as silent as his footsteps.

"Lord Cahsari… What brings you to me? How is your son?" the sailor's deep voice replied in the Common Tongue, his eyes flicking across the alley warily. His words sounded amiable, but his tone revealed a hint of panic as he regarded the council member. What past relationship did they hold that would warrant such concern?

The watcher leaned forward with growing anticipation. There was tension here. A history between the man and elf.

Cahsari's eyes hardened in response, his lips pursing as conflicting emotions danced across his face. He stopped before the barrel, the smile on his face oddly fixed—but a sly council member such as he had probably grown quite used to feigning such amiability.

He began his speech in an almost amused tone. "Far better than you, I'm afraid." He picked up the lyre, turning it over in his hands. "This is a very fine instrument." His hand opened suddenly and he let it drop to his feet. There was a faint crack as the wood split along the side.

The watcher and the human started as one in surprise. There was a terrible temper flaring here…

Immediately confirming the watcher's thoughts, the Helven leaned forward abruptly, slamming his hands onto the barrel to further his threat of aggression. "Let me skip right to the important part, Gaestoran," he growled. "I care not for your dealings. Nilanis may let your captain put through port whatever he wishes, but let me warn *you*. If you ever. *Ever*. Sell to my son again, I shall reveal your name. Your ship. Your captain. And I shall personally see to it that you and your companions are *hanged*."

The man's eyes had gone wide in justifiable panic and he leaned away from the council member. His hand trailed along the wall as though looking for an escape. "Lord Cahsari, I meant no harm. I sell to whoever asks. Your son paid me and I sold to him. The captain does not differentiate between beggars and lords. A profit is all he is concerned about."

Lord Cahsari straightened incredulously at the man's attempt to pacify him. "How much profit do you think he would make if he was hanging from a rope in Eraydon's Square? Ten gold? One hundred? A thousand? Because I would be willing to wager… *none*."

Gaestoran scowled, attempting to draw himself up in equal indignation. The watcher laughed inwardly at his feeble attempt. "Listen, My Lord. You have made yourself quite clear. You want to protect your son—I understand. I shall ensure that none of my shipmates sell to him again." He paused, watching as the council member turned.

"Make sure of that, Gaestoran," Cahsari spoke as he began to depart.

The watcher swiftly leaned into the shadows. *'Close. Pay attention!'* he scolded himself sharply.

"The only reason you're still dealing in this city is because if I had you hanged, Nilanis' business would suffer as well." He took several long strides back toward the open street.

"You know, Ulasum's Tooth is not your son's only vice," Gaestoran called after him. "I'd prioritize, My Lord. The death penalty is far more *permanent* than prison."

*'And I wonder how he gets the coin for such lust-filled endeavors,'* the watcher thought sarcastically. He could see Cahsari stiffen at the words, perhaps realizing the same, subtle implications in the human's words. The watcher's eyes flicked to the slender elven hand which balled into a white-knuckled fist at his side, an outward sign of his inner distress. For a moment, he expected the council member to respond, but without so much as a turn of his head, Cahsari vanished around the building.

"And can I help *you?*" Gaestoran suddenly spoke without turning around, pulling a pipe from his pocket and giving it a good shake. He put it to his lips and lit it, letting a long puff of smoke rise slowly before him in the casual manner of a man at ease. He exhaled heavily, no doubt alleviating his recent rise in stress.

The watcher started then, leaning back into the garden in surprise as he realized the man was speaking to *him*. A human… knew he was there? He scoffed at himself shamefully, running a hand through his short blond hair. *'Amateur,'* he rebuked himself once more.

He stepped out beneath the archway with a long, strong stride. "I want to purchase Ulasum's Tooth," he spoke coolly, with all the airs of a male who never had had any intention of being unnoticed to begin with. It smoothed down the ruffles in his pride.

Gaestoran watched him approach, eyes narrowed in scrutiny. "Not native to Sevrigel, I hear. What brings you to Elvorium?"

The elf stopped before the barrel, reaching calmly into his pocket for the coin. He glanced distastefully at the prying human. "How much?"

Gaestoran leaned back casually and puffed a few more times on his pipe, filling his lungs with the sweet-smelling smoke.

What was that awful stench? Meadow weed?

The human exhaled a cloud and sniffed, ignoring the watcher's question and replying with two of his own, "What's your name? What brings you to Sevrigel?"

The elf paused, studying the curious face indignantly. "Ralaris," he finally ceded. He straightened, irritably waving the air before him to dispense the fumes wafting his way. "And my business is my own," he added curtly. "Do you want to sell your merchandise or question me all day?"

"Both, if I can," the human replied dismissively with another sniff. He reached into the sack at his side and produced a very small bottle, shaking it once. "Ulasum's Tooth. Or, if you prefer, we have it in a more personal form." He raised his pipe. "But I'm going to peg you for the liquid."

Ralaris' emerald eyes narrowed, flashing dangerously in the light. Is *that* what that god-awful smoke was? How and *why* had it ever been created into such a ghastly form? He exhaled through his lips, blowing the smoke clear. What little patience he had was waning thin now. "*How much?*"

Gaestoran leaned forward, resting an elbow onto the barrel and shifting his weight to cross one ankle behind his leg. "A bottle like this? Two hundred fifty silver."

"Thievery."

"Better than murder."

Ralaris leaned forward, pressing his long, smooth hands onto the surface of the barrel much like Cahsari had done moments before. Unlike with the council member, with Ralaris' gesture the human's countenance immediately morphed into fear—not for his position or wealth, but for his life. His eyes darted to the blade at Ralaris' side. With satisfaction, Ralaris smiled inwardly. "And what do you mean by that?" the watcher asked softly.

*Daringly.*

Gaestoran lowered his voice and waved his bottle casually, giving the appearance of an extremely forced calm. Ralaris' eyes narrowed further, preparing for a slew of attempted confidence. "I have been in this business for a long time, and no one who wants to take a pleasure trip buys the bottle. Perhaps you haven't heard," he continued in a suggestive tone, "but there is an assassin running loose in this city, murdering council members and street urchins alike. Now what would a foreigner such as you want with a bottled form of Ulasum's Tooth?"

Ralaris inhaled heavily, as though forcing patience. Internally, he hid surprise—he hadn't expected a male who suspected he may be the assassin to speak so carelessly. His fingers twitched near his blade. "*My business is my own,*" he repeated. "And you're pushing your luck, *human.* I will ask you once more."

The human tapped the bottle on the barrel silently for a moment. "Two hundred twenty-five silver."

"Still thievery." He rested a hand on the hilt of his sword, watching the man's controlled expression waver.

"Look, my friend. Even if you were purchasing this for your personal use, this would be enough for you to have a drop a day for a month. Business is business. I assure you this is nothing personal. Two hundred twenty-five buys silence, as well."

Ralaris reached down for the small pouch at his side.

"And enough to murder half a dozen people."

Ralaris' hand paused over the pouch. The human had gone a step too far. In a sudden motion, he drew his blade and lunged forward, shoving the edge against the man's throat. He watched as the man flailed back, cowering against the wall, plastering his body to the stone in an attempt to avoid the sword's edge. "If I *was* the assassin," Ralaris began softly, lowering his voice until he could practically feel the human's hair rise on the back of his neck. "Do you think it would be wise to declare me so? And *so far from other people?*"

The color drained swiftly from the merchant's face and he coughed once on the pipe. "I was just bartering, my l-lord. Nothing personal. E-everyone enjoys Ulasum's Tooth for personal reasons. And since you are clearly a man well-versed in its pleasures, two hundred silver."

Ralaris allowed the faintest smile to twitch the right corner of his thin lips. He dropped the pouch on the barrel regretfully, unsnapping the top and letting several precious stones roll across the lid before them. The man had managed to play the banter out and maintain some level of pride. *'I suppose he earned it,"* he thought, amused. "Give me the bottle." He sheathed his sword.

The human widened his eyes, pushing the bottle into Ralaris' hands. But his eyes had not left the precious gems. "Your employer is quite generous…"

Ralaris turned. "And do not speak of this to anyone. If I catch so much as a whisper of our meeting, you'll be the first one I use this on." He raised the bottle once before striding toward the open streets of the city. He didn't look back to see the human's reaction, but pocketed the bottle swiftly and glanced warily outside the alleyway. His work here was done.

Seeing only the occasional elf meandering through the street, oblivious to his presence, he stepped out toward the direction of his inn, flicking a strand of golden hair from his brow. He moved across the street slowly, taking a long, winding path off the main road and into the flowered alleyways that ran between his location and the next main street.

When Ralaris re-emerged, his caution remained high. The streets were still quite busy, even as the merchants began to close shop for the evening, but he felt every gaze that passed over his lean frame, every glance that lingered on his brown-leathered garb. The Night's Watch was beginning and the carefree walk of the daytime soldiers became a slow, stiffened slink through the streets, eyes narrowed for the slightest hint of unusual behavior.

*They* were a clear sign of the degeneration of the city that had occurred since the True Bloods' departure.

A few dozen females, a half dozen males. Ralaris made a quick note of their appearances as he travelled; and as a result, it did not take him long to identify a shadow lurking from the corner of his vision. He did not quicken his pace, but carried on in a long, casual stride.

Had he seen something…?

It was only when he turned down the street to his inn that he caught a true glimpse of the man lurking at the entrance of an alleyway. He had embedded himself into the shadows: his face was impossible to define. But no sooner had Ralaris noted that tall, lean frame than the male vanished completely into the darkness.

Ralaris' eyes narrowed, a scowl crossing his lips. Had the merchant followed him? *'No… he wouldn't* dare.*'*

He maintained an even pace to appear unaware, allowing the eyes to follow him to the creaking wooden sign of the inn. He opened the door, closing it solidly behind him, and stepped into the smoky, pine-scented air. The bustle of high-end merchants and traveling elves lit the place with song and talk and music, but Ralaris pushed swiftly past a thick group to the nearest window.

He peered out, keeping his body pressed to the wall, barely allowing his eyes a full view of what lay outside.

The alleyways were empty. The elves moving along the street seemed enveloped in their own interests. *'Damn it…'*

His eyes flicked up to the rooftops and back across the streets. *'Where in Ramul…'* he swore. A sudden shift in the darkness caught his eye and his gaze narrowed; a figure sidled out from the bend in a building, walking slowly, forcing himself to blend into what elves remained on the streets.

'There *you are.'* Irritably, Ralaris hurriedly pushed through the crowd and to the door of the inn, his hand on his hilt. With a swift shove of the door, he stepped out into the street and after his pursuer.

This would be the last night the fool would follow *him*.

# CHAPTER SIXTEEN

A solid knock resounded off the door of the Great Hall in Horiembrig, echoing off the stone and vanishing out through the open windows in a barely observed echo.

"Let me go south for a bit. You will hardly notice me gone."

Saebellus leaned back, regarding Captain Vale solidly for a moment with a forbidding, emotionless gaze. He mused upon the potential absence of his captain and almost spurned his request with a mere laugh. But instead, he foolishly attempted to reason with him. "Vale, Vale, Vale… I need you here. It does not take four eyes to watch an army dying of plague. There are a dozen more uses for you at my side than his."

"And one good use for him," Vale muttered resentfully below his breath.

Saebellus narrowed his eyes in reprimand, causing the male to still.

Vale heaved a sigh. "You told me you would have something for me. Gods, this city grows dull. I am ready for a fight." He stretched out his scarred arms in exasperation. "I'm not made for peace!"

"Not made for peace? What sort of Sel'ven are you?" Saebellus clicked his tongue with a shake of his head. But he smiled inwardly at the jest. The Sel'vi were as peaceful as a Darivalian avalanche… and covered up their destruction just as well.

He would be doing Sevrigel a favor if he killed every last one in the capital for a start.

There was a second knock—this one more insistent than the first and apparently necessary for him to address. Saebellus reclined fully in his chair, gesturing to the windows above them. They snapped shut in unison. He nodded to the guards before the doors. "Let him in."

There was a soft creak of ill-cared-for hinges and then the neglected doors swung open. An elf stepped slowly into the room, eyes scanning the hall in quick, flickering sweeps. Saebellus allowed him a longer moment to cautiously wonder at the interior. It was the first time an outsider had seen the Halls of Horiembrig since Saebellus and his army has seized the eastern capital. He wondered if the elf had imagined some great city of waste, blackened by the siege. He was undoubtedly, in that case, marveling to see that the city was mostly intact.

With steady black eyes, Saebellus regarded the skinny, little male, carefully removing all visible emotion from his gaze. The male was dressed in a simple and yet costly fashion—a suggestion of his master's wealth. But by the nervous manner in which he carried himself, he was no more than a dog.

Saebellus interlocked his slender fingers while his elbows rested on the arms of his chair. He knew the elf was unnerved—he hoped that those he told would be equally as intimidated.

"What do you want?" Vale demanded from Saebellus' left, leaning forward in a bored, dismissive manner, long blond hair sliding over his shoulder. His light-toned abrasiveness broke the silence that the warlord had wished to maintain for just a moment longer.

Saebellus gave another internal sigh. *'Gods damn you, Vale.'*

"Saebellus doesn't have all day," Vale carried on. He picked up his clean knife and flipped it in his hand. His food was mostly untouched. He had eaten very little since the weeks had dragged on without Adonis. No amount of Saebellus' harassment before the messenger arrived had spurred him to do more than poke cantankerously at his plate's contents.

Saebellus raised a hand to silence him. He could be *quite* difficult without Adonis around to rein him in.

"I have a letter here…" the elf began.

Vale swung his legs out from under the table and stood, sauntering toward the Sel'varian messenger in an elaborate fashion. He stroked his narrow chin, stepped around the elf slowly, and surveyed him in an uncomfortably intense manner.

Saebellus rubbed his temple. "Vale. Just get me the damn letter," he barked, waiting impatiently for Vale to snatch the parchment from the elf. He gestured to the guards, "See the male out of the city."

Vale sat back down, turning the parchment over to the back, green eyes focusing on the center. He fell still. "What seal is a ship and crown? Ruljarian?"

"No," Saebellus replied without elaboration. He snatched the parchment from him, glancing briefly at the seal before breaking it. He could feel the muscles at his brow knot in piqued curiosity.

"No?" Vale prodded again, in an aggravated and anxious tone. "Adonis?"

Saebellus could feel Vale's eyes searching his face as he attempted to read the letter. He lowered the parchment, glancing over it to lock eyes with Vale in a steely, annoyed glare. "Vale. Go entertain yourself."

Vale crossed his arms, leaning to the side of his plate to rest his chin on them in temporarily obedient silence. Saebellus knew his harassment was getting to his captain, but by the gods, the male could be so useless at times. His captain tapped his fingers slowly along the side of the table.

Saebellus grimaced slightly. He looked back down at the parchment, taking a deliberately long time to read it just to watch his captain squirm; his slender feet were now tapping as well, his lean frame shifting from side to side. It would do the male some good to learn patient discipline.

Finally Saebellus looked up, folding the letter and setting it slowly aside. He took a long moment to draw his black hair behind an ear and make his tall form comfortable in the high-backed chair.

Vale waited expectantly.

"I almost pray to the gods that the council recalls Jikun just so Adonis can return and *you* can cease your incessant whining. But I already have plans for Jikun." Saebellus heaved a long sigh. He leaned forward abruptly, jerking the knife out of Vale's hands, and slammed the blade into the table. His expression grew more serious, his tone darker. A deathly silence had descended over the room and the shadows along the wall flared and twisted in a mad cackle of delight. "But you asked for a job, Vale. I will give you something to do."

# Chapter Seventeen

Alvena stifled her giggles as she worked, twisting one strand of golden hair around another. She quickly fixed herself with a stoically serious expression as Hairem lifted the mirror to view her progress. She saw his brows knit skeptically.

"Are you sure you know what you are doing? I'm not sure about thi—" he began.

Alvena reached out a hand and pushed the mirror aside. *'I'm not done yet!'* she wanted to reprimand him. She stifled another giggle. No, certainly not done. She felt a little guilty as she worked. But just a little. He was only going to see Ilsevel today, after all.

Hairem settled the mirror back onto his lap, shifting uncomfortably in his chair. "Have you been following the politics as of late?" he questioned, turning his head slightly to see her nod. She waited for his head to go back to looking straight ahead. "I just met the latest council member. Lord Valdor, his name is. He arrived in the city yesterday."

*'And what is he like?'* she would have politely asked if she could. But she was glad that she did not have to follow such conduct. There were benefits, at times, to being a mute.

"He was exactly as I hoped," Hairem continued, as though reading her mind. "A military mind and civil genius. I believe he will contribute greatly to the council. They've been practically unbearable since I 'disobeyed' their wishes about their male of choice." He scoffed, "Of course, that's assuming they were bearable before." He laughed to himself, charmingly amused by his own wit.

Alvena shook her head with a smile. It was cute how he carried on to himself sometimes. She added another strand to the work. Well, this was certainly coming along nicely.

"In fact," Hairem sustained, "Lord Valdor's first political discussion with me was about General Jikun. You know about the plague, right?"

Alvena nodded. Then gave his hair a little tug, remembering he could not see her. Of course she knew about the plague! The servants told horror stories about soldiers' eyes melting out of their skulls and males eating their own flesh in their madness: as though there wasn't another thing in all the world more interesting than that. She shivered, wondering if those rumors were true.

"Well, the council has refused to recall the general, despite the situation," Hairem continued. "Lord Valdor was trained in the same academy as Saebellus—long before the war with the sirens," he inserted. "He became a Droth Guard, but was honorably discharged after receiving the injury that partially blinded him. He has some interesting insights on the warlord from his time at the academy, but I'll get to that later." He paused, as though having forgotten his line of thought. "Right," he started up again. "The council refuses to recall the general. Well, that's the next thing to be done. I heard even his captain has fallen. I should have taken steps earlier, but I kept trying to work with them. The council, I mean."

Alvena hesitated in her braiding, regarding him a bit fearfully. Return the plague-ridden army to the city? Her eyes widened. That was… madness!

"What is it?"

Alvena focused back on the king. He had raised the mirror and turned it to see her expression. She could see the concern in his eyes through the glass and she shamefully looked back to the braid.

What was Hairem supposed to do? Leave General Taemrin and his army to die?

"I know what you are thinking," Hairem spoke softly after a moment, lowering the mirror. "The army will be quarantined outside the city. We have to get them out of the swamp to fresh food, water, and care."

Alvena nodded. Of course. She did not envy him. The decision to recall them could not have been easy, and she did not blame the council for their disagreement on the matter. Or Hairem for choosing to do something other than abandon them in the swamp. She found herself smiling slightly. Even though she feared the plague the army might bring to the city, such compassion was admirable. Or perhaps she was a little biased—it *was* Hairem, after all.

"On to lighter matters," Hairem interrupted her thoughts. "I was talking about Lord Valdor." He paused. "Right, I was about to tell you about Saebellus as Lord Valdor knew him. Really quite intriguing—"

There was a knock on the door of the room and Lardol's voice followed in quick succession.

"My Lord, Lady Ilsevel has come to see you. She is down in the Great Hall."

Hairem straightened, almost pulling his hair loose from Alvena. "Here? I will be down shortly."

"I will inform her, My Lord." His footsteps faded down the hallway.

Alvena pursed her lips. And here she had been having a fine time with the king. The least Ilsevel could do was wait for him to come see her. She hurried through the rest of the braid and tied it at the end.

"Thank you, Alvena," Hairem said, standing and setting the mirror aside.

She frowned as he strode to the door. Was he so wrapped up in his thoughts about Ilsevel that he had not even bothered to check her work? Alvena snickered. Then stopped. Well, wasn't she getting spiteful? *'Shame on me!'* she reached out to catch his arm, but the king was already halfway to the door. She hadn't actually meant for him to go out looking like that!

But too late. The king had reached the door, turned, and vanished out of sight.

Alvena dashed after him as he hurried down the stairs. Well, wasn't he in a rush to see her! It would almost serve him right to show up looking like that if he was in such a hurry! *'I mean, it is not like she is going anywh—'*

"ALVENA," Lardol bellowed behind her.

She drew to an abrupt stop, flinching.

"By Sel'ari, where do you think you are off to? The king's room needs to be cleaned, and it will not be tidying itself. Get back upstairs and do your work."

Alvena turned around and shot him a dirty look. She knew that, *obviously!*

"And do not give me that look!"

Alvena pivoted sharply and headed back up the stairs, watching Lardol vanish back down the hallway. What did he do? Wait all day just for that moment to catch her out of place? By the gods, that old elf was everywhere! She slid her hand along the banister. *'I wonder what Ilsevel and Hairem are doing...'* She gave the hallway one reproachful look as though it was going to warn Lardol, and turned back around.

She reached the entryway into the Great Hall just as Hairem and Ilsevel had finished their greetings. Ilsevel looked a little flustered, her dainty hands wrapped around Hairem's strong arm. "Yes, I would love to see the courtyard."

Alvena leaned back against the wall, watching the two of them walk toward the grand doors leading outside. Once they had stepped outside, she scurried across the room and crouched down before the doors. She could only see the purple of Ilsevel's skirts through the crack.

*'Move over! I can't see a thing!'*

"Oh, My Lord, it is… *beautiful!*" Ilsevel gasped. "Why, I have never seen a garden as lovely! And so vast!"

"This, too, would be yours."

There was silence for a moment and Alvena's stomach knotted.

"Ilsevel, I spoke to your father last night."

They had moved far enough from the door now that Alvena could distinguish the back of the king. And his sloppy braid. He turned enough toward Ilsevel that Alvena could see his deep smile.

"As you know, your father and I do not often agree. But there is something that we share a similar love for… and that is you, my dear Ilsevel…"

Alvena could see Ilsevel's smile broaden as she looked up at the king with sickening adoration.

"I think about you every moment we are not together, and I miss you every minute that passes. Politically, there could be no better match than the daughter of the El'adorium and the king. But if it was only for politics, I would not have given you a second glance. It is not politics that drives my affections, but only complete and ardent love for you.

"Ilsevel, I love you with all that Sel'ari has given me and ask you with all my heart—" Alvena's eyes widened as Hairem went down to a knee before her. "To be my queen, my wife, and the mother of my heir. Would you grant me these greatest of honors?"

Had… Hairem just… Alvena's hand pressed against the door. Hairem had told her Ilsevel was the one… but to see it happen was so…

It was so final.

She could see the elation in Ilsevel's face, the excitement as she clasped the king's hand.

"My dearest king, I could never ask for more!"

Alvena leaned away for a moment, feeling guilty for having witnessed such a private moment. Damn Lardol! He had encouraged the king to begin with—but she found no anger in her heart. Sad. Yes, she was sad. And yet, the king was happy. Not just happy… She had never seen Hairem so blissful.

"The timing of this could not be more perfect," she heard Ilsevel begin. Alvena leaned inward to spy through the crack. The lady was wrapped tightly in the king's arms, nestled into his chest. "I was planning on traveling west in three days to visit an ill relative of mine. The news will surely bring her health! I will be gone only for a few weeks."

Alvena could see Hairem lean back slightly. "How will I survive without seeing you for a few weeks?! Sel'ari! *I shall not live!*"

Ilsevel laughed, smacking him playfully on the chest. "Oh stop! I will be back soon. I have to visit her. They all expect it of me."

Hairem leaned down and kissed her deeply. "I *shall* miss you," he began again in all seriousness.

Alvena felt a bit relieved. At least she would have him to herself for a bit.

Hm. That didn't really cheer her up.

"And I will miss you," Ilsevel replied, giving him a gentle kiss on the chin. "Now… I must ask. Forgive me… but who did your hair? It's…"

Hairem reached a hand up and ran it down the braid. Alvena saw his brow knit in concern. "What? What is it?"

Ilsevel chuckled, shaking her head quickly. "Oh, nothing. It's lovely. Come, show me this garden." She tugged him away from his hair and spun about into the scenery.

Alvena giggled despite herself. Hairem was happy. And… maybe Ilsevel wasn't so bad.

# CHAPTER EIGHTEEN

The dawn was brilliant that morning, golden rays radiating down from Emal'drathar as though the gods themselves had gathered to watch what was about to unfold.

"Your Majesty!"

Hairem glanced up from where he had stopped at the bottom of the steps to the council's hall and raised a hand in acknowledgement to Nilanis' greeting. He returned his attention to Erallus. "Wait here."

"Yes, My Lord," Erallus acknowledged with a bow of his head. A few loose strands fell forward in disarray, coming free of his braid. "And have a pleasant day at the council," he added with a wink.

Hairem gave him a dismissive smack on the shoulder. "Go!" he barked with a smirk. As his bodyguard turned to stand guard outside of the council chambers, Hairem began his ascent up the steps. It was the sight of Nilanis still standing at the top that caused Hairem to shift his smirk into a broad smile—no doubt Ilsevel had told her father about the proposal. The mere thought of their wedding sent his heart pounding. Things had happened so fast… but he had never loved a female as he loved Ilsevel. Even the sight of the snake could not dampen his glorious mood. "Good morning, Lord Nilanis," he spoke as he reached the top. "A very pleasant day, is it not?"

Nilanis beamed back. "Most certainly, Your Majesty. I—"

Hairem raised a hand. "You can refer to me as 'My Lord' now. After all, in a few months' time, we shall be family."

Nilanis bowed his head, but Hairem could see the El'adorium's smile broaden. He knew what the elf was thinking: nothing could add to the male's power like his daughter gaining queenship. But Hairem did not care—Ilsevel would not fall under the manipulation of her father. She was so much stronger than that.

"Ilsevel is thrilled to start planning the wedding when she returns from Elestri. I can only imagine this unusually timed meeting is to inform the council of this most exhilarating news?" Nilanis queried, following Hairem attentively as he turned for the council's doors.

Hairem chuckled once to himself. "Yes," he replied shortly. And that wasn't *entirely* untrue. He *did* plan to inform the council of his decision—but far more important for them to know was his decision to recall the general from the Sevilan Marshes. Now *that* would cause quite the uproar. "I imagine," he began, weaving in a little manipulation in hopes that this meeting would go less sourly than those previous, "that *you* would like to tell the council? Who better to share the news than the speaker of the Sel'vi and Ilsevel's father?"

He broke away from Nilanis before he could possibly disagree and stepped up beside Lord Valdor, who was standing behind his seat in a stoically expressionless fashion: as though the entirety of the events would merely pass him by. Although a morally just male, he was a bit of a dreary fellow; Hairem had yet to see the elf smile. "Lord Valdor, may Sel'ari bless this morning." Or perhaps he should have greeted him by Noctem? Unfortunately, to the other elves present, this would be rather blasphemous to invoke the blessing of one of Sel'ari's greatest foes. No, and he did not need to upset them even further this day.

Valdor nodded his head in solemn greeting. "Your Majesty," he returned in short.

Either way, Hairem doubted it would have made much of a difference to the Noc'olari. He surveyed the hall to pleasantly find that the council's usual punctuality had sustained even this sudden meeting. They appeared quite irked to have been called away from their personal affairs, shifting irritably in their seats and drumming their slender fingers across their desks.

But he didn't need their agreement this time.

Hairem stepped lightly to his own place, passing their grim and aggravated expressions with an unabashedly cheerful smile. It was difficult to be cynical when he was about to wed the most beautiful lady in the land. Even their scrutinizing scowls could hardly put a damper on his spirits. He waited a moment for Nilanis to reach his place before he sat.

"My Lords," Nilanis began, raising his hands to welcome the other council members to the meeting. "This meeting brings with it my greatest pride."

*'Wait until I bring up what I have done with the general,'* Hairem thought with an inner grin.

"As you all know, I am the proud father of the most beautiful and honorable lady, Ilsevel. It is with extreme elation that I inform this council that His Majesty and my daughter are to be wed."

The rest of the council looked to Hairem for a reaction, but he was already meeting their inquisitive gazes with a broad smile.

"Your Majesty, there could not be a better match," Mikanum spoke first, clapping his hands thrice with a nod toward the king.

Cahsari twisted a strand of black hair and sneered softly in response. Hairem felt his smile waver. What reason did he have to sneer? Hairem regarded him with a brief scowl. What an arrogant bastard, even at a moment such as this.

"My family and I are overjoyed for you," Heshellon interrupted his thoughts, gesturing to his heart in the Eph'ven sign of well-earned fortune.

Hairem focused his attention away from the spiteful Helven and smiled once more. "Thank you, Lord Heshellon."

Nilanis gave Fildor, Valdor, and Ilrae a moment to pass their congratulations to the king before he continued, "I am certain His Majesty and my daughter will make the kingdom into an even safer and grander place for our future generations. I—"

Hairem stood slowly and the speaker fell silent. "Oh, if there is more, please continue," Hairem nodded his head.

"No, please, speak, Your Majesty," Nilanis urged.

The king smiled. Why, Nilanis was just where he wanted him. He cast his gaze over the other council members, his smile oddly fixed, not giving them a chance to become defensive. "The wedding will take place after General Jikun and his army have recovered from their time in the swamp."

Nilanis' brow knit. He looked back at the other council members as though to defend himself with visible confusion.

"As I know how pressing the matter of my marriage and future heir is, I shall waste no time in ensuring this occurs as quickly as possible. As such, I have recalled the general and his army from the swamps of the centaurs. They will be isolated to the south until the plague passes. I have already spoken to the proper individuals earlier this morning to ensure their needs are met. I look forward to the coming wedding!" And without a moment's pause, he stepped from his place and strode toward the doors.

Heshellon hesitated. "Your Majesty, why—"

Hairem raised a hand in cool, planned response. "It is Ilsevel and my deepest wish that those fighting for our throne may have the honor of attendance. The wedding *will not* go through without the return of the army."

"Your Majesty," Ilrae started, getting to his feet. "We cannot allow a plague to get so close to the city!"

Hairem only paused to give Ilrae the same false, charming smile that they all had given him on so many meetings before. "If our extensive bridges, cliff sides, bottomless canyons, and vast lake cannot stop the plague, then surely no distance between the Sevilan Marshes and ourselves shall suffice. Lord Valdor, your Noc'olarian people have assisted in the quarantine and dissolution of countless plagues, am I correct? Perhaps you could explain to these fine lords how this occurs. I'm afraid that there are details to manage that I must see to—including the ravens. I'm certain Nilanis will offer you whatever support you need. Thank you my lords. I look forward to seeing you at our next meeting."

The moment of astonishment was absolute; it was only to the sound of his own feet that Hairem left the chamber. With the doors snapping shut behind him, he leaned back on their golden handles with a relieved smile.

*He had done it.*

Political matters were running with ease already. The final glimpse he had caught of Nilanis' open-mouthed shock assured him that the lord was going to be far less trouble with his daughter soon to wed the king.

What a brilliant fate the gods wove.

# CHAPTER NINETEEN

The council chamber remained deathly still. Nilanis stared after the king in stunned speechlessness. How *dare* Hairem ignore the council! How dare he grow so bold as to …*trick* him in this manner! What a fool the king had made of him…!

As he stood in the center of the vast chamber, fuming, he could *feel* the eyes boring into his back. His mouth snapped shut in stunned offense.

"Valdor, Heshellon, see to the supplies and location of Jikun's army when they return. Ilrae, see to the raven dispatch," Mikanum spoke finally, breaking the silence in a tense and almost dangerous tone. "Immediately."

Nilanis did not turn around. He heard the scraping of two chairs and the quiet thud of two pairs of feet descending onto the floor behind him. He watched as Valdor and Heshellon passed by and vanished out into Eraydon's Square.

There was a soft creak and the doors closed behind them.

"He has gotten out of hand," Fildor growled softly.

Nilanis felt his stomach drop, but he turned toward them with face drawn and lips pursed. "I have not—"

"The king, you idiot," Fildor snapped, tossing his uncombed hair about his head as his waving hand caught the ends and whipped them over his shoulder.

Nilanis narrowed his eyes at the brazen disrespect, but internally, relief pushed his panic aside.

"Indeed," Cahsari agreed with a twisted scowl at the corner of his pale blue eyes. They seemed to have sunk further into his skull in his moment of contemplation. "Completely ignoring our will—doing whatever he pleases… We feared this day would come and lo and behold, it has arrived."

Mikanum nodded gravely, his pale, chiseled face contorted in deep thought. He drew himself up and cleared his throat, regarding the room before him with all the command of the El'adorium himself. Yet Nilanis could see all eyes turn to the Darivalian, anticipating what was about to come. "I'm afraid that the king must be disposed of."

Nilanis paled, eyes flicking from face to face. Indifference gazed back at him in solidarity from each of his peers. "Are you all *mad?!*" he finally gasped. "Killing the other council members was one thing, but *the king?*"

Cahsari snorted, deflecting Nilanis' tension with a casual wave of his pale, boney hand. "What do you mean, *the king?* We eliminated his father indiscreetly and we considered that Hairem might become a problem as well. If the True Bloods had stayed around, it would have been them instead. Certainly this may not offer us a long-term solution, but eventually Sevrigel will realize that the position of the king is obsolete."

Nilanis' face hardened and he drew himself up much like Mikanum had done, standing in the center of the room as though he were leading a routine meeting. He raised his voice in command, deciding their course of vote as though he possessed them all. "We *all* agreed that Liadeltris was a special circumstance *only* because he suggested the dissolution of the council. His son has hardly possessed the throne! A second death so swiftly after the first will cause instability within the kingdom. *He has no son.* And we cannot afford this risk. We will shoot down Hairem's ravens, if he sends any. Then we shall send a raven to General Taemrin and order his troops to relocate. Hairem will not be able to find them again to retract our command—"

"Oh, Nilanis! Hairem is about to bed your daughter and you are bending over backwards for the fool. Afraid you'll lose all that power?" Ilrae sneered through yellowed teeth.

Nilanis stiffened. "Hairem is a problem that will soon be under control."

"Your *daughter* is as strong-headed as Hairem. Don't be a fool," Mikanum rebuked suddenly. He raised a hand and gestured toward the speaker. "Nilanis, order the assassin to dispose of Hairem immediately and summon the mages to eliminate the ravens."

Nilanis raised his chin in firm disagreement, weaving his lie without hesitation, "The assassin is currently employed on another matter of great importance. I'm afraid he's unavailable."

Fildor leaned forward, glanced once to his left and right for assurance of the others' support, and locked eyes with the Sel'ven. "We know where he is, Nilanis," he spoke softly, danger etching his tone. "Either you hire him, or we will."

Nilanis remained stiff, his chin raised in stern and unwavering authority. *He* was the *El'adorium!* "This is an unacceptable solution to the problem—"

"I'm afraid that you are becoming an *addition* to the problem," Mikanum interrupted.

Nilanis went still, the implication sending a chill down his spine. He searched his mind for words, but a blank slate lay before him. The room remained silent, waiting for his defense. He opened his mouth and closed it. *'Damn it, Nilanis!'* he lashed out at himself. He inhaled sharply. "The assassin is currently preoccupied on other matters. You will have to find another solution," he replied firmly. He raised his voice once more, willing command into his features—he would not be threatened! "And do not forget who owns his loyalty. *If I should meet an untimely death*, let me assure you that evidence of *all* of your illegal practices *will come to light*."

Cahsari sat back slowly, his face devoid of emotion. The room about him remained silent. "…as you say, Nilanis," he finally stated, heaving a conceding sigh. "I will see if I can talk sense into the king. But if our businesses suffer due to your whim, we will know whom to blame. Ilrae, you take care of the ravens."

Mikanum nodded his head forward in agreement, but his lips and eyes remained uncharacteristically devoid of emotion, even for a Darivalian.

"Then we leave the matter in your hands," Nilanis stated. He could feel the knot of tension in his chest begin to unwind. Seeing only complacency on the faces of the other members, he continued habitually, "The council draws to a close. May the gods alight our future days with wisdom." He turned toward the doors, noting the silence of the elves as they gathered their belongings.

"Nilanis, if I may have a moment," Mikanum called out.

Nilanis stopped, turning to examine the Darivalian as the other members slowly departed. The doors closed with a heavy thud and the two males were left alone in the vast chamber.

*'You have the gall to speak to me in private after your arrogance?'* Nilanis thought coolly.

He watched Mikanum run his fingers along the edge of the desk, pausing as though captivated by the wood. Then the Darivalian looked up, face calm and thoughtful in its regard for the El'adorium, and he stepped down from his desk to walk idly over to him.

"What is it?" Nilanis asked coolly, eyes over-focused on the ornate carvings of the desk the arrogant male had just left. *'Who does that worthless Darivalian think he is?'*

As Mikanum drew to a stop before him, he rested a hand on his shoulder and attempted to turn the speaker to face him. Nilanis begrudgingly complied, looking into the icy eyes of the Darivalian elf with stern rebuke. "I must apologize for my tone back there. Surely you know I meant no threat in my words."

Nilanis' lips curled, glancing once at the hand on his shoulder. "Threaten me again," he began as his gaze locked onto the chiseled face before him, "and so help me, Mikanum, you will be found lying in a ditch."

He saw the Darivalian bow his head, displaying a hint of humility before he replied. "I understand how you must feel with your daughter about to gain the throne and—"

"And you threatened that," Nilanis replied, his voice growing as icy as the hand on his shoulder. "You want a hold on the king? *This* is how you do it, Mikanum. Do not threaten our opportunity again."

He could see Mikanum's eyes flicker with the fierce pride for which the Darivalians were known, the tension rippling along his jaw. But nevertheless, he was wise enough to meet the speaker's demands solidly and passively. "Of course, Nilanis. You *are* the El'adorium, after all."

*

Despite Mikanum's reassurances, Nilanis made for the assassin's inn the moment that the sun first dipped behind the dome of Sel'ari's temple. He would ensure that the council could not possibly contend with his monetary offer! He muttered and scowled to himself as he went. The Night's Watch was crawling throughout the city, hampering his businesses and now his nightly movement as well. Hairem *had* gotten out of hand, but that was all soon to be in his control.

He strode into the inn and stepped briskly up the stairs, squeezing past a large, reeking human at the top without even a moment's regard for the contact against his fine clothes.

"Watch it," the human growled gruffly, shoving him slightly aside.

Nilanis quickly caught his balance against the wall, ignoring the beast behind him. *'Stupid human,'* was his only instinctual thought—the damn thing had only made his mood fouler. He stopped outside the assassin's door, waiting for the rude man to head down the steps. *'This is none of your business,'* he glowered at the fat, dirty face. He pulled his hood down further, feeling rather conspicuous in the bustling hallway. But this matter could not wait.

The human slowly turned about and vanished down the stairs.

Nilanis knocked once, softly at first.

*'Probably too busy whoring himself,'* he thought with exasperation when there came no answer. He knocked more solidly, determined to be heard.

"Ulasum's Tooth?" whispered a voice suddenly beside him. "It will take you far away. A drop for a dream. Two for sleep. Three and your problems disappear…!"

Nilanis started and pivoted, tucking his face further into the shadows. "Get away," he snarled, shoving the fat human back. Gods, did they not know the meaning of distance?!

Several men in the hallway paused to regard him for a moment.

Nilanis paled and quickly turned away, trying to look busy. "*Damn it. Answer the door!*" he hissed below his breath. The man was paid enough to be at his beck and call! He shook the handle subtly and gave it a twist. The door was locked.

He rapped harder.

Still, nothing. *Nothing…!*

An unsettling feeling began to form in his stomach, a chill running down his spine. He hurried down the stairs, ignoring the bustle of humans around him, and leaned over the counter, pressing his hands against the wood. "I need the key for room four," he breathed.

"Checking into it?" the inn keeper inquired, hardly looking up from where he poured ale into a worn, wooden mug with the speed of a Kindarian slug.

Nilanis recoiled stiffly. "Checking in…? Yes. Yes, checking in." He quickly set the coin on the counter, holding his hand out in swift command.

The innkeeper reached down behind the counter and raised a key before him at an intolerably slow rate. "Room four."

Nilanis snatched it without a word and hurried back up the stairs, the pathetic elf forgotten. *'Checking in?'* The words ran through his head ceaselessly as he reached the door. He shoved the key into the lock and twisted the handle with a fervent grasp.

The door swung open and rebounded against the wall with a solid thud. Nilanis stepped in, his eyes adjusting slowly to the dimness, his heart pounding in the thick silence.

The magic orb of light hung dimly from the ceiling, swaying slightly, causing the light to shift shadows at the corners of his eyes.

*'Where…?'*

He closed the door with a snap behind him, taking several long strides forward.

The nightstand candle was new, seated in its brass holder at the center of the table. New logs lined the inside of the fireplace. The ash had been cleared out. The covers on the bed had been pulled tight and tucked in, the rug beside the bed straightened.

The room was empty. The assassin was gone.

# CHAPTER TWENTY

Alvena steadied the stack of clothes in her arms as she peered down the flight of stairs before her. She could just see around the side of the pile and glanced once behind her to Lardol.

"Hurry up, child!" Lardol barked, waving a hand at her from his doorway.

*'They aren't going to wash themselves,'* she predicted.

Lardol pointed firmly. "They aren't going to wash themselves."

Alvena sighed and took an unsteady step downward. With the announcement of the king's wedding spreading across Sevrigel, Lardol was working her harder than ever. She took another indignant step down and lurched forward as the weight in her arms shifted. *'It'd be better to just toss them down the stairs and collect them at the bottom,'* she reasoned.

Of course, the last time she had done that, Lardol had taken punishment to a new level.

She heard the door behind her snap closed as the ornery elf went about his business.

*'I wonder how the king's meeting went today,'* she pondered through several more steps. She hadn't seen Hairem since he had left that morning, but Erallus was standing outside his meeting room looking as ominous as ever. If she hurried through her chores, she could stop into the room on some excuse. Perhaps she could bring him warm spiced wine. He did so seem to enjoy that!

A few more steps down and Alvena stopped to lean against the railing. The clothes in her arms were drooping now, precariously tilting over the side of the banister. She looked back once, quickly, and smiled wryly to herself.

*'Oops!'* she feigned for no one's sake, letting the clothes tumble past the rest of the stairs to splatter in a wide heap of silks on the marble many floors below.

With a grin and a bounce to her step, she hurried down the staircase.

"I *must* see him," a panicked voice rose to Alvena's hearing from somewhere on the floor beyond.

She thought little of it as she reached the end of the stairs, turning to the right to collect the clothes. The guard along the wall looked away from the male before him just long enough to glare at her.

She smiled sheepishly.

"You don't understand. This is an urgent matter!" the male breathed, trying to step past the soldier with a pale and fervent face twisted in indignant anger.

Alvena crouched down beside the clothes and looked up. There was something familiar about... *Oh!* She cocked her head. *'Ilsevel's father!'* she watched him take a sharp, retreating step as the soldier put a hand to his hilt.

"The king is not to be bothered," the soldier replied stoically.

Alvena picked up several shirts, tucking them under an arm.

"I must see him."

"About what?" the soldier challenged.

Nilanis pursed his lips, glancing at Alvena with narrowed eyes. "I cannot tell you."

The soldier heaved a weary sigh. "Lord Nilanis, *please* escort yourself from the palace."

Alvena stood, balancing under the pile of clothes teetering once more in her arms.

Nilanis did not move. "I demand to see the king!" he raised his voice commandingly. "My daughter will soon be the queen. Inform Hairem that I am here! I am *certain* that he will want to see me!"

Alvena snorted. As if titles mattered much to Hairem. She smiled slightly to herself, basking in her personal relationship with him. Why, she could see Hairem whenever she wanted!

She turned down another hallway, the shouting dying down. *'I wonder what is so urgent?'* she pondered. Nilanis had certainly looked disheveled. A little pale, too. She dropped the clothes beside the wash basins and leaned out of the room. His voice was still echoing softly down to her.

Perhaps it was something to do with the meeting Hairem had held about the general. She raised her brows thoughtfully and then nodded to herself. Yes, that was quite probable. Why, just the other day, Hairem had said that the council was angry about the general's troops.

She knelt down beside the pool and slid the clothes into the first basin. As the last garment sank below the surface, the door behind her opened and a young female hurried in to the other side of the water.

She knelt down breathlessly and quickly bowed her head in apology. A tussle of blond curls bounced once about her narrow face. "Sorry I am late, Alvena. Lardol wanted me to pull weeds around the steps. I just finished! Or at least, I hope I did. Gods know it's far too dark to see a thing out there right now!"

Alvena narrowed her eyes in rebuke, wiping a hand across her brow and feigning exhaustion.

"Really I'm sor—"

Alvena grinned and waved a hand dismissively. She liked Mirwen. The female was a few decades older than she, but had just begun work a few weeks prior. As such, even younger, Alvena had found she held a level of command over her. She pushed the silk gently down into the cool water and rubbed it softly with her hands.

"Did you hear the shouting from the hall?" Mirwen asked suddenly, leaning forward. A loose curl twisted into the corner of her mouth, but she didn't seem to notice. "Lord Nilanis is quite distressed."

Alvena looked up as she transferred the garment to the next basin. He was still there? She cocked her head at the female.

"I don't know," Mirwen replied, pausing the transfer of her garment as she pondered this for a moment. She finally spat the curl back out. "Perhaps it has to do with the council meeting? You know how those seem to go sometimes. I wonder what they discussed today…"

Alvena smiled slightly to herself as she pulled the garment out and switched it to the last basin.

Mirwen leaned forward eagerly once more. "*Do* you know? You *always* know!"

Alvena looked up, watching the female balancing over the edge of the water. A little tap and she'd fall right in. Her smile broadened at the thought.

"You *do?!*" Mirwen inquired, her voice rising. "Try to tell me!"

Alvena waved a hand and shook her head.

"Oh *come* now, Alvena. I will make a deal with you. If you tell me what is going on, I will do the clothes. *All* of them."

Alvena tossed her head thoughtfully from side to side. She gnawed slightly on her bottom lip.

"For a week!"

Alvena grinned, holding up a finger and pointing up.

The female stared back blankly.

Alvena gestured to her head impatiently and then pointed up.

"*Oh*. Hairem upstairs. You need to go talk to him?" Mirwen questioned.

Alvena nodded.

Mirwen shoved the garment in her hand into the water excitedly. "Say no more! Leave the rest of these to me!"

Triumphantly, Alvena stood and swept her an exaggerated bow. Her relationship with the king was paying with benefits now! With a hop to her step, she left the room and hurried to the kitchen, quite focused on the wine she would bring to the king to loosen his lips for secrets.

At this hour the kitchen was empty, but she could see a bottle of wine sitting on the counter, no doubt waiting for Hairem should he call for it that evening. She snatched it up and dumped it into the empty pot above the fire. As it began to warm, she gathered his favorite spices and dashed them into the pot, stirring it once with the spoon and waiting impatiently.

After another minute, she dipped her finger into it and nodded to herself. That would have to do! Heaving the pot up, she poured the contents into a golden pitcher and set it on a tray beside a tall, ornate glass.

Now, to answer those questions!

She climbed the stairs to Hairem's room excitedly. What *was* Nilanis in a fuss about? She paused, but halfway up the stairs she realized she could hear nothing below her. Had the El'adorium left? Still, at least she was out of cleaning dirty laundry. She'd make *something* up.

Outside of Hairem's room, Erallus stepped to the side. "Good evening, Alvena. My shift is almost over—is that a gift for me?" he joked with a broad, suggestive grin.

Alvena gave a little snort and giggled.

"Well, alright then. I'm sure Hairem will be thankful. Smells delicious. Spiced wine, I presume? You certainly give him enough of that. Are you trying to get the king drunk?"

Alvena's eyes widened in offense. *'Why of course not! I-I'm just... He really enjoys—!'*

"That was a joke..." Erallus scratched his temple and opened the door. "In with you."

The door closed silently behind her.

Inside, Hairem was seated beside a table near the opened doors of the balcony, watching the night sky as though deep in thought. He did not seem to notice Alvena approach and only moved when she set the tray on the empty table beside him. She raised the pitcher and poured the wine into his glass.

"Good evening, Alvena," he greeted, taking the glass and raising it slightly in thanks. He held it for a moment, still looking out into the night with solemn consideration. "I was just thinking…" he began. He put the glass to his lips and took a long drink. "About what a difference I made today."

Alvena rubbed her arms and looked at him curiously. *'Go on…'*

Hairem's brow knit. "I recalled the general today," he informed her after a moment. "I think I saved a lot of males. But you know, to be honest… I'm terrified of sending plague-ridden elves across the country."

Alvena followed his gaze out into the southwest, imagining what it must be like in the swamps so many leagues away from home. To be sick with your eyeballs melting out of your head. She grimaced. Why, she was uncomfortable enough in the cold summer night air without adding illness to the lot!

Hairem looked toward her as she absentmindedly rubbed her arms again. He smiled faintly and turned away from the outside.

"Alvena, will you close the balcony?"

*'Certainly,'* she thought in relief.

But as she padded toward the balcony, the bedroom door behind her fiercely swung open. She gave an internal shriek of surprise as she whirled to see the intruder.

"Your *Majesty*," the El'adorium breathed as he burst into the room to Erallus' apologetic wave.

Hairem turned in blank surprise. "Nilanis? I thought I told my guards that I wished to be left alone tonight… It is nothing personal, but I have private matters that—"

Nilanis let the doors fall closed and walked forward briskly.

Alvena stopped beside the balcony doors, her brows knit slightly. She could see the speaker's gaze nervously sweep their surroundings. What was he looking for?

His eyes widened suddenly in alarm. "Where did you get that wine, Your Majesty?!"

Hairem leaned back slightly, clearly perplexed by the male's tone. "Why, from Alvena who probably retrieved it from the kitchen where it came from the cellar where one of my servants acquired it from the market where *prior* it had been picked and concocted from some fields…" he trailed off, brow knitting. "You look like you need some. Sit. Alvena, could you pour Nilanis a glass?"

Alvena started. *'Of course—'*

Nilanis shook his head firmly, eyes flitting away from the wine to survey the room once more. "Your Majesty, the wedding preys on my mind. I was wondering if we could discuss the matter?"

Hairem's obvious displeasure at Nilanis' presence seemed somewhat alleviated as his imminent marriage was mentioned. "Well, no doubt Ilsevel is the one to talk to about such matters. I have given her full permission to—"

Nilanis cut him off once again. "It's just that I've been thinking about the guest list. Perhaps you and I could discuss this matter?"

Hairem's smile faded. "Now? Lord Nilanis, I would really like some time alone this evening."

Nilanis moved toward the balcony, stepping past Alvena and causing her to quickly jump aside. He pushed the doors closed firmly, glancing out once before he drew the bolt. "Your Majesty, I also have a concern about security for the wedding. Perhaps we can discuss this as well?"

Alvena saw the king groan inwardly, his face falling in exhaustion. "Lord Nilanis…"

"Your Majesty," the speaker only continued.

Hairem raised a hand, standing and setting the wine glass aside. He took a step toward the door. "If we must. I would like to make this—"

Alvena's glare toward Nilanis' rudeness was quickly cut off with a start as the balcony doors swung open, pushed as though by a strong breeze.

She twisted around, hearing the two males behind her turn as well.

*'I thought he bolted the doors…'* she wondered as she took hold of the frame, pushing them back toward one another.

There was a sudden shadow to her left, like a blanket sliding across the night sky. *'What—?'* But her thoughts were cut off sharply as her body was thrown back by the force of the balcony doors bursting open. She tumbled across the floor with a grunt, sprawling onto the tile with her elbows stinging.

Nilanis gasped and Hairem gave a shout of surprise.

*'What is happening…?!'* Her eyes rose blankly to the new shape that stood before them.

A slick, scarred human stood where it had once been empty, lean of frame and black of hair. Alvena pushed herself up on her elbow, staring fearfully at the human, confusion written plainly across her face. What…? How…? But these questions seemed to drown beneath her fear.

He was shorter than most elves, and yet he was still far taller than she. His body was lean and powerful, his hair black as a raven's wing. Thin brows raised in surprise and delight as the man realized how vulnerable the stunned target before him lay. He raised the jagged blade in his hand and darted forward.

In sudden realization, Alvena opened her mouth in a silent scream. *'Hairem!!'*

Her head jerked around to see Nilanis' face twist in horror, the king beside him reeling back in shock and fear.

"Help!" Nilanis shouted in panic.

Hairem had drawn his sword in time to swing out at the assassin, but the human was remarkably fast, dodging below the blade and driving his hand forward.

Hairem barely dodged in time, the blade slicing through the air where his abdomen had been, snagging just the hem of his silk shirt and tearing it.

*'Sel'ari save him!'* Alvena gasped in terror.

The door to the bedroom flew open sharply and Erallus stood in the opening, his blade drawn at the ready, eyes wide in alarm. "Your Majesty!" he shouted as he quickly grasped the situation. There was hardly time for him to react, but in a swift, fluent motion he had lifted the dagger from his belt and flung it at the assassin.

As though the entry of the king's guard had been nothing to note, the assassin had darted toward Hairem again, swinging his blade once more at the king, slicing eagerly for a fatal opening. He barely noticed the dagger in time; it sailed past his throat, forcing him to cut his strike short. He leapt away from his target as Hairem pressed against the wall, a furious scowl crossing the man's cracked lips.

Erallus' dagger clattered against the stone, bouncing in a solid echo through the vastly vaulted ceiling.

"One of your pathetic soldiers again?" she heard the human breathe in the Common Tongue, scoffing below his breath.

Erallus had taken the opportunity to position himself between the assassin and the king. "Surrender yourself!" the elf guard shouted in Common. Alvena could see his eyes harden as he once again readied his blade. "If you do, you may well be spared from a slow death."

The human laughed, the sound sending Nilanis cowering against the wall. There was a flicker of acknowledgement and surprise as his eyes landed upon the speaker. He sheathed his small dagger and drew a long sword, twirling it easily once as though demonstrating his prowess with the weapon.

He lunged suddenly for Erallus. "I will make your death swift!" he snarled.

Alvena watched in horrified apprehension as the guard raised his blade defensively, parrying with matched skill against the assassin. Their swords clashed in a series of rapid strokes and their feet danced across the smooth marble floor. Erallus kept his feet ever carefully placed, constantly vying for superior balance.

The assassin threw his weight into his blade yet again and Alvena realized suddenly he was as aware of Erallus' focus as she was. The human swiftly hooked a leg around the soldier's and knocked him straight to his back, a sound like thunder ringing out as the guard's armor slammed into the tiled floor.

Erallus kicked out in swift response, slamming his heel into the kneecap of the assassin, breaking the human's fluent attempt to dart forward.

"Your Majesty!" Nilanis gasped as Hairem was left exposed. The king still held his blade and Alvena saw him advance as Erallus lay vulnerable.

*'Don't just lie there!'* Alvena screamed at herself. Desperately, mind blank with fear, she grabbed for the heavy, golden candelabra on the table beside her, heaving it with all her fury at the lean frame of the human.

It collided with a solid thud against his back and he cried out in surprise.

"Why you little *cunt*," he growled in elven as his head snapped toward her. "When I'm done with these two I'll fuck you until you *beg* for death."

Alvena cowered away, hands trembling. *What was she thinking?!*

But the assassin had lost his opportunity to finish Erallus and the soldier was nearly back on his feet. The human seemed to refocus then, grabbing the table where the wine sat and swinging it fast and hard at the elf. It collided solidly with Erallus' body, slamming him into the tile just as he had been regaining his footing. The glass and jug flew to the side, shattering across the floor and spraying it with blood red wine.

Hairem suddenly stepped forward, blade raised slightly. His voice emerged stern and commanding, even as fear flickered beneath his gaze, "Nilanis! Go get my guard!"

The speaker seemed to come to then, eyes widening and head nodding forward. "Y-yes!" he stammered, reaching desperately for the door.

A quick dagger collided with his hand, pinning it to the frame with a swift and securing thud. Nilanis screamed in pain, grasping at the hilt in panic even as he made no attempt to pull it free.

"That could have been your throat," the assassin warned with a hiss. "Move again and I'll *finish* you." He leapt suddenly at Hairem, swinging around in a rapid motion, blade slicing through the air.

There was a flash of metal as the blades clanged thrice, and then the man reached out to grab Hairem by the hair. In that one fluid motion, he yanked the king's head backward and shoved the blade into Hairem's chest.

Alvena screamed silently in horror, getting to her feet, grabbing for the nearest object in desperation.

But Hairem gave a sudden jerk, catching the hand of the assassin and bending it inward. She could see the assassin's grip loosen, his eyes widen in surprise. Hairem slammed his knee upward, causing the man to reel back.

"I trained with the True Blood princes," Hairem breathed heavily, sword still embedded in his torso. He pointed his blade at the man, forcing him toward the center of the room with every ounce of his fading strength.

The human's eyes hardened as he quickly redrew his jagged dagger, but Erallus was swiftly before him. Alvena had become so focused on the king she had not noticed the soldier move. The assassin seemed just as surprised, as though in his determination to impale the king he too had forgotten about the guard. His lips twisted into a scowl of frustration and the bloodlust Alvena had seen before seemed to boil over in a mix of rage and hatred.

He pivoted, barely dodging another furious and swift blow. Again Erallus swung at him, driving his blade toward the human's legs. It was a mere flicker of hesitation—a slight miscalculation that cost him the dodge. Alvena could see it in the man's eyes as the weapon ripped through his thigh, spraying a mist of blood across the tile around him. He returned a furious thrust, half in desperation, but Erallus locked his blade with his adversary's in an instant parry, throwing his weight into the hilt, and, when the human stumbled back, sliced for his throat.

"Fucking cunt," the assassin growled. He dropped to the ground and rolled, scrambled to his feet, and darted suddenly toward the balcony.

Alvena gasped as she realized he was coming her way. She let out a terrified internal shriek and dove away from his path. He rushed through the opened doors, knocking one aside as he stumbled in pain. It smashed against the stone behind it and, with the sound of showering glass in his wake, the human threw himself over the side.

Erallus ran after him, leaning over the railing as though desperate to ensure he had fallen to his death. After several seconds he straightened slowly, turning back in confusion. "He's gone?"

Hairem put a hand against the wall and Alvena could see his knees buckling. Adrenaline was leaving him now and with it, the last of his strength.

"Sel'ari," Erallus gasped as his mind seemed to snap back to the scene around him. He rushed to the king's side, catching him under the arm. "We need to get you to a healer!"

Alvena saw the king's eyes close, but he waved a hand toward her dismissively, even through his pain. "I will be fine, Alvena. Don't look so worried. Help Lord Nilanis, will you?"

She stood, trying to look as strong as he did as the pair quickly left the room.

The El'adorium's eyes fell to her with a scowl. "I don't need your help," Nilanis muttered, gritting his teeth. He yanked the dagger from his hand, gasping in pain, and quickly tucked his bleeding appendage into his silk shirt.

She watched him stumble into the hall. With a nervous glance toward the balcony, she hurried from the room after them.

# CHAPTER TWENTY-ONE

The sky was cloudless, spotted with stars peering down on the still lake like a thousand curious eyes. And Emal'drathar was ripe with curious gods that night—the crescent moon of Noctem was most prominent, shining brightly despite just beginning the cycle of its waxing. Ralaris scowled up at it briefly, imagination turning his mood sour as he pictured the vile god Noctem spying on his actions. Or worse, *Malranus*.

"Good work," the cloaked elf spoke softly, breaking Ralaris from his reverie as he had just begun to imagine mighty Sel'ari smiting down Malranus, one foot atop his corpse with a glowing lance in her hands.

*Gods* was this mission truly so dull that his mind was wandering to senseless apparitions? He glanced to his hand at the latest "evidence" he had managed to gather. Yes, it was.

His messenger paused as he reached into his inner breast pocket, shifting his weight with a frown. "Ah, there it is. Thought I lost it but it was just behind our swatch of fabric here…" He produced a tightly folded piece of parchment. "And a letter from the Realm."

Ralaris reached for the letter and halted, glancing up at the rooftops. He could have sworn that he had heard a noise, but the world above seemed still and silent. He took the parchment and pushed it deep into his shirt. "Thank you. That is all for now. May Sel'ari bless you and keep you safe." He placed a hand on the elf's shoulder and squeezed gently, but his gaze steeled a warning with his words.

"The same to you," the elf replied with a short and solemn nod, eyes flicking upward with the same caution.

Business concluded, Ralaris stole into the alleyway, glancing once more at the rooftops. He had been on edge since the dealings with the illegal merchant:

since that night that he had combed the district for his follower, but had found nothing.

There was a soft patter to his left and he started. Peering into the darkness, his hand instinctively gravitated to his hip where his blade usually sat: but he had left it at the inn. The Night's Watch had grown to take any armed elf at night as a suspect for the assassin.

They had made his job that much harder.

His eyes narrowed and caught sight of a mouse scampering past him along the wall of the building. *'You started for a mouse?'* Ralaris scowled at himself. *'Orcs, elves, council members... and you startle over a mouse. Turn over your blade now—you are an embarrassment to your profession.'* He sidestepped the abhorrent vermin and moved swiftly toward the open road ahead.

At the end of the alleyway, he stopped and leaned slightly into the street. Two males in plate armor marched stiffly in opposite directions. The Night's Watch had become a plague across the city since the increase in assassinations, and apparently they could not make due with just *one* male, but needed two to watch the same damn road. He waited until the distance between their backs had grown large enough and then darted as silently through the street as the breeze that followed him.

He had just slowed his step into the entrance of the next alleyway when suddenly there came a quiet *tink* of metal. It bounced to him from the alley walls—its true direction indiscernible.

"Who goes there?" a harsh voice demanded from somewhere near.

Ralaris froze, glancing behind him. No…? Then… His brows knit and his eyes turned forward again.

No one.

He stepped forward slowly, hesitant to reply. Where was this soldier?

"Who goes there?!" the voice demanded again. This time, Ralaris sensed a hint of panic in the male's voice.

*Where was he?!*

There was a sudden sound of scuffling. Metal scraped against stone and a gurgled cry of distress was quickly silenced.

*'It was not me he was speaking to!'* he realized in alarm.

Ralaris instinctively sprinted forward, forgetting once more that he had left himself unarmed in the event that he was questioned by the Night's Watch. He darted down the alleyway and turned sharply to the right.

In the dim light of Noctem's moon, the sight before him was barely visible. The armored body of a Night's Watchman lay sprawled in the dirt. His helmet had bounced aside and lay against the wall. Something glinted as it trailed from his mouth. And a sword protruded from his gut.

Ralaris surveyed the alley quickly, eyes flicking from the rooftops to the open street not far from him. *'Damn it.* This *does not look suspicious. Where in Ramul did that bastard flee to?!'*

"Did you hear something?" He heard a voice inquire from the street.

Ralaris took several retreating steps, but a sound of shifting metal plates grew closer from behind. *They were closing in!* His eyes moved up, scanning the walls for a way to climb, but there was nothing that would suffice!

"Right over this way," the voices urged one another, closer.

Ralaris tore his eyes away from the rooftops and spurred himself forward. He would have to use the alleyways! He stepped swiftly past the body, his feet splashing into a shallow puddle, and hurried for the path branching off to his right. *'Lead me, Lady Luck...!'*

He spun around the corner and collided solidly with a tall, heavily armed guard.

*'And shit.'* His breath caught in his throat as he attempted to step away, raising an arm before his face to block the imminent attack.

The soldier reached out swiftly, his eyes narrowed venomously beneath the helmet as though guilt was unequivocally bound to the unarmed male before him. Ralaris felt the fingers curl around his arm and his body lurched across the cobbled stones to slam into the wall at their right.

"We have him!" the guard shouted triumphantly to two other members of the Night's Watch, approaching Ralaris from an adjoining pathway. He heard a shout of acknowledgement and their footsteps quickened.

Ralaris turned back to the male, attempting one final, passive attempt to set himself free. "It is not what it looks like," he growled. "I am unarmed." Even as he spoke, the other soldier passed beside them and rounded into the alleyway where the dead soldier lay.

He heard a horrified gasp. "*Sel'ari*, he murdered Talwen!"

Ralaris struggled to avert his face toward the wall as the soldier before him leaned into his back, peering into the darkness in a desperate attempt to grasp a firm look at the "murderer's" face.

"Sorry about this," Ralaris muttered. He pushed his arms forward suddenly, twisting them from the iron grasp of the soldier. As the male cried out in surprise, Ralaris slammed his body into the armor, throwing the suit backwards. The guard stumbled in a desperate attempt to catch his balance while Ralaris swept forward with ease, pulling the soldier's own sword from its sheath.

He could see a moment of fear and alarm spark in the guard's eyes, but just as swiftly, Ralaris turned from him and heaved the blade into the darkness. And delaying no longer, Ralaris fled into the night.

"H-he escaped!!" he heard the soldier stammer after the moment of shock.

The sword clanged off the cobblestones and the alleyway was left in silence.

# CHAPTER TWENTY-TWO

Nilanis started, his eyes flashing open and his heart racing. A faint smell of smoke lingered idly in the air—the fire had died and the new moon left the room utterly and eerily dark.

A death-like silence hung heavily in the room, and not even the sound of his own breath could be heard.

"Is someone there?" he croaked, finding that his voice came out weak and panicked in the sudden silence. He *had* heard something, hadn't he?

There was the sudden, muffled sound of footsteps, barely audible on the marble floor. "I awoke you? You elves and your hearing!" came a soft cackle of amusement.

Nilanis fumbled for the flint at his nightstand, hand throbbing with its still-healing wound. When he finally managed to spark the candle, he recoiled sharply with a choking gasp.

The human had stopped beside the bed, eyeing him casually.

"Gods, you are too close," Nilanis hissed, waving a hand angrily at the man.

His assassin stepped back, scoffing. He tossed his head casually and dismissively to the side as his dark eyes landed on the freshly wound bandages. "Still angry about the hand thing, are we? I already apologized. I didn't know you were having a little spat with your lovers."

Nilanis swung his legs over the side of the bed and ran a hand through his hair, choosing to ignore the comment. He took a deep breath, unable to decide whether the man's successful entry into his bedroom was a testament to the human's skill or his guards' lack thereof. "Did you find out what I asked of you?" he finally breathed, looking up sternly.

The hollowness that met his gaze was unnerving.

Fueled by Nilanis' discomfort, the man sneered softly, the candlelight playing up his hollowed cheeks and sunken eyes like some long-dead wraith that had crawled out of the Pass of the Dead. "Of *course*, my lord." He reclined lazily against the wall. "The elf is going under the name Ralaris. He is definitely from Ryekarayn, if his accent attests to anything about him. Right now, he resides at The Whistling Glade."

Nilanis nodded, leaning forward. "And of his orders?"

The assassin then grinned, seeming to cherish the information that, for the moment, he alone possessed: he licked his lips, clanked his teeth, and paused to dig something out from his teeth. "He meets a man at the docks frequently," he began. "The man often gives him letters. I was able to once catch glimpse of a letter's seal—it was the True Bloods'. I assume that these letters are updated orders or information from them."

The assassin paused and Nilanis' chest tightened. So the male *was* working for the True Bloods. What did the old royals want with Sevrigel now? They may have chosen to part ways with Sevrigel hundreds of years ago, but their potential power in their abandoned homeland was still immense… And just as notorious was their dislike for the council. "And? Certainly you return to me with more than this."

Taking several long strides forward, the assassin loomed closer, dropping his voice.

Nilanis stiffened.

"Oh, certainly, my lord. And what information I have!" His hands extended upwards in triumph and then stopped, freezing in place with his grin. There was a pause, as though he wished to hold his theatrics for effect. Then his hands and grin dropped in a swift and sudden motion. He waved a hand to the bag at his side. "But *first*, my payment."

Nilanis scowled, muttering. These damned humans! Gods, if only he could find an *elf* with the man's skill and mind. He moved to the small chest above the mantel and lifted the lid, producing a small bag that jingled softly in the still room. He tossed it back. "Always the money first."

"Ah, thank you my lord. It's just about priorities," the man inhaled heavily, as though he could smell the wealth he was pocketing inside his shirt. He rested a hand against it for a moment, still savoring Nilanis' tension. "Ralaris is gathering evidence to dispose of the council."

Nilanis' fist clenched. He heart dropped. "What do you mean by 'dispose of the council'?" he demanded through gritted teeth.

"Legally, I'm afraid," the assassin continued with a toss of his hand. The tone was sheer amusement now. "He's been digging around in your—and their—personal business. Quite successfully, I might add. He has enough information to put you, Cahsari, and Mikanum behind bars thus far and he's working on the others."

Nilanis felt the color drain from his face. "What could he possibly have on us?" he demanded, throat tightening.

The assassin chuckled. When Nilanis did not continue, he seemed to grasp that the question was more than rhetorical. "For Cahsari, he has evidence of the Helven's knowledge of his son's involvement in prostitution as well as the councilman's personal dabbling in Ulasum's Tooth. As for Mikanum, he has evidence that the arrogant cunt is being paid off to ignore the problems in Darival. And as for *you,* he has evidence that you are allowing illegal shipments of Ulasum's Tooth—not to mention other valuables—into port."

Nilanis rested a hand on the mantle, staring into the charred wood before him. *'Damn the True Bloods!'* His knuckles tightened, turning as white as bone. "Damn him," he whispered. He swept his hand out, sending the right side of the pieces on the mantel clattering across the floor. "*Damn him!*"

"And as I said, he's gathering information on the others," the assassin continued, seeming to savor Nilanis' panic. "And he is *quite* good at it. It's only a matter of time before he has enough information to put *all* of your pretty faces behind bars. Will your council powers save you *then?*"

Nilanis shook the chill that ran up his spine and inhaled sharply as he rounded once more to face the mercenary. "I have the information I need. There is only one last thing for you to do. *Kill* this Ralaris. And as for the information he has: destroy all of it. *And throw his body from the cliff.*"

The assassin smirked, sauntering toward the window in a nearly silent gait. "*Absolutely,* my lord," the assassin breathed. "Consider it done."

# Chapter Twenty-Three

Jikun leaned over to the damp ground and picked up the bowl of soup beside his chair. He stirred it slowly, staring at the contents with a solemn gaze.

"What is it, General?"

Jikun looked up sharply and forced a smile. "Navon, I don't believe we have the luxury to ask what our food is anymore." He leaned forward, raising the spoon to his captain's lips.

Despite his attempt to rebuff Navon's question, he imagined his captain had some idea of the contents. The food supplies were gone. The horses were gone. There was no food on their hill. The only thing the army now had in abundance was the plague… and dead soldiers.

Navon chewed slowly, a trail of brown liquid dribbling down the side of his chin. Jikun reached forward and wiped it off with his thumb.

"You're looking better," Jikun smiled reassuringly. Yes, Navon was looking better. He had pulled through the worst of the disease and had not relapsed like so many of his soldiers. Yet Navon's body was boney and his skin was taut and clammy. There was dullness in his eyes, a lifelessness that the other survivors had not shaken, either. And more than in any of his other soldiers, Navon's state rattled Jikun far below his emotional barriers.

"I'm feeling stronger," his captain breathed. He opened his mouth for another bite—there was no shame in his hunger. "But if you read me some of your poetry, I'm sure I'd feel even *better*. You know, I didn't mean what I said about it being *awful*. It was kind of charming—in a simplistic, Darivalian sort of way." He chewed again for a moment before speaking, letting Jikun glare at him reproachfully for his poor attempt at humor. Yet he returned the reproach with all its force: "You, on the other hand, do not look so well."

Jikun slowly pulled the spoon away from Navon's lips. He regarded his captain with a firm and almost reprimanding gaze. Of *course* he did not look well. His army was defeated. Thousands upon thousands lay dead. Worst of all, the plague was not finished reaping.

And yet for whatever unfathomable reason, the gods had spared *him*.

Navon swallowed and his head nodded forward slightly. Exhaustion seemed ready to take him back to sleep at any moment.

"I am fine, Navon. Let's get you well-fed before you rest. Open," Jikun barked.

And his captain obediently obeyed, for once, in silence. Jikun had rarely had a moment of quiet compliance on any matter for countless years: since the dark-haired male had been led before him as a token of the council's esteem. A supposedly unequivocal male in skill, Jikun had quickly learned that Navon's knowledge of the real world extended the width of a book and no more. *Necromancy* was proof of that naivety. And yet, if there was a way for Navon to provoke, resist, or query his inner character, he leapt on it like a thakish on a winter wolf. Curiosity… knowledge… whatever it was that drove his inner demons. '*You* are the one who needs to eat,' Navon usually would have said. 'I won't eat until you do,' he should have resisted.

But the Helven said nothing, and Jikun found himself distraught by the lack of confrontation. Even when Navon had first been appointed by the council as his captain, the male had required no time to acclimate to his new authority as captain or subordination to Jikun: he dove right into his stern and opinionated mannerisms, his jests and his taunting. Yet, he had found Navon's sense of the world a welcome and necessary reprieve from the grueling façade of obedience and lack of opinion that surrounded him in the form of simpering Sel'vi.

Navon managed to last through half the bowl before his eyes closed solidly and his head rolled to the side. Exhaustion still took him so quickly.

Jikun lifted his captain's hand and pressed his forehead into it with a sense of relief. He knew he would wake again. He knew he would live.

"General!" came a sudden, distant call.

"General!" Already the second had grown much closer.

Jikun raised his head just as the flap of Navon's tent was thrown open and a Sel'ven rushed in, a dove grasped white-knuckled in his muddy hands. "General!" He paused for a second to pant, his expression clouded in a feverish haze. "General, King Hairem has called us home!"

A moment of stunned silence held Jikun motionless. He clenched Navon's hand firmly and the bowl dropped from his hands, tumbling across the ground. "Home?" he repeated the word dumbly, staring in disbelief at the pallid face of the soldier.

"Yes, General. *Home!*"

"*THANK THE GODS!*" Jikun nearly roared. At the sight of the beaming smile on his soldier's face, Jikun quickly attempted to check his own reaction to what he presumed was more authoritative and appropriate. "Thank you," he breathed to the soldier. "Call Lieutenant Reivel and Lieutenant Seladar to my tent." He paused. Was it really necessary? He knew what he had to do.

The elf hesitated, as though sensing his uncertainty. "Is that all, General?"

Jikun nodded swiftly, masking his hesitation beneath the strong male his soldier needed to see him as. "Yes. That is all. Be quick about it." As the male departed he released Navon's hand and stood. Gods, he wished Navon could share his elation, but his friend would be unconscious for several more hours at least.

Jikun grabbed the bowl, whirling to leave, but then his motions slowed to a crawl. Just as quickly as it had come, his euphoria was fading as another thought crept into the forefront of his mind. Leaving the swamp would not come without a cost. "I could use your support right now," he whispered. "I know what I have to do."

But Navon lay still, his body too weak to keep him awake.

Jikun inhaled, drawing his struggles inside as he so often did, and stepped out of the tent into the brisk evening air. The fire at the center of the encampment burned bright, casting an orange glow across the nearby tents and soldiers.

"Good evening, General."

"You look well, General."

"It's a fine evening, General."

"How is the captain, General?"

But Jikun ignored the soldiers as he made his way to his tent just beyond the fire pit, his mind preoccupied on the task that lay ahead.

"General, is it true that we are going home?"

Jikun stopped at the sudden question, turning to see one of his soldiers leaning out of a tent, a doubtful expression on his worn face. He looked quite ill. Damn, was he next? The council had waited so long to withdraw them!—Sitting in the luxury of the city, enjoying their wines and foods while his soldiers rotted and ate their brothers' flesh…!

"General?"

Jikun snapped back to attention and waved a hand at the soldier to silence him. "Yes, soldier," he replied. "But," he continued forcefully. "Keep it quiet. I will make an announcement shortly."

"Thank the gods!" he heard the male breathe as the general broke away and continued his march past the fire.

Jikun finally ducked under the muddy flap and entered into the comfort of his tent, the air cooler by the frosted mist that he had left hanging before he had left. He took a seat at the chair before his war council's table. Lieutenant Reivel and Lieutenant Seladar… they were the last two males left on his council. Such a deathly silence lay around him. He rubbed the bridge of his nose, resting his face against his fingers as he tried not to think about who was no longer present.

*Gods*, he was exhausted. The activities of the last several weeks had drained him entirely. He had barely had time to eat, let alone sleep.

He closed his eyes, letting his head nod forward.

"Good evening, General."

Jikun looked up sharply, blinking his eyes to clear the fogginess from his mind. "Lieutenants, welcome. Please sit," he beckoned, gesturing to the seats farthest from him; hoping to create some closure to the emptiness.

The two males sat down on either side of one another, facing the general expectantly. They offered little comfort to fill the space that had once been. He felt a flicker of anger rise in him, Hairem's face at the forefront of his rage.

"A rumor is spreading like wildfire through the camp. The soldiers are saying we're being called home," Lieutenant Reivel spoke after Jikun remained silent.

Jikun nodded gravely. He had not truly expected the sickly soldier nor the messenger to keep quiet. Yes. Home. Finally. But it wouldn't be easy. He grimaced as he spoke next. "We must surrender to the centaurs." The words left his lips with a bitter aftertaste, like the remnants of a pale ale. "We cannot fight them in our condition. And we'll have to take our sick soldiers around the swamp. As you are both aware, we have no horses to carry them. We'll have to fill the supply caravan with as many sick males as we can fit within, and the rest will have to be carried."

The lieutenants exchanged looks. "Carried? All the way back to Elvorium?" Lieutenant Seladar queried. "Elvorium is… over one hundred leagues away… And what will draw the caravan… elves?"

Jikun regarded them both steadily, the sickly visage of Navon hovering at the corner of his mind. "My soldiers have sat in this swamp rotting for the damn king and council for nearly two months, surrounded by fucking horse beasts. Do you think that I am going to leave a single one of them behind? Not a damn one, do you understand? We will pull the sick with the well. We will carry the sick with the well."

"Of course not, General. But—"

"If you are proposing some way to make things easier—some way that does not include leaving one of my soldiers—go ahead and speak. If not, then be silent."

He watched the two Sel'vi exchange looks. They had been decent soldiers, but the long months had eroded Jikun's patience. "As you well know, the army is in no condition to fight. If Saebellus learns of our recall… if there is even a chance that he intercepts us on our journey to Elvorium… then this war is over."

Lieutenant Reivel interlocked his fingers, leaning forward. "General, as our information from the capital has said before, Saebellus is no doubt quite occupied with Horiembrig—he barely has enough troops to hold it as is. Even if he learns that we are to move out today—or even several days ago—there is no chance that his army could travel west fast enough to intercept us. And Saebellus would have to consider the plague in his attempt. He can certainly not afford to lose his army to this disease."

Jikun pursed his lips. It was not only Saebellus' *army* that drove his caution. "We can take no chances. We will break the army into divisions. If we are, in fact, intercepted, let it be only one division that falls and not the entirety of this army." He saw Lieutenant Seladar's lips part hesitantly. He paused, seeming to reconsider his thoughts, and then closed his mouth again. Jikun gave a wordless nod of assurance. What came next was harder to say—it was a personal affront to his pride to go groveling before the damn centaurian lord. Still, Jikun bit back his pride with some force and spoke firmly. "I will go and speak to the centaurs about their terms of surrender in the morning. Prepare the army to leave when I give the order."

"Yes, General," they both replied.

Jikun waved a hand wearily, relieved that they had listened with such silent obedience. It had been difficult enough to explain his plans without receiving a comment on their "defeat." "Go." He heard their chairs slide across the soil and their footsteps crunch slowly away beneath his tent flaps.

Perhaps his fatigue was more visible than he realized.

He leaned his forehead against the table, mentally and emotionally exhausted. Surrendering to the centaurs… He had never had to surrender before. But… at least it was not to Saebellus… Elven warlords were known for executing the enemy general as essential and inflexible terms of surrender.

Fortunately, centaurs were not known for the same finality.

*

"The terms?" Hashauel, the centaurian leader, trotted a few steps around Jikun. "The terms…" He stopped, gazing at the dozens of centaurs waiting stoically behind him. They moved ever so slightly as he regarded their attentive faces, shifting from hoof to hoof and flexing their strong bodies as though to remind Jikun how inferior he was. Hashauel himself was flicking his tail to and fro irritably, his great, muscular haunches flexing as he paced. "We have seen the stars, General of the Elves. Never before have our people warred the elves. Dark times lie ahead. But your leaders' days are numbered: as are *yours*, General." He reached forward and drew the blade from Jikun's sheath, turning it over slowly. "Our god has punished you enough. Turn over all weapons and armor your army possesses to my children as a symbol of peace. Then you and your army may go." He leaned forward, pushing the icy hilt back against the sheath. "I will leave you alone with your blade, as a gesture on our half of the agreement."

Jikun felt the weight of the sword drop against his leg. One sword amongst thousands: it was more mockery than leaving him with nothing. He unstrapped his breastplate and dropped it before the horse lord. "Your terms are fair and merciful," he replied stiffly, bowing his head in respect.

But internally, he reeled from the request. To travel one hundred leagues to Elvorium unarmed…? *'Saebellus* must *stay in Horiembrig…'*

"Now go, elf lord," Hashauel ordered, pointing toward the hill. "And deliver the weapons and armor here by nightfall on the morrow. Any actions taken that are anything other than peaceful shall be interpreted as a sign of continued war… and we shall reap what is left of your army."

Jikun tossed his dagger down beside the breastplate. "There will be no aggression from us," he assured. Judging by the appearance of Hashauel's guard, they alone would be enough to finish off what was left of his army. *'Damn council!'*

*

With the pile of armor and weapons behind them as a towering symbol of their defeat in that murky wasteland, Jikun led his army from the hillside of the Sevilan Marshes, out toward Elvorium. A few cautions centaurs trailed them—undoubtedly under Hashauel's orders—but Jikun could do nothing but watch them bitterly as his troops circumvented the swamp. As Jikun had ordered, the caravans sprinkled amongst his troops were pulled by soldiers instead of horses, groaning and straining under the weight of countless bodies of elves.

As the ill died, those that could be spared from the fate of food were burned. And the weight grew lighter. Sixty thousand elves had left to war the centaurs.

Thirty thousand now returned to Elvorium.

In two years of vicious combat with the warlord Saebellus, Jikun had lost fifty thousand soldiers. In a few months entrenched on a hill, he had lost thirty thousand. It sickened him. Every fiber of his being bent under the weight of his hatred for the king and the council. For every soldier who had died retching. For every soldier who had barely survived. And for every soldier who was forced to eat his brothers or starve.

That was what the great and mighty General Jikun and his undefeated army had been reduced to by the council and its pawn.

He scowled in detestation. This was the *council's* defeat, not his! He could so clearly recall the derision in the face of that centaurian beast, mocking his defeat by allowing him to keep his blade. All of that—*all* of that contempt and failure belonged to the council alone!

As they exited the swamp grounds and their escort of centaurs departed, Jikun's predetermined divide to the army obediently split into its three divisions and embarked for home.

"Travel safe," Jikun said, clasping a hand on Reivel's and Seladar's shoulders as the soldiers behind them moved away in their appointed directions.

"May Sel'ari keep you safe as well," Seladar replied heavily. "We shall all see each other in Elvorium soon."

Jikun turned back to the ten thousand males left under his watch. Just ahead, he could distinguish the pale wisp of his black-haired captain, propped up inside a cart, surrounded by ill and feeble soldiers. The persistent sound of coughing between them was as common as the sound of the division's feet trudging toward the capital.

“What if Saebellus does intercept us?” his captain spoke softly as Jikun drew up beside him. He leveled another shameless bark to the males dragging his cart, ordering them to quicken their pace. It was yet another rhetorical question from his captain—a provocation to Jikun’s own feelings, as though he demanded to be shown what lay beyond the general’s carefully composed mask of ice.

Fear. Exhaustion. And in his relief that Navon had found his strength enough to query once more, he allowed those feelings to manifest themselves, albeit faintly, in the creases at the corners of his eyes.

He met the dull azure gaze of his captain with lips pursed into a hard, thin line. *‘What if Saebellus does intercept us...?’* he repeated in his mind. He looked away to the east, a chill running up his spine at the perceived darkness growing at their backs. *‘If Saebellus thinks like me... and gods know he does...’* He inhaled heavily, replying in a grim tone, “It’s not Saebellus’ army I’m worried about, Navon.”

*

Even free of the Sevilan Marshes, Jikun found that the pace of his army remained at a burdened crawl. His attempts to spur on their progress left him raw of voice and his footsteps were reduced to merely a long drag beside the cart. Yet despite their pace, there was no complaint about the heat, the lack of food, or insufficient rest: his army traveled toward Elvorium as though she could be glimpsed on the very horizon itself.

But at their pace, Jikun feared they were yet weeks away. He glanced up into the azure sky, eyes falling to the orange glow radiating from the horizon. The sun was setting, nestling down into the western sea, sending up clouds of smoke as her fiery surface hit the cool waters.

“Halt!” Jikun shouted, his throat twinging in raw pain. He rested a hand on the shoulder of one of the front soldiers pulling Navon’s cart. “We’re going to rest here for the night!”

There was a mummer of relief from the nearest soldiers that spread outward through the troops as news reached them. He could see the army fanning out. Normally, the white peaks of tents would have followed such movement, but such non-necessities had been abandoned in favor of the ill and weak. He looked toward the sky, relieved that there was no rain in sight.

"Here, let me help you down," Jikun offered sympathetically, grabbing the nearest soldier on the cart under the arms and helping him down into the long grass.

"Th-thank you, General," the male stammered weakly.

Jikun slid away to a weak semblance of privacy nearby, and seated himself down near the shade of a tree. Yet, no sooner had he settled back against the trunk than the sound of softly jogging footsteps reached him. He looked up.

"General, I've sent the healthy males out to the nearby surroundings to gather food and water to supplement the…" the soldier paused his pant to trail off.

Jikun did not need him to finish the sentence. He instead let his thoughts reflect on what had been completed, grimacing faintly at the thought of gathering food for ten thousand males. "…Good work, soldier," he finally breathed.

It took many hours before the same male reappeared, offering a handful of berries, wheat, and a sadly pathetic fish dwarfed by the large leaf upon which it lay. "Here, General," the soldier offered. "We have been quite successful."

Jikun took the leaf and nodded his head in thanks, certain to appear quite impressed with their achievement. "Good work, soldier. Now go rest."

The night fell over the plain gradually, turning the world around them to a darkness lit only by the white light of Noctem's crescent moon. It remained cool and quiet, damp and dark. And a few hours before dawn, Jikun roused his men.

The dew drops clung to their bodies and nearby grass, rolling off as they stood and straightened themselves. The ill were once more gathered and placed onto the caravan's carts.

"Alright, move out!" Jikun bellowed, his voice strong after the rest. He watched as the soldiers stepped forward without complaint and moved once more for the north. He placed a hand on the cart beside Navon. "I feel like I had a root shoved into my shoulder all night."

Navon smirked. "I slept on a rock. But I couldn't bring myself to tell the weary soldiers to move me…" He chuckled slightly, but rolled his shoulders as though to push off the ache.

Jikun took a moment to smile in his amusement before he dropped his hand from the cart and barked his first orders of the march. "Do you want to stay in this field all week?" he hollered. "Move it! Elvorium isn't coming to us!"

"You should shout more. I think you're inspiring progress."

Jikun shot his captain a glare. "Don't mock me, Navon. These soldiers need a push to keep going." He glanced pointedly at the cart. "They'd *much* rather leave you behind." And as harsh as his words to his comrade were, he found relief in the venom they spat: soon there would be a council to bite, instead.

Navon's face twisted in annoyance. "I was jesting, but now you're getting a little—"

"Move it! We just started!" Jikun hollered over Navon's rebuke.

The moon lowered in the west as the males pressed forward, but the light of dawn was still indistinguishable below the line of the horizon.

"What did I tell you? They haven't asked to rest yet," Jikun spoke almost triumphantly.

They had indeed made progress since they had risen: all trace of the swamplands was gone and the sour stench of its marshy waters had vanished entirely.

Navon opened his mouth as though searching for a clever response, but his weakened mind failed him and his jaw closed with a surrendering smile. Jikun would take what positives he could from the plague.

Without warning, cries erupted from the south like a howling wind, tearing toward the north end of Jikun's division like a storm. He glanced up once, but the cloudless sky reflected nothing but a dark blue void.

"What is it, General?" the soldiers around him stammered as silence briefly returned.

Navon put a hand to his hip, but his sword lay leagues behind in the heap of battered armor for the centaurian horde. Jikun refrained from clasping his weapon, trying to maintain a calmly rigid composure even as dread clawed at the recesses of his mind. He could spot a male rushing toward them, his face deathly pale. "Scout, what is it?" he shouted to the ragged soldier.

The male stumbled to a stop before him, gasping for breath. "The Beast, General!!"

The cries that had died briefly rose once more, growing louder and more frantic as the cause of their fear drew nearer. Jikun could see his soldiers running to the side, the clean marching line scattered like dust to the wind. A body sailed high into the air before it vanished into the mass of elves fleeing the carnage.

"*The Beast.*" Jikun's pale skin grew deathly white, his composure lost. He drew his sword swiftly from its sheath, aware of how naked the troops around him lay. "Captain, get the army north!"

There was no fighting this time.

Jikun turned away and hurried through the ranks of soldiers who were scrambling away in fear and disarray: he ran toward the beast. He could glimpse a shadow of the creature, even as the nearest males vainly attempted to block its path. The beast tore through them like a blade through water, dispersing their bodies to the side. Jikun was painfully aware that the chainmail on his body was more than all the armor his entire army had left.

The ranks before him parted finally inward with a deafening blow of fear: the beast raised a soldier above its head in triumph. Its skin was brown in the moonlight, its black, knotted hair shimmering with grease near its scalp. It slammed the male down onto the two horns sweeping back across its skull, shattering the male's fragile body on the hard, ridged bone.

The soldier's limp body flopped down into the grass before the creature. The beast raised one tattered leather boot and stepped down onto the male's skull as it advanced. There was a crack of bone and the skull smashed out around its heel.

Jikun's stomach dropped. The beast looked up suddenly, as though sensing his gaze. Its eyes locked with Jikun's even as the soldiers made to regroup before him in a final, desperate shield of protection. Without so much as a glance toward the other soldiers around it, the beast suddenly tore forward, pushing off the ground with a roar, its tattered wings pressed tightly against its back.

"General, behind us!" a soldier nearby shouted, darting in front of him, raising a stick he had managed to find in the open plain—the army's only weapon.

Jikun knocked him aside in a single, swift motion. "FOLLOW THE CAPTAIN TO THE NOR—" But his words died as the beast slammed its body into a nearby soldier, hurling the male into Jikun.

The Darivalian flew backward in turn into the male behind him, spinning head over heel and finally sprawling windless on the grass, his chest aching. Hands grasped for him, but a sudden wall of ice was erected around him, throwing the soldiers away. "I SAID GET OUT OF HERE!" Jikun roared.

There was a moment of hesitation, but as the beast launched itself toward the ice, Jikun could see the soldiers around him stumble away.

"Get everyone out!" Jikun hollered again. The shadow of the beast flickered for a moment outside the wall. His heart froze.

The ice before him shattered, spraying tiny shards across the nearest soldiers. Jikun instinctively closed his eyes, raising his arm to block the fragments.

He felt a hand grip onto his raised arm and his eyes flashed open. The face of the beast was mere feet from him, smooth and unscarred. He could detect a powerful odor of sewage and dirt, with a lingering scent of rotting meat. The black pupils dilated to mere slits as the creature gazed back. Jikun could see the muscles in the creature's thick neck flex. Its top lip curled, revealing several unnaturally sharp teeth vanishing into the darkness of its mouth.

Where the creature's grip tightened Jikun forced his attention, feeling a rush of strength leave him as his concentration increased. There was a sharp cry of alarm and the beast released his arm, hissing vehemently as it flexed its suddenly stiff and frosted hand.

Not nearly as potent as he had intended, but it would have to do.

Jikun swept his hand down as he launched his body forward, picking up a shard of ice that lay in the long blades of grass. He shoved it into the calf of the beast's leg as he moved, diving out of the broken wall of ice at his side. A breeze swept past his skull in deadly force and he imagined that he had just narrowly dodged a bulging fist.

The beast snarled in pain as it turned with him, its yellow eyes narrowed in rage.

The shouts of fleeing soldiers still sounded from nearby as the army gave the two a wide berth, but the beast's attention remained locked on Jikun. It rose up and pushed off the ground suddenly, ignoring the shard of ice still protruding from its calf.

Its rage was far greater than its pain.

*'Damn it! I'm even* less *equipped to combat this creature than usual!'* Jikun whirled to the side, focusing on the earth at the creature's large, tattered boots. Stalagmites of ice burst from the ground, piercing through the legs and feet of the beast, tearing through the other side of its brown, thick flesh, shattering against its powerful bones.

A scream of agony was the only reaction the beast gave. Rather than fall to its knees, it tore forward with greater anger and determination, slamming its fist through the desperate shield of ice Jikun formed before him. Horrified, Jikun could do nothing as the fist carried forward and collided with his shoulder. The general could feel his arm snap clear from its socket, the flesh swelling as blood rushed to the wound. He plummeted into the ground with a shuddering cry.

"Damn. *It!*" he gasped as he used his remaining arm to raise himself from the ground, forcing his body up through the pain. *'Don't stop moving!'* he warned himself. But he didn't need to attach a threat—that was right behind him.

And the creature carried forward, no hesitation between attacks. Jikun raised a hand again, desperately trying to gather the water in the air to form a barrier around him, but he knew his pathetic grasp of magic outside of Darival would not be enough. The ice above him shattered like glass and the fist came crashing down toward his skull.

There was a sudden eruption of smoke and force beneath them, hurling their bodies as one into the air. Jikun felt the weight of his body arch and then drop. Beside him, the beast flailed out in confusion, slamming its wing into the side of Jikun's chest, pitching him back to the earth. With an agile twist, it landed away from the smoke, snarling cautiously at the ground as it retreated a step. Jikun landed clumsily on his feet, off-balanced by the uneven ground as pain ripped through his shoulder. He exhaled heavily and raised his eyes.

*Navon.* His captain was crouched not far from them, trembling slightly as he held himself upright on an abandoned cart, his clammy face twisted in concentration. His skin was deathly white.

Murios' words rushed back to him. Even through the agony in his shoulder, his answer did not waver. "*No*," Jikun whispered, hardly audible to himself.

He could see the smoke vanish into the earth and a sudden, eerie twist of faint, spectral faces rose from behind the beast.

As though sensing the aura behind him, the beast whipped around, stumbling now as though pain seemed to finally reach it. Perhaps it too had been rushing through a fog of adrenaline.

Jikun focused on the ground behind it. "Come on," he whispered. "Come on, damn it." He tried to remember the feeling at the tent when he had formed the stalagmite—the feeling of harnessing his power away from the abundance of water in Darival. But he needed elements larger than the ice he had conjured in his tent. Much larger. He bit his lip, digging his fingers into the soil. "Come on…"

Navon's shadows suddenly burst for the beast and, as it leapt aside, a stalagmite tore through the earth and pierced its chest, pulling the creature inches off the ground and hanging it before the wisps.

Jikun could not see the creature's face, but the cry that it emitted was one of terrible fear and agony, as though for the briefest moment it could feel as mortals did. The blackened, twisted wisps enveloped it in a thin, surreal mist. And the beast's cries grew louder.

Jikun opened his mouth in a shout of triumph, the shock of victory momentarily elating him, but the sound of shattering ice cut off his call.

The ice had shattered beneath the force of the beast's heavy fist and it dropped to its feet on the still and silent earth. As though it had forgotten the pain, it tore away from the wisps, moving across the ground unhampered by its injuries. It hardly glanced at Jikun as it fled away in desperation toward the east.

Jikun felt his chest expand suddenly, his mind recalling the need to breathe. He inhaled sharply in relief, his legs growing stronger as fear fled with the last visible remnants of the beast's form. The troops remained in disarray behind the general, but his attention slowly shifted toward the other solitary figure: the only one remaining nearby. He ignored the tensed muscles flickering pain through his shoulder and merely pursed his lips in an attempt to push the pain aside.

He rounded sharply on his captain, his eyes meeting Navon's. "How dare you…! I told you! I told you!" he breathed venomously, even above the knowledge that the necromancy had saved them once again.

His captain smiled faintly and lurched forward onto the earth, a sudden glaze falling across his eyes as they locked blankly out into the grass.

Jikun's gut dropped. *'The Realms are not a place for mortal men,'* Murios had warned him. *'And souls do not freely leave it.'* Jikun stumbled, hearing the distant sound of soldiers hurrying toward him, their panic just as great as when they had fled. "Navon? Navon?!" He fell to his knees beside him and reached frantically for the captain's neck.

Navon blinked slowly, causing Jikun's hand to snap away in surprise. "Gods, it takes it right out of you, doesn't it?"

"So help me, Navon," Jikun growled in relief. *'He could have died!'*

The soldiers behind them had grown close again, murmuring in nervousness even after the beast's figure had entirely vanished into the distance. "Are you alright, General?!" several called from across the field, but Jikun merely raised his good hand to signal his response. They moved away then, through the chaos left in the creature's wake, to filter through the bodies in order to find the living and burn the dead.

Jikun pulled Navon to his feet and supported him around his shoulders. *'How many soldiers saw his necromancy...?'* he reflected stiffly, eyes flicking across the silent field.

Navon smiled weakly, chuckling as though they had merely tussled with a girl. "Just like the time you got wasted in Raestra and picked a fight with that huge human. And I had to run to your aid and got punched out for it..." he trailed off in an attempt to lighten the mood.

*'No, this is nothing like that time,'* Jikun thought darkly, but he feigned polite amusement as he helped Navon back into the cart. "Stay here," he ordered. "We'll be moving out shortly." He glanced into the distance. The wounds the creature had sustained were severe... still, Jikun did not feel they would stop it for long.

*

The sight of Elvorium on the horizon could bring nothing less than the greatest cries of relief from Jikun's soldiers. He could barely keep himself from falling to his own knees and kissing the earth, even within vision of the arrogant king's palace rising up at the forefront of the capital.

"Navon, do you see that?" he breathed, dragging his ragged feet toward the southern bridge spanning the canyon of the city. Across the way he could see the gates open, but the guards raised hands against their approach. Thousands of tents reflected the sunlight before them.

No doubt the city would place them in this quarantine.

"I've never seen anything so beautiful," the captain replied from his ogling seat on the edge of the wagon.

The soldiers pulling it stopped, collapsing in relief and tears, sickening Jikun with cries of "praise Sel'ari!" that dared escape their lips.

"Two years from home and they cheer. Half a year from home and they weep." But Jikun did not rebuke them. He helped Navon down and held him steady for a moment, feeling a sudden wave of protectiveness for the frail male beside him. He scowled at the palace and away to the scattering of white tents across the canyon. "It appears the city has had the decency to prepare a place for us to be kept." He could hear his own unintentional cynicism as he spoke.

Navon nodded and leaned against the wagon for further support, seemingly ignoring the implications of his statement.

Jikun turned his attention back to the gates of the city. He could see faces peering up over the wall cautiously, as though the plague itself would leap over the canyon directly into their bodies. He scowled in disgust.

Still… his eyes narrowed along the expanse of the capital's canyon bride. One figure had abandoned the safety of the gates and dared approach them.

Jikun felt his heart rate quicken and his gaze harden as his eyes distinguished the male. *The king.* He ignored the shouts of the guards across the bridge as he took several brisk steps onto it.

A sudden clink of metal bouncing off stone brought him to an abrupt stop.

*'Damn it… '* he thought to himself angrily, looking up to the soldier along the wall who had fired a warning shot. He saw Hairem raise a hand to the guards and they lowered their weapons.

"Jikun, stop."

The warning came from behind him this time. Jikun turned to see that Navon had made his way to his side and was leaning precariously on the archway of the bridge. Jikun glanced once over the side and felt his stomach drop like a stone. "Navon, you shouldn't be here," he growled.

"Jikun, they have good reason to keep us away from the city," Navon insisted. "Come away."

Jikun did not move forward, but neither did he leave. He stood quite still, feeling his anger boiling up inside him as Hairem slithered closer.

And when Hairem finally stopped before him, Jikun did not hesitate. The thoughts assaulting his mind were too many to distinguish. But they all chorused the same verse: *Damn the king to Ramul.* He charged in a single, swift thrust of his body to punch Hairem in his clean, healthy face, but arms swiftly wrapped around him from behind and wrestled him back.

"JIKUN!" Navon roared in rebuke.

Hairem paused in a slow, considerate blink, but his face remained quite calm. He raised his hand again against the city watch. "General, there is no apology I can give you for what has happened to your army. But outside the city, they will be well taken care of until the healers can determine that their disease is no longer infectious." He looked past them to the male-pulled wagons and piles of soldiers draped across the wooden plank. "How—"

"WHAT IN RAMUL IS WRONG WITH YOU BASTARDS?!" Jikun bellowed, hurling Navon aside angrily, his fury only heightened by the restraint his sickly captain had managed to muster. "MY SOLDIERS WERE OUT IN THAT SWAMP DYING OF PLAGUE FOR MONTHS." His hand shot out, grabbing the king by the front of his abhorrently clean shirt, to jerk him forward and nearly off his feet. "I lost thirty thousand good elves, Hairem. THIRTY THOUSAND. Do you understand this number?! HALF OF THE MALES I TOOK SOUTH ARE DEAD. And do you know what else?" He shook him, striving to shake some expression out of the king other than calm collectedness. It enraged him further. How dare he look so calm! "The supply caravans? Eaten. The horses? Eaten. The dead soldiers? Eaten. AND THEN WE WERE NEARLY SLAUGHTERED BY THE BEAST! While you fucking bastards sat behind those pretty pearl walls whoring and eating and wasting away on fine wines, my soldiers…" He felt a wave of exhaustion hit him in the chest, the walls of his rage breaking to release his adrenaline as well. He caught the archway for balance. "My soldiers died…" His hand fell from Hairem and he stumbled. "Suffered. And…" His knees gave out and he lurched forward.

Hairem caught him under the arms, a pained grimace splitting his face. "Captain," the king barked to Navon. "Help me take the general to his quarters. He is clearly unwell. I will send a healer to him straight away."

Jikun's head rolled to the side weakly, his mind growing hazy. The strength he had fought to sustain for months was gone. He let his body sink entirely. Damn… into the arms of the king, of all the damned people… Hairem grunted as he repositioned his weight to support him and Navon made his way over to assist.

"General?" Navon asked in concern. "General are you—"

"No," Jikun breathed softly. "I just need rest…"

He felt the two move back across the bridge toward the sprawling array of white tents. They took him into the nearest one on the canyon edge, laying him on a bed of furs and silks. A full pitcher of water was already sitting on the small table in the center of the tent.

"The kingdom spared no expense to ensure that you and your army are comfortable during your recovery. They shall want for nothing," Hairem spoke, pulling the general's ragged boots off and tossing them out the tent flap.

Jikun opened his eyes slightly to catch the horrified expression on Navon's pale face. *'What does it matter, Navon? The king owes us servitude,'* he thought irritably.

"I'm afraid it was not easy to return you to the city… Had I the courage to go against the council earlier, I would have done so. But, if I had, chances are your return would have been unwelcome. I acquired recent leverage that allowed this to take place. The crown doesn't have the coin to cover everything you see here. The El'adorium assisted."

Nilanis? Jikun frowned slightly as Hairem laid his head back. *'I thought that snake—'*

"But I thought the council was backing the return?" Navon inquired.

Hairem nodded. "They are now, but I'm afraid it is primarily to ensure the marriage of myself to Nilanis' daughter."

Jikun's eyes focused. "You sold yourself out to the council?"

Hairem threw his last boot outside the tent. "No. My engagement and love to Ilsevel are genuine. General, is there anything I need to know before I send for a healer?"

Jikun raised a hand slightly. "I'll need thirty thousand new swords, daggers, and sets of armor. And the council's heads on pikes."

Hairem grimaced slightly. "Rest, general. I will send for the healers. I shall pray to Sel—"

Jikun hissed venomously, "Do not ever say that name in my presence."

Hairem and Navon exchanged a look before the king left the tent and Jikun closed his eyes. "Get out, Navon. Go take care of the troops and then get to your tent and get some god damn rest."

"…General… your blasphemy is going to get you—"

"*Necromancer*," Jikun hissed.

Navon's jaw snapped shut and Jikun heard the tent flap fall closed a moment later. Already, he felt himself rapidly slipping into unconsciousness.

*They were finally home.*

# CHAPTER TWENTY-FOUR

"And that is why we will need to pull together in order to pay for the replacement armor and weapons that the general has requested." Hairem leaned forward on his hands, eyeing the council solemnly. He felt guilt sink into him as he recalled Jikun's anger and frustration… and his grief. If he had opposed the council, refused what he knew to be a mistake to begin with, thirty thousand more of his people would be alive today. They were his responsibility. *His*.

And he had failed them.

He remembered his confidence—his *triumph* when he had walked into the council chambers to announce his engagement to Ilsevel and his recall of the general. What a haughty fool he had been. "Even worse than the loss of their gear are the spirits of his—*our*—soldiers. They are fatigued and broken. As soon as I receive word from the healers that individuals are considered 'safe,' they shall not only be allowed into the city, but they will be given whatever assistance they need to recover. The families who lost their loved ones in the crusade shall be given ten years' worth of soldier's pay as compensation for the immeasurable loss they have incurred."

Thunder rumbled in the distance as the room remained silent. Hairem could hear the rain pounding against the glass, dark grey skies looming ominously overhead. He wondered if the general's troops were warm and comfortable. They had not had a morning quite like this in a while, and he counted it ill luck that such poor weather should come just days after the army had made camp.

Cahsari began to stand, but as he caught Nilanis' eye, he returned to his seat, leaning back and scowling angrily. They had been far less difficult to deal with in the last month since he had announced his marriage to the daughter of their El'adorium. And he was relieved for this, if not a little ashamed that it was through Ilsevel that he had achieved their obedience.

Valdor stood instead, his eyes scanning the room briefly. "If the general requires new arms and weapons, then I shall certainly add what I can to the funding of such a request."

The room's occupants were once more silent for a moment as a roar of wind swept past the windows, howling away into the city.

Hairem cleared his throat for their attention, appreciative of Valdor's boldness.

"And I as well," Heshellon finally broke in with a smile, as though refocusing from his own thoughts to join the conversation at hand. "After all, I feel accountable for their condition. And I do not believe the crown should be solely responsible for such a financial burden when it was the crown that attempted to dissuade the council from making this choice to begin with. My people greatly value proof of service and character, and if their steadfast fidelity does not entitle Jikun's soldiers to everything you have said and more, then what does? The Eph'vi will support this motion."

Nilanis gave a slight, grimacing nod before he took control of the situation in his ever-commanding tone. "I will ensure that the council acquires all of the funds necessary to make such—"

There was a sudden roar of wind as the doors to the council room flew open and slammed against the walls behind them with a crack like thunder. Rain pelted in fiercely, showering the chamber in ice-cold droplets as a male stumbled in behind their flurry. He caught his balance swiftly on the railing beside him and kicked one of the pursuing guards squarely in the chest to send him tumbling from the room. A gasp swept through the council and Hairem stepped back, eyes wide as he gaped at the intruder. But shock had frozen all other males in the room.

*'Another assassin?!'*

The elf's clothing clung to his tall, lean frame and his finely chiseled face was knotted in a mix of fatigue and concern. His emerald eyes were vividly bright against the darkness. Hairem had never met the male before, and yet there was something strikingly familiar about him.

Nilanis stood abruptly, his eyes wide as though with fear. "Your Majesty! This male is called Ralaris. He is a known dealer of Ulasum's—!"

The male's cape whipped out past him, tangling around his legs as he pushed away from the railing. "Your Majesty," he spoke out of breath, failing to acknowledge the speaker's rebuke. "Ilsevel has been taken by Saebellus!"

The room erupted with shock and questions. Hairem felt his heart quicken and his complexion pale. His chest tightened, causing the still-healing wound to twinge sharply. Gods, no! "How do you know this?!" he demanded loudly over the others. "I have heard nothing of it!"

The room quieted in desperation to hear the response. The guards had appeared back at the doorway, rain pouring off their armor to puddle at their feet, but Hairem held his hand up sharply. Their weapons were drawn at the male's back—that was enough, even as the intruder gave them no regard.

Nilanis' mouth was hanging open in speechless horror and his lips desperately attempted to form some response.

"You are hearing of it now, Your Majesty," the intruder breathed before Nilanis could speak again. "And if you should wait too long, you shall hear it from Saebellus as well."

Hairem bit his lip. The male's accent was foreign. No doubt he was a Sel'ven, but his speech placed him from somewhere on Ryekarayn. He narrowed his eyes, scanning the male's elegant cotton clothes, sodden and mud-stained from the rain, and his heavily adorned blade. Yet, Nilanis had called him a drug dealer. "Who are you?" he demanded in attempted skepticism. There was something unsettlingly commanding about the male. "*How do you know this?*"

The male's eyes remained focused on Hairem as doubt erupted around him. "I pay well to be informed of anything of interest while I make my stay here, Your Majesty."

Hairem walked stiffly around his desk, making his way toward the elf. "Your vague—"

"DO you want to continue asking me questions of no importance or do you want to save your future queen?" the male demanded sharply, cutting Hairem off.

Hairem was taken aback, drawing to an abrupt halt. Who would dare speak as he did to the king… and openly before the council?!

But Ilsevel's safety forced him to push aside his questions. "How long ago was she taken?"

"Two days. I just received word of the capture and came immediately. Saebellus will no doubt ransom her and use the profit to fund his war against the kingdom. His demands will arrive within a week. Do not allow it. If you send a rescue mission, Saebellus will be caught by surprise. Horiembrig has countless underground tunnels leading into the city. You can rescue Ilsevel and avoid bending to the warlord's demands," the male said, pushing his short hair from his face.

Hairem found it difficult to swallow. Was it true? Ilsevel had been taken? If that *was* true, this male was right—Saebellus would ransom her and use the money to fund the war. He could not allow it—he could not allow more of his soldiers to die for Saebellus' cause!

He ran a hand down his face, noticing how cold his skin felt. This was fear. He inhaled unsteadily. "I will go for her," he breathed.

"What?" Valdor demanded, stepping around his desk as well. "You cannot, Your Majesty. Such a decision is irrational. There are soldiers who—"

"Ilsevel is my *bride*. I will *not* send—"

"Your Majesty," the stranger interrupted sharply, raising a hand adorned in thin, gold rings. "Let me. Your council member is correct. You cannot go into Saebellus' hands and risk your death or capture. The kingdom cannot take the strain of a second bloodline lost in a mere three hundred years. I will go in your stead, if you allow it."

"I do not even know *who you are*," Hairem threw his hands up angrily. "Shut the damn doors already—I can hardly hear myself think!" The guards before the council hall immediately pulled the doors shut and the howling wind was left to beat against them outside.

The room grew quiet.

"I am Sellemar, Your Majesty. This may suffice to answer your inquiries." He reached into the front of his shirt, gingerly pulling out a piece of wet parchment and carefully unfolding it. "A letter written on my behalf by King Sairel, attesting to my credibility." He held out the parchment as Hairem made his way forward, hushed voices following him. "Time is crucial. Every minute you delay, the window of opportunity shrinks. I will rescue Lady Ilsevel. Not for you. Not for her. For the kingdom. There is nothing I want. I brought you the information in hopes that you will not make the mistake of sending some average soldier to do an elite's work—when the ransom demands finally come. If I lie, then it is only myself I put in danger and no ransom shall come. But if you believe me, then when Saebellus' threats come, you shall make no moves to acquire the funds. I will already be at her side. You may select a male to accompany me if you wish. I will provide a second of my own."

Hairem reached out and took the parchment slowly, the male's words causing his mind to slow in disbelief. King Sairel? What association did this male have with the True Bloods? He scanned the page briefly, noting first the unmistakable seal of the royal family. "...hereby attest to the skill and virtue of

Sellemar. His word is my word. His life is my own…" he trailed off inaudibly. He found his mind overwhelmed with shock. He had never heard of anyone bearing such immense approval from a royal member before… let alone a king. *'His life is my own…'* It was not just a sentence—it was a threat. King Sairel not only vouched for the male, but threatened those who meant him harm with his own retribution. Sairel's father may have disowned Sevrigel entirely, but for this male, Sairel was willing to do *anything. Who was he?* He looked up, studying the stranger in a new light.

"You lose nothing by sending me. You have nothing but my word to go on and nothing to lose but the person who brought you the information to begin with," Sellemar continued with confidence.

Hairem inhaled sharply, turning and pacing slowly. The male was right. Ilsevel could be captured. If the male was wrong, Hairem would lose nothing. If he was right, saving her would prevent Saebellus from either harming her or using her against him.

And here… here was the testament from King Sairel himself!

"Alright, Sellemar. I will entrust you with this and pray to the gods there is not some way I can be punished for it," Hairem finally spoke, pressing his hand softly to the wound on his chest.

The male gave a short nod. "And someone to accompany me?"

A roll of thunder rumbled outside the hall, vibrating the glass with great temper. It was as though even the gods themselves roared in fury at Saebellus' gall.

*'Someone…'* Hairem considered for a moment. There was only one male he trusted entirely with Ilsevel's safety, though he had failed to stop the male before them. Still… "My personal guard, Erallus," he spoke finally. "I would have you take him."

Sellemar nodded once. "Then I shall. He is to arrive at room two at The Whistling Glade in three hours' time." He turned and pulled the doors open, looking back once over his shoulder. Hairem caught the confidence in his gaze before the doors snapped shut behind him.

"Hairem, I do not…" Nilanis began. "Ralaris… Or Sellemar—I was clearly mistaken about his business… But I have never heard of him. He's clearly foreign. I—"

"And what do you propose I do, Nilanis? Wait until Saebellus sends a ransom demand and *expects* some action to rescue her? If we fail after his demands I do not expect that we will be treated kindly. Or she. If Sellemar is telling the truth, then this is the best course of action. Jikun took his best soldiers to the swamp and now they are half-dead. I have no other elf of skill except my own personal guard, most of which I have sent to Darival. What would you have me do? *King Sairel* testifies to his abilities. Have you ever heard such strong language between a king and… anyone? 'His life is my own' is hardly a light phrase. I cannot testify to any of my elves with such language. Not even Erallus."

The council members exchanged looks. Nilanis clenched his fists. "I ask that you not risk her life! So Saebellus asks for a ransom! Coin is merely coin! This is my daughter!"

"*And my bride*. There is *no one* who is more concerned about her safety than I am, Nilanis. But I can't send the rebel money to fund his war and sieges against the kingdom. I *cannot*. We have just incurred a tremendous cost from that *damn* war with the centaurs! Too many have died already and I will not be responsible for more deaths."

Valdor slid the rain from the side of his face and wiped his hand across his chest. "The king is right. There are some obvious pieces of information we can gather from this male. He is from Ryekarayn. He is wealthy. He has a close relationship with King Sairel. He knows Horiembrig. And he has clearly done things like this before. We're probably dealing with some cleric of a righteous god; as he is a Sel'ven, perhaps even of Sel'ari herself. Or, less likely, he could be a mercenary. But regardless, I'd wager more money on that male's success than one of Jikun's plagued soldiers."

Hairem raised a hand. "I, for one, do not have further time to discuss this. The decision has been made. I must inform Erallus immediately of his mission." He had to get out of the room. His heart was torn in conflict. But he knew he could not pay Saebellus a ransom. Not… Not even for Ilsevel. He pushed the door open and stepped out into the rain. Gods. *Why?!* He had been trying to do as Sel'ari would want of him. He was battling the council. He was taking a good wife. What benefit did it grant them to punish him like this?

"I am sorry, My Lord. He fought his way in. We were outmatched," Erallus' words interrupted his thoughts. There was a flick of green as his eyes shifted away and his broad shoulders slumped over his lean frame. His voice lowered, "Gods… first the assassin and now this male. I have failed shamefully twice… I don't deserve to—"

Hairem paused, a hand going to the side of his chest subconsciously. His mind briefly churned at the implication of those words. Then he shook his head. "It doesn't matter now. I told you to forget about the assassin. I lived.

You saved my life. Let it go. I need you to go with him, Erallus. You heard what he said about Ilsevel?"

Erallus nodded gravely. Hairem could see the shame on his face at his failure, but the king had no heart for encouragement. Erallus quickly followed Hairem down the steps to the square.

"His name is Sellemar. He's in room two at The Whistling Glade. You are to meet him in three hours' time."

Erallus paused, hanging his head. "I apologize, My Lord."

"Erallus, it's *done*. Next time, you will not let someone into the Hall. I am certain of this. But that is not what matters right now. I need you to do this for me. I need you to bring Ilsevel back."

Erallus looked up, his thin lips pursed, his expression now strong and bolstering with confidence, as though to shake the concern from Hairem. "Yes, My Lord. I will bring her back."

"Then go. Now. I do not need you to walk me back." He gestured to his second personal guard who lagged behind them, no doubt as ashamed as Erallus at having been jointly bested in a fight by a single elf—a male who had refused to even use a weapon.

Erallus gave a sweeping bow and hurried away down the dark, rainy streets. Hairem watched him for a moment. *'Bring her back...'* He started as a flash of lightening silhouetted the statues of the six ancient heroes beside him. He turned to them, clasping his hands at his lips. "Please," he whispered aloud. "Please, help... them... bring her back!"

# CHAPTER TWENTY-FIVE

Sellemar took a seat by the window of his room, watching the rain drizzle onto the cobbled stones below. Judging by the light in the east, it would let up entirely by the time Erallus arrived. He leaned an elbow onto the windowsill, his breath creating a faint fog across the glass.

*Ilsevel captured…* Saebellus was certainly keeping busy. The general and his army were fortunate that the warlord had been occupied on other matters—an interception by Saebellus while they were unarmed would have cost them the war. And consequently, the country. That damn, arrogant council! Sairel's father had been right to refuse to abide their deeds. Would that more elves had possessed the sense to leave with him. But it was too late for that: the virtues of his brethren had been rotting for the last nine thousand years, and many of them had not seen corruption then… and could not now. If such disregard for virtue continued, the Sel'vi would be lost.

He pursed his lips, wondering at the enemy warlord's plans since the capture of Horiembrig. Was Ilsevel worth that much attention? Or had Saebellus simply been incapable of the attack on Jikun?

His brow knit further. And then there was Nilanis, who had recognized him in the council's hall… How? Was he connected to the man who had been following him? Was it *Nilanis* who had hired his pursuer?

There was a loud knock on the embellished door behind him, startling him away from the glass.

"Who is it?" he demanded, looking back along the glossy marble tiles.

The knock sounded again.

Pushing off his knees, Sellemar stood and walked briskly to the door. He threw it open irritably and found himself being pushed aside by a very wet soldier.

"You are early," Sellemar commented, surveying the personal guard to the king. He made no apology for overpowering him earlier, for breaking into the council chambers, or for kicking him back down the steps.

Erallus glanced briefly about at the elaborately painted walls and gold-inlayed ceiling, dropping his oiled sack onto the floor. The beads of water clinging to it immediately slid to the tile and trickled into the cracks between the stone. "There is no time to waste. My Lord's bride is of the utmost concern to me. I was hoping to leave early, but I see your companion has not yet arrived."

Sellemar took a seat on the edge of the large, silk-covered bed, pulling on his boots and lacing them briskly. "'My Lord'? You have a close relationship with the king, then?"

Erallus nodded, pushing the door closed. "I would die for him."

"Yet I heard you failed to defend him recently from an assassin."

Sellemar could see the elf's eyes harden and his lips purse shamefully. "How do you know about the assassin?"

Sellemar waved a dismissive hand. "I said that I pay well to be informed about everything, if you recall."

"...I failed to defend the king. It will not happen again."

"Good," Sellemar replied solidly. He flowed right into the next question. "And what about Ilsevel?"

Erallus paused, briefly hesitant in his reply. "I... do not know Lady Ilsevel other than what I have seen of her interactions with the king."

"Would you die for her?" Sellemar tested.

"I would die for her."

"For Hairem or for Ilsevel?"

He could see Erallus' lips purse and his eyes narrow. "What is the purpose of these questions? What is it that you wish to know? If you can rely on me? Ilsevel is the king's wife-to-be and there is nothing he cherishes more. I would die for her for My Lord."

Sellemar raised a hand. "Touchy, touchy," he muttered, getting to his feet. It was a response he could expect from a devoted soldier. He grabbed his bag and strapped it over his shoulders. "Let us go."

Erallus frowned. "What about—"

"There is no other man," Sellemar replied curtly. "Gods know that you will cause me enough issues on this mission without bringing along a *second* novice."

Erallus opened and closed his mouth in shock. Yes, he was offended. *'Terrible,'* Sellemar thought sarcastically.

"You said you wanted to leave early. Now grab your sack and let us go," Sellemar ordered, opening the door and stepping out into the wide, lavishly decorated hallway.

*Gods*, this was going to be a long trip.

*

Outside the city, across the great expanse of Elvorium's narrow northern bridge, were the two horses he had left waiting since before he had returned to his room—after his intrusion to the council. Sellemar handed the boy at watch a coin and slung his sack over his horse.

Erallus seemed enveloped in his silence, no doubt trying to determine something about him. Sellemar smirked to himself and rolled his eyes. *'He is welcome to try.'*

The guard mounted and turned his horse after Sellemar. "Where are you from?" he finally asked. "Ryekarayn? The Sel'varian Realm? Are you a True Blood follower? One of his younger brothers, perhaps?"

"Prince Hadoream or Darcarus?" Sellemar retained a face devoid of emotion, even as the thought of "following" one of them offended him. "*No*."

"What, to all of it?" Erallus demanded, offended at the tone of his response. "Your accent—"

"Ryekarian, yes, so I have been told," Sellemar replied vaguely.

Erallus inhaled deeply and persisted, "An island off Ryekarayn's coast then? What are you, a lord? A mercenary? …Assassin?"

"Nothing so …low," Sellemar replied. "*Erallus*," he continued before the male could, "I shall play a game with you, if you will. For every *truly* embarrassing detail about yourself that you tell me, I shall tell you a true, albeit *non*-embarrassing, fact about me."

Erallus closed his mouth indignantly, letting his horse trail slightly behind.

For a time, there was the peace of silence between them.

"Have you been to Horiembrig before?" Sellemar finally asked with an exasperated sigh. He turned slightly in the saddle to see the male nod.

"Yes. Once with King Hairem's father—may Sel'ari grant him safe passage," Erallus replied. "I was in the city for about a week. I remember it well enough."

Sellemar turned back. Good. At least the elf knew the city. Horiembrig had become faded in his memory over the years. But hopefully they would never need the information. It would be a sad state of affairs indeed if he had to rely on this novice to escape the eastern city.

Erallus leaned forward suddenly, cocking his head warily. "Why. Why did you just ask me if I knew the city? You said that you knew of the tunnels running below it."

"I do."

"That's hardly common knowledge," Erallus began skeptically once more, prying as best as the male could for further information. *Persistent.* Sellemar wondered briefly if Erallus had been tasked with gleaning information from him. "Even I was not privy to that information during my—"

"Well, that is not entirely true, is it?" Sellemar interrupted him. "I believe that the knowledge of the underground tunnels is fairly common. *Where* they are is another matter completely."

"Are you going to be difficult this entire mission?"

"Are you?"

The two were quiet for a moment. Sellemar could hear the soldier huff a few times before speaking in a forcefully friendly tone, "You know where the tunnel entrances are?"

"One. Just one," Sellemar replied, raising a hand slightly in the air. Finally, the rain had ceased. He ran a hand along the mane of his horse, brushing the droplets away. "And it happens to run to the palace courtyard."

Erallus' eyes widened. "A *palace* escape? That's impossible!"

Sellemar heaved a sigh. "Improbable. Not impossible. Now I would like to travel in peace before you mercilessly continue to sling questions at me. Whatever it is you wish to ask me, I care not."

Erallus rolled his eyes and leaned back in the saddle. A soft melody began to become gradually audible from his lips. "…Men before have lost what they thought they had? Or number your allies in times prewar, when loyalties are not yet bled? Know that the man who stands at your side costs—"

"And *gods* whatever you do, do *not* sing that song."

*

Sellemar halted their journey that night at eighteen leagues east of the capital, in the city of Rialenvas. It was as Sellemar had expected—clean, elegant, and vast, sprawling across the hillside with glittering white towers in the moonlight. He could hear the distant sounds of light music somewhere to the north.

"It hardly feels as though Sevrigel is at war," Erallus spoke as they dismounted outside a three-story inn. "Or that we're going to the center of it."

Sellemar handed the stable boy a coin. "Do not let anything happen to this horse, do you understand?"

The wide-eyed boy nodded and hurried to lead the horse away, as though it was a chest of gold or a delicate crystal vase.

Sellemar strode toward the inn, Erallus' words stinging him with cynicism. "I cannot block out the image of your land covered in white tents filled with dying soldiers enough to notice this 'lack of war,'" he replied tartly. And yet, he knew exactly what the male meant. Times never changed. War or not, most of the land would continue life unchanged—who sat on the throne and what they did with their troops would come and go as city gossip. And that would be the extent of its effect.

He stopped before the inn's polished counter, relieved to be inside and out of the wet and dreary night. "Two rooms." He turned to Erallus. "Get yourself fed and then sleep. We leave at dawn tomorrow."

Without so much as a word of farewell, the weary soldier obeyed his stern command, taking his key and vanishing down the hall.

Sellemar watched as his heels rounded the corner and drew his attention back to the hall about him, regarding the atmosphere of the establishment dismally. He had not missed this aspect of missions. Inn after inn, city after city, one after another, and they soon began to blend together. This particular building with its softly blue-hued walls and elaborate interior was just another building of the "almost homeless." There was no comfort in its elegance. The wide rooms and tall ceilings only helped to emphasize how vast and empty the place truly was.

Sellemar readied himself for sleep and sank wearily into his bed. He had thought cynically of Erallus' open exhaustion, and yet, he had no doubt that at the heart of it, they both felt the same.

He shifted with a muttered curse. Uncomfortable, as he had expected. He supposed that to most travelers, the rooms of such an elite elven establishment were exceptionally elegant, but they hardly reminded him of home. He pressed the back of his hand against his forehead. Erallus had finally stopped asking personal questions, but he still had to give the elf some praise for persistence. With a good night's sleep under his belt, he imagined the male would renew his attempts with vigor tomorrow.

"With blood they fought the trials south, and with blood they fought to flee, 'til silence came from every mouth, for but spared from death were three." He turned over, pulling the sheets up. It was one of those miserable songs that became stuck in his head. "Thank you, Erallus," he muttered begrudgingly to himself.

*

Five days later, the two stopped mid-evening at an inn in the great city of Elisfall. It was a sprawling city with neither walls nor gates, vividly lit by blue and yellow orbs hovering above the streets and encircling the city in an evenly spaced manner. The towers of the temple to Sel'ari were greater than even those of the high lord's mansion itself—as they should be—and waved golden banners through the cool night air in greeting to the two travelers as they passed.

Sellemar dismounted at the inn, handing a coin to the stable youth waiting by the building's columned overhang. "Take care of this horse. Stay here with him." He held onto the reins a moment longer, looking around expectantly. "Is there a white horse with a silver mane and tail in the stables? Particularly tall? No saddle?"

The willowy youth nodded, taking the golden reins in awe, and pocketed the coin silently. Had the country fallen to such waste that stable lads were no longer tipped? He tsked in dismay and turned back toward the golden doors of the inn itself, Erallus at his heels like his half-witted, but loyal, dog. He preferred far more intelligent company, but that was soon to be granted. He pushed the doors open and strode in.

Erallus stepped quickly in beside him, eyeing him suspiciously. "You asked about a rather particular horse. Why?"

Sellemar ignored his question and leaned over the dark marble counter to the innkeeper. "I am looking for a Noc'olarian male. He would be travelling alone. Impossible to miss," he queried, ignoring that the dog at his heels was now yapping indignantly about being ignored.

The slender Sel'ven male behind the counter, tufted with a rather sad state of sandy hair and a hooked nose, still managed to gesture gracefully toward the right. "He arrived last night. He went out back a few hours ago; I suspect toward the stables." He rubbed an invisible smudge from the marble counter as Sellemar drew away.

"You look exhausted," Erallus commented pointedly as Sellemar passed him toward the inn's door. "Are we not stopping here for the night? Who are we looking for?"

"Yes. I *am* exhausted. I have been awake since before dawn. Your breakfast did not catch itself," Sellemar replied simply, pushing the door of the inn open, grimacing slightly at the glare of the evening light. Now where…? The street was stretched with long shadows and yellow light as the sun crept toward the horizon. He leapt aside as a melon cart bounced past him, nearly running him over.

"Watch yourself!" Sellemar snapped, but the driver was as unaware of his existence as the rest of the city. He huffed once, indignantly, and refocused his attention on the street, glancing from one distant, moving figure to the next.

"There is the horse you talked about," Erallus voiced in a tone of mild surprise.

Sellemar drew his gaze back toward the inn as another young stable boy appeared around the side of the building leading the white mare. Erallus met his gaze pointedly and Sellemar turned away. "Itirel," he called, dropping his sack over the back of his own horse. He frowned, looking past the stable hand. Where *was* that male? He narrowed his eyes as he peered down the street. "*Itirel!*"

The door of the inn swung open behind them and Sellemar turned expectantly. Surely it could be none other after he had shouted the intent of his search to half the city.

A tall male halted momentarily to duck an elegantly carved lance below the doorframe. He was uncharacteristically well-built, especially compared to Erallus or, admittedly, himself, but was still a far cry from the thick humans. His pale skin seemed to glow softly, reverberating in the falling sunlight. He pushed his dark violet hair from the contrasting brilliance of his violet eyes, to gaze calmly and sternly at the Sel'ven before him.

*'Here it comes…'*

"Sellemar, patience," the Noc'olari reprimanded with a smile and shake of his head as he let the door fall closed behind him. He stepped out, his movement almost floating beneath the purple-hued robes. "The stable hand informed me of your arrival. I had to gather my belongings," he continued, his tone light. He had adjusted his accent to be almost indistinguishably Sevrigelian and even Sellemar had to admit that he was almost fooled. But Sellemar had never been very good at pretending he was something he was not. The male fidgeted with the upper steel breastplate that was strapped on over his dark cotton robes, shifting uncomfortably as he did so. He raised his head and shrugged, passing an amused smile onto Sellemar.

Sellemar smiled in return. Itirel certainly did look uncomfortably weighed down by the armor, but this time it would be necessary. "I see you have yourself some armor this time. Quite a contrast to running around battling in a cotton suit." And he allowed himself a chuckle, surprised to find how relaxed he had become at the sight of his comrade, and how simple the mission of infiltrating Saebellus' city now seemed. "Ah, Itirel," he sighed, swinging himself onto his horse.

Erallus dropped his sack, his jaw hanging open. "*Gods*, I know who you are!" he gasped. "You're Riphath... the Noc'olarian healer who travelled with Eraydon! Your likeness is carved in statues and drawn in paintings all across the land! But how—why—" he stuttered off into shocked silence, staring unblinkingly as though the apparition before him might vanish.

Itirel exchanged looks with Sellemar, raising a brow in what could only be taken to be further amusement. He moved to the white horse, swinging himself onto its back. "Is that so, my friend? I am Riphath, the great and legendary war hero who travelled with Eraydon and vanished in the war almost nine thousand years ago?" He chuckled to himself. "*I* am the 'great and legendary' Riphath? Is *every* Noc'olari you meet Riphath?—for we are a similar looking people, like yourself. Or am I, perhaps, the first Noc'olari you have seen?"

Sellemar could see Erallus' cheeks grow red with embarrassment as his mouth snapped closed. He picked up his sack in a hurry and swung up onto his horse. "Is this male travelling with us?" Erallus demanded, his words singed in embarrassment-fueled frustration. "You said that you were not going to bring along another elf because he would just be a 'novice' and a 'burden.'"

Sellemar led his horse toward the cobbled street ahead of them. "I distinctly remember stating that I would not bring another '*man*' nor another '*novice*.' Itirel is not a human, nor is he a novice." He flourished his hand from one male to the other. "Itirel, this is Erallus. He's a... *bodyguard*... to King Hairem."

Erallus' lips pursed in irritation, more than likely interpreting that Sellemar was taunting him—and that would be correct. Sellemar swiftly hid his smile by averting his head.

He could see Itirel pass him another reprimanding look. '*Must* you provoke that poor male?' it read.

Sellemar nudged his horse in the side, still suppressing his amusement. Yes, he must.

*

They trotted out of the city in a short ride and turned once more toward the east. Sellemar was aware of Erallus' frustration throughout the final league of travel. At the edge of the forest line, with Elisfall glittering a dwarf's girth away, Sellemar dismounted, patting his horse on the flank.

"We're stopping here for the night," Erallus stated flatly, looking around wearily. He seemed finally worn of asking questions and merely phrased his words as a dismayed statement. He dismounted and picked up his sack, his feet sticking into the earth beneath the long, slick blades of grass. "We've ridden near twenty leagues today. Of course I wish to find Ilsevel, but if we are too weary, we will make a mistake while rescuing her."

Itirel dismounted beside him, dropping the reins of his horse beside Sellemar's, and stretched backwards slightly. He looked toward Sellemar with an amused and understanding smile.

"I am hardly weary," Sellemar countered as his horse took the reins of Erallus' mare in its teeth and began to lead her away.

Erallus' eyes widened in surprise. "Our horses—"

"Are not needed from here on out," Sellemar replied, watching Erallus' wide-eyed stare follow the white mare as she trotted off behind their two horses. "But they shall be nearby for when we emerge."

Erallus turned back, his brow knitting in concern. "We're still near seventeen leagues from Horiembrig…"

"Two days on foot, if you can manage," Sellemar tsked. He glanced behind him, disappointed to see that Erallus was not drawing any conclusions from the situation. "We are entering the underground tunnel I spoke of," he finally relayed. "So keep close and do not speak. I need to remember where it is…"

He heard Erallus marvel to himself at the distance at which the tunnel began from the eastern capital, but he was too focused on a disarray of stones to distinguish exactly what the male said.

"They have been moved," he heaved after a moment.

Itirel stepped up beside him, eyeing the placement of the stars quietly for a moment, his arms crossed behind his back. "Indeed. By quite a great force."

Sellemar straightened. Damn. He walked to the largest stone of the widespread pile. *'I suppose this one is probably in its original location.'* He put a hand against it. *'40 paces north? Or was it 30?'* He glanced once at the stars and then took several long steps into the darkness.

"It might do us better to enter the tunnels in the morn—" Erallus began.

Itirel raised a finger to his lips.

"SH!" Sellemar snapped. "Too many eyes in the day." He took another step. "Twenty-nine… Thirty." He looked around. No, definitely not the place. He moved another ten paces and stopped again. Ah, there it was. He put a hand affectionately against the old tree. *'Then that is 16 paces east…'* Erallus yawned audibly behind him as he began to count. *'6… 8… no, wait, damn it.'* He glanced over his shoulder. "Will you cease breathing down my neck? When I find it, you will know. Itirel, keep him off me." He irritably stomped back to the tree.

Itirel chuckled as he rested a hand on Erallus' shoulder, one eye squinting in Sellemar's direction. "Careful. When he is tired he is even harder to bear. Difficult as that may be to believe."

Sixteen paces later, Sellemar tapped a large, old tree. "This one."

Erallus stared at the tree for a moment. "This one…? This one what?"

Itirel smiled. "It is as he described," he breathed in wonder.

Sellemar took a few steps back to get a running start. "This is the entrance," he replied to Erallus. He ran, pushing off the base of the tree and catching the lowest branch in his fingertips. He swung his body up and took a seat at the branch's base.

Erallus looked up at him skeptically. "You must be joking. I can't jump that high." He stumbled slightly to the side as Itirel ran past him, catching the branch easily and swinging himself up beside Sellemar. "*Most* elves cannot jump that high," he defended himself, regarding the two with narrowed eyes.

Sellemar sighed. He had expected as much. He gripped the branch with his legs and swung his body backwards to hang upside down. He extended his arms. "See if you can reach my hands, at least."

"Why don't we lower a rope," Itirel suggested skeptically. "This is only going to end with one of you two getting hurt."

"I don't know why you are so irritated," the guard muttered, carrying on. "I don't think I know a single elf who can jump that high."

"Now you know two," Sellemar barked. "Just do it."

Erallus moved back to where Sellemar had begun his run and sprinted toward him. His slender body pushed off from the base and he caught Sellemar's arms… at which point his forehead smacked into Sellemar's and he was promptly dropped.

"Damn it, Erallus," Sellemar growled, rubbing his forehead, ignoring the "I warned you so" from Itirel behind him. He swung himself back to a sitting position. "Stay there." *Gods*. If it had just been Itirel and him…!—but he had chosen to make the king comfortable. He heaved a sigh as he stood, leaping up to catch the next branch. "Watch him," he ordered the Noc'olari.

"Watch him for what?"

"…I do not know. In case he does something stupid." Up through the enormous tree he climbed until the ground below vanished in the darkness. Halfway up the tree, he turned and moved along the trunk for a short length. Here the wood jutted out slightly at the side, as though to be a place of a knob. Sellemar halted before it and peered down the large hole into the darkness.

"Found it," he whispered to himself triumphantly. He pulled the sword from his side and held it down into the shadows. "*Hilithae seltaria*." The blade immediately lit with a bright, white-blue light, illuminating the darkness around him. He narrowed his eyes, studying the smooth inner walls of the tree.

Ah, there it was, right in front of him. He scoffed and reached out for the first rung of the rope ladder below him. It was fastened at the top to the tree, but the end hung loose somewhere far below. It was as smooth as silk but as sturdy as steel—like the woven fragments of a spider's thread. He pulled it up slowly as he kept the light pointing into the darkness. The tunnel did not merely extend to the earth, but dug deep and down below the roots, a bottomless pit past the glow of the blade.

He sheathed his sword as the end of the ladder finally appeared, a single knot at the end of its silver strands. He took it and turned toward the ground below. "Alright, Erallus," he muttered to himself as he dropped it down into the darkness. A moment later, he could feel the tug on the rope as the elf began to ascend.

"So this is the egress of the Horiembrig palace escape…?" Erallus breathed as he used the lip of the hole to pull himself up onto the branch. He gave a triumphant grunt as he steadied himself beside the hole.

Itirel climbed up steadily behind him, stepping off the ladder with a bounce to his step once he reached the same branch. He gazed toward the hole as well and Sellemar could see that he was equally as impressed as the soldier. He had almost forgotten that Itirel had never before been to Horiembrig.

Sellemar dropped the ladder back into the darkness. "Go first. I do not want you climbing after and slipping and falling on me and us—"

Erallus leapt nimbly over the side and caught the ladder. "Do not think for a moment, Sellemar, that simply because I cannot *jump* as high as you that I am incapable of fending for myself." His head vanished into the darkness.

Itirel chuckled. "Come now, *Sellemar*. Now you're just pushing him. I remember when you were just like him. Young. Wild. Indignant. Wait, that's still you, isn't it?"

Sellemar rolled his eyes. "You sound like my father." He climbed down into the darkness after them. "You know, I did not ask you along to condone every bite he takes at me," he carried on.

He heard Itirel chuckle again. Well, was he not having the grandest time?

And yet, Sellemar found himself chuckling as well. Gods, how he had missed these days.

*

"Ilra, since you ask," Sellemar could hear Itirel speak of his god as he neared the two at the base of the tunnel. "Purple has long since been the color the Noc'olarian people have associated with him. Hence the naming of the ilralilis."

"You know, I do not believe Erallus cares much for Noc'olarian religion… or plants," Sellemar spoke, touching ground a moment later beside them.

"Do we have a light?" Itirel asked, without taking offense.

"No, I do care," Erallus interjected, and Sellemar picked up a hint of indignation. "Unlike you, he answers my questions."

"Secretive, are we?" Itirel jested.

Sellemar scoffed. "I do have a light," he spoke, ignoring the Noc'olari.

Itirel carried on his conversation to Erallus as Sellemar pushed the rope aside. "What did you ask him?"

Erallus shook his head, as though defending himself from a rebuke. "Nothing. Simple questions about who he is and where he is from. You would think those would be small talk."

Itirel raised his hands slightly and shrugged. "Sellemar prefers to keep to himself. His behavior is nothing personal, I assure you. There are just too many broken hearts pursuing him, I'm afraid."

Sellemar heard Erallus scoff something inaudible and Itirel chuckle. "Oh, you are just damn near hilarious," Sellemar muttered, but he smiled faintly.

After all, if Itirel was enjoying himself, even if it meant taking jabs at him, then he could tolerate it. For a little while, at least.

The air was cool and damp and the smell of soil was all around him. And only darkness looked down at them from above. He drew his sword. "*Hilithae seltaria*," he murmured to the blade.

Their eyes adjusted to the vivid white-blue light that illuminated the world around them.

"Incredible," Erallus breathed as they both turned their heads to marvel at the craftsmanship of the True Bloods.

And what a marvel of craftsmanship it was. The roots of the great tree twisted in and out of the stone tunnel. The floor was a smooth, glassy, golden marble while the walls shone with a similarly golden hue. Gems glittered from their embedded place in the decorative stone arches, which had been carved with tiny royal emblems: a gold-inlaid phoenix with a sword clutched in its talons.

Sellemar could see the faint shimmer of small, floating, white orbs along the arched ceiling. Damn. What were the words for those again…?

"Are those lights above us?" Erallus asked, catching sight of them at the same time. He squinted into the darkness. "*Lutel seltaria*."

Itirel exchanged an impressed look with Sellemar. Even Itirel did not know the words for the magic-fused orbs. With a faint flicker, the little crystal balls gradually grew brighter until the hall was filled with a similar blue-white light as Sellemar's sword.

He sheathed his blade, stepping away from the wall and down the tunnel. "Come. Be quick about it. We have seventeen leagues to cover."

"We are not over-exerting ourselves," Itirel warned in his father-like tone. "I did not come to heal carelessness."

Erallus took step briskly behind him and Sellemar caught the slight, almost triumphant smile that twitched at the corner of his lips.

Well, now he *certainly* was not stopping.

The vast tunnels carried on below the earth, their architecture unchanged except for the occasional pathway leading off to small chambers on their left and right. In the past these were sleeping and storage rooms, filled occasionally by the few select members of the royal family who were privy to the knowledge of the tunnels.

However, as Horiembrig fell from influence, so too did the upkeep of the tunnels fade. The once-elegant storage rooms now consisted of no more than dust, old food, and the occasional rodent skeleton.

"When we arrive out of the courtyard, we will need to capture a soldier in order to obtain information regarding Ilsevel's whereabouts. A male such as Saebellus will not keep her in the dungeons," Sellemar informed Hairem's guard as he stepped over a thick root with an overly compensating step.

The mention of the warlord seemed to pique the soldier's interest. Erallus picked up his pace to fall in line beside him. "What do you know of Saebellus?" he dared to ask.

Sellemar did not glance to the side, but he could feel the gaze intensify on his face. "That he is one of the best generals Sevrigel has ever seen," he replied shortly.

He saw Erallus frown, clearly unsatisfied with the general response. "I meant, what will he *do* to Ilsevel?"

"Nothing," Itirel interjected for Sellemar, in a tone that warned against further questions.

Erallus' lips pursed, his persistence flaring. "He will not defile her?"

"No."

"Ah… he doesn't think that the king will pay her ransom if—"

Sellemar sighed. "No, Erallus. *Simply* because Saebellus is not an animal. Saebellus was a prestigious, wealthy, and elite soldier while employed by the kingdom. He was trained at the highest academies and received the position of second general under the last major general. There has not been the position of second general given since. Even Navon will never achieve anything more than a captain's rank. Saebellus is as cultured as you or I."

Erallus continued undaunted, "And then Saebellus murdered his first general and started a rebellion."

This time, Sellemar heard Itirel's tone change to a sharp reprimand. Erallus was certainly not above his rebukes and the male had crossed even the Noc'olari's patience. "That is still not a reason for which he would defile Ilsevel." He paused as he caught Sellemar from tripping over an outstretched root. It did not stop his stern reply to Erallus for long, "If you want to know your enemy, do not assume that simply because a person opposes your beliefs that he is now subject to entirely evil actions. Saebellus is infinitely more complex than that. I pray that the rest of your kingdom is not naïve enough to misjudge him so carelessly. He has more honor than the entirety of your council."

Sellemar turned back and picked up his pace, adding scornfully, "May Sel'ari take pity on your foolishness; it very well may cost you your life."

"*You* are often no different than Erallus, my friend," Itirel rebuked.

Sellemar's cheeks flushed. He had almost forgotten how much the male's fairness irked him.

*

They had travelled quickly, but even so, seventeen leagues still took the three elves nearly two days.

Sellemar rested a hand on the silken rope leading up into the darkness above them. "This is the end. We shall rest for a few hours and then travel upward. Remember, we take a soldier alive as quickly as we can."

Erallus nodded once in agreement, sliding down against the back wall, gravel bouncing away across the floor and into the shadows. "Alright," he grunted wearily.

Itirel laid his lance aside and made himself comfortable. Unlike himself and Erallus, the Noc'olari still seemed quite energetic. Damn his magically assisted stamina. Even so, he was inwardly relieved that at least one of them would not bear the fatigue of the near-week long journey.

Sellemar leaned back and closed his eyes, at last surrendering to a deep sleep. Tomorrow would begin the real test of their skills.

# Chapter Twenty-Six

"Jikun… should you be up? It hasn't been two weeks." Navon eyed Jikun reproachfully, leaning further into the soft furs of his bed and lowering his weathered tome. The air in his tent was muggy and Jikun wondered how he managed to lie in all that dark, stifling warmth without a breeze or even a flicker of sunlight.

Jikun snorted, holding the tent open above him to let the crisp, mid-summer air scurry in past his legs. "Come. I am going to walk through the city."

Navon slid the covers from his body and rose steadily to his feet, despite the cautious reproach of his gaze. He set the tome on the stand beside him and raised a finger warningly. "Jikun…"

Jikun ignored the reproach this time. He wasn't going to deliberately cause a fight within the city, if *that* was what his captain was thinking—he didn't have such time to waste.

He just had to get away from the crisp, endless sea of stark white canvas flapping about him.

His mind snapped suddenly to the black leather peeling from the spine of the book he had just seen. How was Navon passing *his* time…? "Navon," he suddenly barked as his captain hooked his new sheath to his hip. "That book better not be what I think it is."

He saw Navon glance up almost sheepishly, as though his expression would somehow pacify Jikun's response. "Jikun, it's not another one of your poetry-ridden journals. I haven't touched it since you took it from me before Darival. This is *my* book. You know my practices…" he trailed off.

Jikun stepped in sharply, throwing the tent flap closed behind him. He would have preferred the Helven *did* have his journal. "NAVON," he growled, reaching for the tome even as his gut dropped at the thought of touching such a cursed book. Irrational as it was, his hand urged him to withdraw from the imagined lash that would flare out and sear his soul for his mere proximity to the material within.

Navon quickly picked the book up, stepping toward the rear of the tent. "Jikun—"

Jikun ignored his instincts and reached out, catching his captain stiffly by the arm. There was a brief, pointless struggle as Navon attempted to break free; then Jikun set his jaw, unwilling to tolerate the resistance. His grip tightened on Navon's arm and he drew upon the water in the male's blood. He could feel the skin beneath his hand growing unnaturally chilled as the blood within began to freeze.

Navon dropped the book instantly and clutched his arm with a surprised gasp. Jikun gave him a firm shove backwards and reached down for the tome.

"Damn," his captain growled painfully, rubbing his forearm firmly. "You could kill me with something like that!"

Jikun picked up the book and waved it at Navon angrily. "So could this! *Necromancy*, Navon!" he lowered his voice, fearful that others might hear them. His eyes flicked back once to the tent flap to make certain that even that little barricade to the sound remained in place. "This is forbidden. I let the incident with the beast slide, but gods know I should have turned you in! What if the other soldiers had been close enough to discern what happened?! The penalty is death—if this doesn't kill you first, of course!" He narrowed his eyes angrily, daring Navon to disagree, then wrapped the tome into his cloak and tucked it under his arm. He pressed it firmly against his torso lest Navon should even think about attempting to reclaim it.

Navon turned his head away for a moment. Jikun could see the eyebrows narrowed above his unblinking, azure gaze. He was staring solidly ahead, resentful at having lost.

*'You can't lose on this even once, can you?'* Jikun thought bitterly. He could tell he had not changed Navon's mind about his practices. Not even a little. Did all of Ryekarayn's Helvari have a death wish? Certainly living in an endless canyon of towering stone peaks would do that to any sane male, but here, in *Elvorium* of all places…!

He heaved a frustrated sigh, grabbing Navon's pale arm roughly and pulling back the sleeve. "You'll be fine," he spoke after a moment of examining Navon's reddened skin. He smacked it once for good measure, slipping in his final rebuke.

His captain huffed once, inhaled deeply, and held it. Finally he extended his hand expectantly.

Jikun pursed his lips. Honestly, requesting it back was too far. His fingers twitched, demanding that he send the male sprawling to the earth, but he managed to restrain himself. Navon had been bedridden not too long ago... and he didn't want to test his returning strength by that degree. Still, this was one area where he had to agree with the Sel'vi: and Murios' caution had only propelled his resentment of the dark magic. Any magic involved with the Realms and the dead—whether raising them or speaking with them—was on ground that should never be trod.

*The Realms are no place for mortals.*

Navon's eyes locked onto his and his hand remained stubbornly outstretched. There was the wild Helvarian spirit glimmering behind them, fierce and resolute. Stupidly so.

*'Know when you are beaten, Navon,'* he thought tartly, beginning to turn away.

"We could bring back the males you lost in the swamp."

Jikun's feet drew to an abrupt stop as his body started in a mixture of fear and temptation. He could feel his breath form a lump in his throat, his heart pressing against his ribs with every rattling beat. *Thirty thousand...* His grip on the tome loosened for a moment. *Thirty thousand lives...* He stepped back, turning and pursing his lips in the appearance of determined resolve. "...No." He glanced over, seeing that Navon's persistence would not falter. His body stiffened in response and he drew his shoulders back. "If I catch you with evidence of your practices again, I'll beat you myself."

There was a span of silence between them and what may have only been seconds felt like minutes. Jikun's initial attempts to form a further rebuke stalled and faded, but he was not entirely convinced of the effectiveness of his threat and so he did not move.

"Where are we going in the city?" Navon finally spoke behind him. His tone was slightly grated with aggravation, but he seemed to have finally realized that he had lost that fight.

Jikun's grip tightened on the tome just to be certain. "A walk, that is all. Time away from the troops for a bit would do us both some good. You could use the strength-building after what you lost in the swamp. Saebellus may be preoccupied in the east, but it's only a matter of time before we see him again. *And* that beast."

He ducked out of the tent, Navon tight on his heels.

*The beast…* The weight of the tome grew even greater at the thought of the otherworldly creature. He forced his eyes up and out, away from the plain, stark white canvas around him to the colorful expanse of Sevrigel's glowing capital.

Elvorium was bright and cheerful in the mid-day sunlight. Even the mist from the canyon had subsided substantially, allowing the vast world below to become mostly visible. Jikun walked out onto the bridge, looking over the side as he moved toward the city's gates. He could see small, dark shapes flying above the treetops far below, and the water of the river was as vividly blue as the Kisacaela gemstones that could be found embedded in the walls throughout the canyon. And somewhere along those same canyon faces, Sevrigel's sparse population of human guests was busily chunking away at the serene landscape.

But if the human miners were about, then so too were their prostitutes.

He frowned slightly, feeling an unusual lack of thrill at the thought. His mind whisked him north before he realized it, out across the frozen tundra and through the icy walls of Kaivervale…

"General Jikun Taemrin, your captain is not allowed in the city at this time," a guard shouted as they drew near to the city's golden gates.

Jikun's mind retreated to the warm summer air about him and his pace only grew more determined, the fresh day bolstering his focus. He gestured to Navon to follow him.

"General Jikun Taemrin!" the soldier's voice rose all the more urgently. "We have orders to shoot anyone who attempts to enter the city who is still considered to be in need of quarantine!" He raised his spear slightly, but the male knew it was the threat along the wall and not the spear itself that caused Jikun's pace to slow.

"Navon has already passed the inspections by the temple's healers," Jikun began curtly. "If you do not consider me to be an honorable male, then fetch the priests and we shall wait."

The soldiers exchanged looks—elven tradition no doubt caused them conflict. The council had appointed Jikun as general and, of course, as the "council is honorable," then so too was the male they had appointed. They could not think to challenge his word—or rather, that of the council.

The soldier's spear lowered. "Proceed."

Jikun's pace returned to its natural course and his eyes fell away from the wall to the city's opened gates. Yet as he and Navon neared the egress, Jikun noted the guards leaned slightly away from them.

It was difficult to blame them—he had seen what the plague had wrought firsthand. Nevertheless, he was indignant toward their disgust while at the same time sickened with their unwavering trust.

*'You are in a foul mood today,'* he acknowledged to himself. There was nothing the guards at the gate could do to appease him either way. Whether it was scores of white tents or marble walls, he knew his frustrations were far beyond the scenery.

*The council is honorable.* Jikun scoffed as he stepped through the gates of the city and onto the cobbled street. The buildings towered up above him, and the flowers that had adorned the balconies in the early spring were long gone and replaced by simple vines. It seemed almost surreal, standing once more in the midst of crisp and unmarred civilization.

"What is it?" Navon asked, regarding Jikun curiously.

Jikun rebuked himself for his outward show and attempted to respond in an indifferent, thoughtful tone, "I was just thinking about the council again. What I wouldn't give to put them all to the sword." Well, that had lasted a grand total of eight words.

Navon's eyes grew wide as an owl's, his lips parting to a little 'o' of shock. He glanced quickly behind him to survey the reactions of the guards, but they had created enough distance that Jikun's words were lost in the tumult of the city's streets. "*Jikun*, every word that comes out of your mouth grows more blasphemous by the day!"

Jikun rolled his eyes, grip subconsciously tightening on the book of necromancy tucked beneath his arm. How could Navon even think of rebuking him when he himself had nearly died to the council's corrupt and foolish southern war?—*and* the male himself had been audaciously dabbling in blasphemy mere minutes before?

Somehow, for all he had seen, Navon remained sickeningly loyal to them. *'The loyalty of a conditioned soldier...'* And yet Navon was not originally from the elven continent.

He opened his mouth, desiring to question from where his comrade's unquestioning loyalty had arisen, but the chill beneath his arm drew him to a halt. It would have something to do with necromancy. He knew it before he asked.

"While we are here, I need to make a personal stop," Navon continued, his tone still revealing his ruffled feathers.

By personal stop Jikun could only assume he meant the temple of Sel'ari. "As you wish," he replied with a slight shrug. What did he expect? The culture south of Darival was embedded with blind loyalty. The ice and Lithrian people of the north had long since lost that fault. Life was harsher there. Real. Whereas in Elvorium…

He watched a group of children scurry across the road, kicking a ball down an alley across the street, shouting and laughing as they vanished after it. The image of the young girl in Kaivervale returned to him, seated with her little friends behind the frozen waterfall in the Turmazel Mountains. Seated before the great, yellow eye.

Yes, Darival was far harsher.

He saw Navon give a faint smile as his eyes followed the children into the darkness.

"Do you want one?"

Navon laughed outright, shaking his head. "Gods, Jikun. I have enough children to take care of right now."

Jikun smiled, feeling exceedingly alike on the matter. He watched an older elf rebuke the children for their ruckus as they reemerged with ball in hand. Then they tore off down the street, laughing in defiance as they went.

It was the same rhythm of everyday life here. Nothing seemed to change. Thirty thousand sick soldiers were dying outside their walls, but life across the bridge was as blissfully ignorant as ever. He did not expect them to drag their feet and weep, but what had a single, free-willed elf, not under direction from the council, done for his troops since their return?

The answer was nothing.

*The council was not the only thing corrupted.*

And if war was not enough to shake their complacency, then what was?

Navon drew to a stop beside a pastry stand along a marbled wall, flicking a fattened fly off his hand as he reached for a flaky bun. "These are excellent," he spoke excitedly, the dullness in his eyes abating slightly. He picked up a second, dropping the coin onto the wood of the stall, and handed one to Jikun. "Here. Have you had one of these?"

Jikun regarded him absentmindedly for a moment. How could this light and wild spirit tamper with necromancy? One moment he was looking at the familiar face of his comrade and the next, there was something else shifting darkly beneath his azure gaze. Curiosity was the god's curse on the elves… And Navon had acquired far more than was healthy.

He bit into the flaky bread and wiped a finger across the corner of his mouth where the salty cream seeped past the edge—no doubt it was something from the western seaboard. He raised his eyebrows and nodded heavily. "*Gods* that is good. I can almost forget about how much I hate these people with food made this well."

Navon chuckled at Jikun's jest. "If the next sentence out of your mouth even resembles negativity, so help me I shall wring the rest of it from you with whatever strength I may have left."

Jikun found his smile broadening as the lines on Navon's face ebbed away. "The city of Elvorium possesses only the facade of peace—it lasts only so long as those in power have what they want."

Navon punched his shoulder firmly, causing Jikun to fumble the bread. Jikun threw the remnants at Navon and the male tried haphazardly to smack them away midair. "Knock it off. Act like a general," Navon taunted.

Jikun smirked at their little game and stepped after Navon as he left the side of the booth. But inside his mind was churning as he watched the elves go on with their lives, as seemingly carefree as Jikun had briefly allowed himself to be with his captain. Maybe… that guise of peace was necessary. Outside, the real world was grim: a great weight to bear with little reward in sight. *He* had made his choice to live it.

But he had also chosen to protect these people from it.

# CHAPTER TWENTY-SEVEN

There was a resounding knock on the door to Jikun's room, unfamiliar in its severity and rhythm. He awoke with a start, his icy eyes staring up at the ceiling as his heart lay below, pounding from the rush of adrenaline in his chest. He sat up abruptly, the grogginess of the elven wine gone. Beside him, the woman he had bedded was staring in clear panic, holding the covers to her bare breasts in a state of frozen fear.

"Sh, get under the bed!" Jikun hissed. He hastened from the sheets, kicking her clothes under the bed and yanking the covers from her hand. "Get!"

The woman scrambled to obey, quickly vanishing as the general turned toward the door.

"Who is it?" he demanded, quickly pulling on his pants. He snatched his wine-soaked shirt from the nightstand and hurried toward the door.

"A message," the unfamiliar voice responded vaguely.

Jikun's movement slowed, his face reflexively knitting in concern. "A message?" He glanced once toward the bed. Good, there was no sign of the woman. He rested a hand on the handle of the door, inhaled sharply, and swung it wide. "Why not give it to my messenger?" he demanded curtly, collecting himself under a general's command.

His eyes fell to the elf before him. The male was of the City Guard, donned in clean plate-mail embellished with his arbitrary position. He was armed with a long sword, but Jikun noted that it remained resting in its sheath.

The soldier glanced once into the room, but his eyes seemed disinterested and refocused on the general in an almost apologetic gaze. "It's about your captain, General Taemrin."

*

The Temple of Sel'ari was flocked by a crowd of curious elves. Through the throng of civilians, Jikun could hardly see the speckle of soldiers dotted in their wake. His eyes ran up the steps to the two heavily armed soldiers poised rigidly before the temple's doors. Questions rang out through the air; whispers flitted by as the general passed. Yet the males at the doors remained stoic and still. Jikun drew his horse up beside them, dismounting swiftly and dropping the reins carelessly to the side.

These were not the usual doors, Jikun quickly noted. As unfamiliar as he was with the goddess' temple, these plain wooden doors were clearly temporary and hardly ornate enough to don the entrance to the capital's goddess.

"General," one of the guards acknowledged as the frantic tap of Jikun's boots drew to a stop beside him. He pushed open the door just wide enough to let Jikun through and the crowd leapt forward in a surge of curiosity.

For once, Jikun did not hesitate to enter. As the door closed behind him and the voices of the throng died down, a white-robed male turned toward him from the center of the vast and empty room, catching his attention before his eyes had even swept the unfamiliar interior. The male's hands were clasped together at his abdomen, his thin, weathered face drawn. The gold inlay at his sleeves and hem was the first sign to Jikun that he was not a priest of Sel'ari, but rather a mage of the capital—and a rather high ranking one at that. The intricate detail wove rank amongst its threads and Jikun swiftly deduced he was on the of the capital's leading Seers.

His stomach dropped.

"What happened?" Jikun demanded as his hurried footsteps echoed across the marble tiles. He scanned the carefully composed face of the mage, detecting through his calm guise the tumultuous information rolling about within.

The seer raised a slender hand, gesturing toward the back wall and the interior of the temple around him, sweeping a deliberate arc to rest before Jikun's torso, as though directing his eyes in the exact trail they should follow.

Jikun's eyes snapped away and swept the room, noting for the first time, away from his focus on the elf, the dismal condition of the temple about them. A large, humanoid-sized hole had been smashed through at the back wall and the candles along it were scattered about, unlit heaps of half-burned and stark-white wax. Twisted metal lay in pieces around the hall and a stone hand reached out desperately from a mound of shattered rock, as though grasping desperately for help to regain its once unmarried entirety.

"What happened?" This time Jikun's words were softer, hesitant even. His eyes fell to a splatter of blood on his left and his stomach twisted beneath his rigid frame. Why had a seer summoned *him* to the temple…?

He was not long to receive his answer.

"Captain Navon was attacked in this temple earlier this morning—before the dawn—by Saebellus' beast. Clearly, Saebellus' creature had orders to dispose of your captain specifically. I can only imagine why." His tone through the last sentence was tinted with the faintest traces of stoic sarcasm. The seer raised his other hand at equal height with the first. "I can show you what happened, as I retrieved the events from his mind. The projection will be from his eyes, but it will show you what you want—or rather need—to know." His hands lowered as one. "It is not a pleasant experience."

Jikun had never endured the transfer of events from a seer, nor did he possess extensive knowledge of the method, but he nodded, drawing himself up to demonstrate his solidarity. "Show me," he commanded stiffly.

The world around them changed instantaneously and Jikun found himself kneeling before a seven-foot statue of Sel'ari, the scene projected into Jikun's memory as though he was the Helven himself. He felt a strange sensation through his body as his senses adjusted to unify with the illusion—senses torn between the realities of both vision and world.

Slowly, with growing speed, the reality of the vision solidified about him.

Navon lowered his head once before the statue, in a slight bow of reverence, before he raised his eyes attentively to her face. He studied its calm beauty for a moment, inhaling deeply the perfumed scent of the halls around him: the subtle fragrance the priests had sprinkled above the temple to ease the wandering mind.

His eyes shifted fondly down her arm to her hand, outreached to rest upon the head of the statue of an elven child. And it was with the same fond reverence that the child looked up into the goddess' face and smiled. Jikun felt a sense of peace settle over the captain and Navon leaned forward, reaching a hand out to rest on her foot. Through all of Navon's necromantic tendencies, Jikun had not been able to refrain from doubting his comrade's sincerity to his faith. But here, unwatched and unplanned, the religious fervor he sensed was uncomfortably real.

Navon lowered his head once more and kissed the cool stone. Despite his resistance, Jikun found himself pulled further into the reality of the vision.

There was a sudden thud from his right and Navon raised his head sharply, brow knitting in a mixture of confusion and concern. His hand fell slowly from the stone and he pushed off his knees. "What…?" he trailed off, intrigued.

There was another deep thud and he watched several white-robed priests hurry toward the back wall of the temple, whispering quietly to one another in a blur of rapid theories.

"What is it?" Navon called out, his voice echoing across the high-vaulted ceiling, rising above the whispers with undaunted force. Jikun could feel the concern emanating through Navon's memory, causing his body to tense. And yet, even then there still was rising a level of imprudent curiosity.

Several dozen other worshipers, who were scattered across the temple, had paused in their prayers, raising their heads to follow Navon's inquisitive gaze.

"We don't know, Captain," one of the robed priests replied, stopping before the countless rows of candles lining the wall. He leaned his head forward above the flickering flames, his ear moving toward the wall to determine the source of the noise.

There was a suddenly explosion of stone from before the males, smashing into the skull of the nearest priest to crush it inward in a definitive crack. Shouts of terror erupted from around the room and the sound of feet scattered desperately for the temple's doors.

Navon tensed, and with a soldier's training, pushed his fear aside even as he felt the floor beneath him tremble. He glanced down once to see several small stones bounce past his feet, as though even they were desperate to flee from what now lay before them.

His head snapped up. The unwounded priests had scattered, fleeing into the throng of terrified worshipers screaming, "Sel'ari, save us!" And it was then that Navon stepped back, his eyes locking onto the hole in widening realization.

A shadow loomed before them in the dust. A taloned hand reached out and gripped the stone wall as a body pulled itself through the jagged opening.

"Gods save us!" a nearby female screeched in horror.

Navon twisted about swiftly, the instinct to command seizing him even above his own instinct to flee and survive. He gestured sharply to the people behind him, bellowing above the pounding in his ears, "RUN!!!"

The female behind turned with most of the others, laboring under the weight of her unborn child, stumbling and screaming for the door in a pounding and scurrying of desperate and frantic feet. Yet, several priests stepped forward, inspired by Navon's stance.

There was a low growl behind the Helven and a powerful odor of blood and sewage filled the room. A candle skidded across the floor past his feet, leaving a little trail of smoke in its wake.

Navon turned, his eyes growing wide as his breath caught in the deepest channel of his throat.

With a shudder of bloodlust, the beast shook its great, tattered wings and snorted in the smoke, yellow eyes burning as it scanned the vast room before it; it was seeking its prey. As its eyes landed upon Navon, there was a brief flicker of recognition and hatred, a rising fury of past wounds and vicious encounters. Then its powerful jaws snapped open and it emitted a thunderous roar, reaching down and grabbing the bent candleholder beside it. With a single flick of its powerful arm, the candleholder whipped through the air toward the Helven like a twisted, jagged heap of melded swords.

Navon stumbled back as it sped toward him, diving beside the stone statue at his left. He threw his arms up to desperately cover his head, his shield of flesh and bone rising just as the metal collided with the statue. Rock shattered about him in a crack like thunder, dashing shards across his body.

But Navon did not wait for the dust to settle. He scrambled across the floor away from the wreckage, glancing up in time to see the beast step forward casually, snatching up the injured body of a priest as it went. The male screamed in terror, struggling violently against the iron grasp; then the beast reached over with its free hand and gave the head a swift and final twist. There was a sickening crack and the flailing body went still.

"Goddess of beauty and justice, protect us in our hour of need. The darkness grows about us and we of weak body and mind beg the safety of—" Navon began to pray rapidly as he stumbled to his feet and ran for the doors.

Without so much as a whistle of wind, the dead body of the priest slammed into his back. The sudden surge of pain jolted Jikun back to a sense of self, and yet, he felt Navon's head snap back as the male lurched forward. He slammed into the candles on his right, dousing the flames with his body, and fell backward onto the hard tile.

*'Navon!'* he gasped in horror, feeling the captain's heart pounding, his head spinning. Pain surged through his torso with sickening familiarity. And despite the self-awareness, Jikun could not sever the agony searing his own frame.

Navon rolled onto his chest, coughing and gasping, a hand pressed under his breast against a sharp, warm pain in his ribs.

"—your bosom. Let us not fall to the evil that tests us now but with your help—" Navon gasped, cutting off his recommitted prayer as the beast grabbed the bottom half of the stone statue and heaved it up above its head, its muscular arms barely flexing beneath its weight.

Jikun felt his captain's heart stop and his body freeze in horror.

*'RUN,'* he begged him inwardly, desperate to look away. But he could not. *'RUN YOU FOOL.'*

The beast released the stone and it sailed through the air. Navon frantically dove forward, feeling a gust of air as it smashed into the wall behind him. There was a sudden, excruciating pain through his arm as a remnant bounced off the wall and crushed his forearm as though it was made of soft clay.

Navon looked up, gasping through his pain, seeing the beast's steady pace press forward.

The creature shook the remnants of dust from its wings as it walked, its great boots thudding against the smooth marble.

Jikun could feel his own teeth grit as Navon pulled himself up, his left arm hanging loosely at his side. In his frantic desperation to save his comrade, his sense of self was lost and the vision before him intensified.

The beast bared its teeth in a near sneer of victory, grabbing yet another twisted piece of metal and throwing it forward for the final, crippling blow.

"*Veluhas eserine!*" Navon shouted, raising his good hand into the air. The piece of metal slammed into his leg, ripping it out from under him and bringing him to one knee.

But a whirl of faint faces swirled up before him, unfazed by the injury of their summoner. They howled like the wind through a canyon, sweeping over the beast in screams of delight, growing louder and louder as they twisted about the massive frame of the creature.

The beast let out a terrified roar, the cry of its fear only subsiding beneath its rising anger. He fumbled for the nearest large chunk of stone in his blind confusion, hurling it venomously to where he believed Navon to be.

But Navon leapt to the side, twisting his hand in the air in some occultist symbol. Another roar of black smoke pillared from the ceiling, smashing down upon the creature with the force of collapsing stone itself.

Navon saw a shift within the pillaring darkness and the shape of the beast suddenly burst through on the right, darting across the floor and smashing through the doors of the temple as though they were made of the thinnest parchment.

Navon raised his hand at the doors for another moment, but only faint rays of moonlight returned to him.

"Gods save us," he heard a priest nearby gasp in horrified shock.

The realization of what Navon had done struck Jikun like a blow to the chest and the intensity of his bond shattered like ice. He felt Navon's heart rate slow and an overwhelming grasp of pain hit him. His leg…! His chest…! His arm…! His body failed beneath him and he sank toward the marbled floor. The clank of metal sounded from just out of sight and several guards of the Night's Watch rushed into the room, barreling toward the captain as though he were the beast itself.

Suddenly the general was standing beside the mage once more, panting slightly from parted lips. He raised a shaking hand, wiping a bead of sweat from his temple with all the steadiness he could muster. The perfume faded. The pain vanished. But the images remained.

"Such projections can be quite trying on the witness," the seer informed him, apathetically folding his hands against his abdomen. "But as you clearly saw for yourself, General, Captain Navon used necromancy in his defense. He has been imprisoned beneath the palace of His Majesty. He awaits execution for the violation of Sevrigel's laws against the practice of dark magics."

Jikun stepped back, eyes wide as he surveyed the shattered world around him, now pieces to a scene he had just lived. Even without the vision, the knowledge that his captain… his friend was…

Beneath his mask weakened by the vision, Jikun knew grief riveted his face as plain as the seer's robe before him.

"It's unfortunate that you had no knowledge of his dark ways prior to this public unveiling. Perhaps he could have been turned away from his wickedness," the mage spoke gravely. "But, certainly, a better captain shall replace him. Sel'ari's wisdom knows best."

# CHAPTER TWENTY-EIGHT

"Sellemar. Up. It's been at least four hours," Erallus spoke, nudging the male in the side.

Sellemar's brow furrowed at the intrusion. *'When did he start making the decisions?'*

Even so, the guard's urging was inarguable. On this mission, time was a valuable weapon that they could not waste—although this knowledge did nothing to soothe his aching muscles. Gods, had he really been that exhausted? He opened his eyes bleakly and pushed off the wall in order to rise to his feet. The tunnels behind them still glittered with gold and gems, but the place where they now stood was a long upward tunnel of grey stone—sturdy, unembellished, and unlit. "Sel'ari protect us from what is to come," he prayed briefly. He opened his mouth and closed it, glancing around in confusion. "Where is Itirel?"

"Right here," Itirel called down from above him. He dropped down from the ladder, landing lightly beside Sellemar. "At the top is a stone 'door.' The night is silent beyond it." He picked up his lance and rested it over his shoulder, turning to face him intently.

Sellemar nodded once. "As I suspected. We should have few problems entering the palace this way." He smiled inwardly, pleased that Itirel had taken the initiative to scout what he could before he had awoken.

His comrade placed a hand back on the ladder and pulled himself up. "I assume we are clear to move now?"

Sellemar nodded, feeling slight surprise at the Noc'olari's words. It had been many centuries since he and the Noc'olari had last quested, and yet, Itirel still looked to him for leadership.

Erallus put a hand on the ladder next, but Sellemar pulled it firmly away. "I will be going first." He secured his foot onto a rung of the silken rope and began his ascent quickly behind Itirel.

The air gradually became cleaner and crisper, the scent of damp soil and stone falling away as they neared the outside.

"Ah," Sellemar grunted as he ran his hand into Itirel's foot. He must have reached the top. "Can you open it?"

"Yes," Itirel replied softly. A moment later, a circle of light lit the sky above them, falling down in soft beams to the cavern below. Itirel vanished into the world above.

Sellemar glanced away from the darkness and reached up, feeling Itirel's hand clasp his and pull him through the opening as well.

Moonlight showered the stone around him with a soft and charming glow—though Noctem's sinister gaze was greatly softened by the stone figures about him; he was surrounded by the statues of Eraydon, Tiras, Ephraim, Riphath, Mesheck, and Aura, their bodies creating a circle of stances locked in eternal battle, a protective shield around the three elves within.

He reached a hand down for Erallus as Itirel lifted the sheath of his sword from scraping across the stone. With the statues towering above and around them, he, Itirel, and Erallus were invisible to the world outside.

However, as though looking through a gray haze, the courtyard around them was plainly visible. He could see Erallus' eyebrows raised as he turned around slowly. Even Itirel appeared impressed with the level of magical concealment the True Bloods had invested in their eastern capital.

"We shall have to enter the palace," Sellemar spoke after he concluded with certainty that the vicinity was vacant. Outside the statues, the circular courtyard was a maze of paths lined in flowers and poorly trimmed bushes. An overhang jutted over the first story, upheld by white and gold columns. Above it, the palace walls towered into the night sky, their narrowly arched windows dark. Only a single pair of phoenix-engraved doors at the southern end would allow entrance to the courtyard, and they lay closed and dark.

Sellemar replaced the stone circle over the hole behind them and tapped the statue of Eraydon on the back. "May I pass?"

Erallus opened his mouth to comment dumbly, but fell silent as the statue began to move, silently and smoothly as though made of flesh. It stepped aside. "Do the statues in Elvorium do this?" he whispered in stupefied awe, as though he had never seen magic at work.

Sellemar glanced once more at the statue. "Thank you." It stepped back into place. Sellemar crouched low and hurried along a path toward the doors. He did not make an attempt to answer Erallus.

It would shock the soldier for Sellemar to share what information he was privy to in Elvorium.

At the doors, Sellemar crouched down, pressing his ear against the crack. He heard Erallus move close while Itirel stepped up beside him, his back against the wall.

Somewhere in the distance he could hear voices and laughter, but the interior of the doorway was as silent as the courtyard. Still, Sellemar drew his blade. He expected the halls to be empty—Saebellus would not run a night's watch within an area he suspected to be fully secured from without. He pushed the door open briskly and stepped inside.

He was instantly slammed against the wall and he felt the tip of a blade press against his throat.

"Stay outside or I'll slit his throat," the male hissed to Erallus before the soldier could follow. As he closed the door loudly with his foot, Sellemar caught a final glimpse of Itirel darting instantly out of sight. "Where did you two come from?" his apprehender demanded.

Sellemar leaned back against the wall, his wrist aching from the pressure the male placed on his sword arm. He could make out the elf in the dimly lit hallway—blond hair, blue eyes, ears that curved gently to a point. Undoubtedly a Sel'ven, but that was not all. Sellemar's eyes fell to the emblem on his chest. He was a captain.

"You are Captain Vale, I presume," Sellemar spoke softly. He felt the blade bite into his flesh.

"I am asking the questions—"

"That wasn't a question."

He saw the eyes narrow in irritation. Good—the male was easily provoked.

"Who are you?" Vale demanded. "Is Ryekarayn sending assassins to do Sevrigel's work now?"

Sellemar slid his free hand slightly up the wall.

"I can see you moving. Do it again, and I'll just slit your throat and question your comrade."

He was serious. Sellemar could see the cold assertion in his eyes.

"Sellemar. Acting mercenary. Here to rescue Ilsevel on behalf of the kingdom." Gods, what was Erallus doing? He found himself unconcerned with Itirel's movements: no doubt the male was already putting a plan into effect.

He watched Vale's eyes look him over. "Drop your weapon."

Sellemar obediently let his sword clatter to the floor at his feet.

Vale leaned his body closer, suddenly at ease with his captive's disarmament. "Mm. You look rather familiar. Have I fucked you before?"

Sellemar blinked, shock throwing him off guard. If he had not already been pinned so thoroughly, he would have recoiled in disgust. "What?" he found himself stammering, flustered and appalled by the male's words.

"Oh, as innocent and timid as the other little Sel'varian bitches, aren't you?"

Sellemar refocused, wiping his face of emotion. He had to set the male back on edge. He was getting too comfortable in his dominance: and with it, his focus on Sellemar's movement increased. "It does not surprise me that the best male Saebellus can find—" He flinched as the blade dug into his throat. Damn, it was too late. He had lost any chance of reclaiming his edge the moment Vale had taken it. Where in Ramul were Itirel and Erallus?!

There was a sudden shatter of glass from their left. A rock knocked against the floor and rolled to the side. It was enough. Vale's head turned and Sellemar jerked his throat away from the blade, feeling it slice along the surface of his neck. The door flung open immediately and Vale reeled back from the instant swipe of Itirel's lance.

Sellemar grabbed the captain's wrist even as Vale made an attempt to reposition his control. He kneed him in the groin and kicked out as the male doubled. He bent his wrist back as he ducked under his arm and slammed Vale's head into the wall.

As the captain sank down toward the floor, Sellemar picked the dagger easily from the elf's twisted hand and shoved it into his side.

The door to the courtyard swung open again and Erallus stepped in, sword drawn. He glanced once at the bleeding captain and back up at Sellemar and Itirel. "They may have heard us. We have to move."

Itirel bent down and picked up Sellemar's sword, holding it in his free hand as he stood stoically over Sellemar and Vale.

Sellemar crouched down beside Saebellus' captain and leaned forward. He put a hand over the male's mouth. "Where is Ilsevel?" he demanded. He pushed the hilt of the dagger deeper. "Where?"

Vale cried out, muffled by the palm over his lips.

Sellemar pulled his hand slightly away. "Where?"

Vale let out a gasp of pain as he whispered a weak reply, "Third floor. Turn left. Fourth door… on left…"

Sellemar put his hand back over Vale's mouth and pressed firmly once more on the dagger. "How many guards?" He could hear the male gasp and choke back another cry in a desperate attempt to appear stronger than he was. Sellemar withdrew his hand.

"None."

"None??" Sellemar grabbed the male's hair and jerked his head up, studying his face in confusion.

Vale's eyes were closed tightly, but he could see the pressure lightening. His lips were turning grey. He was fading. "None…"

Sellemar dropped his head.

"I think he at least *believes* he is telling the truth," Itirel spoke with a raised eyebrow. "Anyways, his lack of consciousness now is of no more use to us."

"No guards?" Erallus repeated behind them.

Sellemar pushed off his knees quickly. "Come. The staircase is this way." No guards? That could not be possible. They would never leave Ilsevel unguarded. "And whose idea was it to throw a stone? You want to alert the whole damn palace, *Erallus?* Gods, such a damn novice."

"It worked, so let's not point fingers," Itirel defended the soldier solidly.

They ran as one up the wide, white marbled staircase and as they ascended, it became plain that the second floor was empty. They passed by it and slowed before the third, crouching and moving more cautiously, with Itirel at the rear.

The first glimpse of the hallway coming off the third level was better than he had expected. It was lit with small, golden orbs and a single crystal chandelier along the ceiling, far brighter than the first level passageway. *'Hm… one guard…'* He peered down the rest of the brightly lit hallway. The other dark mahogany doors were closed as well and the elegantly carved, delicate tables spotted across the walls were empty. Unlike so many other elven palaces, there were no pillars or statues, no grand outpouring of wealth. Horiembrig had truly fallen into ruin, and long before Saebellus had taken hold of it.

"He'll see us coming before we even get close," Itirel's whisper came, barely audible beside him.

Sellemar crouched down fully on the stairs. It was not just any guard again. The thick, dark, heavily scarred man was a lieutenant. He frowned. This one he did not recognize. He appeared human: tall and significantly larger than either he or Erallus—or frankly any elf, for that matter. "One of Saebellus' lieutenants…"

"Not Adonis—he's a Sel'ven," Erallus whispered from his other side. "Kraesin, then, I believe. He was a mercenary before he joined up with Saebellus. Incredibly well-known sword wielder."

Sellemar gripped his blade tighter in a rush of adrenaline. "You are sure the man is Kraesin?" The name, at least, he recognized.

Erallus slid closer, his eyes intensely scrutinizing the man before them. It was clear that he was mulling over his options and Sellemar waited impatiently for clarification. "Has to be if he is a human lieutenant," he finally breathed.

Sellemar nodded understandingly, noting that the blade at the human's side was no cheap forgery.

"Oh, and he's an exceptional knife thrower as well."

*'Fantastic.'* The situation was looking dimmer already. Sellemar glanced back at Itirel for guidance, but the male seemed as conflicted about their options as he was himself. Neither he nor Itirel were particularly skilled in long range weaponry, and a quick judgment of Erallus' weapon choice told him the same was true of the guard.

"What is the plan?" Erallus demanded after a moment of uncomfortable silence.

Sellemar paused once more. "…Go break another window. Louder this time. Make some noise. Draw him near the stairs."

Erallus raised a cautious brow. "What are *you* two going to do?" he demanded in reply.

"Kill him. Now let us take care of this and *go.*"

Erallus gave an obedient nod and moved silently back down the stairs.

Sellemar slid his sword into his sheath. Praise Sel'ari the man was a human—an elf probably would have heard the first crash. "Follow me," he ordered Itirel. "And stay out of the fight." He drew out his dagger and crept to the side of the staircase. While he gripped the dagger in his teeth, he slipped over the side of the railing, lowering himself until he was hanging by his hands along the edge.

Itirel moved to dangle beside him, hanging confidently by one hand as his free hand held his lance down at his side.

Sellemar glanced down once, even as his mind warned him against it. He could see the first stairs far below him and his gut dropped anxiously. *Damn*, perhaps Itirel could survive a fall like that, but if *he* fell… that would break more than his legs.

He forced his gaze upward and began to creep up the side of the railing toward the top of the staircase, nodding his head toward Itirel to stay where he was. Sellemar had no sooner reached the top when there was the unmistakable shatter of glass and a loud and definite thud.

"What in Ishkav's name…" Sellemar heard Kraesin breathe in blasphemy, the sound of footsteps padding cautiously toward the staircase.

Sellemar's grip tightened on the narrow ledge, his fingertips aching. *'Faster,'* he willed. He could see Itirel's eyes widen in concern, clearly detecting that Sellemar's stamina wasn't going to keep him at the railing for much longer.

The footsteps receded to the opposite end of the staircase and Sellemar could wait no longer. He pulled himself up enough to catch a glimpse of the man leaning over the side, peering warily into the darkness.

*Finally*: the man's back was to him and Sellemar had his opportunity. He instantly swung himself up, hooking a leg over the side of the railing and nimbly twisting over the edge.

Kraesin swung around and drew his blade in immediate response to the slight sound. "What the—! Who are you?" he demanded, raising his sword. "How did you get through the guards?"

But his questions were merely rhetorical. Sellemar made no attempt to answer, grabbing the dagger from his mouth and throwing it sharply toward the man's chest. As he twisted to move out of the path of the blade, Sellemar drew his sword and met the human's forcefully. He threw his weight into him, sending the lieutenant reeling back into the railing.

*He had one shot at his advantage.*

Sellemar swung his leg out, knocking the human off balance and with a forceful thrust, slammed his left fist into the human's face. With a final, swift kick to the upper chest, the human teetered over the railing and with a piercing cry of surprise, vanished over the side.

There was a sickening thud below as his bones cracked against the marble floor. Sellemar sheathed his blade and hurried to the railing, reaching a hand out to Itirel. The Noc'olari handed him the lance and pulled himself up with ease. "Good work," he praised as Sellemar turned to dash for the door.

"Hurry up. More than one human will have heard that."

"What is going on?!" the sudden panicked voice of a lady rang out from within the room beyond.

Sellemar pushed the door. Damn. Locked. He took a step back and slammed his body against it.

"*Shit,*" he swore, stepping back again. Elven architecture. He rubbed his shoulder.

"Kraesin didn't have the keys on him, if you were wondering," came Erallus' voice behind them.

Sellemar turned—he had almost forgotten about the male. "Come help me with this door," he ordered sharply.

The two stepped back.

"*Stop*, before you hurt yourselves," Itirel barked, pushing Sellemar forcefully aside and taking his position beside Erallus.

Sellemar glared, but remained to the side. Itirel had a lot more power to put into his body—even with magic excluded.

"Go!" Sellemar ordered.

They gave the door a powerful kick, throwing their weight into it. They heard the edge of the door crack against the bolt, the metal no doubt splintering against the doorframe.

"Again."

They could hear the creak of breaking wood.

"Again."

The third kick sent the door flying open. Wood splintered on the other side of the door as the bolt was broken loose, flying inward and clattering against the marble. The door slammed into the wall behind, shaking dust from the engraved moldings and sending a tremble through the floor at their feet.

"Praise the gods!" the female inside gasped in a cry of relief, a hand clutching her chest.

Sellemar hardly had time to assess her condition. He pushed through the two males. She was clothed and appeared uninjured. That was enough. "Time to go," he barked, walking briskly and grabbing her wrist. "Before the palace becomes alerted!"

He heard the sudden, distant sounds of footsteps above them, thudding against the stone.

"They are alerted," Itirel informed unnecessarily.

"Damn, let's go!" Erallus beckoned urgently, running for the staircase. "This place will be swarming in minutes!!"

Sellemar jerked the lady after him as he turned to run, Itirel bringing up the rear. Lady Ilsevel quickly fell into step behind him and he released her to regain his own balance.

No shoes: he could hear her bare feet padding against the marble stairs, but she would have to do without such trifles.

Above them, the sound of rushing feet grew like thunder, a wave of cries echoing through the palace as though the grounds had come to life. As they passed by the second floor, Sellemar could hear her gasp in horror, "Oh my gods… my guard… Kraesin!"

Sellemar hurried past the body, ignoring the open skull beside him. *'Stomach it,'* he muttered indifferently to the lady.

They fled down the final flight of stairs and turned sharply down the hallway that led to their final breadth of escape: into the courtyard.

"And that's Vale!" he heard her gasp again as they approached the body lying against the wall.

If they had needed the identity of the dead and dying of Saebellus' hierarchy, she may have been of some use.

Itirel moved ahead and pushed open the doors. He held them as Sellemar ran past, leaping easily over the overgrown bushes and trampling the flowers beneath his leather boots. He skidded to a stop before the statues and tapped Eraydon twice on the chest. "May I pass?" he panted heavily.

The statue moved aside, all the more urgently as though it sensed the need of the moment.

Sellemar pulled open the stone door and turned toward Erallus sharply. "Go first!" he barked.

The elf quickly lowered himself into the darkness. Sellemar grabbed Ilsevel's wrist roughly and pushed her toward the hole. "Now you. Move!"

Itirel gave him a sharp look of rebuke.

*'Now is not the time,'* Sellemar returned the glare.

Ilsevel quickly lowered herself down into the hole before Itirel, her eyes searching the darkness frantically for some hope in light as she descended without question. Sellemar looked back up to the statue of Eraydon glinting in the moonlight. "Thank you," he breathed, and vanished into the darkness after them.

The stone circle slid closed above.

"Who *are* you?" he heard the lady below gasp. "How did you manage this? Where are you taking me?!"

"Sellemar, my lady. And we are taking you back to the king."

# Chapter Twenty-Nine

"Saebellus!"

The pounding on the door grew more frantic.

"SAEBELLUS!"

Saebellus sat up sharply, his heart racing from the abrupt awakening. "What?!" he replied, throwing the covers from his body. His mind surged with thoughts from the soldier's panicked tone. Was Horiembrig under siege?—Could the elves have gathered troops even without Jikun?! *Insufferably bold!*

The carved door swung open without his further command and a soldier leaned in, wheezing heavily, his hand white-knuckled as he clutched the frame. "General!" Saebellus saw him quickly avert his eyes. "Ilsevel has escaped, Kraesin is dead, and Vale is severely wounded. The men believe the intruders fled into the courtyard, but no trace can be found of them!"

Saebellus stood, black eyes widening as his face contorted in shock, anger, and incredulous disbelief. "WHAT?!" He grabbed his pants from where they hung over the frame of the bed. "Where is Adonis?! And Laethile?!" As though some notion of their whereabouts might lessen the blow of the news.

"I believe they rushed to Vale, General," the soldier replied weakly.

Saebellus fastened the clasp of his pants and swept his sword from the nightstand beside him. His lieutenant, his captain, Ilsevel… He controlled his voice as he breathed, "Where is Vale?"

"At the doors to the courtyard, General." The soldier stumbled aside as Saebellus briskly moved past him.

*'Kraesin…! Vale…!'* No doubt the males who had rescued her were from Jikun's elite forces. How they had discovered her capture, he did not know. The ransom was not expected to arrive to Hairem for another few days! He hurried down the steps, running his hand along the weathered banister as he moved.

"Damn him!" he swore at the mental image of the king's visage as he stopped on the third floor where Ilsevel had been taken mere hours before. He had seen Hairem but once, as a thin, scrawny youth scrambling away with a flock of servants after they had roused the temper of the baker's wife. His general had nearly trampled the little prince under hoof. A foolish child that had grown into a foolishly bold male.

The visage faded as his black eyes, like two churning pools in the Angaulise Swamps, devoured the emptiness around him. Kraesin's body was nowhere to be seen. Perhaps he had been led off? And yet, Kraesin was not one to leave his post. If he had not been overpowered here...

He stopped before the door, scowling at the two places where it had been cracked with near equal force. "Two males...?" he growled, incredulous at the work that only two individuals could do amidst his stronghold. Amidst his men. *'...They must have found a way into the palace using the tunnels.'* He had heard of them, as had so many others. But that anyone on Sevrigel still lived who remembered their points of entry... King Hairem could know nothing about them! When the True Bloods had disinherited the continent, they had taken their secrets with them.

Had the True Bloods been involved?

No. He rebuked his foolishness with a violent shake of his head. It had been his mistake to *assume* the knowledge had left Sevrigel.

His black eyes narrowed at the sight of the broken wood where the bolt had bent away.

If they had entered through a palace escape, its entrance was no doubt somewhere in the courtyard. Two males, no matter how "elite," could not have eluded the company of soldiers he had positioned outside the palace gates.

He turned, moving quickly down the stairs. As he descended the final level of the staircase, he slowed, his lips pursing to a hard, thin line.

Not led away... *thrown.*

"General!" one of the soldiers on the stairs stood, putting a hand to his chest. "Lieutenant Kraesin is dead."

That much was unquestionably evident. Saebellus moved to the side of the man's body and stopped, and yet, his eyes softened. *'Kraesin...'* He would be impossible to replace. He turned back to the soldier. "Move his body off the steps. Lay him in Ilsevel's room."

There would be time to grieve later.

He forced his mind back on the two males. He would make Hairem and Jikun suffer for their audacity.

He stepped off the last stair and walked quickly down the dimly lit hallway. Up ahead, he could see the forms of Adonis and Laethile, their familiar silhouettes crouched low over a body between them.

"General!" a soldier saluted as he passed. But Saebellus gave him no regard.

Adonis looked up sharply as the title echoed down the hall. His smooth face was creased with worry, his pale eyes shimmering slightly in the light. His delicate hands tightened their grip on Vale's narrow shoulders. "Saebel," his voice came to him, no more than a whisper of distress.

Saebellus paused briefly at their side. "Let me deal with the escaped," he spoke firmly, tearing his eyes away from the pool of blood they knelt in. He could see Adonis' chest rising and falling heavily; the male was nearly hyperventilating in panic. He would have to calm him down, but right now…

Right *now*…!

He threw open the courtyard doors, letting them slam against the walls outside. He heard the crack of stone behind the door, the ripple of terror from the troops nearby. He fought forcefully to quell his raging temper, for *their* sake.

The courtyard of Horiembrig was still, even as the guards combed it in the dim moonlight. There was no breeze, no other creatures. He watched their torchlight cast long shadows up the walls. Even the flower buds had closed in the cool night air, drooping in sleep.

It was eerily silent, as though the gods themselves mocked him.

Saebellus inhaled sharply and strode onto the path. His eyes flicked past the poorly cared for expanse of green before him to the large statues erected at the center of the courtyard, their fierce and stony faces still. "I know you were involved," he breathed venomously. "SOLDIER!" he shouted at the nearest male. "Have these statues knocked down. I do not care how you do so, just attend to the matter immediately. When you find a tunnel, seal it."

"What about pursui—" the male began.

"*Seal it.* Do I make myself clear?!"

The soldier nodded in acknowledgement and Saebellus gave the statues a final, poisonous scowl before he whirled sharply and strode away. The briefest flicker of guilt slid in beside him, pushing the ghastly, sprawling body of his lieutenant before his resistant gaze.

*'I'm sorry, Kraesin.'* His troops would not catch them after their head start, and no doubt they would expect an attempt to follow. He would not give them the satisfaction of killing more of his soldiers.

Patience. It had brought him this far. He would not make the mistakes of a lesser general. There would come a time and place for his vengeance.

He stepped back through the double doors and crouched beside Adonis, watching his pale, blue eyes remain locked on Vale's face. Strands of hair had come loose from Adonis' half-braid as though attempting to hide his anxiety. Vale's head was cradled in his lap and he was gently stroking his forehead, avoiding the black bruise swelling on the side. He asked nothing, as there was nothing that could push past his weight of concern.

Vale's face was grey and still, his cracked lips parted slightly, and Saebellus wondered what good even his Noc'olari could do at this point. "How is he, Laeth?" Saebellus asked after a moment, his voice pragmatic. Adonis already bore the weight of his own concern as well.

Laethile sat back slowly, brushing a lock of silver hair from his face. "I used the best of everything I have, Saebel. There is… nothing more I can do for him."

Saebellus let out a deep exhale, even at the expected reply, his temper rising even as his tone remained coolly unchanged. "Then he will die?"

Laethile patted Vale's hand, swiftly glancing from Adonis and back to the general. "He's strong—fiercely determined to see the war to its end. I think Vale will pull through." He smiled slightly, grey eyes failing to match the optimism in his voice.

Saebellus rested a hand on Adonis' narrow shoulder, pushing off him as he stood. Even if his captain did survive, the soonest Vale could be of use to him was two months. "Adonis, I will need you to take over Vale's position while he recovers. I need someone I can rely on to replace him and your unique talents will be invaluable. Kraesin is dead. I will allow Laeth to stay behind and take care of Vale, but you will have to come with me." He paused as Adonis grew still. "He is a Noc'olari, Adonis. There is no one who can do more for him than Laeth can."

Adonis bent his head down and Saebellus saw him slide the back of his hand across his face. He looked up then, eyes firm even as his gentle voice wavered. Beneath that glass-like exterior, the male was strong. "Yes, Saebel."

"We are marching on Elarium in seven weeks."

Adonis' eyes cleared, the caution breaking through his pain. "Elarium? That is Sevrigel's southern capital… Even with part of Jikun's army ill, can we afford to—"

"Yes. Not only can we afford to, but if Hairem makes the mistake of attempting to defend it, *I will crush him* this time. He has had his last 'victory.'" His lips pursed. "As for the necromancer in his presence, he will inhibit us no longer. If Elvorium does not dispose of this male, I want you to see to it that he does not cause Jerah problems *again*."

# CHAPTER THIRTY

"Truly, My Lord," Lardol spoke with a 'tsk' and shake of his golden head, "was it really necessary to put the kingdom in such a frantic state like this? A royal wedding pulled together in a month?"

Hairem found it difficult, even through Lardol's nagging, to cease his broad smile. Ilsevel had borne her capture and bondage with true grace. But her elation at being free had driven her desire for an even more urgent marriage. No sooner had she returned than she had set about planning every detail of the wedding, hardly pausing to consult him in her fervent attempts to rush the otherwise lengthy process.

But this did not bother him. He was overjoyed at her excitement and Nilanis seemed more than willing to grant her every request, no matter how lavish.

"Lardol, what do you expect? Ilsevel was taken by Saebellus—that sort of trial shakes an elf. Can you blame me for agreeing with her desire to marry so swiftly on her return? She insisted, Lardol. If there is one thing I can tell you about love, it is that your life is happy if your lady is happy." He wondered briefly if Sellemar would attend the ceremony—he had seen nothing of him after his initial return, and yet he felt so endeared to him after his mission that he had every desire to see the male present.

"Spoken like a true spouse already. No matter. As you know, My Lord, it puts my heart at ease to see you wed to such a distinguished family… and in love. Your father—may Sel'ari grant him safe passage—was not so lucky. He would be quite proud to see this day."

Hairem fastened the golden buttons of his white silken shirt slowly, staring at his reflection in an almost sightless manner, as though looking far past himself.

How much like his father he looked now. A young king, but how fast the struggle with the council had put creases across his face! He felt a rush of relief that there was a limit to how much, in appearance, an elf could age. His golden hair had been pulled back loosely, much as the True Bloodline had done for wedding ceremonies for centuries, and as his father had undoubtedly adopted in the following of their tradition.

Hairem ran a hand dutifully down his chest, smoothing out the invisible wrinkles caused by his anxiety. He let his hand remain on his stomach as he paused briefly to inspect the gold-laced, silken shirt that shimmered with embroidery and carved buttons bearing the royal crest.

Marriage to Ilsevel! In a few hours' time, she would be his queen. He inhaled sharply, anxiety causing his heart to beat even faster.

"Alvena, no. Absolutely not," he heard Lardol bark, pulling him back to the present.

Hairem looked over his head in the mirror to the girl behind him. She had rolled her eyes at Lardol's rebuke. "What is it, Lardol?"

Lardol sighed, picking up an end of his hair. "This, My Lord. Look at this braid. The public will think you slept in it. Alvena, this is a *wedding*. Do better."

Hairem brushed Lardol's hand away lightly. He smiled back at Alvena, whose bottom lip jutted out in frustration. She was ever defiant to the male—what a wife she would make an elf one day.

He chuckled in amusement. "Alvena, it is perfect." He smiled as she blushed and turned her flushed face away. "Lardol, go easy on her. Trust me, all eyes will be on Ilsevel this day." He stood, fastening the last golden button at his neck, and picked up his sword from the chest of drawers before Lardol could gather to offer it to him. "Please, both of you. Cease fussing over me. I am certain this wedding shall progress despite my appearance. Now, I want both of you to enjoy it! Simply make certain that this room is prepared for us this evening and what else you do with your time today is your own." He turned to focus his attention on Alvena. "And you, my dear. I had Madorana leave a dress for you in your bedroom. You don't have to wear it today, but seeing as how this is such a special occasion and you have done such a fine job of taking care of me today, it is a gesture of my thanks that I hope, at least, you are fond of. Lardol, you will find something similar in your room."

Alvena giggled.

"It is *not* a dress," he heard Lardol snap to her under his breath.

"I'm heading out early. I want to speak with Erallus before the ceremony." He walked toward the door, pausing once to look back at them. "Remember, this room."

"I had better not catch you eavesdropping on the king *this* night," Hairem heard Lardol bark as he closed the door behind him.

He chuckled to himself. The two of them never changed—and he certainly hoped they never would.

"My Lord," Erallus greeted, bowing his head as Hairem turned toward the stairs.

"Come. I want to take one final ride through the city before the wedding. In private. We will take the servants' carriage." Hairem found himself walking with almost a bounce to his step, beckoning his old friend after him. And he wondered briefly why he had never directly thought to think of the male as such before. Erallus was always at his side, loyally and unshakably. Perhaps the mere frequency of the male's presence had somehow delayed the clarity of their relationship, or, more likely, his elation at the world around him: everything was so simple. So likeable. Why, the persistent and over-protective qualities of the male at his back seemed, for that short time, to be his best qualities.

Erallus raised his brows in curiosity. "As you wish, My Lord." He paused and chuckled faintly. "Why, I don't believe I've ever seen you happier, My Lord."

"Erallus, you can't possibly imagine," Hairem beamed. He was quite certain there wasn't another feeling in the world like it!

They made quick work of the walk to the stables. Once in the carriage, Hairem sat back, eyeing the head of his personal guard thoughtfully. He sat so stiffly. So attentively. Yet it was just them and the bouncing servant carriage and no one the wiser to who sat inside. "What are you thinking?" he queried after a moment as the carriage made another bump onto the cobbled streets outside the palace grounds.

Erallus cocked his head, as though surprised for the question. "I am overjoyed for you, My Lord. I was thinking about the splendor of the ceremony. And also how your mother and father looked on their day. I was the personal guard to your father then, as well. I remember the nobility in awe of your mother as she entered the hall, but the look on your father's face was as though he was taking on a duty-bound burden. No matter how radiant she looked, your father could not hide his disappointment. I look at you now and it is quite plain to me that this will be nothing like that day."

Hairem smiled, knowing Erallus felt proud to have seen Hairem take a wife of his own choosing. "He grew to love her. After she passed, he had nothing but good things to say about her." He lifted the curtain of the carriage and peered out onto the wide streets bustling with excited civilians dressed in bright silks and adorned in elegant jewelry. The businesses were closed all across the city—there was not an elf who had not gathered at the temple to celebrate the occasion. White banners waved from all the balconies and every column in the city was wrapped in gold. "Erallus, may I ask you a personal question?"

He saw the soldier hesitate in his surprise. Hairem had, after all, never asked him one. Though the soldier before him was as present as his own shadow, Hairem knew so little of him. "...You may ask me anything, My Lord."

The king regarded the male thoughtfully for a moment. "Anything" was a very long list when he knew nothing. But one question in particular had crept forward in his mind, spurred on by the encroaching wedding. "We haven't spoken often, personally, you and I. And yet, you're practically my shadow. Strange, how that has run its course." He paused, trying to peel back the attentive face before him for some feeling on the matter. "Do you... like your job?—a vow of celibacy seems rather..."

"Impossible?" Erallus finished. He chuckled slightly. "I think of that vow as more of... a vow to not wed."

Hairem gave a little gasp at the implication, hardly daring to interpret the meaning. "*You...?*" He immediately wished he hadn't asked—had feigned dumb to the meaning. Now he would find himself culpable to the crime as well.

Erallus swiftly shook his head, as though he had taken Hairem's tone as misunderstanding. "Since we are being honest, My Lord. And not elves, if that quells your nerves. A human or two." Erallus' attempt at clarification was nonchalant, but Hairem was fully aware that the number was far higher than Erallus was ready to divulge. Though it hardly mattered. One. One hundred. The punishment was the same.

And Hairem did not attempt to mask his surprise. Or his horror. Erallus had dabbled in prostitution? There was no doubt the male was fully aware of the dangers of such a crime; he had been present at his father's side for more than one such sinner's execution!

Hairem opened and closed his mouth. The expression on the male had hardly changed. Where only open and unabashed honesty had been present before, now the faintest trace of concern was knit across the brow, as though the male was suddenly contemplating if he had said too much. And to any other elf in Elvorium, he certainly would have.

But... Hairem pulled his features into a controlled and apathetic mask, hoping to quell the soldier's concerns. Despite his disagreement on the matter, he could hardly see the male before him in poor light. Rather, he found himself seeking a solution to his friend's weakness, internally reassuring himself that Erallus was merely misled or greatly troubled and needed only an intervening hand to gently push him to a safer path. "If... I lifted the ban on marriage, do you think...?" Hairem finally spoke.

But Erallus replied swiftly, as though he had fully reflected on such a matter before. "No, My Lord. I believe that vow is there for good reason. A wife would most certainly force me to give concerns and time where you should be instead. No. Rather, this is a personal trial of my own."

Hairem raised his brows at the frank honesty with which the male responded to him and he felt a sudden desire to protect him from the council and its unhesitating punishment. And Erallus' response had only made this desire fiercer. "While I can in no way pretend to condone such behavior... You are my friend. I'm certain I do not need to order you to keep this quiet. I shall do so as well."

Even as he said the words, he felt a little flame of fear flicker inside of him. He was now aware of an individual committing a crime that was punishable by death—and by elven law, this made him complicit. Should Erallus' crime ever be discovered and Hairem's knowledge made known, even his position as *king* would not save him from the council's retribution.

And yet... he smiled faintly as Erallus gave a brief smile of thanks. He would never let the council lay a hand on Erallus. He owed him his life. And now they were—

"*Even*, my lord," Erallus suddenly spoke, as though he had followed Hairem's train of thought down to the moment. Indeed, the male knew him far better than he could ever hope to know the soldier. "So you can put that whole matter behind you about the assassin—fleeting glances. Politeness. Favors."

Hairem chuckled his amusement, shaking his head. "I see your game," he accused.

"Hardly," Erallus replied firmly, rebuffing Hairem's casual reply to what was clearly intended to be a serious leveling of the matter. "You asked a question and I merely answered it. You just happened to ask the right one."

Hairem closed his mouth, briefly wondering how many others he saw on a regular basis were dancing with death. "And since we *are* on this topic, have you heard the rumors of the general and *his*… similar habit? Is it a rumor or…?"

Here Erallus hesitated, perhaps torn now between honesty and the life of someone not his own. "True, I suspect," Erallus finally gave a dark reply, shifting his gaze slightly away as though this eased his guilt. "I'm quite certain the council is fully aware of these rumors as well and merely ignores them for their own sake. If they garnered true evidence, they would have to sentence him the same as anyone else—and that would undoubtedly reflect quite poorly on Mikanum. Unlike myself, the general has not been as tempered in his sins. I imagine he's playing quite the dangerous game."

Hairem gave a slow, thoughtful nod. Jikun's life too was now safely tucked beneath his secrecy. "Am I the only one who doesn't…?"

"Hardly, My Lord. Our discrepancies are not a reflection on your kingdom… They are more of a reflection of our… weaknesses…"

"And what other weaknesses would you say you have?"

Erallus rattled off without pause, "I can be rather bland… careless, clumsy, childish, apathetic… certainly a bit too progressive—if we're comparing to the council. Unceremonious for certain. A bit too bold. And I have a terrible affection for personal style that simply does not fit the job."

Hairem gave a laugh. "How have we not spoken more?"

Erallus offered a crooked grin.

"As much as I enjoy this conversation, I *do*, in fact, have a reason for bringing you out here like this." Hairem let the curtain on the carriage fall and leaned back against the seat, regarding the male contemplatively. "You said we were 'even' before, and if that is how you wish to see it, so be it. But still, I never *did* thank you properly for saving my life and—"

"My Lord, please."

Hairem leaned back. "No, Erallus. Listen to me. This is my turn to be frank with you. I have no heir. No male blood of my own. Neither on my father's nor on my mother's side." He could see Erallus' eyes widen as his thoughts rushed past his own, daring to finish his train of thought before him. Still, Hairem had the male's obedient silence and he continued, "I have already handed Lardol my will this morning. Marriage makes you realize how much you have to lose. My trust for you runs deeper than to any other—and whatever your personal flaws, you still recognize justice—you're an honorable individual. If anything should happen to me before Ilsevel bears an heir, you shall be instated as king."

He raised his hand to silence Erallus' immediate attempt to vocalize his surprise. "Listen," he commanded once more. "I know this is not a great gift. It's a burden. It has always been a burden. But you are with me every day and so you know this better than anyone. And I know you could rule. Everyone has their sins—granted, not all of them end in the rope—but as king, you could marry and so—I digress. I know you would be a good king—fair, just, and honorable is all one can expect.

"I *do* have one condition—that the palace would remain a home to Ilsevel if she so chose. And the request that you keep her safe," he finished as Erallus' lips parted.

"Your Majesty…" Erallus trailed off, slower to respond as though he had come to realize that Hairem had given the matter true thought. He pressed a hand to his chest, eyes wide, words spoken almost breathlessly. "I am honored… humbled by your trust. I… if you would wish this of me, then I shall do it. There are no words to express the mixed emotions I feel, but above them all is humility for your trust. But, Hairem," he paused, composing his features, then continued in a steady and firm voice. "So long as I live, you shall as well."

Hairem smiled. Erallus had served his family well even before his birth, and other than the countless servants roaming his palace, the soldier was his only friend not bound by any form of politics. "I thought you would say something like that." He raised the curtain once more as the carriage turned back toward the palace. Actually, there *was* one other. "What about Sellemar? Have you heard from him since?"

Erallus shook his head, taking Hairem's change of topic in stride. Hairem briefly wondered if he so frequently flitted topics without any verbal coalescence. "I heard he donated all of his reward to the repairs on the temple from the incident with Captain Navon, and is remaining at the Whistling Glade. However, he still possesses the deed to the estate you gave him."

Hairem frowned, rubbing his chin. "I cannot make sense of this Sellemar…" It had been hard to keep the male off his mind. After Ilsevel's return, he had boasted of his deed in all and well-deserved arrogance—and Hairem could hardly fault him for his pride after stealing Saebellus' most valuable bargaining tool from under his very eyes—but had then refused the reward he and Nilanis had offered. And apparently even after finally accepting their gold, he had given it all to the temple anyway. Perhaps it too was a matter of pride? "After the chaos of the wedding has passed, I shall have to speak with him again," Hairem spoke thoughtfully.

The two were quiet for a moment.

"This may be… out of line, but if I may, My Lord…" Erallus began.

Hairem chuckled. "Erallus, please. You may ask me anything as well."

"Do you have any immediate plans for an heir?"

Hairem nearly choked as he swallowed and felt his cheeks grow warm. He had no doubt that he was blushing. "Now you sound like Lardol."

Erallus smiled. "Someone has to play his part while he's away. I look forward to seeing your son grow after having seen the male you have become."

*

Hairem stood at the top steps of the temple of Sel'ari, feeling small beneath her towering marble form: a reminder of how all things compared to the glory of the goddess. The towering jade columns had been wrapped in golden ribbon and the white marble floor was showered in an assortment of vivid petals. Only the smaller goddess and elven child statue were amiss: the only signs that any damage had been done to the temple at all. Light poured in from the dozens of narrow windows high above them, the pale rays appearing almost tangible. And yet for once, even in all her splendor, as he turned his back on her to anxiously face the mass of nobility, he found her easy to slide from his mind. The halls were shining around the evenly split isles, and there was a female behind him, strumming a lyre and singing softly in the ancient tongue.

He smiled to himself, thinking of how dreadful Ilsevel sounded in comparison.

The new doors to the temple stood wide and, outside of them, Hairem could see a mass of elves standing quietly and stoically for the procession of the bride through the city to be completed. The walk was ever another way for the elves to demonstrate the peace of their city and the grandeur of their royalty, and yet, when Ilsevel was the bride, Hairem could find no fault in the ceremony.

It felt like ages before he could see the approach of her caravan, the royal guard led by Erallus escorting her up the final steps and into the entryway of the temple itself. They parted, vanishing into the colorful crowd and leaving behind the radiant figure of his bride.

The elves were too refined to gasp in awe, but their expressions could not conceal their admiration.

Hairem's anxiety vanished as swiftly as the wind, his eyes locking onto her face with such focus that the elegant gown of greens and golds went almost unnoticed. He stepped down from his stand and walked to her. He could see her fighting back the smile on her pale, pink lips he had ceased struggling against since he had awoken that morning. Let the elves think him unrefined! This was his day.

"Lady Ilsevel," he spoke, bending to a knee before her and taking her hand. He stood, moving to her side and turning back toward the front of the temple at a slow and steady pace.

"My Lord," she whispered.

Hairem led her slowly up the line of nobility, the demonstration of her political ascension from lady to queen. He could see several of the council members stiffen as he passed, but Nilanis' expression was only that of triumph. Hairem's smile broadened.

To think how far things had come!—From that awkward, stately dinner so many months before to *this!*

He stopped with her on the last step, facing her and taking her hands into his own. They turned as one toward the statue of Sel'ari and went down to their knees before her. Ilsevel's radiance seemed breathtaking as the light from a high window cast its rays across her, causing the flaxen threads of silk to gleam as brightly as her hair.

In the light of the sun's golden rays, even surrounded by all the nobility of Sevrigel and splendor of the temple, Hairem could see nothing but his bride.

The priest stepped forward, raising his hands up to the goddess and speaking loudly.

"Goddess of the Elven Kingdom, Second Comer of Emal'drathar, Sovereign Queen of Justice, we, the nation of Sevrigel, stand before you on this day to testify to the holy union of King Hairem, second of his royal bloodline, son of late-king Liadeltris and late-queen Rumel of Elvorium, to Lady Ilsevel, daughter of El'adorium Nilanis Esterel and late-lady Losaldra of Elarium." He then faced them, speaking softer and lowering his hands. "We have testified."

Hairem stood, pulling Ilsevel to her feet. "My body, my mind, and my soul are yours. If you die, I die. If you live, I shall live. Forever and always my life is yours. In the eyes of Sel'ari I have said this. In the eyes of Sel'ari may I be bound to this."

He could see Ilsevel falter, gripping his hands tightly. A glimmer shone at the corner of her eyes, and her lips trembled as she fought back her elation. "My body, my mind, and my soul are yours. If you die, I die. If you live, I shall live. Forever and always my life is yours. In the eyes of Sel'ari I have said this. In the eyes of Sel'ari may I be bound to this."

Hairem smiled gently and tightened his grip on her hands.

"Exchange the tokens of your covenant," the priest ordered, offering his hands to them.

Hairem picked up the golden chain dangling with a phoenix of blue garnet. Alone, it was the elegant and twisted side view of Sel'ari's symbol. Ilsevel offered the mirrored image. Together, they linked as a single completed phoenix.

In unison, they clasped the necklace around one another and interlocked the two phoenixes.

"What Sel'ari has bound is as eternal as the goddess herself. We all hold witness to this. And so it is so."

Ilsevel finally could contain her smile no longer and Hairem swiftly raised his hand to wipe a tear from the corner of her eye. He chuckled softly and turned her toward the nobility, pride swelling in him at the wonder of his new wife.

For the first time they stood as one, King Hairem and Queen Ilsevel of the kingdom of Sevrigel, the first true kings of their age.

# CHAPTER THIRTY-ONE

"The troops are looking excellent, Captain," Jikun smiled at his captain as he handed Reivel the shirt of his indigo uniform. He paused to observe the vast expanse of field before him, spotted only with the occasional small tree that struggled to drop the last of its leaves onto the long grass of the field. Off to his left, the floor of the southern ridge fell away suddenly to the great canyon that lay before Elvorium. That day, the mist had become a cloud of fog over the forest and river far below, blanketing them in a smoky white.

"That's all the training for now," Reivel called back to the large group of troops spread out across the field. He nodded once again, pulling his shirt on over his glistening chest. "Not too long ago I couldn't imagine doing this again—I was certain we were all to die in that swamp!" Reivel continued, his face creasing deeply around his typical blue eyes—he *was* another Sel'ven, after all—as he smiled. "The effect on the soldiers of being out of that swamp and having the care of Elvorium's healers is remarkable. Of course, we're still focused on strength training—they have a lot to regain. But they are alive."

"And looking practically perfect," Jikun reassured his enthusiasm in militaristic fashion. His gaze scanned the males gathering their shirts and swords, groaning to one another about how overworked they were. Despite his frustrations, he had never heard anything more beautiful. Reivel was right—since having returned to Elvorium the recovery rate of his troops had increased ten-fold.

And yet, the smile on his face felt forced and the weight on his chest threatened to pull him down. It should have been Navon in Reivel's place. Navon training the recovering troops.

But Navon was in prison, awaiting execution.

His new captain tousled his long, blond hair to cool his head and glanced across the misty canyon toward the palace. "Did you make it to the ceremony?" he continued in a conversationalist manner.

Jikun scoffed. Navon would have asked such a thing *cautiously*. He could imagine Navon's inquisitive eyes, his almost reproachful tone. *He* knew how he felt about the king. The wedding had been nearly five weeks ago and yet Jikun had not spoken a word about it. "Navon, the ceremony was held in the abominable temple of that witch—"

"*GENERAL*," Reivel gasped in offense, his blue eyes wide in horror, as though the goddess herself was standing beside them.

Jikun carried on as though unbroken, "—and was the ceremony of King Hairem to a female I know nothing of... except she had the indecency to marry him. Of course I did not attend." He started, the voice beside him slow to register. He turned his head, seeing Captain Reivel muttering a fervent and prayerful apology below his breath.

Jikun gave him a moment to reply, unsure of how to correct his harsh words. "You shouldn't say such heretical things," Reivel rebuked sternly. He waved a hand as though attempting to dismiss the blasphemy Jikun had just spewed. "*I* did attend the ceremony. Lady Ilsevel looked stunning. I can hardly imagine a more beautiful lady in all the realms. She is also the first elven queen to be so prominently involved in politics. I heard she even attends the council meetings with the king. ...That is certainly a new direction for my people."

*'My people,'* Jikun thought, noting the possessive. He glanced sidelong at the male before him. *'I preferred you as a lieutenant.'* He turned slightly, muttering below his breath, "Well, beauty does not equal wit."

"What was that, General?" Reivel replied absentmindedly. He was staring off across the canyon, probably lost in some idolatry gaze toward the queen's direction.

Jikun followed his gaze to the towers beside the bridge where, not long before, the city had looked down on the army as Hairem emerged to greet them. He scowled and turned away, his forced attempt to enjoy the pleasant mood quickly leaving him. Hairem *had* come out, despite what he knew of the plague. Jikun could give him some consideration for that had he *also* not been the same male who had sent them to their deaths to begin with... and then left them to rot.

"General. General?" Reivel was saying.

Jikun had not heard him. He *had* been distracted lately. But it was with the knowledge that he was sixty thousand soldiers down and Saebellus had undoubtedly received word of their crippling loss. Even with those that survived on the path to recovery, the condition of the army was hardly comparable to its former might. The next battle with Saebellus would be a battle that could determine the outcome of the war, and he was considerably weaker than ever.

"*General!*" Reivel barked; this time his voice was firm.

Jikun stopped and turned. "What is it?" he demanded, caught off guard by his captain's force. In just a few months, the skinny little Sel'ven had already adjusted to his promotion, barking orders and addressing Jikun as though he had all the familiarity of Navon.

Reivel pointed toward the bridge dusted in the canyon's mist. Jikun followed his finger.

"How coincidental," Jikun muttered, eyes falling where the captain's finger indicated.

"I've been trying to tell you, General," Reivel replied, sighing slightly and shaking his head in almost disappointment.

Jikun straightened and gestured sharply for Reivel to follow. "Come. Someone may need to hold me back from him," he spoke through a warning growl. Jikun had not seen the king since he had attacked him on the bridge. That was over two months ago now, wasn't it? The king had certainly given him a wide berth. In Darival, he had picked a physical fight with more than one of the nobility and had risen the next day without a mark of punishment. But in Elvorium, he knew he was fortunate to not have been put to death—the Sel'varian management of disrespect was far more… *permanent.*

"General Jikun," Hairem greeted with the same, ever-broad and charming smile as Jikun and Reivel came to a halt before him at the edge of the southern bridge. Despite their last confrontation, Jikun still detected what seemed to be a genuine level of affection in the king's voice. Whether he wanted to or not, Jikun found himself feeling slightly humbled by it.

He bowed stiffly in respect, somewhat more readily after his last outburst toward the king. Slipping up twice might be the last time his unruly behavior was tolerated by the southern pricks. "King Hairem, I want to apologize for my behavior when we spoke last," Jikun began before his pride had a chance to stop him. "My soldiers—"

"General, think nothing of it. I asked you to treat me as an equal when speaking about political matters. I would have been offended with anything less than your entire honesty… temper and all."

Jikun straightened, feeling the surprise clearly etched across his face, the ease drawing his shoulders down.

"As I spoke before," Hairem continued before Jikun could offer a verbal response, "it was my own attempts at self-preservation that made me weak to oppose them to begin with. I will forever have your army's blood on *my* hands. There is no apology that I can make equal to the weight of guilt that I feel. The responsibility was mine and I failed." Jikun could see the pain in the king's eyes even as his lips reformed into a politically practiced smile of charm for the captain.

No, not for the captain… for Jikun.

He saw the king's eyes flick toward him and in that brief moment, Jikun caught an unexpected depth of regret and sorrow. For Navon's sake. And, whether he wished to fully admit it to himself or not, Hairem had spared his life when he had attacked him on the bridge…

Jikun felt his hatred mitigated slightly by the king's sincerity. *'It was your people that sentenced him,'* he wanted to hiss.

Hairem turned away slowly and faced Reivel. "Congratulations on the new position, Captain. I am certain you will serve your general well. I have heard excellent things about your days in the academy and even further good reports from the army itself."

"Thank you, Your Majesty," Jikun heard Reivel reply, though his thoughts had pulled him elsewhere. "Your words honor me."

Hairem paused to let his compliment bare some mark on time, then pivoted toward the encampment, gesturing to the white tents. "May we three speak privately?"

Jikun refocused on the world around them and nodded, turning and leading the two toward his tent. After his initial weakness on the bridge, he had been moved into the larger tent of the general's quarters. Hairem had been correct when he had spoken that no expense was spared: his tent was furnished as though it had been made for royalty itself. A long, ornately carved wooden table from the southern cities lay situated in the middle between a shelf of fine, vintage wines and a gold-inlaid chest of drawers filled with political papers and clothes.

"I see you have tested all the wines. Have a seat," Hairem ordered, slowly dropping his lean body into the high-backed chair at the head of the table. He produced a long piece of parchment from his back waistline, tapping it on the table once as though the general and captain were not already at attention. "I have some news of military importance, and I would like to help the army devise a strategy—if I can be of any assistance." His jewel-encrusted hands stretched the crisp parchment out, pressing a finger onto Sevrigel's southwestern coastline. "Elarium. While Ilsevel was captured she heard Saebellus and his men mention Elarium. When she returned, we sent scouts along the countryside toward the city. Over the last two weeks, Saebellus has started to move a small contingent of troops out of the Halls of Horiembrig toward the southwestern coast. It's all very discreet, but we currently assume that the southern capital is his next target."

*'Who is* "we"*?'* Jikun wanted to ask for the clarification of which non-military minds had been consulted before him, but refrained. "A small contingent to take the southern capital?" Jikun sat back, frowning. "He thinks he can take Elarium with a small contingent? Exactly how small are we talking?"

Hairem reclined in his chair, the parchment rolling back together. "Forty thousand..."

Jikun's eyes widened briefly in surprise. *'Forty thousand...?'* he rubbed his chin thoughtfully, imagining the troops slipping from Horiembrig by a southern route, away from prying eyes along the river front. He would have followed his guessed trail along the map, but Hairem had let it fall closed as though its use was merely for appearance's sake. "Forty thousand? That leaves only twenty or thirty thousand guarding Horiembrig..." he trailed off.

Reivel raised his brows in similar surprise. "Forty thousand?" he echoed. "If we take just the troops who didn't go to the swamp, that's ninety thousand soldiers. We could leave the rest here and even *if* the army from Horiembrig marched immediately to attack Elvorium, they'd never defeat the city's defenses."

*'The bottomless canyon. The endless bridges. There is no doubt about that...'* Jikun nodded once, though there was hesitation in his motion. "What is Saebellus thinking?" he muttered to himself, tapping the table. Saebellus was easy enough to find before a fight, but he never entered an encounter he could not escape from: not once had they found his army after a battle. Saebellus was only seen again when he *wanted* to be seen. Had he slipped up, or was he inviting Jikun to engage him at Elarium? Jikun bit the tip of his thumb as his mind whisked him toward the coast. With the sea to Saebellus' back, if Jikun and his army marched from the northeast, the warlord would either be forced

into the ocean or would have to flee south toward the swamps: either way boded ill for Saebellus' troops.

Was Elarium worth it?

"Perhaps… he is making a mistake?" Reivel began slowly, but Jikun could hear the skepticism in his voice. And perhaps even a hint of fear. There was nothing more frightening than the unknown aspect of the battle. This Jikun knew full well—and his recent excursion in the swamp had only helped to emphasize this.

*'No,'* Jikun could hear Navon's words of caution. *'Saebellus is too intelligent.'*

Jikun bit his thumbnail. "No," he spoke after a moment. "Saebellus is too intelligent to make a mistake like that." He unrolled the map again, studying it closely. "What are we not seeing?" *'What terrain is Saebellus playing off of this time…?'*

Hairem leaned over as well, studying the map intensely, his blue eyes straining to see something hidden in the ink. Suddenly he smacked the table, the candles shaking in their holders with his abrupt elation. "The True Blood tunnels! Sellemar and Erallus used one to rescue Ilsevel. It *could* be that Saebellus knows of one leading into Elarium—the coastal capital is no doubt equipped with such a passage. They could use it to take the city by surprise. Add the component of the darkness of night and Elarium would fall within hours." He sounded a bit breathless as he finished, looking up at the two of them with wide eyes. It was clearly a boy's first taste of military planning.

But Jikun had to admit, the plan sounded strong. Owning Sevrigel's sea-bound capital would certainly give Saebellus a strong hold on either side of the continent. Whether he chose to merely seize Elarium's trade or use her ships in future battles, the results would swing heavily in his favor. Jikun pursed his lips. "But… a True Blood Tunnel? How would Saebellus know of the True Blood Tunnels?"

Hairem interlocked his fingers as he bit his lip. "Perhaps he found information of them inside the Halls of Horiembrig. You know that it was once the most influential city on Sevrigel. It would not surprise me that, if one dug deep enough, you could find information about the tunnels. If not that, then I can only assume that Saebellus was privy to this information while in the military. His captain, Vale, was once a close friend of the True Blood Prince Darcarus and received a substantial portion of his training personally from the prince. Perhaps he learned more than combat from him. And maybe that is unlikely, but *how* he knows hardly seems relevant... Of course, I make no suggestion that I understand the workings of war."

So Saebellus *was* trying to remain covert for now. If it had not been for Ilsevel's information, like Horiembrig, Elarium would have fallen without a fight. "This *would* explain why he took so few soldiers," Jikun agreed after a moment's consideration. "If we can be waiting for him when he emerges from the tunnel, or alert Elarium to the egress and then come around behind him, Saebellus and his army will be trapped."

He looked up, his chest growing tight. Was this the beginning of Saebellus' end?

"First, however, if we are going to pincer him in, I need to know where the True Blood tunnel is," he spoke, forcing the exhilaration down.

Hairem hesitated, embarrassment clouding his features. "I... don't know where the True Blood tunnel is..."

Jikun blinked, sitting back against the dense wood sharply. "What? You're Sevrigel's king. What do you mean you *don't know* where the True Blood tunnel is? ...If you don't know, who *would?*"

Hairem stiffened in defense. "When King Silandrus left, his family took the knowledge of the tunnels with them. But perhaps..." Hairem paused. "*Perhaps* Sellemar."

Reivel raised a brow. "Sellemar? Who is Sellemar?"

"I don't know," Hairem admitted, seeming embarrassed further by his growing lack of knowledge. "But he seems to have *very* close ties with King Sairel."

Jikun slid his chair back abruptly, standing. "I can't make any plans to deal with Saebellus until I know about this tunnel. Where can I find this Sellemar?" He could hear the frustration seeping into his tone, but Hairem could not expect anything different. How could the king of Sevrigel *not* know the royal escape and entry routes into the capital cities?! Had everyone failed to ask the information or had Silandrus and his sons simply *refused* to share it? *'Imbeciles, either way!'*

"The old Rilden Estate," Hairem replied, grimacing slightly as though he could read Jikun's rising temper. "He may be there. I tried to convince him to accept it as a gift for his rescue of Ilsevel, but last time I spoke with him he was still residing at The Whistling Glade. Erallus, however, said that—when he went by the inn a few nights ago—the innkeeper said Sellemar had left."

"I would leave too if my reward was that shithole," Jikun muttered.

Hairem's eyes widened and his mouth gaped incredulously. "The Rilden Estate is one of the most prestigious homes in all of Elvorium. It belonged to the brother of the last True Blood king before the Schism. It was *only* left unoccupied because my father was using it for just such a purpose as I granted it to Sellemar."

Jikun raised his hands to halt the king in his winded defense. From the outside, that building had fallen to resemble something of a human *morgue*. "There is no need to justify yourself. I will try the Rilden Estate," he insisted stiffly. *'Gods know I'm relieved to be receiving my payments in* coin.*'*

Hairem stood as well, leaving the parchment on the table despite the number of maps he undoubtedly knew Jikun already possessed. "You have my permission to move out against Saebellus whenever you deem you and your troops are ready. I will leave everything to your plans. And if there is *anything* I can do to assist you, please bring it before me and it shall be granted."

Jikun paused, a thought heavy in the back of his mind. He turned his head slightly away as he spoke, his stomach tightening as a flicker of snow and ice hung at the edge of his mind, "...What about Darival?" he demanded sternly, though he could hear the doubt ebbing into his voice. "...There were no letters since I have been back. No word of any kind..."

There was a long moment of uncomfortable stillness in the room. Reivel himself had looked away, as though he too expected an unfavorable answer.

Hairem's voice fell empathetically. "...The council voted against assisting Kaivervale. I sent my own personal guard, but I have not heard from them. With your troops having been in frail condition prior to this and Saebellus now moving again, I'm afraid I am quite certain that the council shall do nothing about Darival at this time."

Jikun lips twisted sourly as he glanced to his left. He could see Hairem's fist tighten over the map and heard the brief hiss of breath as the king inhaled and held it for a moment.

"But after this battle, I *assure* you, you have my word by Sel'ari that I shall send several hundred soldiers north as soon as you return, regardless of the council's wishes."

Jikun raised a brow at his sudden strength of tone, turning his body in full to face the king. "Thank you... Hairem."

There was a flicker of acknowledgement at the dropped title and Hairem smiled. *'It took you long enough,'* the amused eyes read. "Good luck to you, Jikun. With the blessing of the goddess, this may be the last battle from Saebellus this kingdom has to endure."

Jikun raised his hand against the king even as his mouth closed in what he no doubt had hoped were inspiring words with which to send off his military dogs. The general gestured once to the flaps of the tent, signaling that there was more on his mind. "If you could excuse the king and I for a moment, Captain."

Reivel started, glancing from male to male with a subtle flicker of confusion crossing his features. "Yes, General…" he replied, sliding his chair back and rising to his feet. He bowed deeply before the king, turned, and stepped briskly from the tent.

"There is something else," Jikun dared, his icy eyes hardening as his gaze fixed upon the king. He felt the flicker of light reflect against the chiseled structure of his face and imagined his appearance was not unlike that of a particularly twisted wraith. He leaned forward slightly, drawing on the resolute and powerful picture in his mind. "You said to ask if there was something you could do. There is. I need my captain."

Hairem blinked, looking mildly unnerved. "You have your captain…?" he raised a hand slowly and gestured to the outside. "I—"

Jikun regarded him steadily, knowing he skirted in vain around the topic. "No. Captain Navon."

Hairem's hand dropped. "Captain Navon," his words came out stiff and hollow. Jikun could see the struggle behind his eyes as he sought his next words. "General, Captain Navon has been found guilty of the practices of necromancy and is to be hanged in a few weeks' time. You were requested at his trial, but you did not attend… I thought someone had informed you of the court's decision…"

Jikun remained stoic, not allowing the king to see his emotions. Yes, he had been informed. His eyes shifted warily to the tent flap and he hoped to Ramul that Reivel had been wise enough to distance himself from their conversation. He pushed down his discomfort and forcefully continued, "I heard. However, Captain Navon is the most experienced male I know. Reivel will not suffice to fulfill the position. Not this quickly. Not with imminent battle approaching. Not this time. As you stated, this may be the last battle this kingdom has to endure. Do you want to put that in the hands of Reivel or the best captain this country has seen? Navon is second to no one." His eyes narrowed in their intensity. "And I will not go into battle without him."

Hairem's eyes widened in disbelief. "What are you saying, General?"

Jikun raised his chin, inhaling sharply as he drew himself up. "I am saying, Your Majesty, that if Captain Navon is not by my side, then you shall have to find a new general as well." His breath caught as his sentence finished. Was he *mad?* Putting his career on the line for that damn necromancer…?! He could see Hairem's face contort and twist, emotions flickering in a dozen expressions as he deliberated over the general's words.

Finally the emotions faded and the king's face grew indecipherable. He paced across the tent several times, eyes occasionally flicking to the flaps of the tent and then back to Jikun. "You drive a difficult bargain, General Taemrin," he finally breathed. "But I shall grant you your request. Navon shall receive a royal pardon. This *will*, I hope, make amends between us for past misunderstandings."

Jikun felt the weight on his chest fall away and he exhaled audibly.

"*However*, General, I must caution you. Navon's practices will not be tolerated. He is being pardoned for past crimes, not future ones. If your captain so much as breathes the *word* necromancy, his previous fate shall meet him. And there shall not be a second royal pardon: war or no war. Now, go, get your captain and end this war."

# Chapter Thirty-Two

"This way, General," the voice ahead of Jikun urged him forward, the echo a soft beckon from around a bend in the narrow stone staircase below.

Jikun turned away from the towering windows of the entrance hall; they were closed to the chill of the autumn's breeze that stalked about outside, bellowing against the panes—an unnaturally violent wind for a Sevrigelian autumn. He let his brisk steps pull him down into the darkness, away from the daylight and into the damp stench of the prisons. It wafted up to him not unlike the stench of bloated, rotting corpses on a battlefield. Still, it was faint, as though the elves had tried in great desperation to hide the world beneath them.

But the scent was as familiar to Jikun as the flowers coating their city life.

His eyes strained to adjust to the dim, blue light of the prisons, the illumination steadily streaming down from the small orbs floating near the crevices of the vaulted ceilings. Their magic was merely minor spells of light, just enough to give the stairs a safely visible glow.

"This way," the warden carried on as he stepped down onto the smooth marble tile of the prison hallway that reached out toward them at the staircase's final step.

Here the light brightened and the hallway widened. Great pillars cascaded from the ceiling, ornately carved and lined in gold, as glorious as anything outside the criminals' walls. Vast windows of painted glass spotted the ceiling above him, showering the floor in vivid arrays of color. He had seen something of their brilliance before—in the Temple of Sel'ari. Why the elves would waste such grandeur on this place…

Even in the prisons, the Sel'vi had spared no expense.

Jikun brushed his hand against the side of one such ornate pillar as he passed, surprised by the smooth and dustless surface. "How many prisoners are contained within?" he asked, unable to push aside the awe he felt by the care at which his surroundings were clearly maintained. The hallway stretched away into the distance, seeming just as immaculate as far as Jikun's vision allowed him to see. In Kaivervale, the barracks also housed the city's sparse prisoners. The last time an execution had taken place had been long before his birth. Still, for all of Darival's peace, Elvorium had still touted its unrivaled lack of crime.

"His Majesty's dungeon can hold fifteen thousand prisoners—comfortably. We are somewhere around three thousand right now, I believe. Fairly high for the city. But things haven't been the same since the True Bloods left," the warden spoke longingly, gesturing to the ground at their feet where the marble had given way to tiny colored stones.

Jikun's eyes quickly swept the ancient mural and his stomach twisted suddenly. A lean and regal figure of a True Blood king stood before the body of a decapitated, kneeling male, a red sword in one hand and the head in another. Unlike the council and king now, the True Bloods had been enforcers of justice—unwavering, merciless justice. Perhaps, before Navon, he would have found the scene admirable.

But it could have just as easily been Navon's head the True Blood king held.

The warden glanced back before continuing. There must have been something about Jikun's expression, as the warden's voice grew into a tone of soft reassurance, "In the time of King Silandrus, this prison was nearly empty. And to have men in the lowest cells awaiting execution was rare indeed."

Jikun wiped his face of expression, drawing himself up into a stiff, confident exterior, as he did so well. "Nearly empty, you say? Well," he chuckled, "clearly Hairem is doing a better job than our previous kings."

The warden turned away, giving no reaction. Jikun's brow knit, wondering if his silence was a testament of respect to the general's thoughts or something more personal. They turned to the left, away from the mural, to a staircase leading lower into the dungeons. Here were signs of dirt along the crevices and a mingled stench of urine half-heartedly masked by the aroma of autumn's last flowers.

"How far down is Navon?" Jikun inquired hesitantly, glancing down into the dim light.

"All the way."

Jikun swallowed his anxiety and followed the grim male down the winding staircase as it narrowed deep into the earth. Here, the air grew stale and the smell of flowers was all but lost.

"This is the last floor," the warden informed him as he stepped off the last chipped and beaten stair: it was thousands of years worn and not a day repaired. Here, the vaulted ceiling and great hallways had long been left behind; Jikun was surprised to find that his head nearly scraped along the top of the low stone and the opposing walls were hardly an arm's width apart. It was not a place comforting to those easily vexed by tight spaces. Even the general found himself stifled, pinched in on either side between the old and dirty stone with the ability to move but one direction. He began to want to reach out and push against the walls—demand his space. No longer were there ornately carved pillars and brightly glowing orbs—rather, torches flickered dimly from the walls, consuming what little oxygen had managed to crawl down below.

It was the underbelly of the dungeon for Sevrigel's most heinous criminals: rapists, murderers, human prostitutes and their company—and other bestialitists—and of course, those who dabbled in the dark magics.

Necromancy, namely.

Jikun wrinkled his nose, the stench of decay and sewage hanging heavily in the muggy air. It was unlike the elves to govern such environments of low quality, but Jikun assumed that little care was given for the kind that were housed here; what conditions they were forced to endure were likely seen as a form of recompense for their crimes.

Their deaths, after all, were imminent.

Jikun swallowed, the odor in the air tangible as he opened his mouth to speak. "How long has the captain been down here?" he found himself asking as the warden stopped before a cell door, the iron jangling softly as he raised a key. There was a side of him that did not want to know the answer and he hoped that perhaps even the soft jingle had blocked his words out.

"Since he was convicted at his trial," the warden replied solemnly, glancing once over his shoulder. "That would be over a month ago, I believe. I'm afraid I didn't follow your captain's particular situation."

He turned back and the bolt in the door clicked into the iron. With a grunt against its weight, the warden pushed the door open and stepped aside, remaining still as its unnervingly shrill squeak echoed down the hallway and into the darkness behind him.

He nodded his head forward.

Jikun put a hand to the pounding at his throat, the force of his heart rising up from his chest. He peered into the solemn darkness of the cell and extended an anxious hand. "A torch," he commanded. But he did not wait for the male beside him to react; rather, he leaned to the right and yanked the nearest torch from the wall, ignoring the twisted webs that clung to his hand, desperately hoping for a fate other than the endless and abysmal haze about them.

Jikun raised the light before him. "I can take it from here…" he trailed off, stepping once into the cell. The warden gave a reply, but it fell on deaf ears. At the back of his mind he could hear the armored footsteps fading down the hall, but Jikun's eyes were locked onto the male inside the cell.

Two months without the light of Aersadore's sun. With little food. With little water. If the Sevilan Marshes had been a trial, then this…

"Hello, Navon," Jikun breathed.

Navon was slouched against the wall directly before the Darivalian, one leg stretched out and the other tucked against his chest. His left arm sat on his knee with his forehead pressed against his hand. His clothes were soiled and torn, still stained with blood from the temple. All across the cell, an auburn slime lay smeared, dried and thick, reeking of sewage and rot. Jikun had smelled such a stench before, but here, it was condensed into a windless, windowless prison.

His stomach lurched and he bit his tongue to control his gut.

Navon remained still, yet the rigidness of his posture betrayed his knowledge of Jikun's presence.

Jikun stepped forward with a forcefully strong stride. He waved the torch about the cell, eyes glancing from the worn mat along the right wall to a waste pail and hay along the left. He smiled weakly. "You look well," he jested.

Navon's head snapped up abruptly, eyes flashing from within hollowed sockets. "Get out," he breathed venomously, in a tone Jikun had only heard matched in the necromantic tongue.

Jikun's brows raised faintly, his jaw tensing in preparation. "Navon—" he began hesitantly, his tone becoming softer and solemn. He felt a slight twist in his stomach as the eyes glowered back at him in pure, unshifting pools of hatred.

"Don't 'NAVON' me," the captain growled. "I have been in this prison for nearly two months. You have not come to see me *once*, let alone attend my trial. I have had NO ONE, Jikun. No one! I thought I was going to be lucky enough if you bothered to visit my unmarked *grave*. Beneath the *dirt*, Jikun! Not the catacombs, but *beneath the dirt* like the basest of human scum!" Navon lowered his forehead onto his hand, his voice falling. "Gods…" he choked. "No family. Dead friends. And you *abandoned* me."

*'You're all I have, too,'* Jikun wanted to sympathize. But that would be a lie. And he realized for the first time that while all of the dead soldiers in the swamp had been *his* beloved soldiers and numbers in his army, to Navon, many of them had been genuine companions—friends. While he had lain sick, they had died. Jikun had thought nothing of that; Navon had always kept to his heels, duty bound. But, perhaps better than him, Navon had masked his pain and carried on.

Jikun lowered the torch slightly, letting the silence stand between them for several minutes as his eyes faltered across the frail form before him. His stomach felt tight and the weight on his chest was no less than the force by which the beast struck. He could see Navon's shoulders trembling, his rigid posture wavering in his anguish.

"What a shithole you're in," Jikun finally spoke sympathetically, his voice soft. It was difficult to keep his eyes on his captain, but he forced his gaze to remain. He had seen Navon in trials before: he could still vividly recall the sight of the Helven lying inside his tent, pale and clammy, lapping up the remnants of dead soldiers… but this… was different.

This time, Navon had truly been alone.

He pushed the gnawing in his chest down. "…How are your injuries…?"

Navon let his forehead fall to his knee as he raised his left arm from beneath it. "Healed," came his monotonous reply.

Jikun took several more steps into the cell, fighting the gag that threatened to double him over. Just in mere feet, the air had grown thicker, as trapped and helpless within the small cell as the prisoner. A sour mist grazed Jikun's tongue as he opened his mouth. "I am sorry that you were imprisoned. I told you that dabbling in necromancy—"

"*Really? 'I told you so'* is what you came here to say?" Navon snarled, finding strength once more to lash out. He shifted forward, his voice rising to a near-mad cackle, "'*I told you so, Navon. I told you not to dabble in necromancy. Look where it's gotten you now. Executioner's Row.*'" And just as swiftly as it had risen, his voice dropped, growing solemn and venomous. "Well congratulations, Jikun. You were right. As if I don't damn well know that already."

Jikun cleared his throat, crouching down before the Helven. "Navon, I didn't come here to—"

The movement of his weakened captain surprised him. Without warning, Navon had swung his body forward away from the wall, as though propelled forward by all the rage he had masked, and slammed his fist solidly across Jikun's jaw, snapping his head to the left.

The general fell back, clasping his chin in shock. "Nav—"

But with a cry of fury, Navon fell onto him, slamming his right fist into Jikun's hand, his left moving underneath his swift attempt at defense and back into his jaw. "You *fucking* self-centered... *bastard!* How many times did I fucking tell you to not bed the prostitutes and you did it anyways?! You think I would have abandoned you on trial?! *This is where you would have been thrown!* I served by your side for a dozen bloody years and at my trial they asked, 'Is there anyone here to speak on your behalf?' and *you. Weren't. There.*" He continued through a flurry of punches, his voice cracking, "I don't need your fucking sympathy now. Your sympathy isn't going to save me. I. Don't. Want. Your. Fucking. Symp—"

Jikun grunted, fumbling and catching his captain's right fist as his other hand tightened on his left. He threw him back with a growl, tackling him in the same fluent motion. He grabbed his wrists, slamming them in the damp hay beneath them. "STOP it, Navon!" he bellowed, his hands tightening further. "I told you not to do necromancy! *It is not my fault you were imprisoned.* You think my words would have saved you *then?!*"

Navon looked back, his jaw clenched, his lips trembling. Jikun could see a wave of pain and anguish behind them, fighting to stay contained behind his anger.

Jikun inhaled heavily. "I was... afraid."

Navon's body grew still, his brow knitting skeptically. He pursed his lips into a hard, thin line. "Afraid?"

"Yes. Afraid. Afraid that they'd... somehow find out I knew you were involved in necromancy. That I'd join you."

Navon's eyes hardened and Jikun could feel the Helven's chest tighten beneath him.

Jikun's gaze faltered, finding it difficult to speak as the trembling beneath him stilled. "...And that when I saw you up there, threatened with death... I'd have said things I shouldn't have. Revealed what I did know... That it was my fault for not stopping you." He sat back, releasing Navon's wrists slowly. "And then... I couldn't face that I *hadn't* gone..."

Navon shoved him off, drawing back sharply. Jikun could see the venom rekindle behind his eyes. He pulled his right leg back against his chest and his mouth opened to speak. When no words found their way out, he closed it with a quiet snap.

But Jikun didn't need the words. He could see the sorrow etched plainly across Navon's face. The fear and anxiety riveting him inward. "And… I am sorry, Navon. I am deeply and truly sorry. I …failed. I forsook you when you needed me most."

Navon looked away and Jikun could hear him inhale a deep, shaky breath as though he was finally submitting to his confinement.

"But… what I have been *trying* to tell you," Jikun spoke after a moment, "is that you are to be released."

Navon's head snapped up abruptly, his brow knitting as his head cocked slightly in disbelief.

"You are to be reinstated as my captain." Jikun stood, dropping a hand down toward Navon.

Navon stared numbly at his hand for a moment, and then his azure eyes trailed up cautiously. Doubtfully. He knew he had no reason to believe that Jikun wove a lie, but still, he questioned him. "…But… how?" He reached out a hand hesitantly, letting Jikun pull him to his feet. "How in Sel'ari's name did you win my freedom?"

*'…Still saying her name… even after what her people sentenced him to…'* Jikun steadied his captain before drawing away, grimacing inwardly at the boney frame he had once more been reduced to. "I told His Majesty that you were the best captain I could have… And that I wasn't riding into battle without you. …We go together or not at all."

He saw Navon smile, the creases in his face softening, the anguish vanishing, as though those words alone had made amends for all his wrongs—healed all his wounds. How had he not noticed how alone his captain had become? Did he truly know him so little?

But he understood him now: Navon had become so alone that he was desperate for any inkling of friendship. And though Jikun's apology could hardly make amends for his actions, Navon was so desperate for companionship that he had seized upon the first bit of affection and loyalty Jikun showed as though it was genuinely enough to atone for all his neglect.

Still, Jikun felt his guilt ease somewhat as relief flooded his captain's face. Navon's eyes shifted toward the door. "With regard to the king, you played our friendship pretty close to the chest, didn't you?"

Jikun smiled slightly at his sarcasm. "It was my only card to play."

Navon straightened, rolling his shoulders and rubbing his wrists subconsciously, as though scraping away the feel of the prison chains that must have once bound him. As his new fate seemed to solidify in his mind, he was growing stronger. "We'll see if it has the same effect at your prostitution trial."

Jikun rolled his eyes, but his lips twitched into an amused smile. "Come." He turned and strode toward the door of the cell, aware of the wet fabric pressed against his body where he had touched the floor of the cell. He refrained from outward disgust, knowing Navon was far worse off.

"Gods know we have some planning to do, don't we?" Navon asked rhetorically, stepping alongside his general as he brushed his hands down his body, as though he could wipe away the past months' anguish with the dirt.

"We need to go see the male who recently rescued the queen from Saebellus. I need you in this coming battle, my friend, so after that, you will be ordered to rest and eat until we move out—no room for arguing."

Navon gestured to the door of his cell. "Of course. You'll need me at my best to keep an eye on you in battle."

*There* was the male he knew.

"After you, General."

Jikun stepped out onto the marble of the low hall before them, opening his mouth cautiously. "Navon," he began, allowing his voice to reveal the faintest trace of threat, "I must warn you again. You've heard me say it before. I'm begging you this time. If you so much as say the *word* necromancy, Hairem has threatened that you will meet your sentence."

Navon's smile broadened, but there was an unreadable glimmer from his eyes. "I will not take that risk."

# Chapter Thirty-Three

"This is it?" Navon asked, a skeptical edge creeping into his tone as he regarded the depressingly decrepit estate.

Jikun glanced surreptitiously toward his comrade. *He* was one to make a comment about the lowly state of another's inhabitance. Still, Jikun supposed his captain *did* look—and smell—remarkably better now. The bath had done wonders for him, but he had still not managed to scrub away the clamminess of his skin. "Supposedly it was once a great manor," Jikun replied with a shrug, pushing open the old, vine-covered gates to the Rilden Estate. They creaked noisily, echoing out across the canyon beyond in an eerily solitary ring, as though it was the only noise across the precipice.

And perhaps it was. The edge of the city was quiet in the afternoon light. The surrounding citizens had gone off for the day, to peruse the market square or sing praises in the temple or perhaps sample a bite or two of those cream puffed pastries Navon had given him on their last strut about the square.

But here, the estate was still. Dark. Quiet. It was as he had remembered seeing it years before—a wide, flat land spotted with massive, ancient trees and an orchard nearly bare of leaves in preparation for the coming winter. The back land faced the cliffside—no doubt with a stunning view beyond—while the cobbled road leading up to the estate's doors was overgrown with ivy that crept up even along the pillars and walls of the estate. Jikun imagined that in the summer, the place must be a different sight entirely, but now it was a cold, oddly foreboding structure in the middle of such a grand city; even the shadows of the ancient trees shut out the sunlight. He could glimpse the old Rilden watchtower through the trees, but it appeared in no better condition.

"Are you going to stare at my home all day or are you coming in?" came a call from a cracked window on the second story. A candle flickered on inside one of the dirty panes and a Sel'ven emerged onto the balcony, a silhouette against the light behind him. "The doors are open."

Jikun could distinguish nothing about the elf other than his rigid posture—yet somehow, even that scant illumination conveyed disdain. He quickened his steps into the stained marble of the estate, catching sight only of the short ends of blond hair as the elf vanished into the building above him.

Navon closed the door softly behind them and drew up beside his general.

Although covered in dust, the estate was no doubt a stunning testament to the wealth of the previous royal line. The male from the balcony now stood at the top of the steps, a candle held in his hand. From that single flame and the sparse rays that managed to break through the window's dusted panes, gold inlay glinted off of every carving and unlit chandelier. It was admittedly nothing short of breathtaking.

And if a few orbs of yellow luminescent magic had been released along the ceiling, as the estate undoubtedly had held in its glory days, Jikun imagined that despite the bareness of the manor, it would have rivaled even the splendor of the palace itself.

"General Taemrin, I presume," the male spoke stiffly, drawing Jikun's attention away from the grandiose interior as he took brisk steps down the stairs to stop before them. He drew up sharply and was suddenly slightly taller than the Darivalian, a rare achievement to manage for a Sel'ven.

Jikun studied the male briefly above the yellow glow of the flame. Ryekarian. Nobly-born. Wealthy. And he had rescued Ilsevel from the heart of Saebellus' city. Perhaps he was a foreign military leader of some kind or a member of Sairel's elite forces. "Yes, and you are Sellemar?" he replied, focusing finally on the male's unscarred face. If he was military, his hands were remarkably smooth and his face untouched. There was even an air of luxury about his unmarred skin.

*'He is...'* a frown creased Jikun's features as the Sel'ven's bored eyes stared into his own. *'Pretentious.* That *is the word I am looking for.'* The assessment was not merely due to a flourish of overwhelming wealth across his clothes and jewelry, or the shamefully ornate sword at his side, but rather the look in his eyes as he regarded them. It was unflappably blatant: 'I am better, older, wiser,' it said, and conveyed such arrogance in its certainty that the utter lack of regard for their thoughts was apparent from the start.

The Sel'ven lowered the candle. "Yes, I am Sellemar. What can I do for you and..." he paused, looking down on Navon briefly. "Your captain?" There was the faintest flicker of a smile as the Sel'ven regarded Navon, and Jikun was surprised to note that it was not at all spiteful or cynical, as he would have expected after the recent unveiling of Navon's darker practices. "I am pleased to see that you were released. I apologize for being unable to attend your trial—I was engaged in the mission for Ilsevel's rescue. Welcome back to the surface."

Jikun blinked in surprise, glancing sidelong at Navon to find his comrade had been reduced to the same blank stupor, having been caught off guard. Jikun could feel his mouth gape. This Sel'ven knew of Navon's practices in necromancy… and accepted them? He attempted to recollect his composure as his assessment of the male was addled.

He glanced around, searching for some clue to the personality before him. The halls were remarkably bare and there was no furniture of any kind. Some great prize Hairem had given him—and greater still that the male had done nothing to alter its condition. The unnecessary riches the male wore draped across his body were in stark contrast to the home in which he had chosen to abide. "Perhaps we can sit and discuss the matter at hand somewhere more comfortable?" Jikun began.

Sellemar regarded them stoically. "If you must." He turned back toward the top of the stairs and moved up. "There is little left in this place for comfort," he began, as though they had not already noticed. He swung the candle around briefly to catch their expressions.

Jikun could see Navon's eyes respond with sympathetic agreement. But Jikun knew his own face held a more irritable expression as he recalled Hairem's instance at having given an "unquestionably great reward." He scoffed.

"But," Sellemar continued, turning back around and speaking in a tone unbothered by these details, "there are a few chairs beside the fireplace."

Jikun narrowed his eyes at the male's retreating figure as he reached the top of the staircase. He was harder to decipher than he had expected. As he pursued the male, he scanned the old mural on the wall at his right: a depiction of several elves piercing a dragon through with lances: a scene from the War of the Dragons. It was a rather violent mural for an elven estate and he wondered if the True Bloods had been less obsessed with portraying perfect beauty than the other nobility he had encountered thus far. Still, this male wasn't entirely beyond their tendencies, was he? His eyes fell to the sword at his side.

The worth of that sword alone must be greater than that of the entirety of the Rilden Estate.

"This room here," he heard Sellemar call from the wide hallway beyond.

Jikun jerked his attention out of his oblivious stupor and hastened to follow Sellemar. *'We look like wide-eyed children,'* he thought shamefully to himself, hurrying up the rest of the stairs and stepping briskly to the open doorway.

Sellemar regarded them with the faintest eye roll, as though it was indeed children he was entertaining. "Have a seat," Sellemar offered, standing aside to let them pass into the room before him.

The curtains had been drawn since his appearance on the balcony, but the room was well-lit by a large chandelier and a roaring fire. The dust had been removed, whether by himself or servants, and the marble floors bounced the light back against the glittering walls and crystal vases. Of everything he had seen so far, this room alone held the pristine and royal elegance that was to be expected from the True Blood estate.

Sellemar took a seat before the thick fur rug beside the fire in a stoically formal manner. "I heard that after Rilden was slain here, his family left his room as it was at his death. They considered it a bad omen to move these things with them when they left."

Rilden's death… Jikun could remember that event. He had been murdered shortly before the True Bloods had left the continent, brutally and bloodily by a still unknown entity.

Jikun leaned slightly away from the heat as he stepped past the roaring flames. His blood ran colder than theirs—a Darivalian fire rarely rose so fierce. *'These southerners and their thin skin… Why, even the floor is covered for warmth.'* He glanced down at the rug, raising his brow. "White thakish," he spoke aloud, his mind flickering back to Kaivervale, wondering what had become of the soldiers Hairem had sent.

"Do you hunt?" Sellemar inquired, his voice briefly adopting a mildly intrigued tone. He gestured to the fur. "I have heard that the Darivalian elves are excellent hunters."

Jikun let his boot sink into the thick fur. "Yes. Although my skill has undoubtedly waned over the years away from home."

Sellemar nodded his head in understanding. "I hunt as well… although it is primarily deer, now," he added with a rueful smirk. "Once it was orcs, but that was many years ago."

Navon sank into the chair to Sellemar's left, leaving his thin hands to rest across his thigh. "I didn't think the orcs were troubling as of the last few centuries. In fact, Ryekarayn hasn't heard much from them in many years,"

Navon hedged, head cocked slightly to the right. His azure eyes were inquisitive, piercing as they gazed at the reticent Sel'ven. "Were you on Ryekarayn before the True Bloods?"

Sellemar's face grew impassive and all emotions vanished as though they had never been. He settled further into his chair. "You came to ask me something, I presume," he spoke, his eyes focusing on the general. "Speak." He set his sword across the stand between himself and Navon, letting the two make themselves comfortable as well before he began.

Jikun dropped himself to the edge of a seat, too focused on his mission to recline comfortably. The weight of the topic seemed to dim the flames, but the force of the heat remained. "King Hairem believes Saebellus may use the True Blood tunnel of Elarium to lay siege to the city," he began without formality, watching the solemn expression on Sellemar's face remain fixed. "His Majesty said that you knew of one of the tunnels going into Horiembrig. It seems Saebellus knows of the one into Elarium. If we could find this tunnel—"

"Yes, you would surround him and the war would be won," Sellemar replied. He tilted his chin, studying Jikun's face. "But what makes you believe that Saebellus has knowledge of this tunnel? Such information is hardly privy to Sevrigel's most trusted general, let alone maniacal warlords and traitorous rebels."

Jikun pursed his lips at the interruption and the followed digression. Exactly who did this male think he was? "These are military matters. I cannot discuss the details with you."

Sellemar waved a hand, turning back toward the fire with a gratingly haughty laugh. "Unless I have a good reason to believe Saebellus already knows of the tunnel's location, I will not reveal it to fifty thousand—or however many—males that you intend to lead through it. The tunnels are only of value so long as few people know of them. The moment I tell you of Elarium's is the moment it ceases to be of value. You do not just... *recreate* such vast work."

Jikun leaned forward irritably, narrowing his eyes at the male, yet he couldn't contest his excuse. Still... "Hairem—King Hairem—said he doesn't know about the tunnels. If Hairem doesn't know of them, then what value do they hold?"

Sellemar raised an indignant brow. "I just used one to rescue Ilsevel, as you are undoubtedly aware. That is what value they hold, General Jikun."

Jikun sat back, petulant to the elf's tone.

Navon cleared his throat and Jikun exhaled sharply, swallowing his frustration. "Saebellus never attacks without ensuring he has a way to escape," Jikun replied forcefully. "He's only taking forty thousand soldiers to Elarium and leaving twenty or thirty thousand behind to guard the Halls of Horiembrig. If he does not have a way to lay siege to the city by surprise, he will never take it. He knows this."

Sellemar turned back to face them, a smile of satisfaction crossing his lips. That was the information he had clearly been seeking. "Do you have a map?" he demanded suddenly.

Jikun quickly pulled the one Hairem had provided from his pocket. He offered it to the male.

"The tunnel," Sellemar began, as he unfolded the map, "is located here, fifteen leagues east of Elarium—that's about two days as a soldier marches. If Saebellus uses these tunnels, he will make camp at its entrance and sack Elarium once his troops are rested."

Jikun glanced up, eyes narrowed.

"It is what I would do," Sellemar dismissed. "If you make your crossing at the Galenval River, follow it south until you reach a boulder fifty meters high. Walk due west one hundred paces and north forty-one paces. You will come to the edge of a forest and another boulder. Speak in ancient Sel'varian—'*May I pass?*'—and when you have, '*thank- you.*' That is the entrance to the tunnel. There are no diverting tunnel ways. It will lead you straight into the cellar of the palace."

Jikun was repeating the words in his head. "South past Galenval. At the boulder, one hundred paces west and forty-one paces north to another boulder. May I pass? Thank you." He spoke the last two phrases in ancient Sel'varian, repeating the unfamiliar tongue several more times to solidify the information in his mind.

Sellemar nodded, raising a finger of request. "At least keep the details regarding commanding and closing the entrance between the two of you."

Jikun nodded, rising to his feet. He could sense the elf had more to say, but he had learned what he had come for. "Thank you, Sellemar. This is exactly what I was looking for." Despite the difficulty he had found in speaking to the male, Hairem was right. Whoever he was, however he knew about the tunnels, he was no common noble or mercenary. Was Ryekarayn becoming covertly involved in their war? That was bold, even for the True Bloods.

Sellemar stood as well, nodding his head toward Jikun and Navon with a look that somehow vividly expressed the satisfaction he felt in his knowledge. He opened his mouth and Jikun could hear the pretentious tone before he had even begun to speak. "I would caution you. Saebellus is not a foolish male." He paused briefly, as though to let his warning settle. "Good luck to you. May Sel'ari guide you."

Jikun flinched at the sentence, but he forced his lips into a smile, bitter though it was. "And you. Thank you." He could see Navon grimace as though in preparation for something much worse, but Jikun turned to leave.

"Thank the gods you didn't say anything in there," Navon breathed as he closed the door behind him.

Jikun did not reply. The way Sellemar had said her name was not like the way the council and Hairem spoke it. There was no casual overtone or societal expectation of the phrase: only serious devotion. He had an instinctual feeling that had he spoken anything against her, the male would not have been above defending her honor by the fist… or sword. Perhaps there was some credibility to the theory that the elf was a cleric.

*

Navon let the tent flap fall close slowly behind him before he turned to face Jikun. He had spent the entire walk from the Rilden Estate to their encampment attempting to collect a calm composure, refusing to engage Jikun in conversation. Still, Jikun could sense the anticipation in his eyes and hear it on his elevated breaths. Even as Navon forced himself to sit before speaking and delayed even further to light the table's candles, Jikun could plainly see his impatience. That wild, Helvarian bloodlust—that essence that lurked behind his curiosity. "What is the plan, General?" his captain finally spoke.

Jikun sat at the head of the table, inhaling deeply with all the pretense of solemnity. Saebellus was not making a mistake—at least, not as far as the warlord was aware. No, Saebellus had a plan, and if it was not for Ilsevel and Sellemar, the rebel would have claimed his next city: Elarium may have fallen.

"I am just… trying to deduce Saebellus' thought process," Jikun mused after a moment. "Saebellus is brilliant. Either he realizes the extreme risk of his decision and thinks the chance of success is worth the danger, or…"

Candlelight flickered the shadows across his captain's composed face. Navon placed his interlocked fingers to his lips thoughtfully, concealing his expression beneath. But his eyes had narrowed cautiously. "Do you think there could be a trap? Something we're not seeing?"

Jikun sat back, one arm resting casually across the arm of his chair, the other extended to the map before him. He tapped the wooden figure representing the warlord against the table loudly, turning his thoughts over and over again.

"Play this game with me," Jikun spoke after a moment. "You're Saebellus. You have decided to attack Elarium."

Navon leaned forward. "I would believe that conquering Elarium would be an enormous success: I would gain the strength of Sevrigel's trade and ships. But I would be cautious after what happened with Ilsevel. I would be concerned that you may know about the True Blood tunnels—or would have someone to inform you of them." Jikun saw him pause to give him the opportunity to comment. When the general said nothing, Navon continued, "I would have a portion of my troops lying in wait nearby should we be attacked from the rear while entering the tunnels."

"You would do that?"

"I wouldn't take your chances that I don't."

Jikun pursed his lips. "Then I'll have thrice the scouts check the region for any sign of additional troops. We'll scout outside normal distances." Jikun gave Saebellus' figurine a hard tap. "...But that's not enough. To ensure success, I would wait until half of your troops have entered the tunnel. If you have troops lingering for a surprise attack, then I will surprise *them* instead: I will attack them first after half of your troops have already left. If you are not planning the ambush, then I would siege the remaining troops before the tunnel instead. Those that you had already sent in would have no choice but to continue and emerge to surrender in Elarium, or to retreat and surrender to us." He looked up, releasing Saebellus' figure.

Navon's brow knit, staring at the map. Jikun could see his eyes scanning the parchment, looking for answers, fighting for a solution to the general's plan. He squinted his azure eyes in a final moment of desperation and finally leaned back. "...I would lose," he breathed, almost in relief.

Jikun pursed his lips, forcing back his wry smile as he focused. He would not allow Saebellus to flee again. "We shall send several birds ahead of us warning Elarium of Saebellus' attack and where we believe he will make entry. You shall have your first and second lieutenant oversee this matter." His exhilaration mounted as he spoke the words, despite his attempts to force it away. He could tell that his confidence had crept into his tone and Navon was resonating with it.

"We shall send scouts several days ahead of us to observe the surroundings and monitor Saebellus' movements. Were it not for Sellemar, Saebellus' plan to sack Elarium would have no doubt been successful. But as it is, once Elarium knows Saebellus will come from the palace cellar, his defeat in the city will be sealed. So Saebellus will flee as he always does—back through the True Blood tunnel, no doubt collapsing it behind him. But what Saebellus does not factor in is an army waiting for him, ready to strike when his troops are spread and vulnerable. An army that also knows where and which True Blood tunnel he will use. Even if Saebellus—and I grant him this, he is an intelligent male—suspects an attack and intends to route us from behind, we shall be ready for this as well." He inhaled deeply, looking up. "So I can fathom no successful trap. But our scouts will keep their eyes open."

Navon leaned forward. "What else, General?"

Jikun closed his eyes for a moment. There would be sufficient time to share in their victory later. When he opened his eyes again, they were focused: cold and stoic, all emotion once more vanishing beneath an icy mask. If Saebellus was forced into a corner, there was no telling how bloody their battle would end. But in his gut, he knew the price of victory would be steep. "Order the army to make preparations. Ready their weapons and armor and prepare the caravan. I want everything in pristine condition. Every single soldier and every single horse must be in peak form… this includes you. I believe, my friend, this is the last battle of the warlord Saebellus and his army. We leave in two days."

# Chapter Thirty-Four

Sellemar watched the arrogant general and his pale-faced captain depart, then closed the door behind them and shook his head. Was Elvorium so lacking in skilled soldiers that the Darivalians and Helvari needed to lend their leaders? He scoffed. Times had certainly changed since they had become bereft of the True Bloods' leadership.

And no doubt the council was to blame.

He strode into the kitchen, grabbing a stale slab of bread and sifting through the bowl of fruit beside it for edible remains. He frowned, pushing the bowl aside and leaning forward to grab a half-empty bottle of wine from the counter.

Damn, it was difficult to keep up with own physical needs when the country could not take care of itself without his help for just five damn minutes. What he would not have given for Hairem to hand him a servant or two—to go along with the drafty old building.

Then again, he supposed his secrecy was more important than his comfort.

He picked up a glass as he left the kitchen, returning to the stairs and taking the flight slowly. The light from the windows of the estate was growing dim as the sun began to sink behind the mountain range of the west. He could not see it, but he imagined its soft, grey silhouette against the supple red of the evening sky. Soft rays fell on the mural to his right, casting an orange glow over the scales of the dragons. It glinted off the golden armor of the elves. The general and his captain had stared at the colorful stonework for quite a while.

*'They've probably never seen an actual dragon,'* he mused.

He re-entered his room, setting the wine bottle, glass, and bread on the little table before the fire beside his sword. He raised his hands to the flames, letting them catch a hint of warmth before he moved to Rilden's old desk. Crouching down, he opened the lower drawer. It slid out heavily, sending up an odor of ancient wood and poorly stored susanic nuts that the late lord must have nibbled on as he worked. Still, it was not at all unpleasant. Sellemar inhaled the sweet scent and lifted the small stack of parchment from within.

Nestling back into the comfort of the chair before the fire, he set the stack in his lap and raised an empty parchment before him. He was almost finished. Silandrus may have failed to reform the council, but *he* would find a way to dissolve their ranks without breaking their precious tradition.

And yet, who was he to rebuke Silandrus? If Sellemar had not found illegal evidence on the council, what would *he* have done?

Nothing, truthfully. Nothing at all.

Gods, sometimes he wished he could throw tradition aside as easily as Darcarus was able to do. It would certainly achieve a faster, albeit perhaps bloodier, result.

He raised his quill, scratching along the smooth surface in elegant elven, *'Mikanum: money laundering, knowledge of the transportation of illegal merchandise, knowledge of illegal practices.'* He set the quill aside, picking up one of the papers in his lap and scanning the admission from Nilanis' servant of the El'adorium passing money to Mikanum. For a price, Mikanum had agreed to oppose offering any aid to Darival. He had, in short, left them abandoned in the north—both to the events occurring in the south and the trials they now—or had—endured.

He shook his head with a scowl as the rushing wind of the tundra seemed to sweep across the room, a distant memory of a place he had visited long ago. How could Mikanum have abandoned his own people? But Sellemar knew: the Darivalian had pocketed the price of Darival's assistance for his own.

He flipped through a list of Mikanum's financial keepings he had acquired from Mikanum's bookkeeper, noting that he had circled all but a few of the discrepancies.

Sellemar set the parchment aside and raised his quill once more. *'Cahsari: money laundering, knowledge of illegal practices and merchandise, purchase of illegal merchandise.'* Sellemar had seen much of this first hand.

He paused. Ulasum's Tooth. He stood. *'Damn. I almost forgot,'* he thought to himself incredulously, reaching into the vase above the mantel and producing the still-sealed vial of the repulsive liquid. He tossed it heavily into the back of the fireplace. There was a crack of glass and a venomous hiss of flames. In a brief plume of sweet fumes, all traces of the wicked toxin were lost.

He sat back down, scanning the letters before him. For once, they were not from Sairel or any of the True Bloods. Rather, the small stack of crumpled parchment contained Cahsari's letters to his son, of which the content was primarily a series of furious rebukes. Yet his admonition for his son's infatuation with prostitution and toxins was countered curtly by his son's reproach about his father's own vices, which included and were not limited to Ulasum's Tooth.

The letters had been fairly easy to gather… although admittedly a bit less than legally acquired.

Sellemar set it down on top of Mikanum's papers, lifting the slab of dry bread and taking a difficult bite. He made a face of disgust and set it aside, quickly pouring himself a glass of wine and taking a long swallow to wash the soured contents down.

"Ugh," he muttered. "That probably was bad a week ago." He set the glass beside him with a repulsed shake of his head and raised his quill once again.

*'Fildor: money laundering, illegal drug use, knowledge of the transportation of illegal merchandise.'* He didn't bother to flip through the large stack of Fildor's dealings with the ports along the river ways near Elvorium: he had already spent extensive hours filtering through the condemning evidence. He did, however, set a pipe still stained with ash beside the papers, the wood reeking faintly of the sweet-scent of the leaves of Ulasum. It seemed more than one council member shared that vice.

He raised his glass and took a sip.

"Nilanis," he spoke the name aloud this time, his voice singed with disgust. He set his glass down and scratched heavily on the paper, *'Transportation of illegal merchandise, possession of illegal merchandise, money laundering, murd—'* He stopped mid-stroke, going still.

There was a soft creak from downstairs. He stiffened.

*The door.*

With instinctual speed, he set the quill down, letting the papers fall from his lap. He grabbed his sword, his careless movement knocking the glass from the table, spilling wine across the thakish's thick fur and the corners of his paperwork.

*'Damn it.'* Yet he ignored the stain, stepping over them lightly and briskly striding to the office door. How he wished he had Ulasum's Tooth to coat his blade with now!

He pushed his door slightly ajar.

The light from the sun was gone—the hallway before him had grown dark and cool. He strained his eyes, trying to adjust them as the bright flames of the fire still danced before his vision.

He stepped out, drawing his blade and tossing the ornate sheathe back into the room behind him. It clanged against the marble floor, bounced once, and fell still beneath the desk.

He heard the startled footsteps on the marble below betray the intruder's location: the man was in the hallway between the kitchen and the stairs.

Sellemar slipped forward down the hallway, halting at the top of the staircase. He could see enough in the darkness to make out the entry hall beyond: the door to his estate was hanging open, and what rays of sunlight were left cast a soft, yellow glow across the marble floor.

He leaned cautiously over the banister, but there was no sight of the man. Catching the edge and swinging himself over the side, he landed lightly on the floor before the kitchen with an almost silent thud.

The intruder lunged at him immediately from around the corner, but Sellemar's unexpected entrance had given the elf the edge: it was in reckless, over-zealous bloodlust that the human drove his stroke forward toward the elf's chest.

Sellemar met his blade with equal force, dropping to one knee and swinging his leg out, knocking the human off his feet and onto his back.

"Who are you?!" Sellemar demanded, standing and pointing his blade sharply at the human's chest.

The human gave a grimace in the darkness. "Mercy, my lord," the human breathed, his elven words coming out thick in a Ryekarian accent. He raised his hands as though in surrender and sat himself upright before the blade. "I thought this place was abandoned."

Sellemar's brow knit skeptically as the human got to his feet. *'You should have been able to see the light of my room from the balcony window...'*

The human glanced around, almost sheepishly, before his gaze returned to focus on Sellemar. "I admit I was up to no good... I thought there might still be wealth lying around..."

Sellemar saw the muscles in the man's hand tense suddenly and he swiftly kicked out, slamming his foot into the middle of the man's chest and sending him sailing into the kitchen. The human skidded across the floor, stopping to lie momentarily still upon his back.

"Who hired you to assassinate me? Nilanis?" Sellemar demanded, stepping lightly in behind the sprawled body, careful to keep distance between himself and the man's limbs.

The assassin's face had curved into a deep scowl as he rolled to his chest and leapt once more to his feet. There was a hunger in his eyes equaled only by his hatred. The blow had not softened his lust. He swung his blade to the side casually, threateningly.

"I know who you are, True Blood bitch," the male growled.

Sellemar took a swift step to the left and threw his sword at the man's chest. "I doubt it," he replied calmly, watching as the human darted quickly out of the blade's path.

"Now why would you go and do a thing like that?" the human grinned. "Gods, you're more idiotic than—"

"For this," Sellemar stated smoothly, lifting up the spear leaning against the wall beside him.

The human's eyes narrowed abruptly and he darted forward as Sellemar raised his spear. Sneering venomously, he slammed his sword down onto the golden shaft as though he were wielding a cudgel. The clang rang out across the emptiness and vaulted ceiling, echoing like a crash of thunder against the walls.

Sellemar shoved the shaft back, meeting his every blow, his eyes straining to catch the man's swift movements in the dim lighting.

"Elven eyesight is weak in the dark, isn't it," the human gloated. He grabbed the bowl of fruit from the counter suddenly, hurling it at Sellemar's head as his blade pierced through the air for the elf's abdomen.

*'Yes. Yes it is,'* Sellemar thought incredulously as he twisted his body to the side, the glass shattering against the wall behind him. *'But it does not mean I have to move like a dwarf.'* He felt the blade rip past his side and swung the shaft of his spear out, knocking the man's lunging arm away.

With his path clear, Sellemar slammed the butt of the shaft into the human's knee. In a fluent motion he followed forward with a lunge, twirling the spear before him and smashing the shaft into the human's head. As the human reeled back, he kicked him in the side, propelling the thick body away and sending the man hurling against the counter. Then, with a swift twist, he dropped his body low near the tile, swinging his spear around once again, and shoved it through the man's leather-bound chest.

"If you knew who I was, you would have known there was not a chance in Ramul you were *ever* going to best me," Sellemar stated coolly, yanking free the man's blade as his grip loosened on the hilt. He shoved the blade through the man's throat and pulled his spear from his chest, letting the body fall before him in a crumpled heap. "...And now I have to clean this up," he muttered resentfully.

Sellemar took the man's shirt and wiped the excess blood from the shaft and tip of his spear. The cheap cotton had cleaned it less than was acceptable, but it would have to do for a moment. He leaned it against the wall and grabbed the body beneath the armpits.

*Ugh.* He wrinkled his nose as his face bent near the lifeless figure. Gods, did they *ever* bathe? He ignored his instinctual desire to repel away and tightened his grip.

In an unceremonious fashion, he dragged the bulky mass through the kitchen to the back door of his estate; then, he heaved it across the dry grass of his orchard grounds to the edge of the canyon.

With a final grunt, he shoved the body over the side and watched stoically as it vanished into the darkness below.

# CHAPTER THIRTY-FIVE

Jikun passed briskly through the rows of white tents that his soldiers had staked far from the future battlefield. The breeze was bitter and fast, carrying with it the scent of damp, wet leaves and the nearby river, an odoriferous marker of their whereabouts. He pushed open the tent flap of his final destination with little regard for the inhabitant, stepping in and speaking before the flap had even fallen closed behind him.

"Captain," he began, ignoring Navon's wide-eyed scramble for his armor. "Our last scout was spotted by one of Saebellus' scouts. Our soldier said he believes the shot he fired killed the enemy, but we can't be certain. Saebellus has rested for a day, and he will take no chances. Our scouts have seen no trace of the back line—no ambush in the vicinity—and we have scoured every inch of this land. I expect his descent into the tunnels shortly. Gather the troops. We march on Saebellus immediately."

"Yes, General," Navon spoke, almost breathless with anticipation.

Jikun departed immediately from the tent. There was no time to gloat on their success. Not yet. As usual, he could expect Saebellus' attempt to flee after his loss—however he did it without portals or teleportation. However he managed to vanish an entire army.

But Jikun just had to remain focused and ensure Saebellus could not create the distance he desired between Jikun's troops and his own. He had always used the terrain to achieve this.

He grimaced faintly as his last battle with Saebellus flared in his memory: the searing red light of a bolt of magic plummeted into the canyon wall near Widow's Peak, driving an avalanche down upon him and his men below. And just like every other battle, when the distance between their troops had been blocked by stone or dust or tree, Saebellus and his men vanished. But with

Elarium at his face and Jikun at his back, he would not have his opportunity this time. Whatever magic he was using, this time would be his last.

His boots crunched along the leaf-strewn mud as he strode to his own tent. He stepped in, dismissing the guards outside of it. "Prepare for battle," he ordered sharply.

As the clinking of their armor died away and the tumult of preparations replaced it, Jikun picked up his golden cloak, threw it over his left shoulder, and fastened the sash across his chest. He straightened the sapphire emblem over his breast: his mark as the general of Sevrigel's army. Unlike Navon, he had had his armor bound to him since daybreak. He paused for a moment, resting a hand on the table as his fingers trailed along the curve of the phoenix's arc across his breast. The mark of Sevrigel's general…

Hairem's words flitted suddenly to him, conjured up from some recess of his mind where he had forgotten them. The memory was of his first meeting with the king, when Jikun had dismissed his words as the overeager musings of a naïve prince. *'After the war, what is your ambition?'*

This thought came to him then, as it had on countless nights before. On every eve before a battle. He had never let himself reflect on it, never dared to think that far into the future, but *this* time… with the taste of a possible victory so *near*… His gaze on the emblem intensified. If the war ended… He would return to Darival: *after* Hairem provided the troops he had promised.

Then perhaps he would serve in a time of peace… if that day could actually come to him.

He pushed off the table, dropping his hand to the sword lying on the stand beside his bed. He picked it up, turning it once in the dim light of the candles. The azure gems glittered in the ice-like hilt and he wondered briefly if Mikanum was as corrupt as the rest of the council. But that was a digressing thought—irrelevant to the battle at hand. He let the sheath fall against his side, all resentment toward the council member fading as the exhilaration of war neared.

He pushed back the flap of his tent and stepped out into the cold. "Kutal," he greeted his stallion, running a hand affectionately down the white-flecked muzzle of his horse. Once again, Darival attempted to flicker to life in his mind, dragging him away on the haunches of Nazra, but he forced it stiffly away.

*'One battle at a time,'* he warned himself. He picked up the golden blanket from where it hung over the wooden post beside him and threw it over the creature's back.

He could see the commotion of soldiers hurrying around him, gathering their weapons and armor, barking orders at their comrades. Even though there was a tinge of chaos within its frantic nature, his troops were focused and prepared—they had anticipated his command could arrive at any time.

These were the most highly trained soldiers in the land.

Jikun swung himself onto his horse and trotted to the edge of the encampment. The empty plain stretched into the distance, bisected by a narrow stream that led to the land where Saebellus was encamped. Like so often before, the land's stark contrast to the roiling emotions beneath her inhabitants only filled the coming battle with further anxiety.

There was the soft suctioning noise of hooves pulling up from the earth behind him and Navon pulled his mare along his side. "The troops will be ready within minutes, as you could expect, General," he spoke, nodding his head forward. He paused, wild eyes flickering across the vast plain. "Are you… eager?"

"As eager as any male riding to his enemy's final defeat." Jikun replied with a faint smile, stealing a sidelong glance at the battle-lust rising in his captain. These were words of hope now. The drive of confidence necessary to head forth.

They sat beside one another for a short while as the army gathered around them. Even as the company of troops filed into their military rows, Jikun's attention remained outward, watching the horizon intensely until the seven scouts vanished over her crest.

"LET'S MOVE OUT!" Jikun ordered.

*

"General, Saebellus' troops have entered the tunnel as you predicted. I estimate half are now within."

Jikun waved a hand to dismiss the messenger as he finished, and for the briefest moment, he heard the male's footsteps before the scout vanished into the soldiers behind him. *'So this is it…'* He inhaled heavily as the icy breeze whisked his hair backward, the tempering braids whipping out in the force. His hand slid to the sword at his side, his fingers curling about the familiarity of the ice-like hilt.

Just over the shield of the hill lay Saebellus and his army, exactly as they had predicted.

"Captain Navon, at the ready." He jerked the reins of Kutal harshly, turning to address his troops. "I am not here to motivate you. I am not here to inspire you. If you do not know why you fight or why you kill, then no speech will rile your spirits for the coming battle.

"This is the last battle we shall fight. It is also the last battle our traitorous enemy, Saebellus, shall fight. If we die now, it is in knowing that the glory of the kingdom rests at peace. For every brother we have lost before this day, we shall make Saebellus pay ten-fold—before we toss his body before the throne of our king and burn the corpses of his lost in the fire of our victory. Let the cloud of smoke be so great that the gods themselves must descend from Emal'drathar just to breathe!" He raised his sword in a rallying cry.

The soldiers beat a fist against their chests once and replied in unison. "May Sel'ari grant them safe passage!"

Jikun rounded on his enemy. *'May Sel'ari damn them all.'*

The leagues of rocky terrain separating him from Saebellus' army seemed to fall away in his fervor to engage the enemy; the focused lust behind him echoed the same. He nudged his horse in the flank, the sound of marching feet resounding behind him in the night.

A sudden flicker of movement caught his eye atop the crest of the hill before him. With an instant reaction and a hiss of wind, an arrow shot past him, embedding in the enemy scout's skull.

This was *their* battlefield.

He brought Kutal to a stop at the crest of the hill and cast his gaze outward over the valley below. Like frightened thakish facing the jaws of the wolf, he could see them moving wildly as they hurried into the safety of the tunnel, frenetically scurrying into the darkness.

Jikun smiled wryly to himself. They would find no refuge at the end of it. Saebellus had indeed been caught off guard and for the briefest moment, he wondered what horror the warlord felt as the news reached his ears.

He drew his sword once more, a flash of silver in the faint light. "FOR SEVRIGEL!" he bellowed, pointing his blade forward.

A wave of soldiers surged past him, charging in wide lines of equal speed, weapons tucked against their chests, faces grim, voices silent. Their discipline alone was a sight to see: a seething mass of death ready to swallow the remnants of Saebellus' troops. The dark plain quickly became a teeming mass of soldiers. Cries of triumph rose across the battlefield as ninety thousand elves crashed down upon the residue of Saebellus' frightened troops before them, shadows amongst the still collection of white tents. Jikun could see

Navon raise his sword in triumph from the distance, his horse whinnying madly at the imminent clash of steel.

The last battle of the warlord Saebellus and Jikun Taemrin.

A sudden shadow swept over Jikun and his soldiers, so thick in nature that the valley around them grew dark. Jikun turned on his mount, his smile fading in confusion. Something shimmered to life in the distance behind them—no portal or illusion—just to the right of the empty hill they had just crossed. As if it had always been there. The moon and stars were blanketed by…

"*Oh my gods*," Jikun gasped. He threw himself from Kutal, throwing his arms up over his head in a desperate attempt to shield himself.

He could hear the thunk of arrows piercing armor and flesh, the thud of bodies falling around him. His horse whinnied frantically and reared, kicking out in pain. He dared look up to catch sight of two arrows protruding along its back.

*What in the god's name was happening?!*

He straightened, grabbing Kutal's reins and forcing himself once more onto its back. It screamed in protest, but Jikun swung it around.

"What…" he trailed off in shock. Where nothing but an empty valley had been before lay thousands of enemy troops, volley at the ready as though they had been lying in wait before Jikun had ever arrived. No portal… no illusion… *How then...?!*

There was a sudden shadow above them yet again.

"*NO...!*" Jikun shouted, dropping the reins and once more throwing himself from his horse. Soldiers around him dropped to the earth, covering their heads. Jikun clung close to Kutal in a desperate hope to be shielded by its massive body.

The arrows ripped through his army again while his troops still stumbled in confusion from the first onslaught. The second brought their movement to a stop. Navon was gone. Beside Jikun, Kutal let out a final feeble whinny and collapsed as the second volley left him mortally wounded.

Jikun stood again. A thunderous roar went up around them with the sound of thousands of rushing feet.

*'We're surrounded...!'*

How did this happen?! They had followed the plan. The plan was perfect. *Everything* was as they had expected it! Saebellus had laid camp outside the entrance to the True Blood tunnel, as they had anticipated. He had rested his troops for a mere day before they had begun their descent into the passageway.

And when half of the enemy had entered within, Jikun's army had struck…! *Where had the rest of the army come from?*

Perhaps it was the answer to how Saebellus had been able to vanish after every battle. Why his army could never be found.

By no magic of the gods' design, the enemy had come from behind out of *nowhere.*

*Saebellus had saved this gambit not for minor ambushes or surprise attacks, but for a final, crushing blow.*

Still, *Jikun had more soldiers!* "FIGHT!" he shouted as his troops were pressed from both sides. "FAN OUT!" They attempted to obey, to widen their front and back lines, but as his troops moved out, there were sudden screams of panic.

What in Ramul was happening?! Jikun shoved his way through his soldiers, throwing a male out of his way. "HOLD THE LINE!" Yet, through the mass of seething troops, he caught a glimpse of a pit in the earth.

*'Saebellus' army dug traps…?! When…?!'*

On their right—and by the screams, from their left as well—wide, deep pits pocketed the earth, sending Jikun's unsuspecting soldiers tumbling down into the ground where Saebellus' army dropped arrows into their defenseless bodies.

"HOLD THE LINE!!!" he screamed again, his throat ripping raw.

An enemy tent nearby suddenly exploded in blue-black flames, unnatural, dark fire that was immediately followed by the excruciating screams of his troops. The victims collapsed into the mud as the fire bit their flesh and heated the metal of their armor, burning it with a sickening odor deep into their skin. The agony on their faces was lit by the cold glow of the crackling flames.

Jikun stumbled away, his heart racing. "AVOID THE ENEMY TENTS!" he screamed.

He could hear the clash of metal around him now. A throng of soldiers reeled back in front of him, the back line stumbling into the fire in cries of agony while the soldiers before were cut down in the confusion.

The noise around Jikun was deafening—screaming, shouting, crying… metal on metal and the thud of feet. The night was a blur of moonlight and glinting steel, of firelight and blood.

Another distant explosion of flame lit the scene around him.

A soldier before him was cut down, bleeding profusely from a wound at the base of his helmet. Jikun knocked the falling male away and shoved his blade through the enemy's helmet.

A second enemy swung around beside his fallen comrade, throwing his weight behind his blade. Jikun mindlessly shoved his weight back, watching the enemy stumble from the force. He reached out to grasp the male's wrist and, with the sound of cracking ice, the male's body began to freeze. Jikun slammed his hilt onto his hand as the soldier reeled, causing it to shatter like glass.

Chaos. Burning flesh. Broken bones. Cleaved bodies.

A male not far from him collapsed in convulsions as metal melted into his flesh… as black flames devoured his skin. An almost inaudible 'pop' sounded from inside the helmet before he suddenly went still.

*A slaughter.*

Jikun dropped his sword.

Blood sprayed out from a nearby soldier as the general turned to flee the fight.

Defeated.

General Jikun Taemrin of the great and mighty nation of Sevrigel.

Defeated.

An explosion of flame from another tent cast a vivid picture of the bodies dropping around him.

His army… his troops… Navon… and himself… they were all dead.

*A slaughter.*

# CHAPTER THIRTY-SIX

"Mmm, we need to get up, my love," Hairem spoke groggily, running his hand up Ilsevel's leg, feeling the soft, smooth skin slide against his fingertips. "We'll be late for the council meeting this morning."

Ilsevel smiled, turning her face toward him, strands of her long, blond hair falling across her face. Hairem returned the smile fondly and lifted a strand away from her pink lips. He leaned forward and kissed her softly, inhaling the deep, sweet scent of rose blossoms that seemed perpetually embedded into her lips.

"Oh, must we? That dreadful council!" Ilsevel complained good-naturedly, rolling onto her back and letting the covers fall away from one of her bare breasts. Hairem saw her smile broaden as she followed his gaze to it. "Or we could stay here," she whispered, reaching a hand up to his face.

Hairem sat up slowly, kissing her fingertips before she drew her hand away. "Ah, such are the burdens of a king. I, at least, must go."

Ilsevel smiled, sitting up and swinging her legs over the side of the bed. "Then you shall not go alone."

Hairem turned reluctantly from the gentle curves of her back toward his chest of drawers. *'Clothes now, Hairem.'*

"Who is that mute girl, again? The one that does your hair?" Ilsevel asked as Hairem pulled on his silk shirt and buttoned the cuffed sleeves.

Hairem leaned down and picked up an emerald vest, catching Ilsevel stepping into her undergarments from the corner of his eye. "Alvena," he replied as she pulled a strap across her shoulder.

"Oh, I remember now. Well, I caught her spying and eavesdropping on the nobility at dinner the other night. She is a curious one, isn't she?" Ilsevel nodded as though the name had been at the tip of her tongue. "Lovely girl—quite tragic that she is mute. Why is it that she cannot speak?" She pulled her dress over her shoulders, letting one of the straps fall to rest against her arm. She then pivoted, gliding across the marble floor to his side. Sliding a hand down his waist, she kissed his shoulder. "That vest is very becoming," she whispered.

Hairem winked as he fastened the clasp of his pants. "I wore it to impress you."

Ilsevel stepped around in front of him, leaning up and speaking softly, her breath warm against his lips. "You *know* what impresses me."

Hairem tried to lean in for a kiss but she moved away, sliding her hand down his arm in a tease. He cleared his throat, stepping into his leather boots. "The clerics believe it is caused by a disfigurement of her throat: nothing of the mind. Come." He reached out, catching her wrist as she attempted to swing toward the bed. "The *meeting*."

Ilsevel laughed and allowed him to lead her out. She wrapped a hand around his forearm and took step beside him.

Erallus closed the door, silently following a short distance behind them.

*

The sky was overcast by midmorning, with only the edge of the sun daring to attempt to slip past the clouds' defenses. The walk to the council chambers was a bit cooler than usual for late autumn, but Ilsevel bore it without complaint. Hairem led her up the wide steps of the council's chambers and stepped into the building through the doors that Erallus parted for them.

"King Hairem, Queen Ilsevel," Mikanum greeted with a nod of his head and a polite smile. His eyes flicked intently from one to the other, lingering on the queen as though still uncertain of to how to respond to her presence.

Nilanis ceased his conversation with Cahsari and stood as well, smiling broadly. "My Lord and My Lady, welcome."

How vastly different their behavior had become since Hairem had taken Ilsevel as his wife. He nodded his head toward the two of them in acknowledgement and moved to his seat at the front of the room. Beside the white wooden chair engraved with a blue phoenix and embedded with gems was now a second chair of almost identical appearance.

Hairem allowed Ilsevel the honor of seating herself first before he followed suit.

Without a moment's hesitation, Nilanis strode briskly to his place at the center of the room, raising his hands charismatically, and began to speak animatedly about the condition of Jikun's division of plagued troops, as well as the most recent shipment of silks from the coastal cities. It was as though he had every ounce of energy invigorated by his newfound "power" in blood. And Ilsevel's presence seemed to only spur him on.

Finally he turned his attention to the political matters of the city, twisting toward Hairem as he spoke. "My Lord, today comes a most grave matter. The son of Lord Cahsari was caught in the sin of whoring with a human prostitute from Ryekarayn. We know the sentence of the seized prostitute, but what, My Lord, should be done with Lord Cahsari's son? Carnal debasement has long been a crime punishable by death, but… in *this* case…"

"In this case, you want me to make an exception," Hairem replied flatly. His brow knit faintly as silence returned to him. He thought briefly of Erallus and Jikun and imagined them discovered in a similar situation.

His gaze flicked surreptitiously to the Helvarian council member. There was no emotion he could read from it. Instead, Cahsari seemed to have withdrawn, his lips pursed tightly into a hard, thin line. Was he mortified by his son's crimes? Pained? Hairem couldn't tell.

His eyes lingered on him a moment. He felt Ilsevel's hand tighten on his arm and she leaned suddenly forward. "The law commands that partakers in such an atrocity shall both meet the same fate," she reminded the room sternly. "This is not a matter for exceptions, high noble's son or not."

Hairem rested a hand on hers, pleased with her boldness. Yet he shook his head as he stood. "Release the prostitute. Return her to Ryekarayn. Fine her, brand her, and forbid her from returning." He continued, ignoring the gasps of outrage. "As for Cahsari's son, fine him as well, twice-fold for taking advantage of the state of the woman. Then release him as well."

The council room fell silent, but Hairem could see the eyes of Ilrae narrow in disgust.

Valdor stood promptly. "A merciful decree for both, Your Majesty. However, what is the reasoning for the ruling against the law? Is this mercy to be shown to all infidelity against Sel'ari, even carnal debasement? What about two willing, non-wed elven lovers? For the law commands the punishment is the same."

Hairem felt Ilsevel's hand tighten again, as though she knew that what he was about to say could only kindle further anger, no matter how well it was spoken. Nevertheless, he forced his tension aside and raised his head calmly. "To foster a greater relationship with the humans, we must first see them as equal. This kingdom has seen enough death. And enough arrogance. There are greater evils in this city than the foolish selfishness of a woman and male. Their crime is severe, but a harsh fine should warn them of the consequences of such behavior. If there is a second offense, the male shall find himself on an extended stay within the prison."

Mikanum stood, his eyes cold. "This is a long standing tradition that—"

Hairem smacked a hand down loudly onto the table, finding Mikanum's grasp of tradition now shackling. "I do not *care* that it is a long standing tradition. This kingdom has seen enough senseless bloodshed. Soon we shall hear word of the general's defeat of Saebellus. It is time we start defeating the bloodshed within our own city as well and foster a stronger relationship with our non-elven brethren. Starting with this law."

Mikanum's jaw slacked indignantly.

"Well spoken, Your Majesty," Lord Valdor applauded, the corners of his one good eye creasing with his smile. It was the first Hairem had seen from the male.

Heshellon stood, his expression apprehensive. "Even I must say that this is a bit bold, Your Majesty. But the reasoning is sound—I shall support you in this change."

Hairem surveyed the room, yet it was Nilanis his eyes focused on. The El'adorium's gaze locked with Ilsevel's. His mouth closed and he nodded curtly.

Hairem looked down at her, catching the warning in her eyes directed toward her father. He was surprised how much control she still possessed over him, even after the wedding ceremony.

Nilanis held up a hand against further debate. "This matter shall be written down for a formal vote in two weeks. Until then, the woman and male shall be dealt with according to the king's command."

As the words left his lips, relief flooded Cahsari's face. He ran a hand through his hair and exhaled audibly. As corrupt as the male was, Hairem could not help but feel compassion at his affection for his son. Perhaps the council as a whole would follow Nilanis' example of obedience and understanding—and even Cahsari would see that not all change was to be abhorred.

*

"What you did in there was bold," Ilsevel spoke softly as they left the chambers. Her expression was difficult to read and Hairem found that it seemed more so that she was trying to read his own thoughts.

He raised his brows in a gesture of unmoved confidence. "Bold? For refusing to execute two wayward souls? I believe Sel'ari shall forgive me for my mercy."

Ilsevel turned back toward the streets. "Yes, I suppose she, at least, may."

Hairem frowned, studying the side of her stoic face. "...What does that mean?"

Ilsevel shook her head suddenly, smiling tenderly. "I just worry about you sometimes. I am proud of your fierce heart, but it does not cease my worry at your daringness."

Hairem laughed, throwing his head back dismissively. "I am sorry to cause you worry." He gestured up at the sky. The sun had pushed the clouds aside and the warm rays made the breeze obsolete. "Let me take you to eat. At the place where we dined when we spoke of Lord Valdor's appointment. To take your mind off the matter?"

Ilsevel's smile broadened. "I *am* famished," she admitted. She nodded her head elegantly toward the side. "Lead on, my love."

*

The balcony where they had once sat so many months before—discussing her childhood and Valdor's appointment—had remained unchanged, but the courtyard was now devoid of flowers and leaves, decorated only by the bare branches of the trees, the fiery oranges and reds of fallen leaves, and the lush hedges below.

Hairem raised his glass as the servant stepped out of the deep red curtain to fill it.

"The change to the law—do you agree with it?"

Ilsevel swirled her wine thoughtfully for a moment. "I suppose I had never given it much thought before... but yes, yes I agree." She took a long sip. "After all, Saebellus' defeat is nigh and you were right: the bloodshed has gone on long enough... outside the city as well as within."

Hairem raised his glass as well, pleased with her honesty. Even she had not been able to mask her surprise at his decision, and yet she did not jump to offense like the mulish council members. "Do you find some form of particular consolation at Saebellus' imminent defeat?"

Ilsevel's eyes dropped down. "You are referring to his murder of my brother, I presume." She nodded once. "Yes, Hairem, I do. It eases my heart to know that the murderer will soon die. I wish him all the pain in the world, but I suppose a death at the hands of the military against which he rebelled is a just death, albeit swift."

Hairem reached out a hand, resting it across her own. "Yes, your brother shall be avenged. Sometimes, it is not always the way we expected or wished. But I hope it will bring you peace as well."

Ilsevel looked up, meeting his eyes as she forced a smile onto her full lips. "Yes, my love. I shall soon be at peace as well."

They passed the remainder of their meal pleasantly, and Hairem felt himself nigh-permanently affixed with a contented smile for how matters were falling out. Ilsevel was the greatest gift in his life, and he constantly found himself amazed by her in new ways. When they had finished dining, he took her hand gently and led her out of the establishment.

"I have a few places I wanted to stop before I return to the palace," Ilsevel spoke as they stepped out onto the cobbled street. "You go on ahead. They are a lady's affairs. And—" she winked, continuing almost inaudibly, "perhaps I may pick something up for you to see later."

Hairem blushed. "I will see you this evening then." He kissed her hand before watching her vanish down the street.

"Back to the palace, my lord?" Erallus asked as he turned to face him as well. Although Hairem imagined that the male had heard the subtle comment, his face remained remarkably disinterested. As the male had said, he indeed had a character for apathy, but perhaps it was not as negative as he had originally projected. It eased the otherwise, undoubtedly awkward nature of their sudden pairing.

Hairem's eyes lingered for a moment longer after her. "Yes, Erallus. To the palace."

*

The rest of the day came and went with complacent normalcy. Hairem busied himself under piles of politically-laced parchments and was relieved when dinner brought them all to a close.

As he returned to his room, he breathed a sigh of relief to hear the doors close behind him. He looked around anticipatorily, but Ilsevel seemed to still be gossiping with the nobility downstairs.

The balcony beckoned as its curtain billowed out in the cool breeze, and Hairem obligingly walked out onto it.

The sun had dipped down toward the horizon, red as blood, filling the sky with hues of vivid oranges and yellows. Hairem inhaled deeply, leaning against the railing. The recent rain had left the air heavy with the scent of fallen leaves and autumn's last prevailing flowers. The mountains in the distance were already dusted with snow as winter bore down on them. But in Elvorium, the weather would remain cool and pleasant, the snow vanishing with the grey skies to the north.

He turned his eyes to the darkened city below, the sunset's warm orange hues lighting the gold-slated rooftops with an amber shimmer. He could still distinguish the white wedding banners waving in the distance from the towers of Sel'ari's temple, as they would for the full year after his wedding to Ilsevel.

He found himself smiling. The kingdom was still full of life from the celebration of their wedding. Ilsevel was well-received—her charm, her honesty, her simplicity… Perhaps the people were relieved to find a politician less… masked. Hairem had held nothing back from her. She attended the council meetings with him, she addressed diplomatic matters… She even oversaw the city guard. As unprecedented as a female was in those positions, Hairem found the ability to share the burden of ruling both a relief and a joy.

The council's obedience, a lady he loved… and General Jikun's certain victory over Saebellus. He exhaled heavily. "*Thank you*," he whispered to Sel'ari, watching the white banners twist sharply in a brisk breeze.

The door to the room opened suddenly and closed with a loud snap. He twisted around sharply in surprise.

"Ilsevel? What is it, my love?" he asked, pushing away from the balcony and reentering the room.

Ilsevel's lips were tight, her face drawn. She straightened her dress, as though gaining composure, a crumpled piece of parchment clenched tightly in her right hand. He saw her eyes falter as she spoke. An unsettlement grew within his gut. "Hairem," she began. "I have news from the south…" Her voice wavered.

Hairem felt his stomach twist into a sickening knot, dread filling his chest. "What is it?" Had General Jikun been killed in the battle? Or were the casualties great? How could he have expected a victory without such a terrible consequence?

"Hairem… General Jikun and his army… they were defeated. They…" she lowered her voice to one of deep, almost fearful sympathy. "They were all killed… Saebellus is marching on Elvorium."

The world around him rang with deafening silence. He stumbled forward, putting a hand out almost blindly. Defeated? Dead? The words bounced blankly off his mind.

Ilsevel caught his arm to steady him. "Hairem?" she whispered. "Come, sit…"

He felt a tug on his forearm and slid his feet forward to follow her guide. His mind was numb. *No.* That was impossible. He had misheard. He had misunderstood…! The General… the plan. No!

"No," he whispered in a struggle for breath as Ilsevel sat down beside him. "That is impossible. General Jikun… the army…"

Ilsevel shook her head slowly, empathetically. "No, Hairem. They're gone. A messenger just arrived bearing the news. There is nothing left of his forces. Saebellus has killed them all."

Hairem felt her slender hand slide across his and her grip tighten. His heart pounded in his chest as he fought the numbness back. "No. *NO.* We haven't lost yet. We have the units left here. And I have allies. Allies amongst the other kings. I will ask for their help. They will rise with us…" His voice cracked as emotions began to beat against the wall of numbness. "They will help us defeat Saebellus, if need be!" He found his lips were trembling, his hands shaking, even as a glimmer of hope flickered to life. He drew them up toward his face as fear and defeat fought to overwhelm him. *No. They could still prevail! They had to—*

"Sh, my love," Ilsevel whispered, raising a hand to the side of his face, and pulled him down against her breasts. "Sh…" Her hand slid through his hair slowly.

And he felt a blade slice into his throat.

# Chapter Thirty-Seven

*'Oh my gods... OH MY GODS!'* Lardol had told her not to spy and now she… what she saw! Alvena's lips parted, her heart threatening to tear from her chest. It could not be real!

Hairem's body flailed slightly and Ilsevel pushed him away. His eyes were wide. Confusion. Pain. Shock. A hand went to the gaping hole in his throat as blood gushed forth. He sank down to his knees.

No. The king. Hairem. Her king.

*'Hairem, no!'* Alvena screamed in her mind as her mouth spoke the silent words. She threw the door to the room open, her mind blinded by shock and grief. Hairem's eyes locked with hers briefly before his body swayed and he fell to the side, his hand falling away from his throat.

His eyes glazed over as his body fell still across the blood-soaked tile.

Dead.

Alvena's hand dropped from the door. *'...Hai...rem...?'* She stared numbly at the body of the king, lifeless on the floor beneath her.

"HELP!" Ilsevel shrieked. "HAIREM, NO!"

Alvena started, her mind slowly coming to grasp the situation. Ilsevel had a hand to her breast, another on the winding pillar of the bed, her face twisted into one of shock and horror. "Help! The king…!" The queen narrowed her eyes at Alvena and a coldness glinted beneath their mask of pain.

Alvena stumbled back suddenly. *'How... how could she have...?!'* She choked back her thoughts, desperately turning and fleeing from the room, her bare feet pounding across the stone as she ran. Her body was shivering, but not with cold.

With fear.

She tore down the hallways, their arrays of coloring whipping by in a blur of unrealism. She stumbled, falling before Lardol's door. *'Help!'* She scrambled up, pounding frantically against it as she gasped for breath. *'Help, help, HELP!'*

"Alvena?! Sel'ari, child, come in!" the old elf gasped as he swung the door wide. There was no rebuke in his gaze this time, only concern. "What is it?!" He reached down, grabbing her by the shoulders and pulling her up straight.

Alvena shoved his hands aside, stumbling into the room to lean against the wall.

"Why are you crying? What has happened?"

Crying? Alvena reached up, wiping a hand across her cheeks. So she was. She reached out, throwing herself against Lardol's chest and burying her face into his shoulder. *'Hairem. Hairem. Hairem!'*

Lardol held her for a moment, his hand on the back of her head. "Shhh. Shhh…." He trailed off, no doubt to the sound of the distant clinks of armor and shouts. He pulled her away, turning her chin up and locking eyes firmly with her. "Alvena, what has happened?"

Alvena gasped. She had to get control of herself! Control! She inhaled heavily, his familiar, deep-set blue eyes bringing her some comfort. *'Hairem…!'* She gestured to her head and then her breasts.

"Ilsevel…?"

She stabbed wildly at the air.

"Ilsevel was stabbed?!" Lardol gasped.

Alvena shook her head violently. She raised her hands, gesturing wildly to her head and then drew her finger across her throat.

"Who is hurt?! The king?!"

Alvena nodded frantically.

"*How?!*"

Alvena gestured to her head once more and her breasts. Then sliced at Lardol's throat.

Lardol's features grew tight, his eyes darkening as he settled on her words. "Ilsevel… murdered Hairem?"

Alvena gripped his shirt tightly and nodded sharply. *'Hairem…!'* The image of his last look of hollowness… That final desperate attempt to hang on…

"Does anyone know what you saw?" Lardol whispered, darting quickly to the door and turning the key in lock.

Alvena nodded, lips trembling.

*They were going to kill her…*

Lardol moved back swiftly, grabbing her shoulders. "Ilsevel?"

She nodded again. Why had she…?!

Lardol stood numbly for a moment, his lips parted, eyes wide. A pallor had come over his face and he pressed a hand against the wall as though to balance himself.

There was a sudden array of shouts. Lardol started, his eyes coming to focus back upon her. "Alvena, you must flee. You must flee the city. Flee the country if you can. The queen will find you and—"

There was a sudden knock on the door. "Lardol."

They froze.

"Lardol!" The knock rang out heavily once more.

Lardol let out sudden, long exhale, gasping in relief. "It is Erallus," he breathed, moving to unlock the door. He opened it swiftly, grabbing the male outside by the front of his shirt and jerking him into the room before the soldier had a moment to gather himself.

Lardol closed the door swiftly behind them and turned the key. "Erallus, y—"

Erallus' bright eyes widened even as his arched brows knit in focus. There was heavy pain behind them as he surveyed Alvena. "Hairem has killed himself after hearing about General Jikun's defeat at the hands of—"

"No," Lardol spoke solidly with an unsteady shake of his head. "Ilsevel has murdered the king. Alvena has seen it." He moved quickly to his chest of drawers as Erallus grasped for words. His hand shook slightly as he opened the topmost drawer, producing a sheathed dagger. "And Ilsevel knows it."

Erallus' eyes locked onto Alvena, his lips parting in dread. She could see the shock and horror written plainly in his eyes, the disbelief he too attempted to understand. Beneath those roiling emotions, even the visibility of pain was dimmed. "No…"

"*Yes*," Lardol replied, shoving the dagger into Alvena's hands.

She fumbled to hold onto it as he jerked away. As she looked up at the king's high servant, a new flood of emotion crashed through her. For all Lardol had ever yelled at her and ordered her around, he did not doubt her now, even for a moment.

"The queen demanded that Alvena be brought to her. I—" Erallus began.

Lardol cut off Erallus' words with a firm, dark glance. Alvena could see Erallus pale. "Yes, Erallus," Lardol spoke. "Hairem's will. Ilsevel is no doubt aware that you and I know of it. As well as the council. Perhaps you could find refuge if you went before them… but Nilanis is Ilsevel's father and the

El'adorium. They would never believe that Ilsevel killed Hairem. And I do not believe Nilanis would let you usurp the power of his daughter… as true as your claim may be."

Erallus put a hand against the wall. "*Gods*. I never thought for a moment that it would come to pass…!"

Lardol turned to Alvena, clearly reading the confusion written across her face. Still, Lardol offered her no details. "First, Alvena must flee the city. Flee the country if at all possible," Lardol replied, hurrying back to his drawers. His movement was growing steadier, perhaps due to the urgency of the moment. He reached deep into the back of one of the drawers and pulled out a small bag that jingled softly with the sound of coins.

Erallus stepped toward the door, pressing his ear against it. He pulled away. "I am not the only one ordered to find her, Lardol. There are others…"

Lardol grabbed a pair of his shoes, forcing Alvena to sit. Her mind felt overwhelmed as he pushed her feet into them. She looked down. They were far too large. Lardol carried on without pause. He pulled off his shirt, ripping the sleeves from it.

"We have to get her away from the queen," Lardol spoke as he tied his shoes firmly to her tiny feet with the sleeves.

Erallus nodded immediately in agreement. There was a tumult of pain in his expression and Alvena knew he still struggled to grasp the reality of the situation. As even she did. "…How?" Erallus replied.

Lardol stood, yanking Alvena to her feet. "She must go. Not by water—Nilanis may be involved. The ports are too dangerous. Not by bridge—she'll never escape unnoticed. There must be another way out of the city."

Erallus' eyes lit up. "Sellemar."

Alvena looked up sharply. *'Sellemar…?'* She knew that name. He was the male from the city the day Hairem had asked her to deliver flowers to… Ilsevel….

There was another knock on the door. "Lardol? Is Alvena in here?"

Erallus moved forward swiftly, pulling Alvena aside to stand behind where the door would open.

Lardol took a deep breath and straightened his shoulders. Color had mostly returned to his cheeks. He calmly opened his drawers for a shirt, pulling it on as he replied, "Alvena? No. Why? What has she done this time?"

"Lardol, I have orders to search the room. I apologize. Please open the door."

Lardol gave a loud sigh. "I just got out of the bath. You will have to wait a moment." He looked back at them, gesturing toward the balcony.

Alvena found herself being pulled swiftly away toward the doors and out into the cold night. The breeze bit at her legs beneath her thin dress. She looked out, her eyes filling with dread.

The city seemed small below them, the palace grounds a distant toy. *'Where do we go?'* she thought desperately, looking back at Hairem's guard. They were not like the human assassin—they couldn't just vanish like that!

The soldier leaned over the side, looking down tentatively. "It's about twenty feet to the next balcony. Alvena, can you do it?"

Alvena stared back at him. Twenty feet?! She clasped her hands together.

"Alvena!" Erallus whispered firmly.

She started as a knock rang out behind them.

"Lardol, open the door or I will be forced to knock it down!"

Alvena hurried to the side of the balcony and looked over the edge. Directly below the balcony, twenty feet down, was another. Her heart skipped a beat. How could they?! She turned back to find that Erallus had reappeared at her side, a sheet in his hand.

"Hang on to this. I will lower you down as far as I can. Then you will have to swing yourself toward it and let go."

Alvena's grip on her hands grew painful. Gods, she was just a handmaid!

"Land on the balls of your feet. Bend your legs a little. *Go!*" Erallus whispered.

The door behind them shook.

Alvena grabbed the sheet, her hands sweating and trembling against the soft, silken fabric. She forced her grip to tighten, biting her lip forcefully. *'You can do this. You have to do this,'* she told herself. She stepped over the railing of the balcony and inched away from the side. She forced herself to focus on the wall of the palace as she dangled in the air. Even the gentle swinging tied her stomach into knots. She could hear Erallus grunt above her as he lowered the sheet down. Slowly, the balcony vanished and the lower platform loomed a bit closer.

"Now," Erallus grunted.

Alvena rocked her body gradually until the sheet swung out over the second balcony. With an internal shriek, she released it, her heart pounding, the wind rushing quickly past her ears, and landed with a thud onto the balcony below. Her ankles and feet stung as pain shot up her legs.

She looked up, eyes widening. How was Erallus…?

The male appeared suddenly over the side, dropping along the bars of the balcony to grope along the edge of the marble surface. He swung himself forward slightly, releasing as he moved, and landed with a thud beside her, his chainmail jangling loudly as the little links rattled against one another.

There was a loud argument above them as Erallus straightened with a grimace. "Let's go." He pushed aside the emerald curtain a crack, moving with a faint limp. But there was no stopping now.

The room before them was dark inside. Erallus stepped forward through its vast exterior to the other side. He neither glanced back toward her nor spoke, and when he reached the other side, he opened the door and peered out into the hallway.

But Alvena was right behind him. Through that narrow gap of light, she caught sight of the wide, dimly lit corridor outside—it was empty and silent, in sharp contrast to what was happening just one floor above them.

"Clear," Erallus assured her after a moment of careful consideration. "Come."

Alvena had only a brief time to consider what would happen to Lardol if it was discovered that he had helped her. *'Sel'ari, please keep Lardol safe!'* she begged.

Word of Ilsevel's demands seemed to have not reached the lower floors. And neither had Hairem's death. Erallus and Alvena made a swift flight from the palace and out onto the grounds with hardly another elf in sight. The evening had grown late and most of the servants and guards had retired for the evening.

A sudden pain filled her as she realized that it was the last time she would ever set foot in her home. That she would again see any of them. She glanced back once at the magnificently carved stone doors, now closed and dark.

She drew her attention back to the male beside her, his focus intense as he advanced. Outside the palace doors, Erallus did not hesitate. He slowed to a casual but steady pace, moving and passing through the gates with a polite smile and nod of his head. Never before had the expanse between them felt so narrow. He eyed Alvena silently, as though ordering her to stay close.

"Alvena, aren't you dressed a little—" one of the soldiers began in rebuke.

"I am taking care of the situation," Erallus replied sharply, cutting the soldier off.

They fell silent.

The moment they were out of sight, Erallus stepped into an alleyway and rushed to the nearest sewer lid. "Be quick. These lead to the old Rilden Estate. Come. It is our best chance of escape without being spotted."

Alvena didn't need an explanation. She didn't have a choice. She watched as he pulled the sewer lid up with a grunt and slid it to the side. A thick darkness lay within, the ray of moonlight hardly reaching even the cobbled stones of the alley around them. She took a deep breath and then climbed down into the darkness below. Landing with a light splash, she stepped aside and looked up expectantly. The stars vanished as the male descended behind her and slid the lid back over the hole.

The world was almost completely black around them. A very faint light in the distance pointed them to the next sewer drain. Erallus extended a hand and found hers, placing it against his back. "Run your hand along the wall and keep one on the back of my shirt. Follow me," he ordered as he began to move swiftly through the sewers. "You cannot leave by water—Ilsevel's father controls the Port of Targados. And the city guard has been under Ilsevel's control since the wedding. I would not take our chances there, either. This male, Sellemar, however, may be able to help you."

Sellemar… who was he and how did they know him? But the wonder faded quickly as the cold water seeped into her shoes and the echoes of their breathing and footsteps were the only sounds around them. It was a lonely, unreal world… where Hairem was dead and she fled for her life. They moved steadily, twisting and winding their way through the darkness.

"Here is the entrance to the Rilden Estate," Erallus finally spoke after what seemed like hours. He slowed in the darkness, his fingernails scraping across the stone. "Ah, the ladder is here. Up."

Alvena felt hands grip her own and place them on the slippery algae coating of the metal.

She was really fleeing…

She stepped up, dragging her cold feet onto each rung, and pushed against the trapdoor above them when she reached the top. It fell back with a loud clang and she started, nearly slipping on her hold. Erallus' hand steadied her from below and she swiftly pulled herself from the hole before her lack of balance cost her in a fall.

Her gaze rose to the surface around her. The moonlight fell through the broken stones and small windows, glaring fiercely across the fallen beams and dried leaves. The place was a small room of endless darkness above her; it seemed long-since abandoned, decaying and sinking into ruin.

This was where Sellemar lived?

Erallus closed the door behind them, darting toward a nearby door in a state of urgency that Alvena has almost forgotten in her confusion. She hurried after him, nearly tripping over a pile of shattered rocks nearby.

This was the great Rilden Estate that had once housed the True Bloods' closest relatives? Even though it was merely a watchtower, she was shocked to see its neglect.

Outside the tower, the ancient tree limbs swayed in the breeze and the moonlight lit their way through the shadows like a path from the goddess. They moved swiftly through the ancient orchard, the wind howling fiercely through the canyon behind them. And before them was the old Rilden Estate.

Erallus drew up breathless before the door, pounding loudly on the wood with his great fist. Alvena stepped back, seeing a candle flicker to life slowly from an upstairs window.

*'He's home!'* she breathed in relief.

The door swung wide a minute later and a flicker of emerald gazed warily back at them. "Erallus," the familiar face greeted slowly. He turned, eyes meeting with Alvena's in slow recognition. "You…"

Erallus pushed past him, forcing the door closed behind. "This is Alvena," he began as Sellemar opened his mouth to protest. "There is no time for details. Ilsevel has murdered King Hairem. Alvena is a witness. She must be out of the city tonight. Ilsevel's father owns the port, and Ilsevel herself has had control of the city guard since the marriage. Sellemar, I pray you know of another way out of this city!"

"*Damn*," Sellemar muttered with a grunt, even as he moved instantly away toward a back room. "Stay here."

Alvena looked about nervously. What did they know of this male? How could he know of another way out of the city? Impossible! The city was on a cliff with the lake to the east and an endless drop to the north, south, and west. Elvorium was impenetrable and inescapable!

Sellemar emerged a minute later with a sack, his motion flawlessly focused as he lowered the candle to a nearby table. "Do you know why the Rilden Estate was such a valuable piece of property?" He tossed Erallus the sack and swung about once more. "That is for Alvena," he added briefly, moving through the entryway and into a long hallway beyond. "I doubt your king knew. The king's brother—or sister—always possessed this place until Silandrus and his sons left—at Sairel's appointment, it would have been given into the hands of Darcarus. Its value was immeasurable: only the palace and the Rilden Estate held entryways to the True Blood tunnels out of the capital, the former of which was sealed three centuries ago."

*'True Blood tunnels?'* Alvena had never heard of them. But another way out of the city…? She looked toward Erallus, who nodded his understanding.

"And you know where they both are."

Sellemar nodded. "Of course. It should not surprise you by now."

"I don't know who you are, and yet, it doesn't."

Alvena looked from one male to the other. They seemed quite familiar. Yet Sellemar had claimed to be new to the city when he had met her.

She paused, eyes widening. Wait. Was this the other soldier who had rescued Ilsevel with Erallus? She bit her lip. *If only they had failed!* How foolish she had been to thank Sel'ari for their success! Now…! Her mind felt jumbled, every bit of her thoughts trying to work their way back to what she had seen… Back to Hairem's dying moments.

No, she didn't want to see that again!

"Erallus, what will you do?" Sellemar was asking as he placed a hand onto the wall and ran it down to the marble tiles below. He pressed his fingers against one, speaking in the ancient elven tongue, "*Ha revas?*"

The wall turned inward, a flicker of blue orbs lighting the golden archways of the ceiling beyond. Sellemar stepped down onto the stairs, turning to look back at Erallus expectantly.

The soldier lowered his head. Alvena could see the pain rekindle in his eyes when he finally looked up. "I cannot leave this city knowing that Ilsevel has killed my king. Hairem had a will… I cannot leave without trying to make things right. Yet the guards at the gates saw me escort Alvena out…"

Sellemar's eyes remained steady. "You think you can go back?"

Erallus' countenance reflected the same unwavering determination. "Yes. I will go before the council. They know of Hairem's will."

"Hairem's will?"

Erallus hesitated to elaborate for a moment. "…That I am to be king should Hairem die without an heir," he finally spoke.

Sellemar's eyes widened. "Does Ilsevel know this?!"

Alvena stared at Erallus. King? Erallus was *king?!*

"I am no coward!"

"You *idiot!*" Sellemar suddenly rebuked fiercely. "We are not talking about cowardice! We are talking about common sense! You cannot go before the council! Ilsevel was not afraid to murder her own husband. Her father sits as head of the council. They will *never* believe you that she murdered Hairem.

And it does not matter that they know that you are the rightful king—they will not support your placement as king, and without their support you will fail. Ilsevel will name you a traitor, and you shall be executed. No good can possibly come of you going back!"

Erallus' lips trembled and he pursed them tightly to steady himself. "I must—"

"*Desist* from your stupidity," Sellemar barked, and Alvena stepped away slightly in surprise. He was silent for a moment, brows furrowed in concentration. "There is another way that the remainder of your life may still serve a greater purpose for Hairem."

Erallus cast his eyes aside. Alvena could only catch a flicker of grief from his expression, and yet she knew there was submission in it as well.

Sellemar turned back toward the darkness. "Come, Alvena. I will lead you to the end of this section of path. There is no need for you to die in this city. You shall be on your own then, but I will ensure you make it to Ryekarayn." He turned around a bend in the stairs, his voice echoing back to them, "And Erallus, I shall be back to deal with you after."

Alvena bit her lip, looking back at Erallus. What did he mean—"remainder of his life"? She turned, throwing her arms around Erallus tightly. *'Thank you for everything!'* she whispered. She stepped away, bowing deeply.

Erallus' eyes softened. "You are welcome. You served Hairem well. I will pray for your safety and your future. Stay on Ryekarayn, Alvena. Do *not* come back to Sevrigel," he spoke, forcing a smile. He handed her the sack and Alvena could see the shimmer at the corner of his eyes as he fought back his grief. "I will try to set things right."

Alvena watched as her hands numbly took it. *This was it...* She inhaled sharply, and vanished into the darkness after Sellemar.

"Hurry now," the male called back to her.

The stairs soon faded and the path became a curved tunnel with golden ceilings cracked and faded with years of neglect. From what Alvena could tell, they were descending the length of the canyon and would probably come out at the canyon floor. The palace would be a small thing in the distance far above them then.

And she'd be farther from home than she had ever been before.

"Here," Sellemar spoke firmly. He stopped, turning toward her. The little blue lights above cast his handsome face with shadows. He looked weary, as though what had occurred took some unknown toll on him. Three paths lay before her. "The middle one is the path out. Continue from here. Use the stars to guide you. Head west, for the coast. Follow the river and the canyon. The nearest city is a few days from here." He reached into his front shirt pocket, producing a piece of wrinkled parchment. "When you get to the coast, take any ship bearing the blue phoenix crest—it is the crest of the True Bloods. Show the captain this letter. When you arrive on Ryekarayn, go to the Sel'varian Realm. Show the guards this. You will be taken care of."

Alvena reached out and took it slowly. She looked back the way they had come, her brow knit with concern. What would become of Erallus?

Sellemar followed her gaze. "I am afraid the fate of Erallus is bleaker," he spoke gravely, as though reading her thoughts. He did not try to comfort her. The honesty was chilling. "Erallus' position as Hairem's personal guard commands him to stay and right this injustice. He cannot go with you and do this. By staying here, he might have a final action he can take to make things right."

Alvena turned to him, searching his face for answers. *'What do you mean?'* she wanted to ask. Was that it? Erallus was just…

Sellemar pointed back down the tunnel. "Now flee, Alvena. Leave Erallus' fate to me. And may Sel'ari watch over you."

Alvena turned, hurrying off into the tunnel, glancing back toward Sellemar once. He was the last bit of home she could grasp. The last comfort before she would truly be alone in the world.

# CHAPTER THIRTY-EIGHT

"General! General! *JIKUN!*"

The words fell deafly upon him. He had only ever before been so paralyzed by horror while in the Sevilan Marshes. It was the same carnage again… Everyone was dead. *Dead.*

Jikun found his body jerked to the side swiftly as though he was weightless, causing him to stumble slightly. But… his sword…

He watched blankly as it vanished under a throng of soldiers' steel boots.

What… How…?

Navon grabbed his jaw suddenly, his boney fingers digging into his flesh. "Jikun. Look at me!"

The force of tone caused the fog over his mind to clear somewhat, and yet Jikun felt his eyes strain to focus. "We're defeated, Navon," he whispered numbly.

"What?!" Navon shouted over the tumult of noise. He shook his head as Jikun opened his mouth. "Jikun, we're defeated." He raised a hand, black wisps enveloping a nearby soldier in otherworldly howls. He dropped his hand, placing it firmly on Jikun's shoulder. "Jikun, you have to flee."

Jikun's eyes widened slightly, even as his mind struggled to grasp the concept. Flee…?

"*FLEE*, Jikun! You cannot surrender! If you surrender, Saebellus *will execute* you!"

Jikun looked around at his panicked troops, flinching as a male was thrown to the ground and stabbed repeatedly in his thinly armored gut. Navon pulled him further into the midst of his own troops. "They're almost upon us, Jikun. You must go. If we surrender now, you will not be able to escape."

Jikun eyes shifted about once more, his ears ringing, his heart pounding violently in his chest. There was enough clarity to understand what would result from such an action. *'But in the time it takes me to flee the troops will surely be slaughtered...'*

Navon shoved Jikun forward. "NOW, Jikun. I won't let you die here."

Jikun stumbled, sightless to the ground beneath his feet. The war was lost. Sevrigel was lost. He couldn't die here.

No… not *couldn't*. He didn't *want* to die here.

He turned, abruptly shoving through his soldiers in blind fear. Navon was right. If he surrendered, Saebellus would execute him. Even if Saebellus spared the rest of the troops, for *him…*

The end was a black void. He would simply cease to exist. There was no soul to be saved.

Death… *He would not surrender to it!*

He slammed his hand against the chest of an enemy soldier, knocking him aside as the male's body began to freeze. Navon slashed his blade through the soldier's throat. As his sword ripped free, a nearby tent exploded, showering them with hot sparks and blood.

But Jikun pushed on, his drive for survival propelling him through the chaos of the fight and out to the edge of the battle in a seamless swirl of smoke and blood and screams.

He gasped at the cold breeze, the darkness that lay ahead of them as chilling as the war behind.

Navon turned and enveloped an enemy in black wisps. As the soldier's body flailed, the captain threw the soldier back into the fray, whirling at once and pulling Jikun behind the shelter of a tree.

"*Now flee.*"

Jikun's knees buckled slightly in a sudden surge of weakness. Flee… He gripped Navon's shoulder tightly, seeing his captain's eyes already locked back onto the battle, his body preparing to return. "Come with me," he gasped fervently, his fingers tightening in mad desperation. "Saebellus will execute you as well…!"

But Navon didn't seem to hear him. He was pulling at Jikun's clothes, raising the flaps of the shoulder plates frantically. "*No…*" he trailed off as he pulled back the sash on Jikun's cloak, attention suddenly riveted on the general's chest.

Jikun looked down with him, eyes widening at the trail of blood flowing from his chest.

Navon dropped the cloak, steadying Jikun as another wave of weakness threatened to bring him to his knees. With a sharp intake of breath, his captain turned his back on the battle and numbly sheathed his sword. "Let's go."

The crest across the sash fell loose as the cloak slid across his shoulders, dropping the emblem into the mud at their feet. Jikun glanced back once at the screaming soldiers, barely catching sight of them through the trees, trying to ignore their final cries to prevail against Saebellus' army.

He turned back to the silence of the forest around them. And with Navon steadying his steps, they fled into the trees.

# CHAPTER THIRTY-NINE

The waves beat against the coastline fiercely, as though the violence of war had contaminated the very water of Elarium's shores. The sky overhead was spotted with only a sprinkling of dark grey clouds, but the wind howled along the cliff side with a vengeance.

Almost four days of travel. By now, the army would have been defeated, the bodies raided of valuables, and Saebellus would likely be turning his attention to Sevrigel's true capital.

But no elf now remained to bar his passage—none save the few withered, frail males still recovering from the devastation of the swamps. Jikun had been defeated twice. Disease, the sword—both had conquered him, rendering him powerless in the face of death. His soldiers were dead. *Everyone* was dead.

Jikun felt Navon's hands steady him as he leaned over the side of the cliff, his stomach twisting with the agony of their defeat. Darkness lay before him now.

His hand slid to the wound on his chest, where the hole was now wrapped in the dirty sash that had once hid it. He had not recalled receiving it, but after the shock of war had faded and the pain began to eat away at him, Navon wasted no time in using it to bind the wound. Sill, their pace had slowed to a tedious crawl. Mud, forest, valley… they had trudged through it all to escape.

His fingers trailed up to where the crest of his rank had once lain. *'What happened to it…?'* His fingers shifted across the chainmail and dropped away.

Jikun had made his decision.

He cast his eyes outward over the cliff's edge, lips parted for his ragged breaths. The darkness expanded until even the stars themselves were swallowed along the horizon. "Ryekarayn is across the channel… over fifty leagues…" He followed the glow of moonlight across the deck of a ship far below them. The thin path leading down the cliff side to the narrow shore was empty except for a few small, weather-beaten knarr vessels. In the distance, safe from the possibly shallow waters near the coast, Jikun could glimpse a number of larger ships anchored out at sea.

"I've crossed the channel before. I've seen enough to handle one of those knarrs." Navon replied heavily, following Jikun's gaze. He grimaced once and shook his dirt-splattered face once, keeping sleep at bay. The shadows beneath his eyes were warning enough that the Helven had slept little.

*'Crossing the channel is not the same as sailing a ship... '* But Jikun kept his pessimism to himself. He was weak now. Far too weak to argue. And he could hear the anxiety in Navon's voice. Whether it was due to the unfamiliarity of sailing or the knowledge that the southern waters were notoriously treacherous, Navon's tone was clear enough; he wasn't deceiving anyone. They would be fortunate to survive the crossing in a vessel so small and fragile.

He grimaced as a sudden, acute pain shot through his chest. His knees faltered and he caught his comrade's shoulder for support. "What are we doing for food?"

Navon's face remained composed even as his grip on Jikun's body tightened. He raised the rest of the sash, bound into a sack. "What we've gathered along the way will have to suffice for the journey. Water, of course, will be your responsibility."

*Water... Gods...* The thought of using his magic... Jikun's hand loosened and he sank toward his heels, fighting to appear deliberate about the movement.

But Navon knew him too well. He hooked his hands under Jikun's armpits. "Stay with me, Jikun." He pulled Jikun up straight and began to move toward the path that trickled its way down the cliff side.

Jikun stepped slowly at his side. Navon had to be thinking the same thing. Water, even on the ocean, in Jikun's state was... He looked down at his trembling hand. He wondered if he had the strength to do anything now. His fingers slowly clenched.

The injury had taken its toll on him.

*'Damn it!'* He looked away sharply, drawing his attention from his pathetic form, eyes flitting up the cliff side across the precipice beyond. Through the forest line, he could catch a glimpse of the towers of Elarium, the coastal western capital of success and might a reminder of his failure.

He turned his head away, pushing down his shame.

"Careful now," Navon warned as the algae made the stones slick to their footsteps. "Pay attention to what is in front of you." He steadied Jikun as his legs buckled once more.

"I am fine," Jikun muttered as he pushed off Navon's shoulder. He stopped before the side of the ship, raising a leg as he unsteadily attempted to step in.

"Here, let me—" Navon began.

"I shall do—"

"—help you"

"—it."

Navon pushed Jikun to sit down at the rain-filled bottom of the boat. "That is *enough*. Just sit down and leave me to handle the ship's preparations."

Jikun sank heavily against the ship's hull, letting his head fall against the wood. As his last bit of adrenaline faded, his final state of weakness was beginning to set in. His eyelids twitched and trembled as he desperately fought to keep them open.

Navon couldn't know. If he doubted Jikun's ability to make the journey, he would perhaps insist they remain on the shores of Sevrigel. And he had to ensure that at least Navon made it to Ryekarayn.

He had been a good captain.

And a better friend.

He let his head fall to the side to catch a final glimpse of the southern capital city shining along the cliff side, candlelight dying as the branches of nearby trees swayed before them to block out the light. The wind howled softly into the crevices of the stones, and a final leaf broke free from the branch above and was swept high into the air. Jikun watched it twist and writhe in the wind before it landed onto the froth of the ocean to be swallowed into the water's darkness.

After a short time, Navon pushed the oar into the water and the ship began to cut a gradual pathway through it, away from the powerful gusts buffeting the coast, out toward the human's coast of Ryekarayn. The waves rocked them steadily and with every stroke of the oar, the shoreline receded further into the night. Sevrigel: the only home he had known. He had fought for her, bled for her, loved her.

And he had abandoned her. He could still imagine her silhouette against the black sky, but the darkness had swallowed any last glimpse into the night.

Jikun turned his head away from the coast toward the bow of the ship, staring numbly into the darkness as they made their slow journey toward Ryekarayn.

Sevrigel was forever lost to him.

# Chapter Forty

Sellemar braced a hand against the rough wall of the stairway to steady himself as his foot slipped against a crumbling step—the watchtower of the Rilden Estate was more worn down than he had expected for a place that had only been vacant for three hundred years. He warily glanced up into the dimly lit roof, praying silently that this was not the time it finally collapsed. How naïve of Hairem's family to let such a valuable building fall to ruin!

The fourth trumpet blast thundered from the northern end of the city, and it was but twice more until its call would signal that the enemy had arrived at the city's gates. He felt his stomach twist as he recalled the arrival of Ilsevel's servant at his doorway, ordering him to arrive promptly to the council.

And yet, despite having been told that Saebellus had arrived, he had to see for himself to truly believe it… to *truly* believe that Sevrigel had lost.

He pushed off another step of the old tower's winding staircase and glanced briefly out a narrow window as he walked. The sky was a dull blue-grey in the winter dawn. The clouds knit closely together as though for warmth, bunching together here and there toward the horizon. And with the sun hanging low in the east, Sellemar could see the light spotted through the trees around the tower below him, casting long shadows out before the trunks where little archways of light stretched in a steady pattern into the distance.

Another trumpet blast resounded across the city.

He pushed past the door hanging from its hinges at the top of the stairs, hearing it groan pitifully as it teetered forward.

A final trumpet blast echoed around him.

Sellemar strode forward, resting his hands against the broken ledge of the tower's topmost window. The cool wind whipped his hair back sharply to nip at the tips of his exposed ears. He heard himself inhale sharply, the sound catching in his throat.

It was as he had expected. *Gods*, or was it worse?

Saebellus' army had come from the north, staying clear of the remnants of Jikun's army still camped in their rows of white tents at the south.

But even so, what good would Jikun's troops have done against what opposed the city now?

If the council had withdrawn the ban on Jikun's troops to allow them to defend the city, they could have perhaps resisted. Laying siege to Elvorium from the south or north across the narrow bridge would have meant death for Saebellus, and he had no ships in order to attempt an attack from the eastern port—his losses at Elarium had been great enough for the southern capital to hold.

But then, Elarium had never truly been his objective to begin with, had it?

His mind reflected on the great city around him. Even *now*, if Elvorium closed its doors to the warlord, they could hold out for quite some time. He clenched jaw, frustration seething through his body. The council would never risk fighting and failing—not when their own lives would then be forfeit.

In their cowardice… no, in their *corruption*, they had surrendered.

*'Is this the future you saw for Sevrigel?'* he reflected inwardly toward Silandrus.

Even as his own pride and defiance rose, he could not help but grimace at the sight of them: sixty thousand well-armed enemy soldiers lined up across the canyon. He narrowed his eyes as he saw a flicker of movement from the ranks closest to the bridge. A white flag became visible, an escort of soldiers before it, and then…

Sellemar put a hand to the hilt of his sword instinctively.

The warlord, Saebellus. It could only be the enemy general at the center of the unit, flanked on either side by his captains. He caught sight of a slender, but unusually solid, body of an elf beneath the glint of the finest elven armor and a heavy black cloak. The male stood tall, dark and distinct beside his blond-haired elven brethren.

There was a sudden welcoming salute of trumpets.

"They would not…!" Sellemar whispered in stunned anger. How *far* had his Sel'varian brothers of Sevrigel fallen?!

And yet they *were*. The unit of soldiers, with Saebellus striding toward the front, began to march across the bridge. The city was nearly impenetrable, and yet the council had chosen to *welcome* Saebellus and his army into the city with a military salute. He heard another gesture of welcoming trumpets from the city's walls and with their call, the white banner held by the enemy troops vanished out of sight.

And why should the symbol of truce remain when they were being escorted into the city like foreign guests?

"What in Ramul are they thinking?!" Sellemar growled to himself angrily as he spun about. He sprinted back down the tower's steps, skipping several at a time and catching his balance on the wall as a few of the stony stairs crumbled away when he landed on them. He leapt over a broken beam on the floor as he reached the bottom of the tower and flung open the ancient door leading out to the estate's grounds.

Was welcoming Saebellus Ilsevel's doing? Other than his summons, there had only been silence from her since she had murdered Hairem and he had turned Erallus in to her. The city was left to mourn Hairem's "suicide" and Ilsevel had withdrawn into the palace in "grief-ridden solitude."

Sellemar ran out of the estate grounds to the street, moving swiftly toward the council's halls. Ilsevel's servant had said nothing about the council meeting with Saebellus. She had praised and doted upon him for turning Erallus in to her, but had left out such a detail as this when she had summoned him. He pursed his lips, feeling much like her latest pawn. At least he was aware of it—Hairem had not been so fortunate.

He vanished into an alleyway as he avoided the bustle of the city's streets, brought to life by the unexpected trumpet calls. He could see the fear and concern on the faces of the elves around him as they stumbled from their homes to gather and whisper beneath the balcony overhangs, merely able to speculate at the unprecedented collection of contradictory trumpet signals. He turned a corner and slowed, hearing the sound of armor and marching feet in the cobbled street before him. He approached slowly, stopping behind a small number of elves who had sunk back into the alleyway shadows in hopes of catching a glimpse of the god-cursed warlord.

Sellemar remained hidden as well, watching as the city's watch marched into view, their expressions unreadable beneath their polished helms. Shortly behind them marched a dozen armed enemy soldiers, stiff and steady in their movement as they vanished out of sight after the watch. And then... Sellemar leaned forward slightly.

Yes, *there* was the warlord Saebellus. He was lightly armored, bearing the same crest on his cloak as he had worn before he had rebelled—the emblem of the True Bloods, as though it was *their* cause he served. His black eyes were focused on the cobbled streets, locked in the direction of the council's hall.

There was a visible flicker of triumph burning behind them. His long black hair was braided in the traditional style of Sel'varian males, although any true Sel'varian physical traits had long since left him.

"It is true!" Sellemar heard the male before him whisper in awe, a gangly male, with a smudge of charcoal still stained across his chin as though he had rushed straight from the forge.

"When he abandoned Sel'ari, she cursed him," another lanky elf replied with their kind's speculation—a brief glance at their hooked noses and their sweeping eyebrows told Sellemar they were brothers.

He focused back on their words. *Had* Sel'ari cursed the warlord?—was his appearance a result of his abandonment of their Sel'varian goddess? But then... why not so many others? Nilanis. Cahsari. Saebellus was hardly the first to turn his back on their god.

Sellemar's lips pursed as the two males behind Saebellus came into sight. These two were still Sel'vi and perhaps this made their betrayal all the more grave. His eyes began to travel down the line of soldiers, but then his gaze froze onto the male walking on Saebellus' right side. He had been slow to recognize him in his disbelief.

"*Vale?*" he spoke aloud in surprise. Damn! He had been certain the blow he had dealt the captain had been fatal! Certainly Saebellus had a healer as gifted as Riphath in his ranks!

He turned swiftly and moved back the way he had come, his chest swelling with frustration. He wound his way around the crowds, shoving his way forcefully through as the throng of people grew ever thicker the closer he came to Eraydon's Square.

*The first time he would sit on the council would be to the arrival of Saebellus.*

It disgusted him to think that he was now a part of their corrupted union, but *he* would never give himself over in true loyalty.

Though the crowd slowed his progress, he arrived at Eraydon's Square ahead of the warlord. He could hear the clamor shortly behind at the north, but all signs of Saebellus and his escort were swallowed by the buildings and the countless elves about him. He darted swiftly up the white marble steps, feeling small beneath the large pillars lining his way, as though here, on Sevrigel, he had finally become insignificant.

He paused briefly at the doors, resting his hands against them, hesitating even now at the thought of joining the council; the principle of the matter repulsed him. All of his work... all of it for *months*... The council's self-centered ways had tarnished the dignity of the normally noble and proud Sel'vi! But he masked his anger as he threw the doors of the council chambers open.

Unlike his last forceful arrival, this time the council hardly noticed him. The seven members were arguing loudly, shouting and cursing, moving about their desks in a panic.

They at least still possessed the wisdom to fear Saebellus.

"We should kill him and throw his body into the canyon!" one of the council members shouted above the others, his dark eyes wild, arms thrown up to emphasize his point. Sellemar judged him to be an Eph'ven based on the darkly tanned nature of his skin. "And then barricade the city's gates! Saebellus will never—"

"Are you mad! Saebellus will destroy the bridges and find a way to force a fight by water!" Another elf interrupted, brown-haired and boney of frame. Definitely a Galwen.

"Why do we not have a substantial fleet?! Wait, I know, it is because Nil—" another elf shouted. Cahsari.

Nilanis bellowed his interjection, waving his arms fervently. "Fleets have to dock at the port and Elvorium's port is not large en—"

"—cut into your wealth—"

"—what Saebellus has to say!"

"If we had a sword for every coin *you* make—"

The tumult of shouting quickly grew louder, enveloping all sensible discussion with it. But it was enough for Sellemar to gather the reason for their madness: they were terrified. Terrified for their lives. For their wealth. Despite Elvorium's ingenuity of defense and ability to hold out in water and food for months, their businesses would not survive barricading themselves in. Their wealth and luxury would be sacrificed in the name of defense. And that small chance of failure—that Saebellus would procure ships from his recent fight near Elarium or that aid would fail to relieve the city—that alone was enough to spread the gates of the capital wide. That, and perhaps a firm nudge from... Sellemar turned toward the front of the chamber.

Ilsevel had a hand over her mouth, her eyes wide and feverish, her usual countenance disheveled and worn. He found himself impressed—there was not an elf alive who would have guessed she had killed her husband. He found himself wondering if she truly was afraid of Saebellus' arrival. He squared his shoulders as he released himself from the council's doors.

"Silence!" he heard her attempt to shout, but her high voice was swallowed by the males.

Sellemar regarded her in mild wonder. Even now, her demeanor was of concern and gentleness while her countenance was fragile and passive. His thoughts were quickly broken as the noise of the council only grew louder. He slammed the doors of the hall heavily behind him.

The noise broke just long enough for Mikanum to demand, "How dare you enter this chamber again! Why have you come?!"

"You think rescuing the queen grants you some special permission to just come and go as you please?" a thin elf snarled, turning his chin up haughtily. Sellemar saw the arrogance displayed clearly on every clammy feature of his face as he raised his chin to challenge him.

"Silence!" Ilsevel raised her voice, her slender hands balling into fists that she slammed angrily down upon the desk before her. She inhaled sharply, her body shaking as though racked with fear and anguish. She reached out a hand to her desk, steadying herself upon it.

Sellemar could see Nilanis' lips purse in concern and he drew his gaze back to her. How genuine her vexation truly seemed.

"Saebellus is almost here," Sellemar finally spoke, his voice just loud enough to rise above the tumult of the crowd outside.

Ilsevel looked up, raising her hand before the council could respond. "I have asked Sellemar to sit on the council. Not only did he save me from Saebellus, but he has once again shown his devotion to the crown. He turned in the traitor Erallus."

Sellemar could see the Galvarian council member purse his lips in disgust.

The Eph'ven ventured in a tone that was nothing but cautious, "Hairem's will placed Erallus as—"

Mikanum laughed, throwing his head back. "Heshellon, a common soldier to be our next king? Hairem—may Sel'ari grant him safe passage—surely could not have intended to mock our tradition so. Erallus was simply meant to watch over Ilsevel until she has wed again."

Sellemar could see Heshellon's eyes narrow in anger, his devotion to Hairem dangerously obvious. "We all *know* what Hairem meant. Erallus—"

Cahsari sneered as he interjected, "What you are saying sounds rather treasonous. Are you suggesting that Ilsevel is not our queen?"

Sellemar could feel the tension in the room quiver. Ilsevel's gentle expression had grown hard.

"...No, of course not... I'm merely trying... It's..." Heshellon trailed off as the brown-haired council member beside him gave a faint shake of his head to dissuade him further.

"Erallus misunderstood as well," Ilsevel finally spoke, lowering her head. "He attempted to usurp me the moment Hairem..." she trailed off, emotion choking her voice. The room remained silent for a moment. Ilsevel raised her head. "Hairem wanted me to marry Erallus. I know this. But Erallus attempted to discard me and take the throne for himself. It would have broken Hairem's heart to see his friend betray him so..."

Sellemar felt his cheeks grow hot. Here, her act seemed so forced, every pause a stage for her to bathe in their sympathy. There was a fierceness in her eyes, a fire of triumph burning. Every movement, every trembling fluctuation of her voice seemed carefully controlled to emphasize and sell her anguish. How could the council not realize this?!

Nilanis raised his hand slightly in a comforting gesture. "Let us speak no more of this. Even the suggestion that nobility such as yourself could be bound to a common soldier... sometimes our dear king thought more with his heart than his mind."

"Always," the Galvarian council member muttered cynically.

Ilsevel continued, locking eyes with Sellemar. "I have made a new position for Sellemar. It shall be a position that is granted out of honor. He shall be the first to sit upon it. He shall be the El'ismaldra—the speaker of the honored."

Sellemar drew himself up to begin his carefully composed response, but was suddenly interrupted as the doors behind them swung open. The sound of armor echoed around them into the chambers.

"General Saebellus, Your Majesty!" a soldier announced, stepping aside.

If any small sounds had remained in the chamber—the rustle of fabric or the shifting of feet—they were immediately silenced. Sellemar strode quickly to the side of the marbled hall and out of the doorway as the other council members fell back in silent fear.

Standing in the great and towering doors of the council's hall stood Saebellus—but unlike the elves around him, he neither appeared small nor insignificant. The sunlight fell through from the chamber's high windows, glinting off of his battleworn breastplate. Sellemar could see traces of blood and dirt ground into the filigree and crevices. The light bounced and the shadows dipped off its surface, exaggerating the damage. His black cloak was tattered and stained, falling behind him in a great, sweeping breadth of fabric.

Like day and night, his black-eyed and black-haired form contrasted the gentle beauty and light of the hall, seeming to suck the life from it with a solid, chilling presence. And unlike the other elves in the chamber dark of hair or skin, Saebellus' appearance was a stark reminder of his abandonment to Sel'ari and his people.

With a start, Sellemar's eyes fell on the second medal clasped to Saebellus' chest. It was the medal of Sevrigel's general. He wondered briefly if the warlord had taken it from the general he had killed upon rebelling years ago, or if this was the medal that Jikun had worn the day he was slain.

Sellemar glanced briefly at the huddled council members who were gazing at the general in stupefied silence, uncertainty rippling through their ranks. Ignoring them, Sellemar stepped off the marble floor of the chamber and onto the upraised stone platform beside the desk of a one-eyed council member.

"If they had shown the late general this level of respect, he'd never have lost to Saebellus and we wouldn't be in this predicament right now," the male muttered to Sellemar, his breath cool against his ear.

Sellemar leaned slightly away, glancing once at Ilsevel and feeling his mind call for caution. Despite the mild trust she had demonstrated toward him, she no doubt regarded him as expendable as the others. But for now she was fixated on the parted soldiers, her bright eyes heavily focused.

For several tense moments, Saebellus stood completely motionless, eyes searching the males before him as though looking for something in particular…

Mikanum stiffened as Saebellus turned to face him. "You are the Darivalian council member, are you not? Your general was a fierce warrior. When we find his body, I shall have it returned to Darival. As for the rest of the army," he continued, turning to regard each of the council members momentarily. His eyes lingered on Sellemar curiously. "…No doubt you have been informed that every last one of them is dead as well. This country is now mine. Whether you give me Elvorium or I leave it alone until I build a fleet to take it by force, the choice is yours. I have not come to negotiate. There is no room for negotiation. The end of Elvorium shall either come in bloodshed or through a peaceful surrender. Should you choose to surrender, my position will be solidified immediately; Ilsevel will marry me and formally make me this country's king."

Sellemar's eyes widened as the room sucked in their gasps of disbelief, and he jerked his head to look at Ilsevel. Was *that* her plan all along?

With a start, he recalled the ease with which he had stolen through the halls of Saebellus' palace to reach her. No soldiers save two had given them any resistance, and even the one outside Ilsevel's door had not seemed particularly vigilant for a possible escape by his captive. In fact, now that he recalled the relaxed posture of Kraesin, his bored gaze directed to the ceiling above him, he seemed to have been posted there more as a formality than as an actual guard. Even Vale, under torture, had said there had been no guard... His stomach dropped; he and Itirel had had to force the door down because it had been bolted—from the inside: privacy, not a bolt to contain a captive.

With another flash of anger, he realized just how much time Ilsevel would have had to plan this moment with Saebellus during her "capture." Had this plan come to her after Saebellus had taken her? Had she even truly been captured at all? The unexpected defeat of Jikun and his army... Had she even planned the details down to the general's position and defeat at the end? His mind whirled. As he stared around the council chamber at a scene he never dreamed would come to pass, no theory seemed too far-fetched.

"Why?" he whispered out loud. Her expression read vexation, but he could catch a glimmer of elation behind it. Why turn the country over to Saebellus when she already had been made queen by Hairem? What more had she to gain?

At Saebellus' declaration, the other council members had turned toward the queen as well, their eyes wide, their lips parted in alarm. What she displayed was a mirror of their own shock and repulsion. She seemed to struggle to find words, her mouth opening and closing as her mind seemed to burn for a response.

Sellemar saw the one-eyed council member lean forward, his brows knit tightly as he regarded Saebellus coolly. Saebellus' eyes shifted away from Sellemar toward the Noc'olarian male. "I am Lord Valdor," the Noc'olari informed him. "If you recall, we served together briefly before my troops were recalled to take care of an inner rebellion. I knew you as a good male—but your recent actions lead me to believe that you are quite the different individual. Whatever the reasons for your actions—and I suspect they are driven by the war with the sirens—they have cost the lives of tens of thousands. What will you do if Elvorium is given to you?"

Stoic and withdrawn, Saebellus blinked slowly, taking a deep breath as though Valdor's question was unworthy of a response. He turned, armor plates grating softly against one another. "Do with it as should be done. The laws I give it shall be my own. They are superior to what your self-centered brothers have devised. Either you will give me the city or I will take it. Once again, it is the council's decision for how many must die to reach the inevitable result. If you agree to this willingly, I shall spare your lives. That is the only reprieve you will receive. Refuse, and every head of this council shall be paraded through the streets on the golden platters from which you dine."

Sellemar could see the council ripple uncomfortably. Ilsevel put a hand to her mouth in anguish.

"Saebellus, please," she began.

The warlord turned to face her, his face growing expressionless. "You have the opportunity to spare the lives of your people from further injury. Wed me and I promise no harm shall come to this city."

Ilsevel looked at her father, her expression outwardly anxious, yet for the first time Sellemar could catch the steadiness of her composure. He narrowed his eyes. What was her end goal?

She turned back. "I—"

Saebellus cut her off. "Do not look at your father, Ilsevel. He is a traitor to his own blood. You know what he did to your brother."

Sellemar caught a flicker of hatred in Ilsevel's eyes as she glanced back toward her father. He could see her struggling to mask it and was finally forced to avert her gaze.

What was he talking about…?

Saebellus locked eyes with Nilanis. The El'adorium stiffened, his eyes shifting anxiously to the other council members. "I appointed your son as my captain when we rebelled. Fearing that your name would be tarnished by the 'traitor' in your family, you had him assassinated and *dared* claim my army killed him 'when he tried to resist our rebellion.' When I find the murderer, you will kill him slowly before me and you will leave his head on your gates as a testament of your crime. And you will never take it down."

Sellemar's brows raised in abhorrence that Nilanis was so self-serving as to hire the murder of his own *son*. It was no surprise now the visible hatred that had flickered through Ilsevel's features. And now… He could see the hatred of the warlord evident across Nilanis' face—his pursed lips and narrowed eyes did not try to hide it. Sellemar glanced quickly to Ilsevel for a reaction, but whatever expression she had worn had been quickly masked by pain and plight.

For a moment, there was merely silence as Saebellus allowed the rest of the council to remain focused on Nilanis, to squirm in their unspoken questions. Then he turned back to Ilsevel. "Even your father will be spared if you agree now."

"Your Majesty, you mustn't give in to him," Heshellon spoke forcefully, cutting off her response. "This city shall not blame you for refusing!"

Ilsevel shook her head heavily, hanging it down, as though torn with the weight of her decision.

It sickened Sellemar to see the agreement written on most of the council's faces as they regarded one another, so desperate for their own lives that they did not attempt to object further.

"What about the council?" Mikanum suddenly spoke up. The others turned sharply toward Saebellus, all silently asking the same question.

Saebellus regarded them icily. "The council shall remain as is. I shall not touch you. *If* you surrender to my terms *now*."

Sellemar could see Ilsevel remain standing, head still lowered in what he supposed was meant to be conflict.

He leaned back, regarding the council cynically but carefully. Valdor and Heshellon seemed most conflicted about her agreement. Mikanum seemed hesitant. As for the others… He scowled. Even Nilanis seemed all too eager to cling to his wealth and life.

With each of the elven cities practically independent and the number of truly skilled soldiers minimal at best, it would take weeks to gather a decent force and weeks more for an army to arrive. By then, Saebellus could easily fortify himself in an advantageous position. As for the rest of the elven races, their forces were either insufficient in size or incompetent in battle—thanks to the rules and regulations the council had burdened the nation with in an attempt to ensure peace.

And by banning the Lithri, the Malravi, and the other elven races from the council, those races were not likely to offer any assistance in their time of need.

Elvorium was, in all honesty, without much hope now that the gates had been opened. His eyes narrowed as he withdrew in thought. No, Elvorium was stronger than that…! If the council lifted the ban on Jikun's troops, they could probably hold the city until the sea and Ruljarian people arrived as reinforcements. Potentially, that would be enough to resist. Even if Saebellus built a fleet, the sea and Ruljenari were far more experienced on water than Saebellus could ever hope to be. If he fought them, like a leaf in the ocean, their sheer familiarity with sea-based battle would swallow Saebellus into the depths. What would be left of his troops could be defeated by the other races.

The determination to resist coursed through him. They could do it and *he* could lead them…!

Sellemar opened his mouth, but then hesitated. His gaze slid back to Ilsevel, who was staring up at Saebellus from her still-downcast face, eyes burning with intensity and triumph. No. Even if he voiced his plan, he knew what Ilsevel's choice—perhaps even her plan—would be. His futile opposition, he knew, would lead him to wherever Erallus was now…

Ilsevel suddenly raised her head. "I shall do this. Please, council, I cannot bear the thought of your lives, or those of our people, being placed in any further danger. Or to see your livelihoods wasted away in defense of the city only to have your reward at our loss be the decapitation and defamation of your heroism… No. I shall marry Saebellus." Her eyes met his fiercely. "I shall accept your terms of surrender."

Saebellus' bowed his head slightly, a wry smile on his lips. Yet, Sellemar did not see triumph in it. For the first time, there was a hint of humility. And at the same time, a dangerous, self-appointed importance that so held his own attention that his false smile was nothing but obvious. He was torn in a performance of fierceness for the council and becoming overcome with his own thoughts, oddly comfortable in Ilsevel's agreement and already faltering to put on an act.

Sellemar grimaced. Perhaps this but further revealed that Saebellus had already settled into his position as king before he had even arrived in the city.

The warlord raised his head, his voice echoing solidly across the hall. "Then I shall give my troops permission to enter the city."

The council remained silent, their bodies stiff, even in compliance. Whether they perceived his change in behavior, Sellemar could not tell, but his lips pursed in aversion. Saebellus would not keep his word for safety for the council. There was something personal involved here between Ilsevel and the warlord—Ilsevel would not simply have exchanged one king for another.

So then… *what was the gain?*

Sellemar looked back toward Ilsevel, her carefully composed strength a pillar of hope for the foolish council members that clung to it. How carefully she had chosen her words about the council's lives and wealth. That was all she needed to pull their strings.

# Chapter Forty-One

The soft rays of sunlight filtered through the sheer curtains of the balcony. There they dimmed, edging cautiously forward and out across the wide, tiled floor to peer over the side of the large bed. Ilsevel shifted, moaning softly as she awoke, her body still aching from the force with which Saebellus had bedded her. She opened her eyes, blinking back the bleariness, and focused on the figure beside her.

Saebellus' black hair was wild about his head and he seemed oddly comfortable in the cool morning air, the silk sheets only rising to his firm stomach. She imagined he had spent far too many nights on the hard ground, encamped in Sevrigel's wilderness. He was already awake, eyes staring up into the canopy of silk above them, seemingly lost in thought.

Ilsevel curled up further into the bed's warmth, pressing her forehead against his thick shoulder. "Good morning, my love," she whispered, slipping a hand from the covers to run along the definition of his upper chest. "What captures your thoughts?"

Saebellus started slightly, catching her hand in his firm grip. She inhaled sharply in discomfort and his grip loosened. Without turning his face to her, he stoically slid her hand from his body, dropping it away beside him.

"Saebellus…" she spoke reproachfully, sitting up and letting the covers fall from her bare breasts.

He turned, and Ilsevel could see the hint of desire in his eyes, even as he attempted to mask it. He smiled faintly, taunting her with his self-control. Yet he leaned forward, locking her lips in a long, deep kiss. She felt her heart rate quicken.

Saebellus pulled back and Ilsevel attempted to match his controlled expression. He seemed to enjoy toying with her desires as much as she enjoyed having him follow through. She saw the lust flicker in his eyes and smiled inwardly, reflecting on her triumph. She had won again.

"Where are you going today?" she asked as she watched him begin to dress. He was quick about it, donning simple clothes and no armor. He pushed his crown carelessly to the side on his chest of drawers as he reached for his sheathed blade.

Saebellus pulled the silk across his chest, fastening the centermost button and turning toward the door. He attempted to fasten the rest as he went. "To take care of the rest of Jikun's troops."

Ilsevel cocked her head, aware of how her hair slid down across her shoulder. She reached up to brush it back slowly, watching his eyes trail along her body. "What do you mean by that?"

Saebellus opened the door, holding it ajar with his foot. Ilsevel could catch the disinterested glance of Vale as he looked inside, watching as he turned his attention back to Adonis. She wondered how long they had been waiting for him. Saebellus fastened his last button below his throat. "Jikun's soldiers shall assimilate into my army or they shall be executed." He stepped out into the hall, letting the carved doors fall closed with a quiet thud.

She still heard his apathy echoing through the chamber even after he had left. He would do as his habit and rank required, but his voice was weary.

Ilsevel looked over to the chest of drawers where his crown lay teetering on the edge and his phoenix necklace from their wedding ceremony lay across the ground, barely protruding from a pile of clothes. She smiled slightly. He was nothing like Hairem. There was no royalty in his blood, no mask of behavior, no devotion to the other elven races, no humility, and no compromise. And yet, the war had taken its toll on him—she could see how the long years of conflict had eroded his intransigent hatred, had carved an ache in his soul for intimacy and *warmth*. In his loneliness, he could not resist her.

*He* was exactly what she needed.

She swung her legs from the bed, stepping lightly down and shivering as her bare feet touched the cold floor.

"Galandra!" she bellowed, grabbing her silken night dress and tossing it over her head. Where was that handmaiden? Alvena had always been clinging to Hairem's side like an incurable disease.

The door flung open and a skinny young Sel'ven ran in, eyes wide with concern as she closed the door behind her. "Yes, Your Majesty?!"

Ilsevel heaved a sigh. "I told you to wait until Saebellus leaves, and then you enter. Who just left?"

"Saebel—the king," Galandra quickly corrected herself.

Ilsevel nodded. "Yes. So what do you do then?"

"Enter…"

Ilsevel tossed the girl her brush. She had no patience these days. The kingdom had just fallen into her hands and she did not have time for reminding servants of their basic duties. She crouched down and began to dig through her drawers, not waiting for Galandra to assist her. She heard the female creep cautiously up behind her and touch the brush to her hair.

Ilsevel pulled out a dark red dress, the garment made of silk but lined at the sleeves with thick, white fur. She smiled to herself. Yes, this would do. After all, she had an impression to make today.

She took her time in preparation. *'Let the council wait for me,'* she thought indignantly.

"Is this braid suitable for today, Your Majesty?" Galandra asked.

Ilsevel turned her head slightly, rolling her eyes in disgust. "No. Again."

She looked back at her reflection, watching the strands of hair fall loose from her braid. When she had arranged her capture with Saebellus, she had not believed that things would have come together so perfectly. From the corner of her eye, she could see the place where Hairem's body had lain as he breathed his last; it was unmarked by his death, as though it had never happened. But oh, it *had*, and *Saebellus* was now her king. And without any hesitation, Saebellus had dismissed the power of the council into her hands—something Hairem would have never done! Whether he so easily parted with the power from a lack of interest in the position or from deference to her was momentarily inconsequential. The authority was firmly in her grasp, and she now had all the time in the world to bend Saebellus' loyalty completely to her will.

She had known he would submit to her from the moment she had glimpsed that lust-filled desire in his eyes—that loneliness that had taken its toll as his war raged on endlessly. But she had brought life back to him; he was hungry for her vision. Hungry for her enthusiasm. And more than he desired to end the war, he desired her.

And she had just begun.

How easily Hairem had fallen for her information about Saebellus' attack… and how pridefully Jikun had led his troops to their demise. Even as she reflected on that victory now, a chill of delight crawled up her spine. She stood, pulling her half-finished braid from Galandra's hands. "That is fine," she said, impatience rising within.

She had one last task to do before the council to seal her reign. Just one.

Galandra stammered her apologies as Ilsevel walked briskly to the door. The queen opened it, leaning out to the guard on her left. "Rulwen, bring the item I requested to the council's chambers. Wait outside the doors. I will call you when I am ready." She passed him, hearing the footsteps of the second personal guard fall into line behind her.

Yes, just one last task.

*

As she moved up the steps of the council's chambers, Ilsevel could hear the muffled sound of their raised voices. The consistent bickering grated on her, causing her to purse her lips until they turned white. The fools!—did they *ever* cease?!

The guards before her opened the chamber's doors, bowing their heads respectfully as she passed.

Inside, the council hardly acknowledged her. They were enveloped in their own personal concerns, grappling to be heard over one another. She could grasp the content of their discussion, however: Saebellus' troops were everywhere, spread out across the city streets and dotted along the city's walls. And they were in fear.

"At this rate, even our homes will be filled with soldiers. An elven city has never been so occupied by a military force!" Mikanum spoke resentfully, stiffening in offense.

Ilsevel could hear the rare murmur of agreement.

"*My concern*," Cahsari began, interlocking his fingers, "is the fact that he has seized half of all our wealth to pay for accumulated war costs against Jikun and the kingdom. He said he would leave the council alone. I hardly see this as a follow-through to his promise."

Fildor scoffed, reclining in his chair and flicking a strand of brown hair behind his ear. "Traitors do not keep promises."

Ilsevel turned her attention to the one male in the room who was withdrawn and silent, standing to the side stiffly, leaning away from the other council members as though this removed him from their inclusion. She found herself smiling slightly, watching his emerald eyes flick from face to face. He said nothing, but she could sense the tumult of thoughts racing through his mind, the tension pulling at his lean, muscular frame. She narrowed her eyes, studying his face. Who was he?

She *would* find out—whether he told her willingly or she had to force it from him. *'He will not keep secrets from me,'* she thought indignantly, stopping before her throne. She pivoted, facing the council silently for a moment. They seemed to notice her then, the noise quieting as she raised her hand. She noted that every eye lingered upon the empty throne beside her, no doubt surprised that Saebellus had refrained from accompanying her.

But the council was *her* business. As was everything else in the city. She owned Saebellus and thus owned Sevrigel. She smiled wryly.

"Your Majesty," Valdor began, bowing his head respectfully to her, his one eye rising to meet her own. "I am pleased to see you looking so well. You bear the concerns of this entire city with you. You are a strong lady. We honor you."

Ilsevel let her smile soften. Hairem had chosen this male correctly. He was not like the others—not full of deceit and corruption. He would be obedient. Or like Hairem, he would die.

Mikanum looked around, frowning faintly. "Your Majesty, Nilanis is not here yet—it is unlike him to be late. Shall we wait for him?"

Ilsevel shook her head, the corner of her lips curving wryly once more. "Lord Sellemar, please have a seat in the El'adorium's chair for now." She watched his brows arch slightly in surprise, but he walked steadily to her father's desk.

"Thank you, Your Majesty," Sellemar spoke with a brief bow of his head.

Ilsevel regarded Valdor. "Thank you for your concern, Lord Valdor," she replied, ignoring Mikanum's inquiry.

"Indeed," Fildor began, eyeing Sellemar briefly as he passed. He turned back to Ilsevel. "Your marriage to Saebellus has saved—"

"Silence," she cut him off sharply the moment Sellemar had taken his seat. She stood, rising up above them, looking down with a cool, steely gaze. "The time of your corruption has come to an end. No longer shall it be tolerated. For every male, female, or child that speaks against, disobeys, or deceives the throne, they shall be executed in Eraydon's square and their heads displayed on Ephraim's lance." She watched their eyes widen in speechless shock, their lips parting as their jaws slacked. Sellemar's eyes flickered incomprehensibly. "For countless years I have watched this city pander to your whims, bending as you make senseless demands against the will of the king and queen—the Sel'vi chosen by Sel'ari to rule the rest of the elven people—as though you were *equals.* The True Bloods never would have left if not for your self-centered scheming—you drove them from our land! And so as of today, your votes no longer hold power.

"We were once a pure people—a people of strength and nobility who valued the survival and peace of our own kind over the affairs and wills of the outside world. Now we have allowed lesser beings such as humans to walk our land and we war with the beast-kinds—the sirens and the centaurs." She leaned forward, inhaling sharply. The silence in the room was deafening. Their eyes were locked onto her—there was nothing that could tear their attention away. "Nilanis was a traitor to his Sel'varian blood." She glanced once towards the doors, feeling her chest swell with triumph as she called to the guard outside, "Bring it in!"

The doors to the council chamber pushed open and the elves craned their necks with baited breath.

In a wave of nausea, she saw their faces twist in visible horror, heard a unison of strangled gasps. She felt her smile broaden, her eyes light up. "This is the punishment for those who disobey the crown. This is the punishment for selfishness. You shall serve me in every way or you shall join my father's fate." She spread her arms wide as the head of Nilanis was carried to the center of the room, impaled through with a wooden spike that protruded from his skull. She stared coldly back into his unseeing eyes, her vengeance finally realized. "No longer shall the elves be separate peoples in this land! No longer shall they be ruled by lesser beings—Sel'ari's chosen shall once more be the kings of their brethren! We shall bring assimilation to this country! The reign of kings has returned."